ONE BRIGHT DAY

in the Middle of the Night

GARY AUMAUGHER

ONE BRIGHT DAY

ISBN: 0-9833548-2-0
ISBN-13: 9780983354826
Library of Congress Control Number: 2011909875

First Edition - July, 2011

ONE BRIGHT DAY

Cover photography by Jonathon Nevedal
Cover design by Gary Aumaugher
Thanks Isabella for a great cover shoot

Special thanks to Kathy Pass, Kathy Swallows, Becky Smith and Susan Nevedal for their editorial comment and support.

A character list is provided at the end of the book for reference.

Contact the author at gaumaugher1@gmail.com.

Rachel

July 1752
Pennsylvania, the American Colonies

Chapter 1

Rachel felt the impact slam against her face, crushing her nose and dislocating her jaw. The force of the blow threw her against the wall behind her, leaving clumps of chestnut hair and bloodied scalp embedded in the rough wood grain. Before she blacked out, her mind took time to be disgusted at the taste of manure in her mouth.

Rachel choked and coughed blood out of her windpipe, jarring her back awake. She opened one eye but it refused to focus. Although her daughters were far away, Rachel sensed their fear as the pain from the cow's hoof radiated throughout her face. As the blood flowed from her crooked nose and seeped through her coarse work dress, she knew help was on the way. She lost consciousness again.

Mary, Rachel's oldest daughter, was with her father in the field, clearing stones before plowing. A gasp escaped her lips and her hands flew to cover her face. "Papa! We must go back to the house... Now!'

The forcefulness of her voice startled her father. "What did you..."

"It's mother..." She lifted her skirt and ran towards the house. "She's hurt; bad I think!" she shouted over her shoulder.

"What in the devil are you talking about?' he called as he followed.

"She's hurt... She needs us... Hurry please!"

He caught up with Mary and could see fear in her eyes. Rachel and her daughters shared something that Thomas Delings had witnessed many times before but never understood. His wife and daughters had the unsettling ability to perceive events over distances beyond any rational explanation. When he would ask his wife how she knew of her daughter's scraped knee, she would look at him square in the eye and ask, "Do you doubt me?" Thomas had learned not to.

He ran faster.

Elizabeth and Isadora were with Mrs. McWethy on a blackberry-picking excursion. The stains on Elizabeth's seven-year-old face and hands hinted of a near-empty pail. Isadora, three years her senior, chastised her again about how so many berries would give her the trots.

Elizabeth dropped her pail, covered her face with her hands, and moaned. The same instant, Isadora's eyes grew large and vacant. "Mrs. McWethy" she yelled, "We have to go home... Now!" She grabbed Elizabeth's hand and pulled her towards the trail.

Mrs. McWethy peered out from behind a blackberry bush, puzzled and irritated. "No you do not, young ladies! I told your mother we would be out until noonday. You shan't be walking all the way home by your lonesomes. She forced her plump form through the thick berry bushes with authority.

Isadora turned and looked over her shoulder at Mrs. McWethy. "I'm sorry but we can't stay. Mama is hurt and we have to go help her."

Elizabeth, her hands firmly clamped over her nose and mouth, could taste blood. She coughed and spat blackberry juice on the ground, staring at it in awe. She looked at her older sister and begged her to hurry. "Come on, her mouth is bleedin', come on." Isadora ran after her little sister.

"You can't leave; I have to take you home! You girls come back here or you'll not sit for a week!" Mrs. McWethy left her two buckets and set out to catch the girls. "What on earth has gotten into you two?" By the time she reached the narrow dirt road, the girls had a good head start. "You may move through the woods better'n an old woman, but I'll catch you now," she muttered. "Then we'll see who runs off from whom!" But she didn't catch up with the girls until they were back to the rough-hewn log home, watching their father carrying their mother back from the barn.

Sarah reached their mother first. At twelve years, Rachel's strongly rebellious second daughter could, and did, wrestle any boy her age and came out on top. When Thomas became frustrated with her shenanigans, his wife would smile and say, "I thought you wanted a boy?"

The feeling struck Sarah while she was searching out the hen's new nest. Her stomach rolled as a wave of nausea passed through her. A cold sweat broke out on her freckled face. She knew with certainty that her mother was hurt, but where was she?

"Mother!" she yelled out "Mother!"

There was no reply. Sarah swung out of the loft, skipping most of the rungs of the ladder and dropped to the dirt floor. She crossed to the other side of the small barn and found her mother lying back against the wall, blood flowing freely from her nose and mouth.

Rachel was only semiconscious. Sarah lifted the bottom of her dress, thrust it in the water trough and started to wash off her mother's face. Rachel seemed to recover her senses and tried to stem the flow of blood from her nose. Moments later, Thomas and Mary ran into the yard shouting for Rachel.

"Over here, over here," Sarah called back.

Thomas burst in the door and caught sight of his wife. "Oh my Lord in heaven," he mumbled. Her nose was cocked sickly to the right and her jaw hung sprung like a bad door. He carefully lifted Rachel and carried her towards the house. As he approached the door he saw his youngest two daughters running up the road followed by a puffing Mrs. McWethy. Good, he thought. I sure can use her help about now. The girls were right smart to bring her back. He could hear her shrill voice calling after his daughters as he shouldered the cabin door open. Rachel moaned weakly at the jostling.

Sarah followed her father in the door while Mary rushed down to hurry Mrs. McWethy to the house. She was the village midwife and the closest thing to a doctor they had. Mary shouted instructions to Elizabeth and Isadora as she passed. "She's been hurt bad but she is awake. Go see if you can help in the house! Hurry up! Elizabeth, you stay out of the way."

"But I want..."

Mary assumed her mother's tone. "Do as I say. Stay out!" Mrs. McWethy was still fifty yards off. As an afterthought she yelled over her shoulder, "Elizabeth, pump some water." That will keep her out of the way and make her feel useful she thought.

"Don't try to stop me," the old woman gasped as she approached Mary. "I'm going to redden their behinds just as they deserve!"

"Please hurry, ma'am," Mary panted, sweat streaming off her face from the long run. She took the woman's arm, pulling her towards the house. "She's hurt bad."

"What are you talking about, girl, who's been hurt?"

"Didn't Isadora tell you? Mother is hurt. The cow has kicked her. Come to the house. Please hurry!"

Mrs. McWethy stared dumbfounded at the young woman. Comprehension flickered across her face before being replaced by fear. Her eyes darted side to side, as if looking for a way to escape. She saw the tears in Mary's eyes. The old woman swallowed hard, drawing courage out of her gut by force of will. "Come on child, take me to her."

Rachel lay on the bed, blood staining her hair and dress. Thomas turned to Mary. "Take your sisters outside."

"No!" Mrs. McWethy said sternly, "They need to see this. They'll learn nothing out there." Mrs. McWethy leaned over the bed. Her callused fingers tilted Rachel's head forward, exposing the wound. The bleeding had stopped for the most part. "I've seen worse." She cautiously lowered the injured woman's head. Rachel yelped in pain as the wound touched the pillow causing Mrs. McWethy to duck, as if she expected a bolt of lightening to strike her down. She took a deep breath and continued. "Hold her head steady," she commanded.

Thomas nervously placed his large hands on Rachel's temples and looked at the old woman's lined face. Mrs. McWethy's knotted fingers felt the jawbone. "This will hurt." Rachel's glazed eyes showed no reaction. Thomas's stomach churned and his face whitened as the midwife forced the jawbone back into place with a wet pop. Rachel grabbed at the old woman and let out a strangled scream. Thomas reached for his wife's arms and brought them back to her side. "Hold her head not her hands!" reprimanded the old woman.

The girls, who until this moment had kept their distance, surged forward in unison. "Give her room to work!" barked Thomas. He released Rachel's arms, which had again gone limp and gripped her head. Practiced, but shaking, old hands straightened the bloody nose as much as it could be. Rachel's hands tightened to fists but stayed at her sides.

"Mary, clean her up as careful as you can. She's had enough hurt for one day. A dislocated jaw and broken nose is painful but not likely fatal. Cut her hair away from the wound on the back of her head. Then wash it out with saltwater."

The midwife tiredly pushed herself up from the side of the bed. Rachel weakly squeezed Mrs. McWethy's wrist. "Thank you," she whispered, barely moving her swollen lips.

The midwife backed away without speaking. "Thomas, I'd speak with you outside." The tone was one that could not be ignored. Thomas followed her out as the girls surrounded their mother. A few paces from the house, Mrs. McWethy began in an even tone, "Can you explain this?"

Thomas's mind searched for an escape. He hesitated, looking out over his fields. "She was milking the ..."

"Not that, you fool! How did Elizabeth and Isadora know she was hurt?" She looked at him with fear in her eyes. "Your daughters knew she was hurt bad and bleeding from the mouth when we were over half a mile from here! Is this a house of witches?"

"Isn't a message from God just as good an explanation as a message from the devil?" he shot back with such violence he surprised himself. He wondered who he was trying to convince.

"This isn't the first I've heard of the Delings family's powers, but it is the first time I've seen it with my own eyes. Never gave it no mind until now. Just thought it was idle gossip."

Thomas clenched his fists at his side. "My wife is not a witch, and neither are my daughters." His voice was quivering.

"Then what are they?"

Thomas stood and looked at the sky for a long time before responding. "Blessed," he said quietly.

"Well, do not send your 'blessed' children to my home again. They are not welcome. And that goes for you and your wife also."

"If that is the way you want it." Thomas' anger showed in his words. "We wouldn't want to bring a curse upon you. What do we owe you for your services?"

The old woman looked truly frightened at receiving a curse. "I'll take nothing for what I've done today." She turned and hurried away without another word.

In the two weeks since the accident, the whispers had become louder. Other children were no longer allowed to play with Rachel's, people stared when they went to town, stepping aside as they approached. The few who did greet them were quickly stared into silence by the others.

And now this. Fear crept back into Rachel's heart. Early in the afternoon, the three oldest girls had accompanied Thomas to town to purchase supplies. A short time later, Rachel felt her daughters' embarrassment, fear and anger. Now all Rachel could do was wait for her family to return. She paced the small house, trying to concentrate on her chores but it was no use, every noise brought her to her feet to peer out the door, searching in vain for the wagon coming up the path to the barn. Now she heard it for sure. Rachel fought the urge to rush for the door. She set her mending aside and waited for her children. She unconsciously rubbed the knuckles of her right hand.

Sarah stormed through the door first, her lips tight and the sleeve on her dress torn. Thomas followed, carrying Isadora. She wiggled out of his arms and ran to her mother, clutching her leg as if to squeeze into her very soul. "I'm not a witch am I?" she cried.

Rachel's heart ached. "Of course not!" She crouched down and hugged her little girl. She looked up at her husband. "What happened?"

Before he could answer Sarah burst out "It was that pig George Hemmingford. He called Isadora a witch. He said we were all witches! So I told him to apologize. He said he didn't apologize to witches. So I hit him."

"Oh no! Are you alright?"

"I'm alright mother."

"Much better than he is," snickered Thomas in her ear. "His nose looks like yours now. I think she broke it good." He sounded proud. Thomas straightened and continued "The girls were waiting outside while I was in with the blacksmith. When I came out, Sarah was standing over George, screaming at him to apologize."

"Sarah, did George strike you or Isadora?" There was no hint of sympathy in her voice.

"No... But he called…"

"I don't care what he said!" Rachel hated appearing cold hearted to her daughters but they had to learn to control their emotions or they would never be able to carry through the plans she had made for them. She stood and looked down on Sarah. "An insult is not a reason to strike someone! I'm sure your father agrees. Now go to the barn and get your chores done. We will discuss your punishment later."

"I didn't do anything wrong!" protested Sarah, tears starting down her cheeks.

"Enough! Now go!" She watched as Sarah defiantly marched out the door, fighting back the sobs. Rachel's strength left her as she fell into her husband's arms. "This has got to stop," said Rachel, more as a plea than as a statement of fact.

"I don't know how to stop it. I wish I did," Thomas sighed as he shook his head.

"I think I do. I think we both know." There was a tone of resignation in her voice. Thomas held her close but made no response.

That night, after the children were asleep, Rachel led Thomas outside, out of earshot of the children. "We have to move from here," Rachel said firmly.

"It's not that bad. It will blow over in time." Thomas looked at the tears welling in Rachel's eyes.

"No, not this time. I can handle their fear and spite, but the girls can't." She began to sob softly. Thomas put his arms around her shoulders. "It's not their fault they know things. It's not my fault.... My children have been cursed at, spit upon and now assaulted."

"I think it was Sarah who did the assaulting." The words came out before he had time to stop them. Rachel did not see the humor in the altercation that afternoon.

"You know she was defending her sister. Don't you understand? It's over for us here. We have to go where no one has heard of us. We have to start over."

"I can't start over. If you haven't noticed, we have no sons to help clear a new farm. You think I can do it myself?"

"We had no sons for this farm and it was cleared wasn't it? We have four strong girls who can help. And if you hadn't noticed, they are rather pretty. I think you will have your four sons sooner than you wish. Have you forgotten the time you spent on my father's farm being 'neighborly', winning his favor before asking for my hand?"

"Yes I do remember, but do you remember how hard it was? Remember that no one will offer a fair price for this farm because we're of the devil."

"I know," Rachel replied. "I think it best if we rent the land to someone for a year before we sell it. By then greed will dull their memories and the price should be fair, especially if you have your father sell it for you."

Thomas sat in silence for a while. "Yes, it could be done. But you tell me, how will the next place be different? Something will happen and it will start all over again."

"No!" Rachel's voice was as hard as a blacksmith's anvil. I swear to you and God above. I will never again reveal my gift to another living soul. Nor will my children for they have seen the results. I will teach them to suppress and hide this gift so no one will again suspect us of being anything but ordinary folk. This I promise you."

Irene
October 1938
Chicago

Chapter 2

The world had provided a beautiful, crisp, late October day, but Dr. Irene Moore had seen little of it. Dr. Moore had been working since seven AM without a break and it looked as if it might continue well into the night. But then that wasn't unusual for an assistant coroner in the bustling city of Chicago. The body that had arrived this morning was a rape/murder victim who had been found in a vacant lot, hastily buried under a pile of trash. The chief coroner had already decided that this case was a low priority, probably a prostitute who tried to rob her client and paid the price. The body was found near the red light district, it was completely nude, no jewelry, no evidence found near the scene and no witnesses. The chief passed the job on to one of his young assistants so he could concentrate on more important things; currently a political fundraising dinner to support the party bosses who controlled his budget.

Dr. Irene Moore had never intended to spend her life examining the dead. She had high hopes and expectations when at the age of twelve she decided to become a doctor. Her teachers at school had patiently explained that nursing was an admirable career. She, equally patiently, explained that a doctor and a nurse are not the same. After all, this was 1920, not the dark ages. Her mother and sisters supported her but her father considered it foolish to buck the system. As far as he was concerned, women belonged at home like her mother, and if they did work, it shouldn't be a man's career.

Graduating in the top third of her class at Loyola University Medical School by performing in the top five percent proved her suspicion that the rest of the men in the medical profession agreed with her father. The effort had required almost complete sacrifice of her social life but Irene considered the rewards worth it. Irene was pretty but not beautiful. Her dark brown hair and blue eyes were from her mother; her tendency for being 'down right skinny' as her grandmother put it, came from her father's side. This was emphasized by being taller than average.

Harold didn't seem to mind her career choice or her appearance. Irene and Harold had met when she was a sophomore and he was a senior. They had dated for a year, at first occasionally, but later it seemed they were never apart. Things were getting more serious than she had planned. She wanted to graduate medical school before getting married but Harold had other ideas. Irene's grades were beginning to suffer and what was worse, she didn't seem to care. Being with Harold was the focal point of her life. She still wanted her dream of becoming a doctor, but not at the expense of losing Harold. He, on the other hand, did not want to be responsible for Irene not attaining her dream. They spent hours discussing, arguing and persuading, trying to find the perfect solution to the problem. They both knew the strain they would be under during internship. Irene didn't think it was fair to start a marriage out that way and was afraid she would quit rather than destroy their marriage. Harold felt if they planned properly, they could both intern and still have enough time for each other.

Harold was meeting her at their favorite restaurant and she was sure that it was to celebrate making a decision. She began to worry when he was thirty minutes late. Harold hated being late. Irene started making calls after another 30 minutes. Then she took the bus to the university and started her search. She collapsed in her room two hours later, still unable find Harold. It was early the next morning when she received word. There had been a high-speed chase through the streets, the police in pursuit of a bootlegger. A police car had lost control, jumped the curb and crushed him against a wall. He probably never saw it coming. Irene was devastated. She threw herself into to her schoolwork to block the pain of losing Harold.

Her internship was spent at Washington General Hospital, a third rate facility serving the immigrants and poor of the south side Chicago slums. It was made clear to her that she wouldn't have been there if they had been able to find a male graduate who knew which end of a stethoscope to put in his ears and was willing to intern there.

She spent two years handling nothing more complex than colds and the flu. Anything more difficult was assigned to a physician better equipped to handle the patient (translation: had a penis). The best (translation: only) job she could find after completing her internship was at the Coroner's Office. Now after three long years, her boss was finally starting to treat her as a doctor, not a nurse. If only she could get the rest of the world to understand that she was Dr. Moore, not Dr. Moore's secretary.

The body she had been working on told her little that was useful except that this woman had not been a prostitute. She wore little makeup, there were no signs of alcohol in the stomach and no signs of venereal disease. There was a ring mark on her left hand, probably from a wedding band. A blow to the left side of the head split the skin and chipped the skull but was not the cause of death. The wound had stopped bleeding before the time of death. The bruises around the throat showed where each finger was placed as they collectively choked the life out of Jane Doe. There were signs of forced entry, sperm in the vagina and evidence that the woman fought back, hands bruised, nails broken and flesh that did not match the victim's under the nails.

One interesting find had nothing to do with the crime. The victim was also a man. Dr. Moore had found a complete set of male sex organs along with the usual female organs. She examined the testicles and confirmed they did indeed contain sperm and they were connected to the urethra as would be normal in a man. Rather than being located externally as on a man, the testicles were in the lower body cavity. She had noted this abnormality and continued her investigation.

At five-thirty, Dr. Moore was about to leave for the day and stop by the clinic where she did volunteer work. A detective arrived with a woman who wanted to see the unidentified body. It matched the description of her sister who hadn't come home last night. The detective pulled Irene aside. "This lady might not be all there upstairs, if you know what I mean. She keeps trying to tell me she knows her sister is dead, knows when it happened, has all kind of details yet can't tell me how she knows. Says it was a vision."

"Then why did you bring her here?"

"Her description matched the body we found this morning and I figured what the hell, it's worth a shot."

"And if it isn't her sister, it gets her out of your hair."

The detective gave a sly smile. "Yeah, that thought crossed my mind too."

"Come on. Let's get it over with."

"If you don't mind," he injected nervously, "could you take her in there? These places always give me the creeps, you know?"

"Wait here. I don't want to come out to find you gone and me stuck with a lady who's 'not all there upstairs'."

Dr. Moore and the detective stepped out of the office to meet the woman waiting in the hall. "Mrs. Ramsey, this is Dr. Moore. She will take you in to see the .. uh .."

"Thank you detective," said Mrs. Ramsey.

Vera Ramsey followed Irene down the hall and through the door labeled Morgue. Irene, noting the resemblance to the Jane Doe, prayed she was mistaken. She hated standing there, holding a cold sheet while a family member dissolved into a weeping heap. She never knew what to say. The room was cold; Irene could see her breath as she spoke. "Is this her?" Mrs. Ramsey bit her lip and nodded her head. "She died sometime last night. I can't put it exact but I believe ..."

"She died at 10:17 PM last night. A little after eight last night, he grabbed her. I'm sure it was a man because of what happened later."

Doctor Moore thought the detective was right, she was a few bricks short of a full load, or she was there when it happened.

"He hit her on the head here," she said pointing to her head at the exact spot of the wound on her dead sister, even though she could not see it from where she stood. You could see her wince with the remembrance of the pain. "I felt him rape her at 8:48 and again at 9:35. I think she was choked to death, at least that's what it felt like."

Irene stood staring in disbelief at Mrs. Ramsey. She recognized the descriptions of her feelings. It was exactly the same way she had felt when Beth, Irene's little sister, had her fingers slammed in a door at school. She had felt it happen but didn't feel the actual pain. It was more as if she had remembered a hurt from the past. Irene remembered how it felt when her grandmother died, the mental hug she felt and then the disconnection, that certain knowledge that her grandmother was dead. Irene had to take a chance, to know for sure if this woman was like herself. Trying to keep her voice as steady as possible she asked "You felt her say goodbye at 10:17 P.M.?"

Vera answered automatically "Yes. I had taken my husband's watch and ..." She paused and looked at Irene suspiciously.

Irene grew bolder. "You felt her fear when she was abducted. You not only felt the fear but knew who it belonged to. The same goes for the pain as she was struck in the head. You didn't actually feel the pain; it was more like remembering a pain you experienced before, but worse because you knew it was happening to someone you love." By the time she finished her voice was trembling. If this woman was like Irene, she would recognize the description instantly. If not, Irene had just taken a gamble and possibly exposed herself.

Vera stared at Irene. "But how did ..." Vera's voice trailed off. Dr. Moore had described her feelings exactly. There was only one way she could know those feeling so well.

"Have I missed anything?" Irene asked. "Oh yes, you only have sisters, no brothers."

"Oh my... you are...like me I mean," Vera stammered.

"Yes, I believe so."

"Thank God," Vera whispered and started to cry. Vera had never imagined meeting someone else like herself unless it was family. It felt as if a terrible weight was lifted, this woman would know she was telling the truth about her sister.

"I'm sorry," Irene said. "I didn't mean to say it that way. It's just that once I got started I had to finish quickly before I lost my nerve. Taking a chance is a very hard thing to do after having it drilled into me ever since I could talk to never reveal myself to anyone."

"I know," Vera replied. "My mother was the same way. 'People won't understand. And they fear what they don't understand.' I must have heard that a hundred times a day when I was a child. Right now the detective thinks I'm crazy."

"You better hope he keeps thinking that way. After I confirm everything you've been telling him, you'll be considered to be involved up to your neck, an accomplice, or at least a witness."

"I told him I had a vision. It seemed to satisfy him so far," Vera said defensively. She began to understand what kind of trouble she was in.

"That's because up until now you were just a crazy lady. When he reads my report, you'll be the only person who appears to know anything about what happened to your sister last night. That's all he'll need to investigate every detail of your life looking for clues of your involvement. Meanwhile the trail to the real killer will be getting cold."

"I don't care about me," Vera cried, "I just want the bastard that killed my sister caught and punished!"

"Just remember there are a few thousand of us who don't care to become sideshow freaks in the process." Irene said harshly. Catching herself, she softly said "I'm sorry; you just lost your sister. Just please be careful, OK?"

Vera nodded just controlling her tears. "I'll do my best."

Irene got Vera's home address and took her back to the waiting detective. "What kept ya? Well?"

"Yes. It's my sister."

"Christ, I'm sorry. I really thought she would turn up OK. Well we better go back to the station and get some questions answered. You all right?"

"I'll be fine officer. Let's get it over with. I need to call my brother-in-law and let him know what's happened."

"Sure, you can call from the station." He guided her down the hall.

Vera looked back over her shoulder and said "Thank you Dr. Moore. Thank you for everything."

Irene went back to the office and called the clinic where she volunteered when she could. "It's doesn't look like I'm going to make it in tonight. I'll be in tomorrow, I promise."

"One of the advantages of working for free," she said to herself. "Nobody fires you for not showing up."

It had been six days since Irene's encounter with Vera. Irene shouldered her way into her apartment, juggling her armload of packages. Carol was already home, creating something questionable in the tiny kitchen. Carol had been a nurse at Washington General while Irene had interned there. They had moved in together to cut cost and had been living together ever since.

"How did it go at the clinic?" inquired Carol, though she never asked about Irene's work at the Coroner's Office. "Too gruesome," she always said.

"A red letter day. I stitched the result of a knife fight and cured a case of the clap." Irene piled her packages on the kitchen table. "And got paid by the recipient of the stitches!" Irene opened her black doctor's bag and with flair withdrew four bottles of beer.

"Have you no shame!" Carol said in mock horror. "Alcohol? And you a doctor. I shall report you immediately!"

"That's why I drink it. We operate better after a shot and a beer. It's in all the medical journals."

"Put them in the icebox. We'll have them after dinner." Carol walked over while wiping some kind of goop off her hands onto her apron and gave Irene a long kiss on the mouth.

"Careful; the shades are up," Irene whispered.

"Don't worry. They can't see in here in this light."

Irene had never intended to let her life get this crazy. Her relationship with Carol had just happened, one of the few things Irene had allowed to just happen. She was usually very analytical in her approach to life. If it was known that she was involved with a woman, she would lose her job, her apartment and probably her license to practice. It was Carol who had initiated the relationship and Irene had not resisted. Irene had been attracted to both men and women ever since her teens. The stigma forced her to never reveal even a hint of those feelings, not even to her sisters.

Carol was pretty, a couple of inches shorter and three years younger than Irene, and contagiously cheerful. She had been a nurse for three years when Irene came to the hospital to intern. They hit it off well from the start and soon became good friends. When Carol's apartment house was sold, she was told to move on short notice. Irene asked her to share her place until she could find another and Carol accepted.

Several weeks passed while the normal roommate relationship prevailed and their friendship grew. Irene admired Carol's seemingly unlimited compassion. She cared for everyone as if they were family. Carol was constantly amazed by Irene's ability to absorb the massive amounts of technical material required of a doctor. She always had a journal or text book in her hands reading snatches whenever her schedule allowed. Both women had little social life, Carol by choice, Irene because her work schedule left no time for one.

Irene had just put in a sixteen-hour day, worse than usual because of an outbreak of a nasty strain of influenza. Her steps echoed hollow on the nearly empty streets this late at night. It made her nervous to walk alone through the neighborhood at night but everyone ignored her in the typical city fashion. As she dragged her tired body up the two flights of stairs to their third story apartment she heard muffled cries coming from inside the apartment. She fumbled for her keys and then realized she hadn't even tried the door. It swung open easily. As she stepped in she heard scrapping and thumping coming from somewhere off to the left, then a whimper in the darkened room. She rushed in to find a man on top of Carol pinning her to the floor, one hand on her throat, the other trying to grip both her wrists. Carol's blouse was ripped away. He looked up to see Irene coming towards him and looked back to Carol, trying to decide what to do. His hesitation cost him the half-second he needed. As he tried to jump away a fraction of a second too late, Irene's heavy black doctor's bag struck him in the face, the force of the blow sprawled him on his back, allowing Carol to scramble away.

Irene jerked open the bag and removed a scalpel. "I've never done a castration without anesthetic before, but I'm willing to give it a try."

"Get away from me you crazy bitch." He rolled over, pushed to his feet and jumped away from Irene. He picked up a chair and held it like a lion tamer, keeping it firmly between himself and this mad woman with the scalpel. "She asked for it!" he yelled.

"That's obvious," Irene snarled. "That's why you were choking her, because she asked you to. Get out of here before I slice you open." The man had circled to within escape distance of the open door and bolted for it, throwing the chair at Irene as he ran. She deflected the chair painfully off her left arm and it crashed into a lamp on the end table, sending glass fragments skittering across the floor. After he dashed out the door, Irene ran to it and slammed it shut behind him, throwing the lock. Irene's hands were shaking uncontrollably and her legs had turned to rubber, no longer capable of supporting her weight. She slid down the door, dropping the scalpel on the way. Irene crawled on her hands and knees to Carol who sat sobbing on the floor. Her chest heaved as she tried to talk. "We went to ... the picture show and ... came back ... and he pushed inside ..."

Irene cradled her like a child and tried to calm her down. "It's OK. He's gone now. I'm here. It's OK now."

"He wouldn't ... leave. I told ... him to go and ... he wouldn't leave."

Irene held Carol's head on her chest and rocked her like a baby as she sobbed. "It's OK, you're safe now."

"What if he comes back?" Carol cried.

"Don't worry, his type are too scared to come back. But if he does then I'll have to perform the operation I promised him," Irene joked, trying to sound self-confident. A momentary smile flickered across Carol's face. They sat on the floor a long time just holding each other. That night Carol woke screaming from a nightmare, and Irene barked her shin on an out of place chair running to her. Carol was soon her usual self, more worried about Irene's shin than her own nightmare.

"Why don't I stay in here tonight," Irene suggested, "it might help your nightmares and I know it will help my shins." Carol just kept apologizing for Irene's new injury.

While they lay wrapped in each other's arms in the dark, Carol kissed Irene goodnight, but it was not a goodnight kiss. It was a full soft kiss on the lips with more than a hint of passion. What surprised Irene the most was how easy it was to return it. Irene realized she was in love with Carol and that Carol felt the same way about her. Carol and Irene shared the same bed from that point on. That was five years ago.

Irene was sure her mother knew about Carol but was very careful not to raise the subject. She had tried once and her mother had made it clear she did not want to know about it. Oddly enough, her sisters did not condemn her. If there was more than one present, they clearly showed their disapproval. If they were alone with Irene she could sense their excitement as they asked her all sorts of questions. Sadie her youngest sister even said she was envious of Irene's courage to risk so much for love.

"Carol's the courageous one," Irene had said. "I never would have made the first move when there was so much to lose. I only wish we didn't have to hide our love as if it was something to be despised." Maybe it was as evil as everyone else thought it was, but when she held Carol close and felt her hair on her cheek, Irene knew it couldn't be bad.

Irene's mind snapped back to the present. "What's for dinner, beautiful?"

Carol looked at the smear on her apron thoughtfully. "I don't think it has a name. But I'll come up with one before we eat. It's gauche to eat anything without a name."

While Carol went back to the stove, Irene put the beer in the icebox and looked through the mail. There was a letter from Vera Ramsey:

Thanks for calming me down last week. I really needed it. I know you understand, being 'family'. The detective doesn't have any leads so far, but I pray every day.

As you asked, I've enclosed all my family history that I have been able to discover. I hope it helps in your research. I told my sisters about you and they want to meet you. Elgin is only a short drive. I hope you can come visit us.

Thank you for everything.

Irene wished she could call and tell her that the police had arrested a man trying to pawn the wedding ring of Vera's sister. She was sure that Vera had heard by now. It appeared that Vera had avoided suspicion despite her indiscretions. Inside the envelope was a handwritten family tree going back four generations. Irene had thought about little else for the past few days. She so wanted to talk to people like herself. She hadn't realized how much she missed her talks with her sisters. Irene examined the family tree. There was no link up with her family that she could see; it must have been farther back. Irene's mother had given her "the talk," when Irene was sixteen. Her mother had told her that their special abilities and female only offspring went back at least nine generations.

"Come on, clear your junk off the table. I can't get dinner on if I can't see the table. Set it quick. We eat in five minutes."

"We can't eat it yet. You haven't named it."

"It's 'Chef's Surprise'."

"That's what we had last night."

Carol kissed Irene on the nose and smiled. "Surprise!"

That night they lay on the old threadbare couch listening to the radio and sipping their beer. The feel of Carol's skin under her fingertips made Irene tingle all over. "I think I'll love you for a thousand years."

"Is that all?" Carol pushed out her lower lip in a pout. "I already decided to love you forever."

"Let's take it a thousand at a time. If the first thousand goes well, we can decide on eternity." Their lips met in a deep passionate kiss. They made love.

Irene felt totally relaxed, just floating in the aftermath of the orgasm. That's when she remembered what she wanted to do. She reached over to the night stand grabbed the empty pill bottle that she set there earlier. She unscrewed the top and used it to collect a sample of the cloudy liquid from her vaginal area.

Carol leaned up on one elbow and looked at Irene as if she had lost her mind. "What on earth are you doing?"

"Taking a specimen. I need to check something out, an idea that's been bothering me for a few days."

"Boy, you sure know how to ruin a moment. I want to cuddle and you're running a science experiment. What are you doing? Taking a sample for your physical here to save time?"

Irene realized how she looked. "I'm sorry. I know this looks crazy but I need this to check something. I can't tell you now but tomorrow when I get home I'll explain everything."

"You're OK aren't you? You're not sick or anything?"

Irene put her arms around Carol and soothed her. "I'm fine. Tomorrow this is going to look damned silly but I just have to do this. Honest, I'll explain tomorrow."

Chapter 3

When Irene arrived at the office the next morning she headed straight for the lab without even stopping to hang up her coat. She tossed her things on a chair, removed the bottle and prepared a slide. She had just slid it into the microscope when Jake Best burst into the room in his usual overbearing manner. "Hey sweetie, what are you doing here so early?"

Irene answered through clenched teeth "I'm not your sweetie and it's none of your business." Jake was one of the most irritating people she had ever had the displeasure of working with. As an afterthought she added "And if it was your business you'd louse it up."

"You're going to have to learn respect for your fellow doctors, honey. You can start by getting your things out of my chair." Jake stood tapping his foot gesturing grandly at Irene's coat and bag.

"Sorry," she said. "I was a bit rushed this morning." She picked up her things and carried them over to the coat rack. When she turned around Jake was twiddling with the microscope.

"What you doing here anyway? A little government work?" Jake leaned towards the microscope.

"Just a quick favor for a friend," Irene replied nervously trying to push between Jake's bulk and the microscope. "If you don't mind, I'd like to finish."

Jake leaned down and put his eye to the scope. "Sure, no problem." He leaned back and looked at Irene. "Just tell him it's a bit lower in count than normal," Jake leered at Irene "but still plenty to do the job."

Irene's cheeks flushed as she waited for him to move away so she could look in the microscope herself. He had already told her the answer but she had to see for herself. She looked at the slide a long time. Irene was confused. She didn't know if she felt happy, sad or even scared. One phrase from her youth kept running through her brain, "Mother Nature's not too smart, is she." Mother Nature was a lot smarter than Irene had given her credit for.

Chapter 4

"I'm going to have a hard time telling you this, so please bear with me."

She's going to leave me, thought Carol. Irene had been so formal and stiff ever since she had come home.

"What I have to say is very difficult for me." Irene nervously looked at the table.

Carol felt tears growing in her eyes. The moment she feared for the last five years was about to happen.

"Ever since childhood I've been taught to trust no one with this and it's very hard to get past that." Irene paused for a moment, not sure that she could go through with it. "I'm different than everyone else. My whole family's different. There are three very important differences, two I'm sure of, one I strongly suspect. Before I tell you, you must promise me you will take this secret to your grave. I'm not kidding around, I'm serious."

Carol looked at her puzzled. "If you ask me to, you know I will. I promise never to tell another living soul."

"Look. I have a hereditary anomaly. I'm telepathic and I can only give birth to girls," she blurted out. "... sort of," she added as an after thought.

"What on earth are you talking about?" Carol was really confused now. Maybe Irene wasn't leaving her after all; maybe she had just lost her mind.

"Do you remember the night that jerk you went out with tried to rape you?"

"Sure, how could I forget? Him trying to rape me wasn't nearly as traumatic as kissing you. I was scared to death you'd hate me and throw me out. I was petrified."

"Do you remember the phone calls right after it happened?" Irene asked.

"Yeah, you said it was one of your sisters calling and then she called the others. Then each one called to get the scoop."

"I lied. My family didn't talk to each other that night. They didn't need to. All three of my sisters and my mother felt every bit of my fear that night. If you remember, I was so scared I wet myself. My mother and my sisters felt everything as I did and they called to find out what happened." Irene paused to let it sink in.

"You mean you each feel everything that the other person feels? Everything?"

"No, not everything. I wouldn't know where I left off and they began if that was the case. We learn to sort of filter things that we send out and receive. Block the radio static if you see what I mean. Only really big things get through. The connection is strongest to my mother, next is my sisters and then my grandmother." Irene reached across the table and squeezed Carol's hand. "Later I got questioned on what went on that night. No one could understand why I was so scared at ten o'clock at night and so happy at midnight. I couldn't very well tell my mother I just found the woman of my dreams."

Carol started to giggle. "She would have fainted dead away." Carol was giddy. Irene wasn't leaving her, she was just telling her some dark family secret that wouldn't change the way she felt. "It doesn't matter. I love you and this makes no difference. It's strange, but it doesn't change the way I feel. I'm also not sure if you haven't just lost your mind, and if that's the case I'll visit you every day at the institution."

"Look, I'm serious." Irene bowed her head and took a deep breath. "I know I'm asking you to accept a lot just on my say so. But you know me, and you know I'm not crazy. Being telepathic makes people scared of you. They want to know how you do it and when you can't tell them they think you're hiding something.

"There is a lot more. When I say we have female babies, I mean always. This has been going on for many generations, at least nine so far. A boy has never been born to us. Don't speak with your heart, think with your head. This is a dominant trait. That means that left alone long enough, there would be nothing but women like me and my family left in this world."

"That's not possible," Carol said. "There have to be men to get you pregnant. And besides, it would never get that far. The lack of male births would be noticed far before then."

"And what would be done about it when we're discovered?"

A dark cloud passed over Carol's face. She was just beginning to understand the impact of what was being said. "They can't kill you. People wouldn't stand for it even if they did feel threatened by you."

"No, I agree. There are too many of us now to be murdered. Even the federal government couldn't pull that one off without protest throughout the world. But they would have to do something."

"They might quarantine you. You know, like what's done for people with tuberculosis."

"They don't do it *for* people with tuberculosis; they do it *to* people with tuberculosis. They do it for the rest of the healthy world so they don't get infected. Quarantine is just a nice way of saying concentration camps, jails. Is that where you want to live?" Irene looked down at her hands unable to look into Carol's eyes. "There is a far more effective and cheaper solution ... sterilization. It's simple and fast. Snip snip. A nice neat solution to the problem."

"That's not what we fear most though. The government's solution for us will be far more humane than what the general public will do. Think about the fear, prejudice and hate that will surface when we are discovered, and I do say *when*, not *if*. It's just a matter of time. The more of us there are, the quicker that time will come."

Carol now had tears running down her cheeks. "If this all broke in the morning papers, I'd stand by you. I love you with all my heart and I'm not leaving because of anything the world could throw at us. The only thing that could get rid of me is if you no longer loved me. Then I'd die of a broken heart."

Irene got up and walked around the table and rubbed Carol's shoulders and neck with gentle, practiced fingers. "There's one more thing, and if you thought the rest of this was crazy, you ain't seen nothing yet."

"There's more?" Carol looked over her shoulder at Irene. "I don't think I'm ready for this. Maybe I should climb up on the roof and jump off now to avoid the rush."

Irene took a deep breath. "I'm a man."

"What!"

"Wait, listen for a minute. Do you remember in biology class, there were plants that were male or female and some plants that were both."

"Yes. A monoecious plant has both sexes in a single plant and ..."

"Dioecious."

"Dioecious plants have male and female in separate plants. But what's that got to do with you?"

"I'm monoecious. At least I'm pretty sure."

Carol swung around in her chair. "You mean you're both a man and a woman? How is that possible? You sure don't look like a man to me and I've given you some pretty thorough physicals. Just last night I checked your plumbing and there was no penis in sight."

"Do you remember Vera Ramsey?" Irene asked.

"Whoa! Now I'm having a real problem here. Who is she and what does that have to do with anything?" Carol was frustrated and nearly to the breaking point.

"Please try to hold on a little bit longer. I hope this will start to make sense in a minute."

Irene started again slowly. "Vera's sister was murdered here about a week ago. I did the autopsy on the body. During the examination I discovered that Vera's sister had two sets of sex organs. Even though she was outwardly a woman, inside she had a set of functional testicles. I even checked and everything appeared functional."

"What about a penis?" Carol asked. "Isn't that needed?"

"Not to produce sperm, it's just the delivery truck. Her testicles were connected to the urethra as would be normal in any man. It stood to reason that if she ejaculated during orgasm like a man does, it would appear as an excretion on the outside of the vagina."

"I still don't see what all this has to do with you?"

Irene rubbed the back of her neck as she paced around the table. "When Vera came to identify the body, we talked and one thing led to another. Well, I figured out she was like me, telepathic I mean, and only girls in her family. She confirmed it. That meant her sister was too. I started thinking about all this later and combined it with a comment you made about me."

"What comment was that?" asked Carol.

"One of the first times we made love you said that I smelled like a man," said Irene a little embarrassed.

"Last night, you were taking a sample to check today, right?"

Irene looked into Carol's face, watching for the reaction. "The results were completely normal ... for a man. Lots of healthy active sperm. The count was a bit low but otherwise normal as far as I could tell." Irene was shivering.

Carol stood and wrapped her arms around Irene's waist. "Look at it this way, we're not really homosexuals any more." Both women started to giggle, then began to laugh until tears were running down their cheeks. The tension had built to the breaking point and they dealt with it by laughing at the ridiculous situation they were in. Their sides began to ache.

They tentatively regained control. Their eyes met. A smirk formed on Carol's lips and they again launched into uncontrolled laughter. Irene dried her eyes and then dried Carol's. "This was just a way to lead up to my next question. I wanted you to know the facts before it was asked."

"You sure take a twisted path," panted Carol, struggling to halt the last of her giggles. "What's the question?"

"Carol Ann Jacobs, will you marry me?"

Carol just stared at Irene. "But how would we..."

"I didn't ask that, I just want to know if you'll marry me."

She hugged Irene. "Oh yes!"

"Getting married is between two people and God. The government is only interested for tax purposes. We can dispense with that portion," said Irene.

The following Sunday, Irene and Carol attended church together as usual but this time they joined the crowd at the altar to pray. Each made her silent prayer as the minister paused to touch their heads. They stood and returned to their seats, each had confirmed her decision in her own heart. After the service, the walk home seemed to take an eternity. It did little to calm the butterflies in their stomachs.

The marriage ceremony was a simple one. There were no guests or bridesmaids, no one to witness the ceremony. Still in their Sunday dresses, they each lit a candle and faced each other.

Irene started "Carol, I love you with all my heart. I promise to love, honor, and protect you, in sickness and health, for richer or poorer, forsaking all others for the rest of my life. With God as my witness, I give myself to you with no reservations."

Carol repeated the vow to Irene. She then produced a simple gold ring. "With this ring, I thee wed." She slipped the ring on Irene's finger.

Irene also slid a ring on Carol's finger and repeated the words "With this ring, I thee wed." Together they lit a new candle from their individual candles and then extinguished the individual candles. Together they intoned "I now pronounce us bound as one for eternity." They met in a gentle kiss.

"I know it's not much of a honeymoon but since you have tomorrow off I arranged to have it off with you," said Irene. She held up two train tickets. "Care to go to Milwaukee for dinner? We don't have to be back until tomorrow night."

"I'd love to," accepted Carol.

It was about a week later that Irene arrived home after work to a surprise. "Hello, I'm home..." Irene looked around the room. There were vases everywhere with fresh flowers. The small dining room table was set with the good china and candles burned in the center. A bottle of red wine sat open, breathing on the end table.

Carol stuck her head out of the kitchen. "Did you have a good day?" Carol had on her Saturday night dress, silk stockings and a lace apron. The apartment was filled with a wonderful aroma.

"Oh I'm sorry ma'am," Irene mugged. "I live in apartment 304. I must have come in here by mistake."

"Be quiet, you poop! Come in and sit down. Dinner will be ready in a few minutes." Carol ducked back into the kitchen, the obvious source of the wonderful smells.

Irene set her bag by the door and gingerly walked around the small living room. "What's the occasion?" She pulled off her shoes and rubbed her tired feet.

"Whatever do you mean? Does there have to be an occasion?" Carol asked slyly. "Isn't this how a good wife should treat her mate?" She laid a plate of hors d'oeuvres next to Irene.

Irene eyed Carol with well-founded suspicion. "OK, whose cooking is this? You have trouble with anything more complex than spaghetti." Irene regretted her words when Carol looked genuinely hurt. "I'm only kidding. It's just that you've never done anything like this."

"I've never had a reason like this before," said Carol. She reached out and caressed Irene's cheek. Irene took her hand and kissed it gently. "You have just enough time to sample one or two and pour the wine." She hustled back to the kitchen.

Irene watched her go and then tried the appetizers. As she nibbled on a second, she filled the two wineglasses and placed them on the table. Carol returned, minus the apron, carrying a platter of roast beef and vegetables in one hand and a gravy boat in the other. "You even made gravy," exclaimed Irene.

"Yes, and there aren't any lumps either," proclaimed Carol proudly. "Well, at least not too many."

Irene enjoyed the wonderful meal and tried to keep Carol at the table but she flitted around the apartment like a nervous butterfly, making sure everything was perfect. Finally, after Carol cleared away the desert dishes, not allowing Irene to lift a finger, the two of them retired to the couch. "Thank you, it was all wonderful," whispered Irene.

"You're welcome but I have to admit that I did have an ulterior motive," responded Carol.

"Ah ha! So that's it," exclaimed Irene. "This is just a plot so you could have your way with me. Well, it worked."

Carol gave a nervous smile. "In a way, yes." She toyed with her empty wineglass. "I wanted to ask your help with something."

"For you, anything. Whatever it is, it's yours."

Carol fixed her gaze on her glass. "I want to have your baby."

Irene stared at Carol. After several seconds she realized she was spilling her wine down her dress. "You what? I don't think it's ever been done."

"People do it every day."

"You know what I mean. What if there's something wrong with it." Irene was trying to think up reasons not to do what she so desperately wanted to try. Ever since she discovered that she produced what appeared to be normal, healthy sperm, she had been thinking about it too. "If it works, and that's a mighty big if, when you go to the hospital, who are we going to say the father was? Don't you think someone might think it odd to have me as the father?"

"I've been working on that. The easiest is just to say I was raped and was too ashamed too report it. They will believe it. It happens all the time." Carol could see the hesitation in Irene's eyes; she was weakening. "You have good job with steady pay. I could go back to work after she gets old enough."

"Not until she's in school. She will have to be raised and taught just as I was," Irene said. "You'll be taking on a very heavy responsibility having a daughter by me."

Now for the clincher thought Carol. "It may not be a she. You only know that it will be a girl if you supply the egg. If you supply the sperm, we just may produce a boy."

"Yes. You may be right." Irene had already thought of that. "But are you sure you want to do this? What if the child is deformed?"

"The sperm looked completely normal, you said so yourself. I want to do this more than anything else in the world." Carol cupped Irene's face in her hands. "And if we don't try, we'll never know will we. I'm not getting younger. I don't want to give birth when I'm forty."

Irene gave up her last feeble resistance. "I'll need to come up with a way to deliver the packages, so to speak."

"Already done." Carol held up a syringe with the needle removed, leaving a long tube with a small hole in the end. "I figure we can collect the little guys just like you did, put them in here, slide it inside me and push. I think it will make a very good penis replacement."

Irene looked it over for sharp edges where the needle had been removed. "I think you're right but I suggest we add a tiny bit of warm water to add volume. It might help them on their way."

Carol gave Irene a kiss that could melt an iceberg. "Ready to make a baby?" She took Irene by the hand and led her into the bedroom.

Chapter 5

At four months pregnant, Carol was starting to show even to the casual observer. The comments and whispers had already started at work. Being an unwed mother was not an easy thing to do in 1940. Carol decided to continue to work at the doctor's office until she was forced to quit. Every dime she could save would make life that much easier when the baby came.

Irene had been researching the Monoecion family trees ever since her discovery. She called to Carol "Take a look. I've been trying to calculate how many there are of us. With the data I've collected I've tried to make a guess as to how many children were born to the lost branches and estimate how many will be born in the future."

Carol came and stood behind Irene looking at the chart on the table. "I know you keep all this stuff in a safe place but it worries me to see it all on paper. What if something happened to us?"

"You forget. My family would know the instant it happened. One of my sisters would be here within hours to collect anything sensitive. I've already told her where it will be.

"Besides, I don't know any other way to notify everyone I can of what I've discovered. We were all making the assumption that there was no visible physical difference between us and the rest of the human race. Now I know every time one of us goes into surgery there's a chance of discovery."

"Why would anyone suspect anything? It would just be considered a fluke of nature."

"I shrugged it off the first time I saw dual sex organs. The second time would have raised my curiosity and a third would have triggered papers in medical journals. All it would take is one doctor making the heredity connection and the game is over. The investigation would be short and sweet and we would be front page news."

Irene knew there was another important reason to contact as many of those with the genetic monoecion strain as possible, their mental health. As a teenager, Irene had been tormented by her guilt about her sexual urges. She would have given anything to know that her sexual feelings were normal, that it was no more unusual for her to be aroused by the female form than it was for a normal man to be. After all, she had the same equipment as a man, the same hormones. And it worked the same way for her attraction to men.

This line of reasoning upset Carol. To Carol, it was saying that it was normal for Irene to be attracted to Carol but Carol was perverted to be attracted to Irene. No matter how hard she tried, Irene couldn't help Carol eliminate the guilt she felt. Irene had a medical excuse and Carol was jealous.

Carol looked at the figures. "You mean there are over three hundred thousand of us already?" Since she had become pregnant, Carol considered herself part of Irene's family tree. She was a Monoecion now too.

"That's a very conservative estimate." Irene closed her black leather journal. "We need a plan if we wish to remain undiscovered much longer."

"What? I need to keep the shades down more? I think the neighbors have already figured out I'm pregnant."

"I didn't mean us, although it's getting harder to keep that a secret too. I was talking about Monoecions. It would be nice if we could keep it hidden as long as possible and the way to do that is to have us in jobs where we can stand a chance of hiding it if it does start to show up."

"You mean like medical examiner's office?"

"And the police, and the FBI, and the state and federal governments, not to mention newspapers. If we have people in the right places, at least we will get a little lead time when we are discovered."

Carol stopped rubbing Irene's shoulders and sat down at the table. "So tell me, what would you do if we found out that tomorrow's headline will be 'Women with balls take over the world'?"

Irene thought for a few moments. "I don't have the slightest idea, but maybe with a few hours notice I would think of something."

Carol felt the child growing inside her but it was Irene who informed her that the child was definitely Monoecion. Irene felt the connection growing stronger every day as the fetus developed into a conscious being. It started as a whisper barely heard when she was just over three months. By the time she was in the womb six months, Irene could feel the child respond to her emotions. Carol chose the name Sally, after her mother, but just in case she also picked out the name Randolph. Irene was thankful that she knew it was a girl.

Carol went through all the mood swings of an expectant mother as her stomach grew and her mobility disappeared. The two flights of stairs to the apartment became the south slope of the Alps, scalable only with great effort and determination. She reminded Irene daily that she was at fault for Carol's current condition, only half in jest.

The sweltering heat of July in Chicago was upon them. No matter how she tried, Carol could not get comfortable in bed. Irene was banished to a mattress on the floor so Carol's broadening frame had enough space to sleep. Saturday night Irene was preparing for another night on the floor when Carol asked her to come to bed.

"Are you sure I won't disturb you," asked Irene. "You have such a hard time sleeping as it is."

"I miss having you next to me at night. I'll be all right."

"Well, considering the size of your belly, you'll still miss having me next to you!" remarked Irene. Carol hit her with a pillow.

At five o'clock that morning the first contractions woke Carol. She sat up in bed and started timing them. By six o'clock she was convinced that this was the real thing and woke Irene. "Irene, wake up."

A muffled snore escaped from Irene's mouth and a mumbled "Hmmm?"

"Irene, wake up! We need to go to the hospital."

"What!?" Irene leaped from the bed. "Where's your bag? I'll call the cab; you get your robe on!" She tore into the wardrobe, clothes flying in all directions.

"My bag is at the foot of the bed, right where I told you it was every time you ask. Tell the cab to be here in half an hour. I'm going to take a bath first." Carol observed the glazed look in Irene's eyes. "There is going to be another doctor at the hospital isn't there?"

"Of course there is but don't worry, I'll take care of you," replied Irene while searching for her shoes.

"It wasn't me that I was worried about." Carol eased herself into the bathroom for a quick sponge bath. A few minutes later, she emerged with her necessities bag, hair brushed and proceeded to calmly get dressed.

"Hurry up. We need to go!" urged Irene.

"Is the cab here?" Carol asked simply.

Irene looked back at her a bit confused by the question. "Ah, no."

"If you don't mind, I'd rather not walk to the hospital. Let me know when the cab pulls up." Carol went back to getting dressed. Irene paced back and forth in front of the window muttering under her breath. "Would you please try to calm down," Carol pleaded. "You're getting the baby all excited."

"I'm sorry but I can't help it," apologized Irene, "I've never been a father before."

The cab finally arrived. Irene grabbed her doctor's bag and Carol's suitcase and rushed out the door leaving Carol to turn out the lights and lock the door. The streets were nearly deserted as the cab rushed them to the hospital. Irene paid the cabby and helped Carol into the emergency room doors. Being back in her element calmed Irene and she began to give instructions to the nurse on duty. Carol was taken to a private room where she was poked, prodded and prepared for the birth. Despite the steady strong contractions, by nine o'clock Carol had only dilated to three centimeters. It began to look like it was going to be a long day.

At 10:30, Carol announced "I want to go home. I can come back tomorrow and we can finish this then."

"I'm afraid that it doesn't work that way," Irene explained patiently. "You're just going to have to stick it out."

Another contraction gripped Carol as she clutched the bed frame. "You stick it out! I'm going home!"

Irene checked Carol again. "Sorry, but you have dilated another two centimeters. You're going to have a baby."

Up until this point, Carol had not really come to grips with this fact. Now it seemed all too real. The pain began to climb with the contractions. "This hurts, this really hurts," cried Carol.

"I know," soothed Irene. "You just…"

"You don't know anything!" screamed Carol in a burst of venom. "When did you have a baby?" Carol started to sob.

"You don't have to slam your thumb in a door to know it would hurt," explained Irene defensively. The pain of Carol's accusation cut to her soul.

The nurse saw Doctor Moore wipe a tear from her eye. "That's why most doctors stay out of here as much as possible. It gets a little emotional when the pain really starts."

"Yes, I know." Irene squeezed Carols' hand. "I have to check on the delivery room. I'll be right back."

"I'm sorry," said Carol between sobs. "I didn't mean it."

"It's all right. This isn't the first time I've done this. Now just hold on for a little bit longer. I'll be right back."

"I'm sorry," Carol cried again.

At 10:40, Irene announced to Carol that she was ready. Moments later she was transferred to a gurney to be rolled to the delivery room. Carol began a nervous giggle between the grips of pain. "I'm going to have a baby!" she called out to nurse they passed in the hall and resumed giggling. She regained control on the delivery table.

"It's all up to you now," Irene coaxed. "You need to give me a good push." Carol strained in time with the contraction. "Very good! I see a head with a nice patch of brown hair. Let's try that again." Again Carol pushed with the next contraction. "The head is out! Just one more is all it should take."

"I can't do it. I'm too tired. Let me rest a minute," begged Carol.

"You can rest later. Right now we need one last big push. Come on, I know you can do it." Irene gently rotated the baby as Carol pressed down once again. The baby's shoulders cleared the birth canal and slid out into Irene's waiting hands. Seconds later, little Sally Jacobs let out a cry. "Thank God you're a girl, little one. If you were a boy she was going to name you Randolph." Irene cut the cord and passed the baby to the waiting nurse to be cleaned up.

Irene completed the post delivery duties, removed her gloves and held Carol's hand as the attending nurse finished the cleanup. Carol was rolled to the post delivery room and Irene sat on a stool resting in the operating room. The nurse returned and addressed her. "Excuse me doctor, but I just want to ask if you would be my doctor when I start my family. I've been in here for many births and I've never seen a doctor treat a patient like you did today."

Irene smiled at her. "I would be honored but I can't claim great compassion. The mother, Carol Jacobs, has been my best friend for years." Irene added with a laugh "She also told me that if I loused this up that she would make my life hell."

"Just the same, I'd still want you for my doctor." The nurse turned to walk away.

"Hey, you did a great job too. I'd be happy to work with you again anytime."

The Great Depression was slowly loosening its hold of the country. War once again broke out in Europe and Irene became politically active, campaigning for United States involvement in the blocking of the growth of Fascism. When France fell, she went to England as a volunteer at the height of the Battle of Britain, returning home to Chicago nearly two years later. A second child was added to the family. The wear and tear of the war years and life in the big city had taken its toll. Carol and Irene started looking for a small town to move their family to where the pace of their life could be slowed.

The Journal

July 16, This Year

Chapter 6

Charlie Wilkens had been remodeling homes in the Benton Harbor, Michigan area for 17 years now and each one was different. That's what he enjoyed about his work. He loved to watch the new take shape from the old. The people on the other hand were usually a pain in the ass. They never understood what was necessary to hold a house together and why. This job was a perfect example. To the couple who lived here, it was simply cut some holes in the roof and put dormers in. Knock some two-by-fours out of the way, slap some studs and sheet rock up and you have a guest bedroom. The only problem was if he removed the two-by-fours as requested the entire roof would collapse with the first heavy snowfall. He didn't care if Hank Smally had told them his outfit could do it, it wasn't safe. Charlie had drawn some sketches of the way it could be properly done and discussed the design with the owners for forty-five minutes. He finally nailed together some boards and showed them the structural weakness of their design by sitting on it. He got a bruised butt and an OK to do the job his way.

His crew had finished for the day and Charlie had hung around to check the wood around the new hole in the roof. If there were any rot, it would have to be replaced before they framed in the dormer tomorrow. He pushed his ball cap back over his rapidly expanding bald spot, exposing his gray temples. With the skill of surgeon, he used a screwdriver to poke and probe the wood, feeling the flesh and bone of the house, searching for any signs of disease. The blade hit something soft.

"Shit," Charlie cursed under his breath. He slid up the blade of the screwdriver expecting to see shards of rotted wood. Instead it was a flap of leather attached to a book. He carefully eased it up out of the crack between the attic floor and the roof. The old leather bound notebook looked to be in pretty good shape. He absently started leafing through the pages, checking the dates of the entries that ranged between October of 1938 and April of 1944. He took the book and slid it into his toolbox. He didn't think the new owners of the house would miss something they didn't know they had and his wife Gloria would sure love to read somebody's old journal. She always got a kick out of such things.

By the time Charlie had arrived home, he had forgotten all about the notebook. It wasn't until late that night when Gloria asked him how the new job was going that the notebook floated its way to the top of his mind. "It's going OK now that they let me do the job my way. Oh, and I found something you might be interested in, an old diary or journal I found. It was stuck between the roof and the attic floor. It looked like it had been there a long time."

"What, you just took it?"

"Well, yeah. They just bought the place, haven't even moved in yet. It was probably left there years ago by who knows whom. That place has been through at least three families since we moved here."

"Still, you should have asked permission." Gloria looked at her husband expectantly. "Well."

"Oh, it's out in my tool box." Charlie got out of bed, pulled on his robe and headed to the garage, tripping over the cat on the way. "Damn it, cat. I wish you'd learn to sleep somewhere other than in front of my door." He retrieved the notebook from his pickup and returned to the bedroom, searching the hallway for UFO's (unidentified furry objects, as his daughter called them) along the way. "I'm not sure what it is, I didn't have time to look at it too close."

He offered it to his wife. "Go clean it off first. It's filthy." Charlie blew the dust off and brushed the mouse droppings and spider webs into the wastebasket.

"There you go my lady," he intoned with a grand gesture.

"Thank you my lord. Now wash your hands before you get back in bed." As Charlie stood at the sink in the bathroom, Gloria started to flip through the pages. "Looks like it was written by a doctor, a woman doctor unless you know a man named Irene."

"A doctor of what? She could have been a doctor of English literature."

"I don't know yet, I just opened it."

Charlie crawled back into bed and started to read over his wife's shoulder. He looked at the alarm clock, 11:15. He should have been asleep an hour ago. He turned off his light, rolled over and in minutes was dead to the world.

Charlie opened one blurry eye; the clock said 3:42. Gloria's light was still on. He attempted to say, "Good God woman, go to sleep." What came out was one long mumble followed by renewed snoring.

When the alarm went off at five in the morning, the first thing Charlie noticed was that the bed was empty. He turned off the alarm and staggered to the bathroom. Halfway through his morning ritual, Gloria came in still looking fresh, bearing a cup of coffee. "Have you been up all night?"

"It's your fault. You're the one who brought that notebook home. That thing beats any soap on TV." She handed him the cup.

"Oh, what's so interesting?"

"From what I could tell, this Dr. Moore, whose first name is Irene, is married to Carol. At first I just figured it was a guy with an unusual first name but now I'm pretty sure it's a woman."

"How can you be so sure?" Charlie asked between sips of coffee. "Lots of guys have strange names."

"How many men do you know who menstruate?"

"There have been several I've suspected" chided Charlie. "Still, it might have been a figure of speech."

"It sure didn't sound that way" mussed Gloria. "But you know what else, more than once he says it's a miracle he could father a child. Figure that one out."

"I don't have time." He rinsed his razor and dropped in the drawer. "I've got to go to work. If I'm not there before the crew arrives they just sit on their butts and wait. You'll just have to work it out yourself."

"I've been trying to all night. I'd like to give up for now and go to bed except I drank enough coffee to keep an army awake."

Gloria went to the county court house and checked on the house's previous owners. She had dealt with the clerk many times before in the line of duty for Charlie.

The clerk disappeared into the basement, returning fifteen minutes later. "I found it. Dr. Irene Moore purchased the house in June of 1961. Looks like it was sold to a Carol Jacobs in 1972." She paused for a moment. "No, no, Miss Jacobs inherited it from Miss Moore. It appears Carol Jacobs sold it in 1979 to a Phillip Klausman."

"Does it say if Dr. Moore was a man or a woman?"

The clerk checked over the forms. "Not on this one but I assume it was a woman, there's no Mr. or Mrs., just doctor. If she voted, it would show up in the voter registration."

"Thanks, Louise. That covers the time period I was looking for. Do you know of anyone who might have known Dr. Moore or Miss Jacobs?"

"No, that was well before my time here. Jack Speilding might know something. He used to work here until he retired four years ago. He lives over near there. I'll get you his phone number, hold on a second."

"Great, thanks." Gloria could hardly contain herself. It all fit. Dr. Moore and Miss Jacobs were live-in lovers. Then, when Dr. Moore died, she willed the house to Miss Jacobs. Gloria felt like a private eye. Nothing this racy had happened in her life in years.

"Here's his number. If he doesn't answer just keep trying. He spends most of his days on the lake with a fishing rod in his hand. Well, good luck. I hope you find what you're looking for."

Gloria tried his phone repeatedly until three o'clock that afternoon when she finally fell asleep on the couch, which is where Charlie found her at six-thirty that night. He covered her with a blanket and went to the kitchen to see what he could find for dinner.

While Charlie munched on his sandwich, he flipped through the notebook and read snatches here and there. The more he read, the more confused he became. Charlie went back to the beginning and started over, reading and re-reading each entry. The entries mostly made sense up until November of 1938, that is, if Dr. Moore was a man. He mentioned several times that he missed or loved a woman named Carol. Charlie was sure Carol was a woman because Dr. Moore referred to Carol as "she." Then their wedding ceremony was described. That proves he's a man, thought Charlie. But then there were a couple of entries about trying to get Carol pregnant and how impossible it seemed. The next entry completely lost Charlie, "We will have to stop trying for a baby for a week now because I'm menstruating. That's something men don't have to deal with." That's got to be a figure of speech, Charlie thought. It has to be.

There was one reference that showed up throughout the journal that Charlie wasn't familiar with. He pulled out his copy of the American Heritage Dictionary that he and Gloria always used as the bible for their Scrabble games and looked it up.

mo•noe•cious adj. 1. Botany. Having male and female reproductive organs in separate flowers on a single plant.

This is crazy, he thought. According to the journal Dr. Moore was monoecious. That means either she's a plant, he figured he could throw that one out, or both male and female, which was almost as crazy as being a plant. But if it were true, it would explain a lot of things in the journal, like being so surprised that she fathered two children. He was absently flipping back and forth through the journal looking for anything that would help him make sense of it all when he noticed the loose binding.

It was around midnight when Charlie woke his wife. She didn't wake happy. Her neck hurt from lying on the arm of the couch and she was still tired. "Why did you let me sleep there? Now I'm going to be sore all day." She tried to focus her eyes but it was a losing battle. "What time is it?"

"It's 12:10. Come on and wake up, I've got something to show you." Charlie helped Gloria sit upright. "Come out to the table."

Gloria couldn't get her eyes to focus or her mind for that matter. "12:10? Show me in the morning." She flopped back down on the couch.

"It concerns our Dr. Moore and the journal. Come on, please?" he begged. "I want you to see this." Charlie reached his hand out to his wife.

Gloria gave in. I'm awake now, she thought. "Hold on, I've got to pee. Just wait." She headed for the hall bathroom. Gloria hadn't seen Charlie this excited since he started his contracting business, though it wasn't excited exactly, it was more like nervous. She flushed and opened the bathroom door to find Charlie standing outside waiting. "I wish you wouldn't do that. I feel like I'm being timed. Now what are you so fired up about?"

"I want you to see what I found inside the cover lining of the journal. I think I figured out Dr. Irene Moore and it's either a grand hoax or the discovery of the century." They went to the dining room table where Charlie had laid out four large sheets of rice paper. He pointed to the first one and asked her "What's wrong with this picture?"

"Please Charlie, I'm too tired for guessing games and I'm no medical expert." She looked pleadingly at Charlie. She hated it when he got this way. She looked at the drawing on the table more carefully. "It's a drawing of a woman's reproductive system, so what?"

"Close, but no cigar. What are these?" he asked tapping the paper with the eraser end of a pencil.

Gloria moved her face close to the paper to read the faded printing. "It's labeled testicles. But that can't be right, the rest of the organs are female."

Charlie handed the journal to her and pointed out a passage.

Being monoecious opens up so many new possibilities I don't know where to start. It also brings about an answer to the dilemma my sisters and I discussed so many times. We used to say that Mother Nature was such a fool for creating us, especially with the trait 100% dominant. Here we were, doomed to just having girls and no boys, generation after generation. After a short time, at least in the grand scope of things, there will be nothing but girls and no men to fertilize them. Now I see that Mother Nature was not so dumb after all. She provided each of us with the ability to both carry and fertilize the egg.

Charlie then handed her the dictionary and pointed to the definition. Gloria read it with growing comprehension. "You think she was both, like this drawing?"

Charlie said, "I'm almost sure of it. I think she was some kind of medical freak. It would explain everything, why she has menstrual cramps and yet claims to have fathered two children." Now is where she sends me to the funny farm he thought. "And you know what else I think? I think that the world is in danger."

"Don't be so melodramatic, how's the world in danger?"

"These Monoecions, as she calls them, can produce only girls, no male children are born, right?"

"I guess."

"Trust me," Charlie said. "That's what she says in the journal. Also she says the trait is one hundred percent dominant so every child has the trait too. Got it?"

"Yes, I think so. But how does that endanger the world?" Gloria asked.

"Just look at her numbers." Charlie flipped to a bookmark and pointed to a passage for Gloria to read.

This is an estimate of the total monoecious population. There is no way to know how accurate it is but it should be close. The starting date is based on my mother telling me it has been nine generations. Because the trait is always dominant, the numbers are easy. I have tried to adjust for the birthrate changes over the years.

Year	New births	Deaths	Population
1720	1		1
1743	4		5
1766	16		20
1789	64	1	84
1812	256	4	336
1835	1,024	16	1,344
1858	4,096	64	5,376
1881	16,384	256	21,504
1904	65,536	1,024	86,016
1927	262,144	4,096	344,064
1950	1,048,576	16,384	1,376,256
1973	4,194,304	65,536	5,505,024
1996	16,777,216	262,144	22,020,096
2019	67,108,864	1,048,576	88,080,384

"It doesn't take a rocket scientist to figure out as they increase in population, we will decrease" said Charlie.

"Why do we have to decrease?"

"Look here." Charlie flipped the journal open to another marker. "She figured it out here."

In a closed system with a population of 1000, it would take 13 generations to completely convert the population from dioecious to monoecious. When the population is raised to 100 thousand, the number of generations only increases to 23, and at a population of 100 million the number of generations to convert is 31. I find it hard to believe it would take such a short time. At first glance it would seem that these numbers do not apply but they do. We must keep in mind that the world is a closed system and that population increases apply to human and Monoecions alike.

I realize the numbers do not take into account any social reaction to the process and are therefore inaccurate but they do point to one definite fact, we cannot remain undiscovered for much longer. I expect that will happen within the next two or three generations.

Gloria looked up at her husband. "It's probably not for real is it? I mean this is probably just a hoax."

"Well, the first thing to find out is if this woman really did exist."

"She lived in the house you're working on from 1959 until she died in 1972" said Gloria. "When she died she left the house to Carol Jacobs. I assume that it's the Carol that's mentioned throughout the journal as her wife."

"How do know that?" asked Charlie.

Gloria explained what she had found out that day. "That's as much as I've been able to find so far."

"Find an address on any family members?"

"I've just started! I think I've done pretty well just getting this far. Maybe Mr. Speilding will remember something. What's the rest of this?" she asked pointing to the other papers spread on the table.

"I think they're family trees of monoecious families. Of course they're all ancient. It will be tough to find anyone of them still alive. Some of the kids should be." Charlie became concerned. "You haven't said anything to anyone about this book have you?"

"No, I just told the clerk at the deeds office that I was trying to get some history on the house. Why? What's the problem?"

Charlie held up an index finger. "First, if you were one of these monoecious people, what would you do to keep this from getting out?"

Gloria looked frightened. "You don't think they would hurt us?"

"I don't know. I just don't want to take any chances." He ticked off the remaining points. "Second, if this is a hoax, I don't want anyone to know I fell for it. And third, if it is true, this book could be worth a whole mess of money."

In the morning it all looked pretty foolish. Charlie was upset with himself for falling for the obvious hoax that the whole affair had to be. He wanted to tell Gloria to forget trying to talk to Mr. Speilding but she had already left by the time he got up. They had decided last night that she should try to catch him on his way out fishing rather than risk his wrath by calling after midnight.

Now Charlie's thoughts went to who could have pulled this one on him. It couldn't be any of the guys on the job; they didn't know him well enough to invest the amount of time it would take to create the journal. Not to mention that none of them had the smarts to come up with it in the first place. No, this was the work of a master, someone who really wanted to get even. That line of reasoning led him to only one person, Willie Schmitt.

Charlie grinned to himself. Several years ago, Willie had been the victim of the most elaborate practical joke ever attempted by Charlie. It had required months of planning and the cooperation of several friends, including an old school chum who worked at the IRS office in Chicago, but it had worked. Charlie's grin grew as he remembered Willie slowly walking to face him, and humbly saying "Wilkens, if I had a hat, I'd take it off to you." Willie bowed to Charlie. "But remember this; I'll get you for this one. I don't know when, or how, but I'll get you for this."

That had been over ten years ago and he had forgotten it, until now. This was something that Willie was capable of doing. Charlie decided it was time to look up Willie.

Gloria reached Mr. Speilding's house a little before seven in the morning and parked the car. She didn't want to disturb him so she parked on the street rather than in his drive and watched the house for signs of life. It took only minutes before the side door opened and a cat curved its way out. Gloria got out of the car and walked up the drive. An old man came out of the door carrying a rod, fishing tackle and a small cooler. He was a bit startled to see a woman in his driveway at this time of the morning.

"Can I help you? I was just on my way out." Lord, he hoped it wasn't another Jehovah's Witness. It took him near an hour to get rid of the last pair. But then that was his fault. He just liked to talk religion almost as much as he liked to fish.

"Are you Mister Speilding?"

"I'm Jack Speilding. And you are?"

"I'm Gloria Wilkens. My husband is Charlie Wilkens, the contractor." He just looked at her blankly. "The lady at the County Clerk's Office said you might be able to help me. I'm looking for some information on a house my husband's working on over on Clayborn street. It won't take long. Do you have a few minutes?"

"Young lady," Jack started, "I am old, but I hope I have more than a few minutes left." He gave her a grin. "I'll be glad to help you if I can as long as you don't call me mister. The name's Jack."

Gloria blushed. She hadn't been called a young lady in a long time. "How do you do Jack? My husband's working on the old two-story house at the corner of Clayborn and Walnut and we became interested in the people that used to live there. Do you remember Dr. Irene Moore and Carol Jacobs? They moved there in 1959."

A smile slowly grew until it seemed as if it were going to cover his entire face. "This old mind can't remember much, but I may be able to help you a bit." He turned and looked up at the porch. "If you don't think the neighbors will gossip too much about a lady sitting on my porch this early in the morning, come on up and sit a while. I'll tell you what I can."

After they got settled on the porch Jack remembered his manners and offered Gloria a cup of coffee. "No thanks. I already had two cups this morning. Did you know them?"

"Oh yes! Better than most people know their elders. I was about eighteen when they moved to town. I wouldn't have noticed two old women moving into town but every young man in town noticed Miss Jacobs' daughter Becky. My, my, she was a looker." Jack noticed Gloria was listening intently. "She was the first girl to break my heart. You may forget the second or the third, but never the first."

"You called her mother Miss Jacobs. Was she ever married?" Gloria asked.

"No, not as far as I know."

"Dr. Moore, was that a ... I know this sounds silly but was Dr. Moore a man or a woman?"

"Well, that's a good question" he quipped. "No, Irene was a woman all right, but when I took Becky out for our first date, Dr. Moore put more fear in me than any girl's father ever did. That was the first time I ever met her, Dr. Moore I mean, and by the time she was done questioning me, I thought J. Edgar himself had been at me."

"Wasn't it a bit odd having two women move into a house together?"

Jack immediately lost his smile. "Look ma'am, there was a lot of talk around town back then, but let me make sure you understand this. They were two of the nicest ladies I ever met. And if you just want to dig up an old scandal, I think our conversation is done." He rose from his chair, his hands clenched tightly at his sides.

Gloria was taken aback by his agitation. "I'm sorry" she stammered. "I didn't mean to pry into their personal lives. I have no intent to debase their character. We had found some letters in the attic and I was just trying to understand them. I'm sorry; I didn't mean to upset you."

Jack sat back down and shook his head. "I'm sorry ma'am. I got so use to defending them back then when I was dating Becky, it just came back naturally."

"Was Becky the oldest?"

"No, that was Sally. She was four years older than Becky and was already off to college by the time they moved here." Jack paused for a minute pondering. "I think she was a lawyer living in Washington DC back then. Who knows where she's at now?"

"Did Dr. Moore have any children?" Gloria asked.

"No, not as far as I know of. She just treated Carol's kids as her own."

If you only knew, thought Gloria. "Did Carol have any more children?"

"No. Two was it. Becky said they kept their mom plenty busy all by themselves."

"Did Becky ever mention her father?"

"I think he died in the war." His eyes focused on some point in time far away. "I don't remember her telling me that. I think I may have assumed it since so many kids lost their dad or brothers in that war. I don't remember her ever mentioning their father. I'm sure the girls had the same father, it was obvious by how much they looked alike, and they didn't look that much like their mother."

Gloria took a chance. "Did the girls look at all like Dr. Moore?"

Jack looked surprised at the question. "Yes, as a matter of fact, they did look a sight more like Dr. Moore than they did Miss Jacobs. Do you know something I don't?"

"Nothing definite. Just something in the letters made me think it was possible." The time slipped away as they sat on the porch and talked. Gloria checked her watch and excused herself. "Thank you for your hospitality. The way you talk of them, I wish I had a chance to meet them."

"Well, if you promise to say hello from me, you could talk to Becky yourself. I believe she lives over in Kalamazoo now, and her name is Mrs. Rebecca Lovett but she always goes by Becky, hated the name Rebecca. Her husband died a few years back but the last I checked, she still lives on Locust over by the college campus. Her number is in the book."

"Thank you. I'd love to talk to her about the house and its history. I really need to get going, I promised my husband I'd only be gone an hour."

As Gloria was driving home, her mind was churning with ideas. She needed to locate Becky and find out if all her children were girls. This would be touchy though. Becky wouldn't be as easy to fool as Jack was when it came to questions about her family. If Mrs. Lovett knew they were on to them, who knew what would happen.

Gloria came home to find Charlie on the phone, which frustrated her greatly. She wanted to tell him what she had found out from Mr. Speilding. Charlie brushed her away when she tried to get him to cut it short

Finally she heard him wrapping up. "Yeah, you know how it is, Willie, I've just been thinking of you lately and had to see what had happened since I talked to you last... five years is a long time... Yeah, you too. Keep in touch. Goodbye." Charlie hung up the receiver. "Well, if this is a practical joke, I'm sure it's not Willie. He had a stroke two years ago and can barely sign his name now."

"That's what I've been trying to tell you," flustered Gloria.

"What? How did you know Willie had a stroke?" asked Charlie confused.

"Oh shut your trap for a minute or I'll give you a stroke. I've been trying to tell you that I saw Mr. Speilding and he confirmed the information in the diary. Dr. Moore was a woman and she lived with a Miss Jacobs in that house." Gloria shushed Charlie as he tried to interrupt. "He also gave me the address of one of their children, Becky, the youngest one. She lives close by and he thought she would be glad to have us by to talk to her about the house."

It began to really sink into Charlie. "My God Gloria, do you realize that this could be real."

Chapter 7

Gloria reached Becky that afternoon. Gloria explained that they were restoring the old house to the way it was back in the fifties and wanted to know if they could get together and ask her about the details. Becky said she would be glad to help and set a time to meet at her house on Saturday.

Charlie and Gloria arrived in front of the house fifteen minutes early. "OK, remember the play, I'll do all the asking about the house and details like that. You take the lead in asking about the family. She'll think you're just making conversation."

"I know, I know. We've been over it a thousand times. Just relax or you'll have a heart attack in the middle of the conversation."

As Gloria and Charlie stepped up on the screened in porch, a pleasant looking lady opened the front door. Her hair was white, peppered with a few remaining brunette strands. "Hello, you must be the Wilkens. I'm Becky Lovett. Come on in." She led them into to a warm but simple living room filled with books. There was at least one bookshelf on each wall. "Welcome to my library. You'll have to excuse the mess. I don't get to clean like I used to."

Gloria looked around the room for anything out of place. The room was immaculate. If my house ever looked this neat Charlie would have heart failure, she thought. "This room is lovely," said Gloria.

"Can I get you anything, coffee, tea? There may even be a soft drink left in the fridge."

"No, not now thanks," Charlie answered. "We stopped for lunch on the way over. We just appreciate you talking to us. The new owners of the house wanted to rebuild it back to the way it was," he lied, "and I could only tell so much from looking." Charlie pulled out his note pad and started to ask questions about the colors of walls, what rooms were wallpapered and the like.

Gloria sat quietly and looked around the room. There was a collection of pictures on the mantel and she went to look at them. "Is this your son?" she asked indicating a picture of a young man.

"Well, it's my son-in-law but he doesn't seem to mind if I call him mine. The picture next to him is my oldest daughter Diane. They live up in Grand Rapids."

"Do you have any family pictures of the house in Benton Harbor?" Charlie asked. "That could give us some information on the way the house looked and may jog your memory on some details."

"That's a good idea. I'm sure I have some. I'll be right back."

After she left the room Charlie hissed in a low voice "What are you trying to do, give us away? Don't be so direct."

Gloria hushed him. "I know what I'm doing, now be quiet."

A few minutes later Becky returned with three boxes of photographs. "I'm afraid they aren't organized very well. I hope you don't get bored to tears finding what you need."

Gloria smiled at Charlie. "Oh, I'm sure we won't. We love looking at family pictures."

They spent most of the afternoon looking at the pictures, Becky telling Charlie about long forgotten details of the house, Gloria asking questions about the family pictures. "Is that your sister?"

"Oh yes, that's Sally. She and her husband live in Florida now. They keep asking me to come down there to live but I won't go. I like it here, even the dreadful winters. Oh, and there's a picture of my oldest, Christine, the lawyer. I always have to add that to the end, the lawyer. We were so proud when she graduated. That's her husband Robert with her. She works for the Justice Department as head of the Research Department. Sally helped Christine land the job in Washington."

Gloria kept an eye out and it didn't take long before she saw an envelope with the name Christine Landis on it. "Being a lawyer is such a full time job. Does she have any kids?"

"Yes, three."

Gloria waited for the names but they never came. "It must be rough raising a family in Washington DC."

"They live in Arlington and commute. It still bothers me having her and the kids there. Washington DC is such a high crime area."

"Yeah, and most of it is committed by Congress," added Charlie.

A few minutes later while looking at pictures of Carol and Irene in front of the house, they came across a much more recent shot of Christine, Robert and their three lovely daughters. Gloria continued to flip through the pictures appearing to ignore it. While Becky was occupied elsewhere, Gloria slid the picture in her pocket.

When they had finished, there were two dozen pictures set aside of the interior and exterior of the old house with various family members as the center of attention. "If it's all right, we would like to borrow these long enough to have them copied," Charlie said. "I'm sure we could find a one-hour photo service here and have them back to you tonight if that's OK?"

"Oh, don't do that. That's much too expensive. Just take the pictures with you and mail them back after you have them copied."

"That would be great. Thanks."

With the information supplied in the family tree charts from Dr. Moore's journal and the more recent data provided unknowingly by Becky Lovett, Charlie began the task of tracking down Dr. Irene Moore's descendants. The results of Becky Lovett's branch were strongly supportive of the contents of the journal. He had seen pictures of all three of her daughters and their families and not a boy among them. Becky's older sister Sally was more of a problem. The early pictures they had seen had shown three girls but then a boy had appeared that Becky had referred to as "Sally's youngest." This was an obvious problem.

Armed with Sally's husband's name and a few references as to where they had lived supplied by their talk with Mrs. Lovett, Charlie began his quest. It took three days of careful detective work before he found the Lansing court record of an adoption by Sally and her husband.

Charlie was ecstatic at his find, but Gloria was strangely unmoved. While Charlie had become driven in his investigation, Gloria had withdrawn. She had remained fascinated by the journal, rereading it several times, but since the visit to Becky Lovett's home she had not lifted a finger to help Charlie.

That night while Gloria was fixing dinner, Charlie raised the issue. "We have all the evidence we need to prove what's going on. I think it's time to go public. What do you think?"

Gloria wouldn't look him in the eye. "What ever you think is best," she said, showing her distaste in her voice.

"You don't sound much in favor of it."

"I'm not. I'm afraid of what it will do to Mrs. Lovett and her children. I like her and I like Irene and Carol. From everything I've found out, they were people I wish I knew."

Charlie couldn't believe his ears. "They're destroying the human race for God's sake! And you want to be their friend?"

"Becky didn't seem like much of an ax murderess to me. She seemed like a nice old lady who cares about her children and grandkids. You want to hurt her, just go ahead, but I'll have nothing to do with it." Gloria turned her back on Charlie and returned to cutting broccoli for dinner with renewed vigor. Charlie winced each time the knife slammed down.

"Oh, this is just great." He tried to reason with her. "You know that if they're left alone, they'll wipe out the human race? There won't be anyone left other than people like them."

Gloria snapped back "If you mean no men, it might be an improvement. Look where men have gotten us so far. Men will probably wipe out the planet before the Monoecions will ever have a chance take over."

"So, you want to have sex with other women, is that it? Because there won't be any men left in this new world of theirs. Nothing but a planet full of queers!"

Gloria turned to face him, a satirical smile on her face. "So that's what it comes down to, homophobia. You're scared of gays."

"Bull shit! I am not scared of gays. I've had queers working on my construction crews."

"Yes," Gloria said, "and you made sure they moved on after you found out."

"I never fired any of them but you can't expect me to give them the choice jobs at the expense of the rest of the guys." Charlie paused and thought. He switched to a new tactic. "OK, what do you think these nice people are going to do if they find out that we are the only other people who know their dirty little secret? They are going to protect themselves and we're going to be found dead somewhere!"

Gloria put down the knife. "For some reason, I can't picture Mrs. Lovett gunning us down in cold blood. Get a grip, Charles!"

"There's also the factor of money. We spent a lot of money tracking down this evidence and I'd like to get paid for my efforts."

"What's it worth, Charlie? Five hundred thousand? A million? Judas did it for thirty pieces of silver. You do what you want, but I'll have nothing to do with it."

Charlie slept on the couch that night. Early Friday morning he was at a lawyer's office trying to convince him that he was sane. The lawyer really didn't care one way or the other as long as his fee was paid.

Jasmine

Chapter 8

The car sputtered to a stop. Damn it, Marci McBride thought, how could I be this dumb? It was dark along this stretch of interstate 75 north of Chattanooga. She had never run out of gas in her life, yet here she was, not only out of gas but fifty miles south of home with her five-year-old daughter asleep in the back seat. She felt her fear rising but struggled to control it. Scaring little Jasmine and thus, Alicia, wouldn't do anyone any good.

Marci struck her fist against the wheel. This telepathy wasn't worth a damn. When you really needed it, all you can say is help, I'm in trouble. "What I really need is to talk to Alicia, what I need is my stupid cell phone." Unfortunately, her phone was currently sitting on the kitchen counter.

"It's OK," Alicia soothed. "We all do stupid things sometimes."

"That's easy for you to say, I'm the one sitting on the shoulder of the interstate out of gas. You're curled up on the couch watching the tube." Marci let out a short yelp and Alicia was gone from her head. Jasmine stirred in the back seat. Marci had just heard Alicia. No, she thought, not heard, I was inside her head. But Alicia was fifty miles away. This was not the normal telepathy where she sensed fear or excitement or love. Plus, that only worked with blood relatives. She knew exactly what Alicia was doing, what she was wearing, even what movie she was watching. She wondered if she imagined the whole thing.

Alicia had finished putting little Jessica to bed and had plopped down in front of the tube. She idly surfed through the channels and stopped on an old Marx Brothers movie, pausing to listen to one of Groucho's classic high speed verbal exchanges with Chico. The next thing she knew she was sitting on the side of the interstate, feeling Marci's anger and frustration for running out of gas. Out of habit, Alicia soothed her even while finding the situation a bit humorous. That's when she realized her mind was actually inside Marci, sitting on the north bound side of Interstate 75 at mile marker thirty-six. The link that bound their minds together snapped so quickly that she winced.

Alicia sat stunned for a few moments trying to pull herself together. She popped open her laptop and pulled up the Tennessee map. The closest town was a little burg called Athens. She did a quick search and found a service station with a towing service. Alicia called and gave them Marci's location, explained her situation and asked them to hurry. Alicia didn't like the thought of the two of them sitting on the side of the road alone. The attendant promised to have someone there inside ten minutes.

"Didn't you want to talk to 'Licia?" Jasmine murmured sleepily from the back seat.

Marci whirled around in her seat. "Honey, did you know I was talking to Alicia?"

Jasmine rubbed her eyes. "Uh huh."

This is too weird, Marci thought, all three of us had been connected. "Did you hear Alicia too?"

"Uh-huh," Jasmine answered, "I just put you together. I thought you wanted to talk to 'Licia."

"What do you mean you put us together?"

"I just put you together." Jasmine was waking up now. "Was it bad?"

"No, it wasn't bad, it just surprised me," she soothed. The connection had been so short that now she wasn't sure if it was real or if she just imagined it. "Can you do it again?"

Jasmine frowned and stared at the dash for a few moments. "I don't 'member how," she said yawning.

"It's OK honey. Mommy ran out gas. I wasn't paying attention to the gas gauge and now we're stuck here for a little while. When a policeman comes by, he will stop and help us. You want to come up front?" Jasmine nodded her head setting her thick, light brown mane in motion. Marci never understood where she got all that hair. It certainly wasn't from her side of the family. Jazz crawled between the seat backs and plopped into the front passenger seat. Marci felt Jasmine starting to get edgy. "You know, when I was a little girl, my mommy taught me a poem to say when ever I got a little scared. And it's such a silly poem that you just can't stay scared when you say it. Would you like to hear it?"

Jasmine nodded her head.

Marci started slowly "One bright day in the middle of the night..."

"It can't be bright day at night!" Jasmine exclaimed.

"Of course not, it's supposed to be nonsense. That's what keeps your mind from noticing it's scared. Now just sit back and listen." Marci made a big production of preparing to recite the poem, Jasmine making an equally big production of smoothing her dress and folding her hands in her lap in her most ladylike manner. Marci recited in a librarian voice:

"One bright day in the middle of the night
Two dead boys got up to fight
Back to back they faced each other
Drew their swords and shot each other
A deaf policeman heard the noise
And came and killed the two dead boys"

Jasmine giggled "That's silly. Who told grandma the poem?"

"I believe she heard it from her mommy and I have no idea where she heard it. Would you like to learn it?"

"Uh-huh. I already know the start. One bright day 'n middle of night," Jasmine recited proudly.

"Let's get all the words in there. Poems sound so much better that way." Marci spoke the lines over and over as Jasmine repeated them back. The car rocked gently as the semis rolled past, kicking up little dust clouds as they flew by. Marci studied her little girl while she tried to get each line right. Jasmine's deep blue eyes focused somewhere in space as her mouth struggled to form each word perfectly. Marci had a hard time accepting that she was five already; a big girl starting school. As far as Marci knew, Jasmine was the first child born where both parents were monoecious. Maybe she and Alicia were getting more than they bargained for.

Eight years before, Marci McBride's mother had taken her and her sister to a park for a "family" reunion. This reunion was a loose collection of other monoecious families in the area that had maintained contact over the years. While she was there she had met Alicia Inman. They were both on the rebellious side and were immediately attracted to each other. Even though the parents knew that attractions were normal, it was still treated like leprosy. "If you have to have a fling with a woman, have an affair and get it out of your system, but marry a man. It attracts less attention." Both sets of mothers tried to talk the girls out of a permanent relationship with no success.

While Alicia still had a year left before graduation, they decided to have Jasmine. For most couples the decision ends there but for Marci and Alicia it went much farther. They spent weeks deciding who should be the father and who the mother. In the end, economics decided. Even though Alicia was still a year away from graduation versus Marci having completed her undergraduate studies, Alicia's degree in electrical engineering would earn them much more on the open market than Marci's history major.

Marci became "Mom" and quit her job in her eighth month to stay home with Jasmine. Careful saving and Alicia's part time job carried them through to Alicia's graduation. It had been rough. They occasional drew a raised eyebrow by those who suspected their relationship went beyond roommates but found they were mostly ignored. There were exceptions but they were rare.

Alicia was very careful not to let her personal life be known where she worked at an engineering firm. Being an activist on campus was a badge of honor, but in the conservative job market, it was the kiss of death. Their second child, Jessica, was born three years after Jasmine. They were just now getting out of debt from the second birth since Marci was not covered by Alicia's insurance.

The headlights glaring in her back window brought Marci back from her daydreams. The yellow flashing lights meant it was some wrecker driver out to make a buck. She would have preferred a state trooper. Her imagination was working overtime tonight and she felt very vulnerable sitting by the side of the road. A young man climbed out of the truck, his hair fell down to his shoulders from under his cowboy hat. Marci rolled her window down a couple of inches.

"Are you Mrs. McBride?" he asked, a chipped front tooth adding a whistle to his Tennessee drawl.

Marci nodded confused. "Yes, that's me."

"An Alicia Inman called and said you ran out of gas. I got a can in the truck. We'll have you on the road in no time. It's just three gallons but it will be plenty to get you to the next exit. There's an Exxon station on the right as you exit." He turned and headed back to his wrecker.

"Alicia did get the message." Marci sat in wonder. "It wasn't a dream."

"'Licia got the message, right mommy?" Jazz repeated.

Marci looked at her daughter, not knowing what to think. "Yes, I guess she did."

After he poured the contents of the can into the tank, the mechanic approached Marci's window again. "That will be twenty dollars."

"Sure." Marci fumbled through her purse, pulled a twenty from her wallet and passed it out to the mechanic.

"Ma'am, better crank it up while I'm still here to make sure it starts."

Marci turned the key and the engine fired, sputtered and died.

"Pump the gas pedal a little," he suggested.

She pumped her foot and tried again, this time it caught and idled smoothly. "Thanks for everything."

"No problem. It's just a good thing you had your cell phone with you when you needed it. I forget mine all the time, especially if I really need it. Well, goodnight." He turned and headed back to his truck.

Marci looked at her little girl. Yes, it was a good thing I had my phone, she thought.

Thoughts and theories raced through Marci's brain on the drive home. When her confused mind finally started to slow and wander, she caught herself thinking how hard it must have been for Alicia growing up with an alcoholic mother. Then she realized Alicia had never told her about her mother's problem. Not only did we connect on a conscious level, she thought, I also picked up some of her unconscious memories. It was tough enough to have your emotions out and available to whatever sister or daughter or mother that cared to sample them but this was a whole new ball game. This could be a very humbling experience, to have all your motives and desires hanging out for others to see. What buried secrets of hers had been exposed to Alicia? Her brain again was reduced to chaos as conflicting thought and ideas plagued her for the rest of the drive home.

Alicia held the front door open as Marci struggled in with Jasmine draped over her shoulder. "What the hell happened tonight?"

Marci shushed her and carried Jasmine into the girls' room. Alicia went out to the car and carried in the menagerie of items required to keep a five year old content for a four hour car trip. By the time she carted it all in the house, Marci had Jasmine tucked into bed.

"I don't know," Marci said picking up the old conversation as if it never paused, a talent developed by all parents within their first year of servitude. "I had just run out of gas and I was so upset with myself and wanted you so bad. The next thing I knew you were hugging me telling me it was going to be all right, except you were here on the couch watching TV and I'm in the car."

"I know," Alicia said, "mile marker thirty-six. I was sitting here on the couch watching ..."

"The Marx Brothers."

"Right, the Marx Brothers and the next moment I'm inside you. I mean really inside you. What caused it?"

"I thought Jasmine was asleep in the back seat when it happened. When I realized what was happening I cried out, I was so shocked. As she was waking up she said she put us together."

"What did she mean, she put us together?" Alicia was more confused now then ever.

"I don't know and she couldn't tell me. I asked her if she could do it again and she couldn't remember how."

That night as they lay trying to sleep, Marci whispered "I'm sorry about your mother's problem."

Alicia stiffened slightly. She had been thinking about her mother's alcohol problem tonight, about the time when Marci had burst into her brain. Alicia allowed one tear to roll down her cheek. "It was no big deal. We all have problems growing up." She was so ashamed and at the same time so relieved that she wouldn't have to hide it any more.

Chapter 9

Charlie and his attorney were led to a small office. It reminded him of the ones at car dealers where you're shoehorned in while the salesman puts on the pressure to close the deal. So far so good, he thought, at least he was past the lobby at the Nation's View, a national tabloid style newspaper. Though they were not as respected as the mainstream press, they did carry some hard news, usually in the form of exposés. They also paid much better. The woman who led them in sat down behind the desk and motioned for them to sit down. "Well, you requested something more private, so here we are. What do you have?" she asked.

Charlie's lawyer opened "I'm here to represent the interest of my client, Charles Wilkens. He has discovered something very hot, which until it is published, will keep him in possible danger. It will also blow the top off the evening news for weeks to come. Because of the sensitive nature of the information and the obvious value of this information, I would like you to sign this non-disclosure agreement." Charlie's attorney pushed a piece of paper over to the woman. "It's pretty standard, it just states that you will not use the information that is shown to you unless approved in writing by Mr. Wilkens."

"Before I bother to have our attorneys check this over, you need to supply me a reason. What's this all about?" She sat back in a bored fashion. She had seen this a hundred times. The scoop usually turned out to be all in the participant's mind and of no practical value to the newspaper. Her job was to sort the few real stories from constant flow of drivel that came across her desk. "I'm authorized to give you a verbal assurance that any information given to me for evaluation will go no further without your approval."

Charlie began the tale making sure to leave out all details. "How's the end of man in the next hundred and fifty to two hundred years? Completely wiped out by a dominant genetic defect. And there is a group of people who are keeping it a secret to allow it to spread wide enough so it can't be stopped."

She put elbows on the desk and pressed her fingertips together. "Do you have any documentation, evidence, proof of the defect?"

"How about a journal by the doctor who discovered it. The journal details the physical factors and projects the effects on the population. There are also three family trees of some of the people affected and we have the names and addresses of people alive today with the defect."

"Where's the doctor?" She was getting interested but this wasn't the first time she had been told of the end of the world.

"Dead."

"Pity. How's the genetic defect work? Does it make you sick, do you grow an extra arm or what?"

"It's much more subtle than that," Charlie said. "Women who have it can only bear female children. In all the families affected, no male child has ever been born."

"So all these people who have this defect are women?" This was starting to get interesting... if there was proof.

"Yeah, in a way."

"What do you mean?" she asked.

"We can't go into that until the agreement is signed," Charlie's lawyer injected before Charlie had a chance to answer.

"What kind of proof do you have?" This is where they all fall apart.

Charlie pulled out copies from the file folder in from of him. "Three generations documented from current birth records and the good doctor's notes explaining that it went on for nine generations before her."

"And the people affected with this defect, any of them famous?"

"Not that I know of but there should be over twenty million of them by now according to the doctor's calculations. Some of them are bound to be famous or the wives of someone famous." Charlie could see she was listening more intently. "At least one of the women involved in the cover-up works for the justice department in Washington DC."

She opened the desk drawer, pulled out a piece of paper and slid it to Charlie's attorney. "This is our standard non-disclosure form. Check it over, fill it out and I'll sign it. It will save time. Excuse me." She picked up the phone and dialed three numbers. "Yeah, Louis, do you have a few minutes? I want you to listen to a possible story." She twisted the phone cord as she listened. "OK, ten minutes, and you might want to bring Danny with you. He has a good ear. Bye." She hung up the phone. "Let's move into the conference room where there's more room to spread out."

In the conference room, Charlie was introduced to Louis Gardner and Daniel Nash. The journal was laid out for examination along with the drawings and family trees. Charlie patiently explained the text references he had marked and showed the research he and Gloria had done to confirm the journal's descriptions. Louis listened carefully to the story questioning Charlie frequently especially when anything sounded inconsistent. Daniel Nash stayed more in the background, intently listening and watching.

After an hour of discussions, Louis excused himself and signaled Danny to follow him. In the hall Louis asked Danny "Well, is it real?"

"He thinks it is." Daniel Nash could spot a fraud at hundred yards. He was forty-six years old and had been a reporter for twenty-two of them. In that time he had built up an ability to see inside a person and know their motivations better than they knew it themselves.

Louis flagged a secretary. "Phyllis, have you got the background checks?"

"Right here," she replied as she handed him the printouts.

"And he doesn't appear to be crazy. At least if he is, he has good credit and an excellent rating from his local Chamber of Commerce." Louis flipped a page. "No warrants or complaints with the authorities." Louis scanned the report on the lawyer. "His attorney looks the same. As far as I can tell, they are who they say they are; reputable, rational people."

"Except this guy thinks these psychic women are out to exterminate all men from the planet and take over."

Louis nodded slowly. "That's it in a nut shell. And if it's true, what have we got?"

"If it's true?" Daniel ran his hand through his thinning hair. "If it's true we've got the biggest story ever published. The circulation will triple on an exclusive. And the public won't go away in a week. This will hold 'em a month at least ... If it's true or at least mostly true."

"What do you think, with what you know now?" Louis asked.

"It's crazy. Women who can reproduce without men! Pure science fiction. Chances are it's some kind of mistake, over simplification, quirk of nature thing that can be explained. But if it is true, and it could be, he's got a lot of evidence to back it up; well... it scares the hell out of me."

Louis gave Daniel a hard look. "You've got forty-eight hours to let me know one way or the other."

"I'll need at least a week to prove it conclusively. In forty-eight hours I can give you a ninety five percent probability."

"Do what you can. Let's get back inside." The two men strode back in the room.

"Mr. Wilkens, why are you bringing the story to us?" Louis asked.

"I'm worried about what the government would do with this information if the public didn't know. I think they would label the whole thing as top secret, I'd never be heard from again and the CIA would try to find a way to turn the telepathy thing into a weapon. Basically, I don't trust it." Charlie paused for a few moments and added "They also don't pay as well."

Louis laughed. "And just what would you like for an exclusive on your story?"

Charlie's attorney jumped in. "The fee for an exclusive on the story and the rights to all the documents to be used in any way you wish, TV, movies, news specials, will be one million dollars. Two hundred-thousand up front and the rest at one hundred thousand a year for the next eight years."

"Let's get a few things straight. We don't know if the documents are real, we don't know a thing about your Dr. Moore. She is probably just a crackpot. On top of it there is the question of ownership of the journal, it may not even be yours to sell. You're completely out of range for what you have."

Charlie's lawyer started to earn his pay. "First, the ownership of the journal is not in question. I can prove his claim in any court in my sleep and you know it. Second, Mr. Wilkens is only asking for payment when the story proves to be accurate and truthful. Third, you can get two thirds of the money back just selling the story to various TV scandal shows which will just increase your paper's circulation. And last, this will be front-page news for weeks. With the head start in collecting information, you can stay a step ahead for three or four issues."

"Sorry, you overrate your story; it's not worth a hundred-thousand."

The lawyer listened to the meaning interwoven with the words. "If we open this up to a bidding war, Charlie will make out much better, but the story will leak and things could get ugly. But if we have to, we will."

"If this story leaks before it's released, it won't be worth a nickel. Two hundred thousand is the best I can do. And I'll throw in a ten thousand retainer that you won't have to repay no matter how it comes out, except for fraud of course."

"That's still too low," intoned the lawyer. He felt a sudden sharp pain in his ankle as Charlie kicked it under the table. The startled attorney looked sharply at Charlie who was glaring back at him. He returned his attention across the table. "Please excuse us for a moment. I think I need to discuss your offer in private with Mr. Wilkens." Twenty minutes later, a figure was agreed on and the documents signed.

Daniel looked over the evidence that had been supplied by Mr. Wilkens. He assigned various staff members to verify the accuracy of what had been supplied while he searched for the quickest way to confirm or deny the whole story, in a single step if possible. One of his researchers hit upon it a few hours later. One of the family tree branches had just been pruned less than a week ago by cancer.

Daniel showed his false identification to Herbert Klausman. "I was wondering if I could talk to you for a few minutes about the circumstances surrounding your wife's death?"

"Certainly," the old man responded. He led him inside and offered him a cup of coffee, which Danny gratefully accepted.

"There is something I need your help on that must be kept in the strictest confidence. We fear that a doctor has been acting improperly and we are searching for evidence to prove it. What we need is to perform an autopsy on your late wife."

Mr. Klausman looked shocked. "Do you mean someone did something to harm Linda? What happened?"

"As I'm sure you understand, I can't tell you the accusation or the individual involved until it is proven, but I can tell you that you will be the first to know the results of the examination." Danny put on his most sympathetic face, perfected with years of practice. "I know this is a very difficult thing I'm asking you do and if there were any other way, I promise we would use it."

"Will it be handled properly?"

"Absolutely. If you can tell me who took care of the arrangements, we'll even have a new casket available in case there is any damage to the original. We must stop this person if this allegation is true. To do this we need your signature."

Danny slid a piece of paper from his briefcase and laid it on the coffee table in front of Mr. Klausman who read it over carefully, asking question about the details. After about ten minutes of study, he signed it. "When will you do this? I'd like to be there."

"As soon as possible, maybe even today if it can be arranged. I'll send a car for you if you'd like."

"Yes, I'd like that. Is it all right if my daughter comes with me?"

Danny stopped and rubbed his chin. "I don't have any major objections. We would prefer not, only because of the trauma it could cause, especially if this turns out to be completely false. We just don't want to hurt anyone if we can help it. If you could, we would prefer not to worry anyone else until we know if a crime has been committed or not."

"I understand." Mr. Klausman said. "It will be just me. I'll stay here until I hear from you."

"Thank you, Mr. Klausman. I'll call you within an hour." Danny planned to do everything he said. Thirty minutes later he had the gravediggers and the medical examiner arranged. Of course, for the money they were getting paid for a few hours work, they both could take a month off in the Bahamas while they kept their mouths shut.

Danny picked up Mr. Klausman a little after three in the afternoon and drove him to the cemetery. There was a tense moment when the gravedigger just about dropped the casket. It was only Danny's fast reflexes that kept the casket upright. When Danny returned to the car Mr. Klausman eyes were filled with tears. "Thank you for maintaining her dignity," was all Mr. Klausman said.

After a quick cleaning, the casket was loaded in the rented hearse and taken to the examiner's office. Danny and Mr. Klausman waited outside the lab while the examiner performed his task. "You know," Mr. Klausman said, "in August it would have been fifty-one years. What I really miss is not having her there to tell me I'm ignoring her. I always said I'll do it in a little while, we can go out to dinner tomorrow, we can drive to Alaska next year. I don't know what to do without her. She was a good woman."

Danny liked Mr. Klausman. He reminded Danny of his father after mom died. Just like pop, Danny thought, he won't last a year without her.

The medical examiner came out of the lab. "Everything is on the up and up. There was no problem at all."

Danny turned to Mr. Klausman. "I'm sorry we had to do this only to have it turn out as unnecessary."

"It's all right. If it had protected another life, she would have wanted it that way. I think I'm going to walk for a while. I'll meet you at the cemetery if that's all right."

"Certainly," Danny said. He looked at the doctor. "When will we be there?"

"In about an hour to an hour and a half."

Mr. Klausman nodded and shuffled out the door.

After Mr. Klausman left, the doctor said "It matches the picture exactly. How did you know this?"

Danny gave the doctor a cold stare. "I thought we already discussed the matter of questions. Did you collect samples and photographs?"

"All done. The samples show the body was still producing sperm at the time of death. All I have to do is close her back up and put her back in the casket."

"Good. Let's get her back in the ground where she belongs. I feel like a damn grave robber." Danny went in one of the offices, picked up the phone and dialed the direct number. A secretary answered the phone. "Tell Louis it's Nash." In a few seconds he came on the line.

"What's the results?"

"Irene was right, all the way. I've got samples and photos from the medical examiner."

"Hot damn!" Louis said. "I say we go. What do you think?"

"Yeah, we go," Danny said quietly, almost to himself. "You know what else I say?" There was no answer so Danny continued. "If I ever have to do this again, I quit."

"Don't worry Danny, never again." Louis hung up the phone. Louis had heard it before on several occasions. You'll do it again, he thought, just like you always do. If it means getting the story, you'll do it again.

Chapter 10

Monday, August 5

Marci was in line at the Food City grocery store, with Jessica in the cart and Jasmine hanging on one pant leg. The line was short but the clerk seemed to be moving at a snail's pace. Marci knew what would happen if Jasmine had to stand here too long. First there would be the "can I have ..." followed by the "I'm tired, will you carry me?" and then the grumpies would set in. As the check out clerk asked for her second price check in as many items, Marci started looking for a shorter line. Unfortunately, they all looked about the same or worse.

Out of boredom, Marci browsed the usual collection of rag magazines always kept at the counter along with the candy bars and diet pamphlets. "I had an alien's baby!" yelled one in bold black letters. Under the headline was a poorly faked picture of a woman holding an ET-looking creature. *Where do they come up with this stuff?*, thought Marci. She was looking over the one claiming to have found Adolf Hitler's illegitimate son when another headline caught her eye. "RACE OF DUAL-SEXED WOMEN PLOTS DESTRUCTION OF MANKIND."

"Mommy, can I have some gum?" Marci's heart started beating faster. She reached out and gingerly pulled the Nation's View from the rack, her hands starting to tremble ever so slightly. She tried to convince herself it was just another farce as she rapidly flipped through searching for the story. Her heart leaped to her throat as she turned the page and saw three drawings of sexual organs, one labeled male, one female and the last clearly marked monoecious.

"Mommy", Jasmine's voice was quiet and filled with worry, "are you OK mommy?" Jessica began to squirm and fuss in the grocery cart.

Marci struggled to regain control. She took a deep breath and in a shaky voice said "I'm OK, honey. Don't worry," but she could feel the rising emotion of dread. It was all she could do to send a little feeling of reassurance out to her children. She read the first lines of the article.

There is a race of beings out to destroy mankind. They appear to be normal women but inside they are very different. They call themselves Monoecions and within a few more generations, they expect to control the world.

"Ma'am ... Ma'am, are you ready?"

Marci looked at the clerk with a total lack of comprehension. "What?"

"Move your cart up. I can't reach it back there."

Marci realized where she was, dropped the paper in her cart and moved up to the cash register.

She felt as if everyone was staring at her as she ran her debit card, messing up the pin number twice before finally controlling the shake in her fingers and completing the transaction. A bag boy carried her purchase out to the car while she carried Jessica with Jasmine in tow. She strapped Jessica in her car seat while the bag boy put the groceries in the trunk. She directed Jasmine to the back seat, put on a weak smile, and muttered a quick, "Thanks." Once inside the safe cocoon of the car, she broke down and cried. She cried for the life she was losing and the normal life she feared her children would never have.

When Marci made it home she called Alicia at work. Alicia had already been calling Marci every few minutes. She had been picking up a great deal of fear coming from Jazz. It was such a strange feeling, she didn't know what to expect. She just knew something wasn't right. When Marci explained what it really was, Alicia took it well. "When I imagined all the terrible things it could be, this doesn't seem quite so bad." After a pause Alicia said "Think about what we should do. We're going to have to make a decision on when to come out of the closet."

"If we ever do. We'll talk tonight. Love ya."

Alicia wasn't very productive for the rest of the day. She had a hard time keeping her mind off Jasmine and Jessica and what their life would be like in the new world.

The alarm clock exploded into Christine's mind. *Why did I have a cigarette?*, she thought, I quit months ago. Slowly the fog lifted and she realized it was a dream. *Thank God*, she thought, quitting again was not something she would look forward to. It was disconcerting to realize she was still hooked enough to dream about hiding behind the shed just to have a cigarette.

She reached over and shook her husband. "Wake up, oh love of my life. It's morning."

He opened one eye enough to see the alarm clock. "I've got another twenty minutes. Go away."

"Is that the way to talk to the woman who bore your children?"

"You bore everybody. You're a lawyer, it's your job." With that he covered his head with his pillow.

Christine pulled herself out of bed. "It takes a lot of gall for an economist to call a lawyer boring." She headed for the bathroom. After her shower she looked at herself in the mirror. She longed for the days when she could convince herself that she was only ten pounds over weight. It had been three months since she promised herself to make time for tennis three days a week. She played twice the first week, once the second week. Then the Hollingfield case hit and she hadn't picked up a racquet since. There just isn't enough time, she thought. She listened as the girls started the morning ritual fight in the hall.

"You don't get the bathroom until seven!"

"You weren't using it."

"I went to get my brush!"

"It's been empty for ten minutes."

Robert stuck his head out the door. "Quiet!" he roared. "Any louder and you'll wake Congress." He closed the door and muttered to himself "And I don't want to be blamed for the mess that would cause." The voices in the hall dropped to a low growl.

When Christine walked in the office two co-workers jumped her. "Where have you been?"

"Good morning, Anne. Good morning, Roger. That is how civilized people greet each other."

"Yeah, right," the woman replied. "This is Washington. I repeat, where have you been? Larry wants you."

"There was a traffic accident on the trunk. What's the big deal? I'm ten minutes late," Christine asked.

Roger broke in "Fifteen, but who's counting. An article in the Nation's View claims to have uncovered a plot to wipe out the human race. And it says that there is at least one woman involved here in the Justice Department." Christine looked at him with a raised eyebrow. "Yeah, I know. This paper also reports on UFO conspiracies. The thing is they seem to have some solid evidence, at least enough to get two FBI types here asking questions. Larry is already meeting with the other department heads and wants you to join them as soon as you come in. He wants to make sure we at least make the appearance of complete cooperation and get them out of our hair as quickly as possible."

"Great," Christine said, "just what I need, another damage control crisis. Anyone have a copy I can read before I go in so I can know what this is all about?"

"I'll bring you a copy," Anne offered. "Just bring it back, there's an article I want to read about a new diet."

Christine waved her off and went in her office to unload. She dropped the notebook computer in her chair and hung up her jacket. She had just finished plugging into the network when Ann returned with the copy of the Nation's View.

"Which article is it?" Christine asked.

"Well, I realize that it could be any of the end of the human race articles but this one starts on page twenty-four. Hurry up, I saw Larry's secretary in the hall and told her you were scanning the article and would be there in five minutes. Bye." Anne hustled out the door.

Christine opened the magazine to the article. As she read, she felt the panic well up inside her. She tried to calm herself when she realized she had simply stopped breathing. She gasped in a breath and tried to slow her heart rate. Her daughters must be worried by now, that was a jolt of fear if she ever felt one. She did her best to send a soothing message. Now she would have to make a decision. She read enough of the article to convince her that she was the Justice Department employee the article spoke of and picked up the phone and called her mother, Becky Lovett.

"I know all about it," her mother confirmed. "If you check your voice mail, you'll find two messages telling you to call me. Two reporters have been camped on my doorstep since I woke up this morning. They might have been here all night for all I know. They gave me a copy of the Nation's View and started yelling questions at me."

"What have you told them?" asked Christine. "Don't tell them anything until you talk to a lawyer."

"I am talking to a lawyer, I'm talking to you. And no, I haven't said a thing to them. I told them I would read the article and then let them know if I would respond."

"Good job, mom." Her mother confirmed that a couple by the name of Wilkens had visited with her, asking questions about the old house and going through family pictures. "If they have Grandma Irene's journal, they have already traced all of our relatives. I guess it's over, mom."

"No," her mother answered, "it's only just begun. What are you going to do?"

"Not much I can do. All of our deep dark secrets are right here, big as life in the Nation's View. I'll just tell them who I am, if they don't know already, and wait for the shit to hit fan." Christine continued to scan the article as she talked. She had to admit that if you looked at the raw facts presented in the article, much of it was true. Unfortunately it had been twisted to appear to be a dark and sinister plot to subjugate the world rather than an attempt to protect themselves from persecution.

"If you don't mind, I'd like to come and spend some time with you," Becky asked.

"Of course. Just be careful it doesn't look like you are fleeing. Could you call Robert and explain? I'm going to call him right now but I won't have much time. Tell him I'll call him as soon as I'm allowed. Then again it may be up to the warden if any of you can visit me."

"You think it could come to that?"

"Anything's possible, Mama. It's not nice to fool Uncle Sam."

"Please don't joke about this, I'm worried."

"So am I, mom. I have to go. Tell Robert I'm calling Ben Davis to represent me. I'll call as soon as I can." After finishing her conversation with her mother she called a close friend, Ben Davis, who had a private practice in town. Christine asked him to represent her in a matter here at the office. She didn't explain what it was all about, only that it was serious and she needed him here as soon as he could get here. He promised he was on his way. For this, she needed someone who had experience fighting the government and Ben Davis was the best. Christine was already fifteen minutes late when she went to Larry's office rather than the conference room. He was already back.

"What kept you? Have you had a chance to read it?" Larry asked.

"Yes, I've skimmed it."

"Good. Sit down. I'm going to tell you the same thing I told all the other department heads. First of all, it looks like a bunch of BS to me but we need to make sure before we tell the public that. The official line to any reporters is 'no comment, we are currently investigating the allegations.' I need you to get with…"

"Larry, hold on. I need to tell you something."

"Yeah, what?" He waited for Christine to say something. "Well?"

"I can not work on this investigation because of the possible appearance of conflict of interest." She couldn't bring her self to look him in the eye.

"What? What conflict of interest? You got some involvement with the Nation's View?" Larry truly didn't understand.

"No. No connection with the paper. I have reason to believe I may be the object of the article. That's all I can say right now."

Larry looked down at the article and back at Christine with dawning comprehension. "Are you the person referred to in the article, the one employed by the Justice Department?"

"I may be, so it is best that I withdraw myself from this investigation to avoid all appearances of a cover-up."

"Are you really one of these creatures?" Larry asked tapping the magazine article. "That's insane. You're as human as I am."

"I think it best if I wait for my attorney before I answer any more questions." Christine folded her hands in her lap and prepared to wait.

"Jesus Christ." Larry shook his head as his brain tried to force this round idea into a square hole. "Jesus H. Christ." He picked up the phone and rang his secretary. "Track down those two FBI agents and tell them I need them in my office pronto." He hung up the phone and stared at Christine.

"Can I call my husband? He doesn't know anything about this and I'd like to be the one to break it to him rather than the reporters who are probably already on their way to his office."

"What, you've already called the networks?" Larry asked with concern.

"No, I just assumed the Nation's View knew who I was long before this morning. They have already identified my grandmother. It won't take much research to find me. I'm on page twenty-six remember?"

Larry nodded his head. "I guess so. It will take the agents a few minutes to get here and screw everything up. Use my phone. I'll be right out side." Larry stepped out closing the door behind him.

Christine picked up the phone and held it to her chest thinking of what she would say. "Hi honey. You'll have to pick up the kids tonight. I'm being arrested for attempting to wipe out the human race," or maybe "Dear, I've decided that I'll father the children from now on." The phone started beeping loudly in her hand, startling her so she dropped the receiver. She picked it back up and depressed the switch hook and tried again. This time she dialed.

"I'm sorry, Mrs. Landis, but he's in a meeting. Do you want me to put your name on top of his stack of messages?" asked his secretary.

"No, I think you better get him out for this one. Have him go to his office and transfer me in there."

"All right, if you think it's necessary." There was an edge of concern on her voice.

As an after thought Christine added "Tell him no one has died," but she was already put on hold.

A few seconds later Robert came on the line. Christine could hear the voices of the meeting going on in the background. "Yes Chris, what is it?"

"You couldn't step out of the meeting for just a few seconds?"

"Sorry, but it's going really hot right now and I need to stay close." Robert paused for a second as he became distracted by the meeting chatter and then continued. "What's wrong?"

"It's pretty hot here too. I think I may be arrested."

"You're being arrested!" All of the voices around the table behind Robert stopped. "Let me transfer you to the office." The line went silent.

"That's why I get the big bucks," Christine said out loud mocking her husband's favorite expression for whenever he screwed up. *Sometimes he could be such a jerk,* she thought.

Robert came back on the line. "What's going on?"

"Mother will give you a call and fill you in on the details. I'll tell you as much as I have time for. I'm probably going to be accused of being part of a plot to destroy the human race. As crazy as it sounds, that's it."

"How ..."

"Please be quiet and listen. As I said, mother will fill in the details. I have a different genetic structure that is passed on from mother to child. I'm not capable of producing male children and neither is any of my family or offspring... Look, this is way too complicated to explain in the few minutes I have. I've asked Ben Davis to represent me and he's on his way over to the office now. I'm here waiting to be questioned by the FBI."

"Questioned about this so called plot?" Robert asked.

"That and being telepathic and a few other things I'm sure. I've tried to reassure the girls as much as I can but they need to know what's going on."

"Whoa! What do you mean telepathic?"

"I told you mother will explain." The office door opened and Larry walked in followed by two suits. "Get a copy of the Nation's View, page twenty-four, or turn on the news. I'm sure I'll be on it any second. Get someone to pick up the girls and get them home. I don't want them subjected to the press until they have a chance to sort things out in their own heads." Larry gave her the sign to hang up the phone. "I've got to go now; I think it's time for show and tell. I love you."

The phone at Senator Gordon Fenton's office started to ring early on the morning the Nation's View broke the story. Most of the calls were from his loyal conservative revolution calling to see what he was going to do about this new menace to America. It took several calls before his secretary could figure out what they were talking about. She reported it to Todd Lindell who sent a staff member to the newsstand to buy several copies. The staffer ran all the way back and handed the stack to Todd. "Great. Have you read it yet?"

The staffer looked at Lindell in disbelief. "I just ran the mile in four minutes and twenty-five seconds, fought fifteen other staffers for copies, ran another four and a half minute mile, and dropped them in your hands. And you have the nerve to ask me if I've read it yet?"

"A simple 'no' would have sufficed." Lindell flipped through the pages until he came to the article. "This looks like it would go better with Elvis and UFO sightings. Distribute these around to the staff and see if anyone can confirm a trace of truth to it. I want it debunked in twenty minutes. We need to get some real work done. Until we have an answer the official line is that 'it's under investigation by the Senator'. Nothing more is to be released until more facts are known." He took two copies and went in the Senator's office and closed the door.

"Here they are, Gordon." Todd handed a copy to the Senator. "Starts on page twenty-four."

"What I want to know is if it's real or not. Who have you got working on it?"

"I put Stan, Henry and Plakett on it. If it's true, we'll know in a few minutes."

As the self-proclaimed leader of the conservative revolution, Senator Gordon Fenton loved anything that got the right riled but this had hoax written all over it. "Have we received anything back from our inquiries at the FBI?"

"Not a thing. I think they were caught with their pants down just like the rest of us. They would rather say 'no comment' than 'I have no idea what you are talking about'. If this thing is true, some heads will roll there but this looks way too much like a load of BS."

They each read in silence for several minutes, only an occasional expletive breaking the silence. "Where's the mention of a Justice Department involvement?" the Senator asked.

"On page 26, third paragraph in the right hand column. All it says is that it's a Mono."

"A what?"

"A Mono. It's on the first page of the article. The reporter used as short for monoecion, a person with monoecious properties."

"OK, I get it. According to this they look completely normal. So what are they going to do, x-ray every woman in the department? See which ones have extra equipment?"

"Beats the hell out of me. I know a department head over there pretty well, we play golf occasionally. I'll give him a call and see what's happening." It took ten minutes for Todd to get through to the Justice Department. His golf buddy informed him that two FBI agents had been questioning Christine Landis, head of Research Resources, since before nine AM and they looked like they were setting up for an all day session. No additional information was available on Mrs. Landis.

"I want everything you can get me on her, just in case" the Senator told his chief aide. "If she's involved, I want a file started on her immediately, what trips she's been on lately, copies of expense reports, the works. I don't want one piece of data missed. Make sure her private life is gone through also, drugs, divorces, ever had an abortion, any affairs, you know the routine."

"If they have this Landis woman already, you can bet Mr. Nash and Mr. Wilkens have been having a good time feeding information to the FBI since early this morning."

Actually Daniel Nash and Charlie Wilkens were at the Nation's View's DC office still waiting for the agents to arrive. It had taken the FBI over an hour to find out there was a Washington, DC office for the Nation's View. Two agents had just arrived at the receptionist's desk.

"Well, Charlie, are you ready for this?" Daniel asked.

"I don't know. I've never been interrogated by the FBI before. I presume it won't be on my list of favorite things to do with a Monday."

"At least you didn't break any laws getting here."

Charlie looked surprised. "What laws did you break?"

Daniel gave a sly smile. "What you don't know won't hurt you, and it sure won't do me any harm either." The agents entered the room.

Christine replaced the receiver and looked at Larry. "My attorney isn't here yet."

The first FBI agent spoke up first. "I don't think you'll need an attorney Mrs. Landis. We just want to ask you a few questions about the article. There are no charges being considered at the current time."

"Just the same," Christine answered, "I think I'll wait for my attorney before we get into this. A publication has accused a group of people of some very serious offenses and I believe I will be linked to this group. If I were representing a client in a similar situation, I'd advise her to wait until I had a chance to review with her. I hope you don't mind but I would like to follow my own advice."

"That's all well and fine, Mrs. Landis, but could we get some of the less sensitive preliminaries out of the way?" asked the first agent.

"I think that would be in order."

"Fine. Your full name?"

"Christine Ann Landis."

"Are you married?"

"Larry," Christine called, "get these fellows my personnel file. It will save them a lot of time."

Christine's boss produced the folder from under his arm. "I figured you wouldn't have any problem if I gave it to them, so I brought it along just in case. With your permission?" Larry looked at Christine. She nodded and he gave it to the agent.

The second agent spoke up. "Is it up-to-date? You know how it is, these files rarely get updated."

"It should be," said Larry.

"Now, are you still married?" the first agent asked.

"Yes, to Robert Edwin Landis." By the time they went through the information on file, Ben Davis had arrived.

When he came in the room, Larry let out a low whistle. Larry slid off the corner of his desk where he had been sitting and extended his hand to Ben. "Hello, Ben. Gentlemen, may I introduce Benjamin Jefferson Davis. You better pray that everything you've done so far is on the up and up, because if it isn't, Ben will find it." He turned to Christine. "How did you ever get Ben to represent you?"

"Easy," she said. "I just promised to lose to him at racquet ball at least twice over the next month."

"Gentleman, if I may have a few minutes with my client, you can get back to what you were doing." Ben waved his arm towards the door.

"Why don't you and Christine move into conference room D? It's getting a little crowded for my office anyway," Larry suggested.

Christine and Ben spent the next fifteen minutes covering the situation. "I don't see where any laws were broken," Ben said. "I think it's safe to answer whatever you feel comfortable with. If a question feels like the answer could be twisted to their advantage, we'll offer to provide the answer in writing. Then we will go through it with a fine tooth comb to make sure they can't use it against us later. The real problem is going to be public opinion. There is going to be a major public uproar over this with heavy pressure to do something about this problem and I'm afraid you're going to be the focal point for a while."

"I don't see what I can do about it. Ready to do battle?" she asked.

"I'm always ready when it's with the FBI. This will be the most fun I've had all week," Ben added with a hint of sarcasm.

The questioning ran all day long as the two FBI agents, who had been reinforced by several more, played tag team with Christine. While one team questioned her, the other conferred with a task force hastily assembled in another conference room. They then traded places and started the process over. Sandwiches were brought in as they worked through lunch. At seven o'clock in the evening the task force had to make a decision. "Have they completed the search of the Landis house yet?" asked Woody, the leader of the FBI task force.

"They just finished up," an aide injected.

"OK, do we hold her overnight or do we let her go home?" asked Woody.

"I say we let her go home but keep four agents on her around the clock. Tell her it's for her own protection," put in one agent.

"It just may be," said a second. "The feedback we're getting from the outside is pretty ugly. We have no idea how the public will react but right now they don't seem to be inclined to be polite about this."

"Another approach is to send her to a hospital for tests. That keeps her confined and under our watch."

"But we're not ready for tests," pointed out Woody. "We better do that once and only once. Plan it properly so we don't leave out anything. If we ask her a second time, she may refuse. I'd much rather we have a cooperative patient than an abused martyr."

"Who says she'll do it the first time?"

"She will," said Woody. "She's trying to show us that there's been no conspiracy, only an attempt to keep themselves out of freak shows. I think she'll go along just to reinforce the point."

"Assign four agents to her for tonight, two shifts of two and send her home. Have them escort her to our office tomorrow. Tell her we'll start at nine o'clock. Jack and Hickok, let's go get something to eat and see if we can plan tomorrow a little better than today's mess."

"Can I let her husband up? He's been waiting in the lobby since four thirty."

"Sure, send him up," said Woody. "Let's get going. I want to get home before my wife gets remarried."

The ride home was a quiet one, just some small talk mostly, as if neither wanted to breach the real topics until they were safely home. "Where are the kids?"

"Janice from next door picked them up. She's keeping them until we get home."

"Good, maybe the press won't find them there."

"They have to come home when we get there. She made it clear after she saw the news on TV that they needed to come home tonight. She wants nothing to do with this whole affair." They rode in silence for a while longer.

"My mother can come and watch the kids, I'll call her," Christine said.

"That won't be necessary," Robert replied, "My mother is already on her way."

There were at least a dozen news trucks filling the street. Reporters and cameramen piled out of them as soon as they spotted Christine. Robert forced his way through the crowd and parked the car in the drive. As the reporters rushed forward shouting questions, Robert stated once for the record, "We are not going to make a statement tonight or in the morning so you can pack up and hit the road." Christine ran to the neighbors with several reporters following her. Janice opened the door and let the kids out as strobes flashed and video cameras rolled. Christine protected the children as best she could and herded them back to their own home where Robert held the door open.

"Get off my yard of I'll charge you all with trespassing! Good night!" Robert closed the door. He threw the bolt and stood waiting for Christine as she hugged the girls. "Why don't you get the girls taken care of and then we need to talk."

Christine nodded her head. "It will be a few minutes, I need to explain a few things to them."

Melissa, Christine's oldest at fifteen, hugged her mom. "Why are all the news people out there?"

Christine guided them all into her bedroom where they sat on the bed. "It's just like we talked about. We knew the news would break eventually but I prayed it would be a long time from now. Now it's just that we are the only monoecious people they know so we get all the attention. It won't take long for them to spread out." Christine looked at her two youngest, Stacy twelve and Terra ten, as they huddled on the bed. They aren't ready for this, thought Christine, but then neither am I. She explained what had happened at work and why the FBI had searched the house. She tried to tell them what to expect over the next few days as best she could. "My emotions will be up and down like a roller coaster for the next few days so try not to over react."

"We'll be OK, mom," reassured Melissa. Christine hugged each one goodnight and sent them to bed.

Christine and Robert were having it out in the bedroom. "Please keep your voice down. I don't want the children listening to this."

"The children don't need to be here to listen, they're telepathic." Robert was pissed. He had dated Christine for two years, been married to her for eighteen years. He had trusted her and shared his secrets with her only to find out she hadn't been straight with him. "Look, I love you but why didn't you tell me? Why did I have to find out this way?"

"Because I'm not the only one involved! If it was only me I would have told you." Christine was running out of patience after spending eleven continuous hours of being questioned by the FBI. "Just think this out. If every Monoecion told her husband, we would have been freak show material a hundred and fifty years ago. Then we would have been none too politely exterminated. If you haven't noticed, most people don't enjoy that."

"Look, I understand what you're saying but look at it from my point of view. I think I'm marrying one person and then find out that you're not who I thought you were."

"I'm no different now than when I married you," Christine said. "You may think of me differently but I'm not the one who has changed. I was a Monoecion when we were married and I'm a Monoecion now. If I had told you before we got married, would you have married me?"

"Yes, I would have, but then it would have been my choice, made knowing the facts."

"Now you know. So you want a divorce?" Christine was near tears with anger and frustration.

"No. I don't want a divorce. But you know, when we got married, I thought I was the only one with balls and it's a bit irritating to find out I was wrong all these years." Robert dropped into a chair. "Look, I love you and the kids very much. I'm not rejecting you. I just need some time to get over the shock of all this. I just don't want any more secrets between us."

Christine put her hand on Robert's arm, afraid he would shrug it off. Robert put his hand on hers. "We'll get through somehow" he reassured her.

"You're not the only one in shock. We knew this would happen but we had no idea when. It's like waiting for the Second Coming; you never expect it to happen during your life time."

Chapter 11

Tuesday, August 6

The morning routine went off just as it always had at the Landis house. They had decided the night before that they were not going to hide like hunted animals. Robert stayed home with the girls until it was time to pick up his mother at the airport then he would head into the office to clean up some details so he could take a few days vacation to help keep things running. Christine prepared for another day of questioning by the FBI and whoever else showed up.

Christine gave the girls last minute instructions. "Remember what I said last night. If you are verbally attacked by anyone, ignore it, no matter what they say. If you are attacked physically, defend yourself but try to get to someone for help instead. If someone asks a question, even if it sounds stupid, answer it as best you can, we have nothing to hide anymore. The only chance of our lives returning to normal again is for the public to lose interest and forget that we're different. The sooner they understand us, the sooner they'll get bored with us."

Christine's words seemed empty. She knew the public wouldn't get bored for a long time to come. She wondered if her children would still be capable of love and compassion by the time they lived through all the hate and suspicion that was ahead. When the FBI was through with Christine at the end of the night, she figured she would feel mighty low on love and compassion herself.

Robert's mother had insisted on coming to help out in any way she could. Christine hoped this would work out with her own mother coming in Wednesday. There had been hints of friction between the two mothers before but no real conflicts had arisen. She hoped it would stay that way.

Christine kissed Robert and the girls good-bye, then slipped out the garage side door with the two agents. Some of the reporters were caught napping as the agents cleared a path for her to the car pulling up on the street. Only three or four reporters managed to shout questions and take pictures as she was hustled into the waiting car and driven away. A second FBI car ran interference while several news vehicles followed them.

The Spotlight show aired with half the show devoted to the Monoecion situation. It started with the usual over-dramatic introduction that was a trademark of the show. "The human race is under attack. An alien race is attempting to destroy man and take over the planet earth. Are little green men coming from Mars or three-headed slime monsters from Alpha Centauri spearheading the attack? Well, here are some pictures of them in action." Film footage of Christine Landis trying to protect her children from reporters as she hurried them home from the neighbors was shown along with shots of her mother Becky, walking in her front door. "You didn't see them?" The pictures reappeared with circles around Becky, Christine and the children.

"If we are to believe Charles Wilkens, these innocent looking people are just a few members of the new species that is threatening man's existence. They call themselves Monoecions and they carry a genetic defect that if ignored, will spell doom for Man." They interviewed Charlie and he told the story of the journal discovery and his follow up research.

The scene cut to a doctor's office where an "expert in the field" described the condition. "Apparently these people carry in their bodies two complete sets of sexual organs, one male and one female. Even though they physically appear to be normal women, they are capable of both fathering a child and carrying a baby to term. At this point in time, all of this is conjecture since I have not had a chance to examine one of these people myself. I have seen the x-rays and photographic autopsy results combined with the writings of Doctor Irene Moore, who discovered this condition in nineteen twenty-eight and the evidence seems to support the theory."

The show ran a quick history on Irene that managed to get at least some of the facts correct. Pictures of her high school and college yearbooks were displayed along with excerpts from her journal. They returned to the doctor. "Now this is a genetic defect, not a disease. You can't catch it from contact with someone who has it like you can catch AIDS. It can only be passed from parent to child. What is so dangerous about this particular defect, if we are to believe Doctor Moore's journal, is that it is one hundred percent dominant. That means that if either parent has the defect, all offspring will have the defect and will pass it on to the next generation.

"Is this a real threat?" asked the host.

"Oh yes. If the information we have is true and if nothing is done to change the situation, the world will go the way of the calculations. Mankind would disappear to be replaced by these hermaphrodites, or as they prefer to refer to themselves, Monoecions."

"How long would it take for this to happen?"

"Dr. Moore estimated it at a little over thirty generations. It has already been eleven by her count."

"How could you tell if the woman you are talking to is really a woman and not a Monoecion?"

"Just by looking you can't. I haven't had the opportunity to test a living Monoecion yet but from the information I have been able to collect, the only way to tell would require some sophisticated medical equipment. You can get a good clue however, by looking at the family history. If the family has only produced female offspring for the last three generations then there is a high likelihood that they are really Monoecions, not females. Now this is not a guarantee, normal people can have only female offspring for three generations just out of pure chance. Also, the Monoecions try to adopt male children to make the pattern appear to be broken. This trick is described in Dr. Moore's journal."

"Probably the most knowledgeable person on Dr. Moore's journal is Charles Wilkens." The camera cut back to the studio. "Are the Monoecions really trying to remain in hiding?"

Charlie appeared back on the screen with the host. "Absolutely. Dr. Moore described in detail various methods the Monoecions could use to avoid detection. One we have already covered is adopting male children to hide the female only birth pattern. Another is making sure that there is a supply of Monoecion doctors available so a normal doctor wouldn't accidentally discover the pattern of the dual sex organs. Dr. Moore also recommended others to take positions in the media, the American Medical Association, and in government at all levels. This would put them in position to squash any attempts at investigation of the story."

The host didn't seem to take the story seriously. He considered the whole thing a farce that would soon be uncovered as such, but he continued with one last question. "Are there any estimates of what the Monoecion population is today?"

"The journal estimates that there are over twenty-two million alive today," Charlie said, "but I think the estimate may be high."

The host let out a low whistle. "We will be following this story as it develops, but when we come back, a glimpse into the backstage lives of supermodels Candy Kriss and Cynthia Haley. Stay tuned!"

Chapter 12

Wednesday, August 7

The United States legislature hadn't moved this fast in fifty years. After the revelations in the Nation's View two days prior, no less than eleven separate investigations were begun. This did not include the covert operations by the CIA and several other equally secretive organizations from around the world. Investigators were tripping over themselves questioning the known Monoecions as well as Charlie and Gloria Wilkens, Danny Nash, and anyone else they could find who may have even a shred of evidence. Becky put on a large pot of coffee and set out a jug of tea every morning just for the steady flow of investigators.

Six different reports had been uncovered that described the condition, all published in the last forty years. Some even implied a hereditary link but none had caused any alarm and were simply considered a medical oddity. The FBI had gone into the genealogy business. Their task was to identify when this genetic defect occurred by tracking back the families to a common ancestor who had natural-born males in the family. Another group of agents took the information from the first group and went forward in time in an effort to identify every living Monoecion in the world. No small task considering there was an estimated fifteen million in the United States alone.

Senator Fenton's investigators had only one goal, find every piece of dirt, accurate or imagined, and have it ready for the Senate hearings. "It's all pretty simple," he explained to Todd. "The public loves to have an enemy. They want it personalized, not some concept that they can't get a hold of. Look at what Hitler did in Germany. He focused the hate of the nation on a target, the Jews, and they weren't even doing anything to harm the country. Here we have an alien race of beings, bent on the destruction of the human race. They are taking our men away from our women. Hell, they're even taking our women away from our men."

"Every dyke's dream come true," Todd added.

"Hey, remember that line, I may use it."

Todd tried to get the game plan clear. "But what's the political gain out of this? You really think the public is going to back you when the aliens you're attacking all look like their grandmother or their cute little niece?"

"That's your job to make sure that their actions speak louder than their looks. There's going to be a bunch of liberal goofballs out there trying to muddy this whole thing up. We need to show that I can lead us out of all this indecision, that I can take the bull by the horns and kick its ass. If we leave this up to the liberals, they tell the damn Monos 'Now don't go screwing the humans if you can avoid it. You be good and don't wipe out the human race.' And while they debate how to fix the problem without offending anyone, the Monos will be out there breeding like rabbits. Hell, we won't last another five generations unless we exterminate the Monos now." Gordon Fenton's face was red, there was sweat glistening on his balding dome. He had found the perfect rocket to propel him into the next presidential race.

"Senator, you'll be committing political suicide if you go out and propose exterminating these people."

"I know we can't propose killing them but we can propose eliminating the disease. If we can enact forced sterilization, no one is hurt and the problem is solved. The liberals will have a fit and come off as coddling the creatures that are bent on destroying mankind. We show the American public that we have a humane method of eradicating this scourge and provide the leadership to carry it through; we will be able to walk into the White House after the next election and call it home. We've got to fire the people's hate for these creatures and at the same time provide them the feeling that they are doing the right thing for all mankind in the process. We have to make it a patriotic duty to sterilize these creatures and turn them back into humans." The Senator went back to studying his copy of Irene Moore's journal.

"For God's sake, Gordon, just don't use the phrase 'final solution'. Hitler beat you to it."

Marci and Alicia had talked for hours the night before. The topic had been whether to go public or not and if so, when. Marci was dead set against it. She was convinced that they were going into a period just like the Japanese Americans after Pearl Harbor was attacked. "No one is going to give a flip about what happens to us." She was convinced that if they were discovered, they would be opening themselves up to attacks from all directions, especially since they were the only Monoecious couple in the area, and as far as they knew, in the world. They would be an oddity to be looked at like animals in a zoo.

Alicia was sure that Marci was blowing the whole thing out of proportion. The world would get bored with them in a few weeks as soon as the next major crisis comes up. Until then, things would be rough with the media attention and the gawkers but it would be over soon enough. After all, they couldn't keep it quiet for long. As soon as one of their relatives was discovered, they would be discovered. It wouldn't be hard to trace them from any number of cousins and aunts. Alicia was sure that she would be looked at differently at work if she volunteered the information rather than have it discovered in some investigation. They went to bed without coming to a consensus and the decision was delayed.

The next evening, Marci watched the local news and prayed that Alicia had kept quiet. The reporter stood in front of a neat brick home describing the assault that had taken place there. "An admitted Monoecion, who had revealed herself on Monday after the news broke in the Nation's View article, had been staying at this house here in east Knoxville with a friend for the past two days." They didn't mention that her husband had beat her and thrown her out of her own home when she told him about herself. "About an hour ago, three people wearing ski masks jumped her and beat her severely here in the driveway. She was still alive when the ambulance left but her current condition is unknown. There were several witnesses but no one could identify the attackers."

They then cut to another reporter at a local high school where he told of a teacher who had revealed to her students that she was a Monoecion. "She was attacked in her own classroom at the end of the school day by an unknown number of attackers. She has been stabbed multiple times and was currently in guarded condition at the University Of Tennessee Medical Center."

Just then the door swung open and Marci screamed in surprise. Alicia stood in the doorway staring as if Marci had lost her mind. "I realize that I may not be beautiful after a day at work but I hope I don't look that bad."

Marci let her breath out in short bursts as she calmed herself. "I was wrapped up in the news when the door opened. You scared the crap out of me." Marci got up off the floor where she was sitting and went to Alicia and gave her a childlike hug. "You haven't told anyone have you?" she asked nervously.

"No, we haven't decided yet. I wouldn't say anything unless we both decide in favor, you know that." The hurt was evident in Alicia's voice. Marci told Alicia what she had heard on the news. Alicia shook her head. "This is insane. Has the world completely lost its mind?"

"I'm scared."

Alicia felt Marci tremble in her arms. "I'm scared too. I'm more worried about the girls. Anyway, that decides it. We don't reveal ourselves no matter what, and if we have to, we go underground. I think you need to go shopping and get some little boys clothes for Jasmine and Jessica. It will help throw off suspicion if one of them can pass for a boy."

"That will be easier with Jessica but I'll try it with Jasmine too."

"I better get a set of men's clothes myself and see if I can go butch." Alicia looked in the mirror as she tried to mash her breasts against her chest. "There are times when it would be nice to be flat-chested."

"We will need everything here and waiting. I'll get some fake facial hair like we used in the theater group. With a little padding to give you a gut, we might be able to hide your boobs but it won't be easy." Marci placed a throw pillow on Alicia's stomach. "We'll also need to pad your lower back. Not many men have that nice curve like you do."

"There's something else we will need." Alicia stopped, not sure how to say it but sure of how it would be received. "We'll need a gun," she said quietly.

"No!" There was fire in Marci's eyes now. "A gun wouldn't have helped either of those women on the news today. They were both jumped and didn't have a chance even if they had a gun. I'm not going to live in fear of Jasmine finding it and shooting herself or someone else."

"And what are you going to do when there are four men beating down the door, say don't come in or I'll hit you with a dirty diaper? This is getting ugly and it's going to get worse. Now you can try to hide behind your rose-colored glasses until some butcher decides it's your turn to be crushed under his heel but I'm not going to wait until you, me, or one of the kids becomes a victim."

"There has to be another way," Marci said quietly, her voice barely above a whisper. The anchorman was again on the TV talking of the "Monoecion Problem." Alicia and Marci listened as the newsman reported that the FBI would be spearheading the effort to identify the extent of the Monoecion population by tracking back through the family trees of the growing number of known Monoecions. "That's right, track us down and identify us to the general public so the gangs of thugs can come and finish us off. Use our own damn family trees to kill us off!" Marci grabbed the china candy dish off the end table and threw it at the TV before Alicia could stop her. Luckily, her aim was poor and the dish shattered into a thousand pieces against the wall. "What good would a gun do me?" Marci's voice had an edge of madness. "I can't hit the broad side of a barn with a scoop shovel."

Chapter 13

Thursday, August 8

Christine and Ben Davis sat together at the witness table before the joint session of Congress. "Well, Ben, are you ready for the biggest circus to be held under the big top since the McCarthy hearings?" Christine asked Ben.

"You underestimate yourself. By the time this is done, no one will remember Joe McCarthy. I bet you never thought you'd be on TV with hundreds of millions of people watching around the world."

"Want to trade places?"

Ben shook his head. "I don't care how many games of racquet ball you throw, I won't go for that one."

A page turned on their microphones and the Speaker of the House asked "Are you ready, Mrs. Landis?"

"Yes sir, I think I am."

"Good, I'm glad one of us is." The gallery laughed as the speaker rummaged through his papers for thirty seconds until finally giving up and sending a staffer to run up and get a new copy of his notes. "Now, Mrs. Landis, if you haven't grown too old waiting, I was hoping you could answer a few questions for me." Another round of laughter broke out on the floor.

He's good, thought Christine. He just turned what could have shown him as an old forgetful fool into an image of a warm hearted, quick-witted leader. "I'll try, sir."

"Good. Are you a Monoecion?"

"The term monoecious is in the dictionary but the term Monoecion is not. Could you give me your definition of the word?"

"I'm sorry counselor, I forgot you were an attorney. Let's decide that it means a being who has both male and female sex organs in one body. Is that an acceptable definition?"

"Yes, it is," Christine said.

"Now. Are you a Monoecion?"

"I don't know the answer." There were ripples of excited voices across the floor. "I have not been medically tested for this condition."

The speaker looked at his notes obviously concerned. He covered his microphone and conferred with his aides. He returned his attention to Christine. "Didn't you have tests run yesterday afternoon?"

"No, sir," Christine answered. "The tests were scheduled but they were called off because the doctor forgot to have me consume only clear liquids for twelve hours before the test. He didn't think my Ruben sandwich and side salad would go well with the barium. They have been rescheduled for tomorrow morning."

"I see. Has anyone ever told you that you were monoecious?"

"Yes. My mother told me when I was fourteen."

"Then why did you just say you didn't know if you were monoecious?"

"My mother also told me that Santa Claus came down the chimney and left presents around the tree." Christine paused as the snickers died down. "I do think there is a higher probability of her being correct about the monoecious characteristics but I have still not been tested to confirm this."

Marci watched the hearings on CNN as she did her ironing. "Give 'em hell, Christine!" Marci shouted to the TV. Jasmine looked up at Marci from the couch where she was playing with her cars. "Oops, mommy didn't mean to say that. That is not a good word for you to use, OK?"

Jasmine nodded and went back to her cars. Jessica rolled over in her playpen where she happily slept off her lunch.

The speaker became a bit more cautious. Mrs. Landis was playing this very well. "Do you have children?"

"Yes, I do, three daughters ages ten, twelve and fifteen."

"Three daughters. Is it unusual to have all girls in your family? On your mother's side I mean."

"No sir. You might say my family has a tradition of having girls," Christine responded.

"That, I believe, is probably the greatest understatement I have ever heard. Has any female ancestor of yours given birth to a male child as far as you know?"

"No sir, not as far as I know." Christine noticed the mood of the spectators growing more serious.

"Do you mind if I ask you a few questions about your childhood?"

"Go right ahead."

"When did you realize that you were different from other children?"

"When was I told? As soon as I could talk and understand. I'd say around the age of four. But it was very subtle during that time. My mother would let me know if I was saying anything inappropriate."

"What do you mean inappropriate?"

"Any reference to being telepathic, to knowing things I shouldn't."

"Are you telepathic?"

"In a way, yes. I can't read what you are thinking. It only works with blood relatives, my sisters, my mother and my children."

"Would you be so kind as to tell me what your children are thinking about?"

"No, I wouldn't. First, I can only sense feelings and emotions. Even then they have to be very strong. Second, a person's feelings are their own. I would never try to tell you someone else's feelings without their permission."

"Very noble of you Mrs. Landis."

Jasmine perked up her ears at this exchange on the TV. She looked at Christine very intently. "Who's that?"

"A lady who is trying to defend herself when she hasn't been bad." Marci stopped ironing to listen to the TV.

"Do they think she's been bad?" Jasmine asked.

"That's the way it sounds to me," Marci said.

"So you can sense the feelings of your children and siblings. Doesn't it get confusing as to who you're feeling?"

"No, not at all. You always know who it is. Don't you recognize your wife's voice?"

"I'm not married." The Senator squirmed in his chair. He didn't like being reminded of the divorce after his ex-wife caught him with that twenty-five year old office aide. "Does distance have any affect on this ability?"

"None that I'm aware of. When I was in California two years ago, I felt Terra, my youngest, break her foot playing soccer."

"I thought you only felt feelings?"

"No, we also will sense when someone is hurt badly. You don't feel the pain exactly but you know where it was inflicted."

Jasmine was terribly excited. "Mommy, mommy! She's like me! Christine, she's like us!"

"Yes she is. Now settle down. Mommy wants to hear what she has to say to these ... people." Marci came over and sat next to Jasmine. Jasmine was so excited Marci could feel her small body trembling.

Senator Barkus of Illinois began his questioning. "Could you tell me who your grandmother was on your mother's side?"

"Carol Jacobs."

"And your grandfather?"

"Dr. Irene Moore." Christine felt a little strange for a moment. She looked over at the TV camera on her right and realized she was looking at herself. She was sitting on the couch with her mother ... no, not her mother, Jasmine's mother, watching herself on TV. But who was Jasmine?

'I'm Jasmine' came the answer.

A sudden fear gripped Christine. They put something in the water to make it look like I'm crazy. Or maybe I am crazy. What's happening to me?

Christine felt the warmth of a five, going-on-six-year-old smile fill her entire being. It was a feeling she hadn't felt since childhood. Oh no, she thought, I'm probably grinning like an idiot. She looked at herself through the eyes of Jasmine, watching her on TV. There she sat next to Ben with the most pleasant, innocent smile she had ever seen spread across her face. This was certainly not the normal Monoecion telepathy. It was a child that she was connected with, of that much she was certain. Christine wondered who this child was but before she could complete the thought, a flood of Jasmine rolled over her, images of Marci and Alicia, her bedroom, Bingo the stuffed dog. Jasmine was definitely a Monoecion, Christine was shown the experiences in Jasmine's short life that confirmed it. Christine lost her fear and carefully showed some of herself to Jasmine, being careful to give her only things she could understand. The whole meshing of images and ideas took less than a second. It was as if their minds had gone into overdrive when they were connected.

Jasmine wanted to know if Christine would be her 'bestest' friend. Christine let Jasmine know that she would be honored. Christine gently let Jasmine know that she was busy right now but she hoped ever so much that Jasmine would visit her again real soon.

Jasmine let Christine know that she thought she could since she knew how to do it now. With that she was gone.

Christine felt the jerk back to normal plane of existence. She whispered to herself "Incredible."

"Christine is nice, mommy. She hasn't been bad at all," Jasmine said.

No, I'm sure she hasn't," Marci said.

"She likes you, too. She wants me to visit again," Jasmine said as a matter of fact.

"What?" Marci looked down at Jasmine who was now busy again with her cars. Marci looked at the TV just in time to see Christine look up at the camera. For a second she could have sworn Christine was looking straight at her.

"Mrs. Landis, are you saying your grandfather was not a man?"

"Dr. Irene Moore provided the sperm that combined with the egg provided by Carol Jacobs. That process created my mother, Rebecca Jacobs. I believe that fulfills the requirements for Irene Moore to be considered my paternal grandparent."

"So your paternal grandparent, Irene Moore, was a Monoecion and lived with your grandmother, Carol Jacobs, as… Monoecion and wife?"

"I presume so. Grandma Irene died when I was quite young so I don't remember her much."

"Was Carol Jacobs a Monoecion like your Grandfather, excuse me, paternal grandparent?"

Christine realized he was playing a game. He wanted her to say 'no, she was human'. He had been trying for some time to get her to separate Monoecions and humans as two different races. She wasn't sure how she knew or why he felt it was so important, she just knew she didn't dare make the distinction. "As far as I know, my grandmother was never tested to see if she was monoecious but I assume that she had only one set of reproductive organs."

The questioning went on for six hours. The main focus of the initial three hours was her telepathic abilities and sexual differences from "normal humans." But then things began to turn a bit more nasty. Questions began to center on why she chose to work in government when private practice paid more. Wasn't it a fact that she was there to try to kill any investigations before they had a chance to get started? She had done a pretty good job deflecting the attacks until they brought up a case she had helped to research concerning the murder of a doctor. He was collecting data on hereditary defects in humans. One of the areas he was collecting data on was the tendency towards single sex births within a family. Christine had felt that the murder had nothing to do with his research and recommended the investigation look elsewhere for the motive. A small time crook was later charged for the murder when he was busted for a drug charge and had the doctor's watch in his possession. It didn't matter that the man was placed at the scene and was convicted of the murder. The

Senator strongly implied that it was a setup to cover up the real murderers who were probably Monoecions.

When Christine felt she was finally making headway in defending her actions in the murder case, several discrepancies were brought up in her expense reports and personal bank accounts. She turned to Ben and whispered to him, "What's next, I'll be accused of stealing scotch tape from the god damned government. I don't know how much more of this I can take before I tell them where to get off!"

Ben tried to settle her. "I know it's tough. Take a few minutes break to regain your concentration. You're due a break. Don't let them push you into saying something in haste."

"Every time I think I can't handle any more, I just picture having each committee member on the racquet ball court, running them into the ground one at a time." She sat up and leaned into the microphone. "Senator, if you took time to do your homework, you would find that the per diem charge was well within department limits for the city I was in. The reason it appears to be excessive is that I had to charge my partner's expenses because he lost his American Express card." The questioning droned on for a few more hours.

Christine and her mother walked down the sidewalk a block from the house. They had decided that there was no place safe inside the house to talk without the walls listening. They were sure the house was thoroughly bugged by now. "Mother, you wouldn't believe it, there I sat concentrating on the questions, and bang, there's a five year old child sharing my brain." The excitement in Christine caused her to pick up the pace.

"Slow down, Christine. I'm too old to run." "We need to keep this short. It's not safe for us to be on the streets like this. Some nut will want to make a name for himself and blow us away."

"I know, but I had to tell someone or I was going to bust. I mean I know all sorts of things about her, how old she is, her mother's name, someone else named Alicia who I think is her father."

"Monoecion?"

"I think so but I didn't ask. I know her mother is because she said that she was like us, only she didn't say it with words. It's so amazing the way it feels that I'm not sure I can describe it. Imagine I'm holding a picture of something in my hands and I want you to see it but I can't show it to you. So I'm going to stand here and describe every minute detail until you have a perfect vision of the picture. Now imagine that instead of describing it, I just turn it towards you and you can see it for your self. If talking is like a bicycle, this form of communication is like the space shuttle."

"How long did the connection last?"

Christine thought for a moment. "It seemed like twenty or thirty seconds but after viewing the video tape, I think it really lasted a second or two."

"Don't let anyone know this ever happened. You would be placing that child and yourself in great danger," Becky said. "If the government knew you could pass real information back and forth, you would be the ultimate spy, more valuable than a real James Bond. And possibly too valuable to allow to exist."

"I know, mother. You didn't raise a fool."

"I know I didn't." They hugged and finished the walk in silence.

The agents assigned to watch them couldn't get their listening gear in place in time to hear the conversation. They were sure it was nothing of consequence and noted the walk in the log.

The silence was oppressive as Robert and Christine lay in bed after watching the news. The lead story was the congressional investigation of the Monoecions, specifically the investigation into the actions of one Christine Landis. "What's wrong?" Christine asked. "You haven't said three words to me in the last hour."

Robert sighed. "I've been trying to find a way of avoiding the subject."

"Which one, your wife's a witch, your wife's a traitor or your wife's a crook?" Christine asked sarcastically.

"My mother thinks it would be a good idea if your mother stayed at a hotel." Robert rushed ahead to get it all out at once. "She thinks that your mother is a bad influence on the girls and adds to the media circus going on around this house."

"Oh, she does! And do you want to know what I think? I think my mother is going to be here as long as she wants to stay. I need her and she needs me right now."

"I know that. Mother wasn't trying to be cruel; she was just trying to protect the kids as much as she could."

"Has it slipped her mind that they're Monoecions too?" Christine sat up stiff in bed clenching her fists. "Doesn't she understand that we need each other right now?"

Robert put his hands on Christine's shoulders. "Look, I'm not siding with my mother against you. I understand. I'll talk to her. I just didn't want her to take you by surprise if she mentioned it. I figured you've had enough surprises lately."

Christine crumpled against his chest. "I'm just so tired... so damn tired."

It had been only four days since the news hit the streets in the Nation's View when Rae Ann Baird made the decision to tell her husband. Their marriage had not been the best lately but she had little choice. She had talked to both sisters and the decision had been made to tell their husbands. The effects would ripple out from there but it was only a matter of time before they were traced from another family member.

Rae Ann talked to her twin girls before hand. "Don't make any judgments about your father based on what happens tonight. This is going to be a major shock for him and he's going to feel betrayed and angry. Just give him time to get used to the idea." They'll understand, Rae Ann thought, they're good girls.

The girls were nineteen and sophomores at the community college. They chose to stay in Macon, Georgia, and go to school to keep the cost of college within reach of their parent's income. The girls were identical twins, at least physically. They were the average American dream girls, good looking, five foot nine, with medium length natural blonde hair, Carla's hair cut a little longer than Kathy's. They were the type you expect to see on the cheer leading squad except they preferred to be on the field rather than beside it. They both ran track and cross country through high school and continued to run on their own now that they were in college. Emotionally they weren't the match they were physically. Carla, the youngest by ten minutes, was easy going and forgiving. Kathy on the other hand was a hell raiser. She was strong-willed and self-confident, bordering on egotistical. Rae Ann had no idea why she was so headstrong.

"All you have to do is remember how you felt when you were fourteen and I told you the whole story. You were so mad at me for keeping secrets that you could have spit nails. Daddy's going to react the same way if not worse. Just give him a chance, OK?" The girls nodded. "Don't come out unless I call you."

Now it was time to do it. The girls were in Kathy's bedroom and Randy was in a good mood watching TV. It had to be tonight or he'd hear it from a brother-in-law. Rae Ann did have the good sense to wait for a commercial break.

"Honey, could we talk?"

"Yeah, sure." He pressed the mute on the remote. Things had been rocky lately but he had been trying. He hadn't been out with Hank and Tom in a week, and his drinking had been cut way back. One of her complaints was he was always too busy to talk to her. Tonight he would make time; the show had been a lousy rerun anyway. "What do you want to talk about?"

"What do you think about the stuff on the news about the Monoecions?"

Randy looked at her and half-laughed. "That leaves a lot of room, which stuff do you mean?"

"You know, just what do you think of it?" Rae Ann rubbed his arm as she spoke.

"Well, first, I think all this bleeding heart civil rights crap is a bunch of bull." He shifted in his recliner so he could look at her. "Hell, they'll wipe us out if they have half a chance. I agree with Hank and Tom, the best way to deal with Monos is to exterminate them." He watched as a look of horror came over Rae Ann's face.

"Good plan. Just put 'em up against the wall and shoot the bitches, right?" Rae Ann spit out. She hadn't intended to put the venom in her words. This was not going the way she wanted it to.

Randy recoiled from her. The only other time they had discussed this was when it first came out and she hadn't really seemed to have an opinion. Obviously she had one now. "I don't mean it that way. You know, mandatory sterilization. I'm not an animal, even if you think I am."

Rae Ann looked down at the floor. "I don't think you're an animal. I didn't mean to say it that way."

"Well, Christ, you asked me what I thought and I told you. You don't need to tear my head off." Randy stared at the silent TV screen.

"Do think that should apply to your children also?" Rae Ann asked.

"If they were Monos, you bet it ..." Randy looked at wife with his mouth open. Her jaw was set and her eyes locked on his. "You can't mean ... They're not Monos."

"The trait comes from the mother," Rae Ann stated. "It's one hundred percent dominant. They didn't choose to be monoecious."

"You bitch." He slapped her hard across the face.

She rocked back and regained her balance. "I had that one coming... But if you ever hit me again, I'll break your neck."

Her word carried the weight of truth. Randy knew she could do it. Ever since she was a child she had been training in the martial arts. He knew that even at forty-one years old, she could take out any three men without working up a sweat. She had been training the girls since they were six. "Get the hell out of my house. Take your little witches with you and get out of my sight."

"I guess that may be a good idea tonight." Rae Ann went in to get the twins. They had been glued to their door, listening to the whole exchange.

The first night Rae Ann and the girls spent in a hotel but Rae Ann knew they couldn't afford that for long.

Chapter 14

Friday, August 9

The next morning Rae Ann returned to the house to talk to her husband before he went to work. She knocked on the door, it felt strange to be knocking on her own door but she thought it best.

Randy looked through the window then opened the door. "What do you want?" His voice was harsh.

"I thought maybe we could talk."

"The time for talking is long past. You had twenty years to talk to me but you never said anything!" Randy snarled.

"You've got to understand. I couldn't say anything without putting thousands of innocent people in danger," Rae Ann explained. "I couldn't do that."

"And I can't talk to you now." Randy slammed the door.

Rae Ann found a little two bedroom apartment she could rent by the week and checked out of the hotel. Surely, she assumed, Randy would cool off soon.

Christine sat at home watching the continuing live coverage of the joint session of Congress, waiting to watch her mother testify. Unfortunately, she had no special privileges and had to watch it on TV just like everyone else. She couldn't even sit at the table with her to lend moral support. Her physical wasn't scheduled until one o'clock in the afternoon so she had two whole hours to herself until they showed up to escort her to the hospital.

Christine felt the presence of Jasmine just as she had the day before. When Jasmine made the connection, Christine immediately recognized it as Jasmine just as she could recognize one of her own children. The only difference was that this connection came with images and ideas, not just feelings. Christine gave her a rather formal greeting. "Hello, Jasmine. It's nice to have you visit again." Then Christine received what could only be described as a mental hug, that same warm feeling you have as your mother wraps her arms around you and squeezes. If only the world could feel this, she thought. "Oh, thank you," Christine responded and returned a hug of her own. She was amazed at how easy it was to do. Christine checked her watch.

This time the conversation seemed to last many minutes, giving Christine a chance to analyze what was happening to her. On one level, her mind was continuing to capture what was going on in the world around her while, on another level, she was experiencing an exchange of information with this child at a speed she never dreamed possible. She began to realize how limited her thinking had been before this. The saying was right, two minds are better than one, but no one had grasped how much better. Christine began to think of things she could do in her defense with a clarity she had never imagined.

A rather desperate cry of "I don't understand!" startled Christine.

"I'm sorry, Jasmine. I forget how young you are and how confusing the world can be." Christine was astounded at how easy it was to explain complex legal concepts without words. The conversation ceased as quickly as it had started, a simple "I have to go now," and Jasmine was gone. Christine looked again at her watch, ten seconds had passed. In that time they had "discussed" pets, parents, going on a trip to the Knoxville Zoo, legal definitions of human and the concept of human rights as it relates to the United Stated Constitution.

Christine saw that they had started questioning her mother. She wished that Ben could have been her mother's attorney also but he felt he had his hands full with his current caseload. He figured it would help having another viewpoint anyway. "God, how I wish I could be there with you," she whispered, pushing loving reassurance with all her might.

Senator Fenton had asked for and received the honor of starting the questioning. "I've been confused about Doctor Moore's use of the term monoecious. Why didn't she use the proper term, hermaphrodite to describe your condition?"

"In most human hermaphrodites, one set of organs are underdeveloped. Irene was also a bit of a flower lover, and she just liked the term monoecious better." Becky paused a moment and added, "She used to call my sisters and I 'her flowers'."

The Senator allowed a short snort of disdain escape. "How did your 'father' get your mother pregnant?"

Becky looked over her glasses in disbelief. "I always presumed it was done by putting sperm in her vagina, just like everyone else."

"Everyone else had a father who was male," the Senator replied. "Since Irene Moore wasn't, many of us are confused as to how this takes place."

"Since I was the youngest, I wasn't present at the conceiving of any of my sisters but I doubt that my parents invited them in to watch." There was a round of laughter in the hall. "They never discussed it with me and I never asked."

"The details are described quite thoroughly in Doctor Moore's journal. Are you saying that she never discussed it with you?" asked Fenton.

"Did you ever discuss the details of impregnating your children's mother with them?" asked Mrs. Lovett. It took a while for the room to calm down again.

The Senator tried to regain his composure. "Did your father ever encourage you to have lesbian affairs?"

"If you are asking if Irene encouraged me to have sex with a woman, the answer is no. That was always strongly discouraged. I was told to not be surprised if I felt a sexual attraction to a woman because of the dual sex organs in my body."

"Oh, I see. And did you experience any sexual urges toward women?"

"That's none of your damned business!" her voice burning with indignation. "I refuse to discuss my sex life on national TV. When I agreed to testify here I thought I was to appear before Congress, not Doctor Phil!"

The Senator looked around nervously, he had lost the first round and he didn't like it. "Did your father indoctrinate you with her philosophy of control?" came the question.

"I'm not sure I know what you mean. She talked to me about life like any parent does. Trying to teach me right from wrong." Becky Lovett looked the part of the kindly grandmother.

"Did she ever tell you to get into the proper positions in local and state government to discredit anyone suggesting investigation into all female births or telepathy?"

"No, she talked of the importance of being in the right places to be able to pickup advance notice if we were discovered but never to discredit anyone. She was sure that our traits would be discovered within a few years and she hoped to delay it as long as possible."

The questioner raised his voice. "I see. She wanted to make sure your kind had enough numbers to control the government, or at least keep it from taking action against your race?"

Becky took a deep breath, concentrating on maintaining control. "My parents were sure that if our traits and abilities became public knowledge, we would become persecuted by people who would fear us rather than try to understand us. It seems to me their fears were well-founded."

"Oh, I see." The Senator spread his arms wide. "If we just showed your kind compassion, you would stop reproducing and mankind would be saved. Is that it?"

"It would be a step in the right direction," Becky spoke quietly. "It beats having gangs of thugs murdering suspected Monoecions on the streets while the police look the other way."

"Are you accusing the US government of supporting these acts of violence?"

"No. But both the actions and lack of action by this body allow it to happen."

The Senator shook his head in disbelief. "You sit before this body of government and accuse it of murder while your race documents its attempts at extermination of all humans on this planet!"

Christine watched the exchange. It was getting ugly and it would get worse. Then her FBI escort arrived to take her to the hospital. Try as she might, they refused to wait so she could see a little more of the questioning. She reluctantly turned off the TV and followed them to the car.

Marci had told Alicia that it would be dangerous to buy a handgun right now. With the background checks, it might bring suspicion on them. This had pleased Marci to no end, she did not want a gun in the house. Alicia had another idea. The law did not cover replica antique firearms such as Civil War revolvers. Her father used to shoot them in competition and in reenactments. It was the only kind of gun that her mother would allow in the house, also. They were just as accurate as modern guns at ranges up to 100 yards and if they used it in self-defense it would more than likely be at a range of ten feet or less. Her dad had taught her to shoot with a Colt 1851 Navy replica. It was small and light enough for her to handle but still potent enough to scare off an attacker. Alicia stopped at the sporting goods store after work and went to the firearms counter. She caught a salesman's eye and he came over to her. "Can I help you?"

"I was looking for something for my little brother's birthday. A friend in a Civil War reenactment group has convinced him he needs a Colt Navy cap and ball revolver." She hoped the clerk wouldn't notice how nervous she was.

"Sure. Got just the thing." He walked down to a glass case that contained floor display models. "Did you want steel or brass frame?"

"What's the difference?"

The salesman let out a sigh. He wanted to say "the brass frame model has a brass frame and the steel frame has a steel frame, you dumb broad" but then he remembered his commission. "The brass frame isn't authentic for Civil War enactors but it is easier to take care of because it won't rust. The steel frame is stronger and won't wear out as quick if the gun is used often."

"Give me the steel frame and if he doesn't like it, he can exchange it if that's OK. What else will he need to shoot it?" Alicia saw the grin appear on the salesman's face. He was counting the dollars already. Alicia tried to remember what her dad really used and what was just extra crap the salesman was trying to unload on her.

When Alicia left the store, she had the minimum requirements to use the gun, a hundred percussion caps, a hundred .370 lead balls, a pound of 3x black powder, powder flask, ball grease, nipple wrench, cleaning rod and patches. "I'm never going to remember how to use this thing on my own," she said to herself. "It's time to call dad."

Chapter 15

Saturday, August 10

Six days after the disclosure, Congress enacted an emergency measure proposed by Senator Fenton. From that moment forward, all Monoecions were required to report to their local drivers license bureau and have an identification card made for each member of the family regardless of age. The more moderate members of Congress were able to muster enough support to remove the fingerprinting requirement and to allow a sixty-day waiting period before any criminal penalties would kick in. The FBI was to be responsible for implementing the system ASAP.

Senator Fenton was pleased that he was able to muster enough pull to bring the issue to a vote on a Saturday special session. He had suggested that the states use a modified driver's license but the implementation method was left to the individual states. There were only a few cries of another unfunded federally mandated regulation. Fenton was also pleased because a firm from his home state was the prime supplier of the equipment used by many states to produce these cards. The company had contributed generously to his last campaign and he was sure this would ensure their continued support. The law was slated to go into effect as soon as the states could be set up to handle it. Most states could go to work within a week using the modified driver's license forms.

There were outcries from all over the world about the new US policy, mostly from countries that had no known Monoecion populations. It was compared to Nazi Germany rounding up of Jews during World War II. The US government patiently explained that no gas chambers were being built and that the Jews had not attempted to wipe out the human race. Ironically, most nations made it a crime for Monoecions to enter their country without approval.

Early Saturday morning, Marci and Alicia loaded up the girls and headed for Alicia's parent's house in Chattanooga. They wanted to be able to spend the day and still get back at a reasonable hour that evening. An hour later Grandpa and Grandma were making a fuss over Jasmine and Jessica.

Alicia's dad, Carl, had a hard time accepting his daughter's lifestyle. He had liked Marci when he met her but then she was just Alicia's college roommate. A short time later Alicia announced that they were in love. Carl lost control and raked both of them over the coals. When he accused Marci of leading his daughter astray, Alicia told him she was the one who seduced Marci, not the other way around. That comment seemed to break him. He felt that somehow this was all his fault and was the result of his failure as a father.

In time he learned to accept the fact that Alicia and Marci were truly in love but he never could bring himself to think of his daughter as a lesbian. The real conflict began when Marci announced that she was pregnant. Alicia told him that she was artificially inseminated using an unknown donor. She couldn't very well tell him she was the father. Carl's anger flared anew. He could not accept them raising a child in their relationship. It was bad enough to have his daughter 'living in sin' as she was, but to expose a child to that lifestyle was too much for him. He banned them from ever coming into his house. Alicia's mom came to see the baby after it was born but Carl refused to come along. It took six months before he consented to talk to his daughter again. For another year, every conversation seemed to end in an argument.

The one thing Carl did not have a problem with was loving the sweet little baby that came to visit. Alicia's mother was the one who finally got through to Carl. She explained that Jasmine needed a male father figure and the only way she was going to get one was by spending time with him. Carl couldn't argue the logic and soon things began to become routine. If two weeks went by without a visit he let them know that it better not happen again.

When Marci became pregnant with Jessica, he objected again. There was a rough period but he had already been through too much. He attended Jessica's birth and was the first to hold her after Marci and Alicia. He played the role of the proud grandpa to the hilt.

Alicia's mother never really forgave her for the pain she caused her father. She also didn't like the precedent she set for her younger sisters. If either of them had followed Alicia's lead, it would have torn Carl apart. He always thought it was his fault Alicia 'strayed'. He was sure he had failed to give her what she needed when she was growing up. Even when the younger sisters were safely married off to nice young men, Alicia's relationship with her mother was never fully restored.

As grandpa carried a giggling Jasmine into the house, tossed over his shoulder like a sack of feed, Alicia managed to delay outside with her mother. "Have you told him?" Alicia didn't need to be more specific, her mother knew just what she was talking about.

"No, not yet, but I'm sure he already knows, even though he hasn't said anything yet." She picked up Jessica and rocked her gently. "Have you or Marci told anyone yet?"

"No and we're not going to. It would be too dangerous for us. We've already decided to go into hiding if any of the relatives disclose. I think I could pass for a man well enough to get us out of the country to some place where we wouldn't be persecuted."

Alicia's mother shook her head in disbelief. "Now just exactly where is this magical fairyland that you'll be running off to because I'd like to go too!" The sarcasm was obvious.

"I don't know yet," Alicia said "but there must be someplace. There has to be."

"Let's all pray the world comes to its senses before it comes to that."

Alicia pulled Jessica's necessity bag out of the back seat of the car. "Now who's living in a fantasy?" she asked sarcastically. Her mother did not reply. They walked into the house in silence.

After an hour of catching up on what the neighbors have been up to and touring the new flowerbed with mom, Alicia brought up going shooting with dad. "Do you go out shooting anymore?"

"Oh I go out every now and then but not enough to keep in shape for competition. You always had potential but you just weren't interested enough to practice."

"Too much noise and the ear protectors always messed up my hair."

"Not to mention that boys didn't like girls who could out shoot them," Carl said. He realized how strange that sounded with his daughter sitting there holding another woman's hand. God how he hated to see them showing affection for each other. What upset him even more was the fact that they continued to do it when they knew it bothered him so much.

Alicia sensed her dad's frustration. "Want to go out and punch some paper this morning? I was telling Marci about it and she wanted to give it a try."

"Don't see any reason why not. I think I've still got some powder and balls around here. Your mother can watch the kids for a couple of hours while we go over to the club practice range. That OK with you, dear?"

"I can handle them for a while but don't be gone too long or dinner won't be fit to eat," said grandma.

"Get your tail in gear then, girl. Come on down stairs and help me carry the stuff out to the car, you remember how much junk you need to shoot cap and ball." Carl signaled to Marci "You too, missy. If you want to try, you have to carry your weight." Carl led them down to the basement and pulled bags and boxes from the shelves.

"What do you want to shoot, the Remington or the Colt?" Without waiting for an answer he decided to take both.

"Marci, get the spotting scope and tripod.... They're on the second shelf behind those paint cans," he said waving his hand in a vague direction.

Marci was flabbergasted at the amount of equipment Carl was pulling out. "The gunfighters of the Old West carried all this junk around?"

"Only when they went target practicing. When they went into a real gunfight, the only thing they carried was their trusty Colts, fully loaded."

They carried the equipment out the back door and Alicia told her dad to put it in her car. "We'll drive mine today." She opened the trunk and they piled the stuff in.

"I hope your shocks are in good shape because the road back to the F.O.P. pistol range isn't." Carl saw the new reproduction Colt Navy revolver still in the box confirming his suspicion that this was not just a fun outing.

When they pulled into the Fraternal Order of Police pistol range, there was only one other person on the firing line, a policeman practicing for his annual department exam. Carl set up the loading stand, spread out the paraphernalia on the bench and hung the targets on the frame. The policeman had been shooting at the typical man-shaped targets and holding a respectable eight-inch pattern. He came over to see what Carl was setting up.

"What the hell is that thing?"

"Black powder revolver. It's a replica of the type used during the Civil War."

"I've seen the Hawken deer rifles but I've never seen the revolvers before." He started to snicker as Carl went through the rather complicated loading procedure. "I suppose they aren't very accurate."

"Oh, they're better than most people think," said Carl and stepped up to the firing line, twenty-five yards from the targets. "Put your ears on girls. I'm going to warm it up." He pulled the hammer back to full cock and seated the revolver firmly in his right hand. He put his left hand in his pocket and concentrated on the target while breathing deeply. He raised the gun in a slow deliberate motion and slowly squeezed the trigger, timing the pull with the hardly visible weave of his arm. The first shot went high and to the right in the eight ring, three and a half inches from the center of the target.

"That's pretty good for an antique," the policeman said, obviously impressed.

"Which," said Carl, "the gun or the shooter? For the gun, that's terrible, for the shooter it's pretty good considering how long it's been since I've practiced." Carl settled his breathing down and placed the next shoot in the black in the nine ring at six o'clock. The next three shots were in the ten ring, one dead center on the X. The policeman had quit snickering and was now standing with his mouth open. Carl went back to the bench and started to reload. The policeman mumbled something about it being time to go, packed his equipment and left.

"I guess he didn't like being shown up by a hundred and fifty year old gun," Alicia said.

"There was a time when I would have considered that poor to average shooting. Now I'm thrilled to death with a score of forty-seven." Carl proceeded to instruct Marci on the theory of how the gun worked.

Marci took note of how long it took to complete the loading process. "It's obvious you can't wait and load these guns when you need them. How long can it remain loaded and still be trustworthy?" Marci asked.

"The loads will remain good for years as long as you don't get it wet," explained Carl.

"Wild Bill Hickok used this model gun for years after the cartridge guns came out and you don't get a reputation like his using an unreliable gun," added Alicia.

"By God, you do remember some of what I taught you," said Carl. "It's all in how you load it and how you take care of it after it's loaded. If you treat it like your life depends on it, it will work when you need it to save you life."

Carl got into one of his favorite subjects, old west gunfighters. "Think like a gunfighter for a moment. This gun has a couple of advantages over a modern firearm. The first is the sound it makes when it goes off. Black powder gives a lower muzzle velocity so the sound is lower pitched also. That makes for a low pitched boom rather than a high pitched crack."

"I'll say," said Marci. "It sounds like cannon."

"Exactly," said Carl. "At close range, that low pitched boom and flame spewing from the muzzle will scare the hell out of anyone even if you miss them. The next item is the cloud of smoke. It acts as a smoke screen, just like the ones used by the military. If you are just inside that cloud, you can see out much better than your opponent can see in. Check it out while you shoot, it really doesn't obscure your view of the target that much but to someone up there looking back at you, you nearly disappear." Carl loaded one of the Colts and started with Alicia, reminding her of her grip, commenting on her stance and pointing things out to Marci for her to watch. Then it was Marci's turn shoot. He kept them going as fast as he could load.

Marci and Alicia had been shooting for over an hour when Carl pulled his daughter aside. He wasn't sure of how he was going to broach the subject, he had never found a way with his wife. "Honey, I think I understand what this is all about. You didn't just suddenly get an interest in the Civil War, I know that. It doesn't take a genius to figure what it means that your grandmother had all girls, your aunts had all girls, you have no brothers and I haven't seen a grandson yet..."

"Yes, Daddy, what do you want me to say?" asked Alicia.

"I just want a straight answer, but first I want you to know that I love you and your mother and nothing will change that." He waited expectantly.

"You already know the answer, dad." Alicia added "I love you too."

"I just wanted you to know that, as much as I can, I understand. I would like to know one thing though." He paused, not sure if he would go on. "Is Marci like you or is she... you know..."

"A lesbian?" Alicia said. Her dad winced. He always had a hard time with that word. "For what it's worth, she's not a lesbian."

"That's great," he said with a broad smile. Somehow it was so much better that his daughter and her lover were Monoecions rather than gay. "That means Jasmine and Jessica are really my grand-daughters?"

"They're really your grand-daughters no matter what, but yes, I am the father, if that's what you are asking."

Carl hugged his daughter. They hadn't noticed that Marci was done shooting and was standing there smiling at them, lost in their embrace. Carl looked up at Marci. "Come here daughter and give your other dad a hug."

As they packed up to head back to the house, Carl said "Why don't you leave your new gun with me and I'll tune it up a bit. You know, smooth out that trigger pull and properly sight it in. You can take mine with you until I get it done."

"Sure," Alicia said. "That would be great." She had noticed how hard it was to pull the trigger compared to her dad's gun. And on his, the pull was smooth and consistent. "Are you sure you don't mind?"

"No, not at all. It's been years since I've tuned one and I'd like to see if I can still do it." He swapped guns with her and they headed home. When they got there, Marci was introduced to the other joy of shooting black powder, cleaning the mess up.

"Strip her down and put it in the sink in the utility room. You can wash it out there."

Marci looked up at Carl. "Who, me or the gun?"

"The gun, nitwit. You saw me do it just a few hours ago. What do we do first?" Carl patiently worked with her, guiding her steps explaining how it all worked again and again until he was sure she had it down pat. After both guns were cleaned, he dried and oiled them and put the new one away. He then took meticulous care in loading five chambers of his old gun. After making sure the hammer was on the empty chamber, he produced a long plastic cable-tie and strapped the hammer down.

"To make this gun fire, cut this strap off, put the hammer in half cock and press on the percussion caps. The whole process shouldn't take over thirty seconds if you practice a little. But it's damned near impossible for one of your little ones to do it accidentally."

"Thanks, dad," Marci said and kissed him on the cheek.

"Go on girl, and put it in the car. Mother has almost got dinner on the table and I'm starving."

The family sat down to a table that put Christmas dinner to shame. "Mother, this is the most beautiful sight these eyes have seen in a long time. What's the occasion?" asked Carl.

"There's no occasion, I just thought that with this family's schedule, who knows when we'll have a chance to get together again," his wife replied.

Alicia knew her mother better than that. She knew her mother was thinking that this could be their last dinner together for a long time. The talk was mostly small, discussions of the sisters and their kids, what was happening at the water treatment plant where Carl worked, and the like. Dinner was finished but everyone stayed at the table, afraid that if they got up, that wonderful feeling of warmth and safety would evaporate into the mist. Finally it couldn't be delayed any longer so Alicia helped her mom clear the table while Marci changed Jessica and helped Jasmine pick up her toys. Carl disappeared into the basement for a few minutes and returned with his hands in his pockets.

"We need to get going," said Alicia sadly.

"I wish you didn't," her mother said, truly meaning it for the first time in many years. "We love you all, be careful."

Carl put his arm around Alicia's shoulders and walked her towards the car. As they circled to the other side of the car, Carl pressed an object into her hand. She looked down at it, a tiny single shot pistol no bigger than her palm. "It's a gambler's boot pistol," he whispered. "Works the same, just put a cap on and it's ready. Just in case."

Alicia slipped it in her pocket. "Thanks Dad. Let's hope I never need it." They strapped in the girls and headed home. Five minutes out of the drive and both little girls were fast asleep.

Chapter 16

Sunday, August 11

One of Rae Ann's daughters, Carla, pushed open the screen door and let it bang shut behind her. She did a couple of quick stretches and set off down the street. She hadn't made it a block when a young man stepped out from a van and shouted "Hey Kathy, hold up a minute."

The twins were used to be called by each other's names. It took a second for her to recognize Keith. He was not somebody she wanted to run into. He had tried to get both Carla and Kathy to go out with him but both had shut him down. "Hey Keith. I'm in a bit of a hurry. I'm trying to get quick run in before I have to go work," she lied. Two guys grabbed her arms from behind and another came around the front of the van. "What are you doing Keith? Are you out of your mind?"

"No, but you're going to be, you fucking Mono bitch," said Keith with a lewd grin. "Get her in the fucking van. Hurry up before somebody sees us!"

"You're a lunatic!" Carla hawked and spit in the face of the boy holding her right arm. She then lurched to the left pushing the man holding her other arm into the open van door. He released her arm as he fell backwards, vainly trying to break his fall. His head struck the door frame with a sickening thud. Keith, seeing her arm free, lunged foreword to grab her. Her left foot swung in a perfect arc catching his cheek bone with her heel. Keith's head snapped sideways. Using the man's hold on her right arm as a pivot, Carla rotated her body on the follow through. Her right foot following her left caught Keith's head on the rebound like a basketball. Keith dropped like a sack of feed.

Carla was now face to face with the man who was still held her right arm. His eyes were wide with surprise as her left hand thrust foreword catching him in the throat crushing his larynx. He released her arm and dropped to his knees gasping for breath, his eyes dancing wildly, hands clawing at his throat.

She looked over her shoulder just in time to see the last man standing lunging at her with a knife. Carla dodged sideways avoiding the tip of the blade but the edge sliced along her rib cage. She kicked at him as she backed away but missed as he ducked back.

He nervously surveyed his friends laying like broken toys, moaning in pain. This was not in the plan. He had no desire to take this hellcat on in a one on one fight. He saw the blood soaking her left side. This gave a boost to his courage. Maybe she wasn't as sharp now that she was hurt. He circled carefully never taking his eyes off her.

Carla backed slowly along the side of the van, feeling carefully for footing. The last thing she could afford was a stumble. He was following cautiously waiting for an opening. Just as he reached the end of the van Carla reached her hand to her bleeding side, grimacing in pain. He lunged forward at Carla.

He didn't see Carla's sister, Kathy, until it was too late. Her foot caught him in the right knee, which popped like a dry stick. He dropped in agony cursing at the top of his lungs. Kathy grabbed Carla's hand and pulled her towards home yelling "Come on, let's get out here while we can." They sprinted for the house looking over their shoulders making sure they were not being pursued. Just as they reached their front door, the van motor started and it pulled away with tires squalling.

Carla was gasping as they stumbled in the door. "Are they coming after us?"

Kathy watched the van speed away. "No, they're running. What happened?"

"I had just left to run a couple miles before dinner when this van pulled over and four guys jumped out. One of them was that bastard, Keith, from high school."

"I ran out the door as soon as I felt your fear," said Kathy. "I think I set a new record for the two-twenty."

"Thanks. I needed your help," croaked Carla, holding her side.

"Like hell you did. You had already taken out all but one of them by the time I got there. You did that one all by yourself, girl. Come on and get in the bathroom so we can see how bad it is." Kathy guided Carla into the bathroom grabbing the phone as she went by. It rang almost immediately. She answered it with, "We're OK mom."

"How's Carla's side?" It still amazed Rae Ann that even though they were identical twins, she could always tell who was hurt or scared. She knew it was Carla as soon as it happened.

"I'm checking now, hold on." Kathy set the phone on the floor and helped Carla lift her sweatshirt. "It's bad. Not real deep but its long." She grabbed a towel from the rack and pressed it against the wound. "Hold this to reduce the bleeding. We need to head to emergency." Kathy picked up the phone. "Mom?"

Rae Ann said "I heard. Take her to the hospital, I'll be there as soon as I can. I'll call the police from here and have them meet you there. Now go."

"OK, bye." Kathy looked at Carla who's face had now turned white. "Lean against the sink. I need to get something over the cut." She wet a hand towel under the tub faucet and pulled a belt from the bathrobe hanging on the door. "Hold this while I tie it on."

Carla began to wobble as Kathy tied a knot. "I think I'll need some help. I wasn't feeling too bad until a few seconds…" With that Carla passed out.

Kathy tried to catch her but she slid through her arm to the floor. Kathy struggled to pick up her sister in the confines of the cramped bathroom. It was like picking up spaghetti with a single chopstick. She rolled Carla onto the bathroom throw rug and dragged her into the living room. Kathy contemplated dragging her out to the car but it still didn't solve the problem of getting Carla into the car. Kathy remembered the first aid kit and dug it out from under the bathroom sink. She found the smelling salts.

The instant Kathy snapped a capsule under her nose, Carla slapped it away and moaned. "Come on and stand up," begged Kathy. "I need your help here, stand up!" With Kathy's help, Carla unsteadily made it to her feet. Carla's arms locked around Kathy's neck and the two of them staggered into the driveway. "Damn girl, either you need to lose weight or I need to lift weights."

"I'm going to be sick," muttered Carla.

"Oh God, not now," pleaded Kathy as Carla's head lolled on Kathy's shoulder. In another three feet they reached the car door. Kathy gently eased Carla into the back seat.

Within ten minutes she was at the hospital emergency room door. Two police cars were in the parking lot. Kathy opened the car door and saw Carla was awake again. She looked up at Kathy and gave a weak smile. "I'm back. I don't know for how long."

Kathy carried Carla into the emergency room entrance and flagged down an orderly. "She's been cut on the side. She's lost some blood and she keeps passing out."

The orderly helped Kathy put Carla in a wheelchair. "I'll take her back right now. See the nurse at the counter." With that, he rolled Carla toward a set of double doors.

"Can't I go in with her?" called Kathy after him.

"Not until she's checked in at the desk," he replied over his shoulder and disappeared through the double doors.

Kathy went to the front desk and joined the line of people waiting for their turn with the receptionist. After several minutes, she finally made it to the front of the line. She had just started giving the medical information to the woman behind the counter when a policeman approached the woman Kathy was talking to.

Kathy put her hand on his arm and said "Officer, I need to report an assault."

"Just a minute young lady. I'll be right with you," he said to Kathy and turned to the woman at the counter. "We're looking for two women, a Kathy and Carla Baird. They're sisters..."

"Officer," she again placed her hand on his arm. "I'm Kathy Baird, Carla is in with the doctors now."

Startled, the policeman whirled around and stepped back placing his hand on the butt of his gun. After looking at Kathy and deciding he wasn't in immediate danger of being attacked he relaxed a little. "Are you Kathy Baird?"

"Yes, I said I was. I was trying to tell you about the assault."

"Yes Ma'am. Would you please turn around and face the wall, put you hands up as high as you can reach." The policeman pulled his radio from his belt and keyed the mike. "I need assistance at the ER registration desk. I have one suspect. The other is in with a doctor."

"What are you talking about?" Kathy's voice raised an octave. "Four men attacked my sister, one of them stabbed her. Why are you calling us suspects?"

The policeman stepped back and put his hand back on the butt of his gun. "Ma'am, I'm asking you to turn around and put your hands on the wall."

"What are you talking about!" Kathy screamed at the policeman. "My sister was just attacked and I brought her to the hospital."

The policeman drew his gun. The people standing near Kathy parted like the Red Sea, each looking for cover. "Turn around and put your hands on the wall!" demanded the officer.

Kathy whirled around to face the wall. "Sweet Jesus! These guys jump my sister, they stab her while she defends herself and now you treat us like criminals!"

"Listen lady, there's four men in the hospital, one concussion, one broken leg, two more with severe head and neck injuries. It looks to me that the assault was in the other direction." The policeman saw his backup arrive so he holstered his weapon and moved in and cuffed Kathy. He took her out to the patrol car and read Kathy her Miranda rights. He was just putting her in the back seat when Rae Ann arrived.

"What is going on?!"

"Mom!" Kathy yelled. "Carla's inside. They're arresting us, not the guys who attacked Carla!"

"Please move away from the car, Ma'am." The policeman closed the car door. "You can see her at the station. I advise you to get your lawyer down there."

"And I advise you to release my daughter!" retorted Rae Ann. The officer stood between the car and Rae Ann with his nightstick in his hand. After several tense seconds glaring at each other, Rae Ann looked at Kathy and shouted "I'll be down as soon as I can. Don't say anything to anyone until I get a lawyer there!" She then turned on her heel and marched towards the hospital door. "Jackass!" she added in a voice just high enough for the officer to hear.

Rae Ann forced her way up to the front of the line at the counter and demanded to see her daughter. "We don't even have the required information on her yet," responded the clerk. "The other young woman was giving us the information when the police took her off. Now if you'd finish filling out these forms, we can get you back to see her." The receptionist gave a smug smile and held out a clipboard.

Rae Ann leaned in real close to the woman behind the counter and in a low whisper said, "Look lady, first, I want to see my little girl and make sure she is all right and then I'll come back out and fill out all the paper work you want. So, if you don't let me back there right now, you'll need your precious doctors to remove that clipboard from a very personal, and by then painful, part of your body." Rae Ann smiled sweetly and winked.

The receptionist paled slightly. "Follow the blue line, third door on your right," she said in a trembling voice.

"Thanks ever so much." Rae Ann rushed down the hall following the blue line. When Rae Ann entered the room she saw a nurse cleaning the wound on Carla's side as a policeman was asking her questions. Carla was crying, in obvious pain. Rae Ann marched over to the policeman. "Get Out!"

"What?" He noticed her for the first time.

"You heard me. Get out of here.!"

"Look lady, I'm a policeman with a crime to investigate."

"Yes, and I'm a mother with a child to take care of. You can ask all the questions you want after the doctor finishes and with our attorney present. Until then, get out."

"I can't leave the room. Orders." He squared his shoulders and set his feet.

Rae Ann moved in nose to nose with him and poked him in the chest with her finger hitting a pressure point. The pain was so intense it made his eyes water. "Then get in the corner and stay out of my way."

The doctor and nurse were staring at them. "Yes Ma'am!" He stepped back out of the way, rubbing his chest.

Rae Ann moved in next to Carla and held her hand. "It's going to be OK, Baby," she said squeezing Carla's hand gently. The nurse and doctor went back to work.

It took over forty stitches to close the wound in Carla's side. The doctor had used Valium along with the local anesthetic so she was feeling pretty high by the time they started. Rae Ann slipped out to call her lawyer and finish off the hospital forms as promised. She and Randy had only used a lawyer once when Randy was involved in an automobile accident. She looked up the attorney's number in the phone book and called.

"Horton and Avery. This is Gerald Avery, can I help you?"

"Yes, this is Rae Ann Baird. I don't know if you remember me but you defended my husband, Randy, about a year ago in a civil suit."

"Yes, of course I remember you." There was a little edge in his voice.

"I'm calling because I have a problem that I hope you can help me with. My daughters were attacked earlier today by four men."

"Oh no," Mr. Avery said. "Are they all right?"

"Carla got cut on the side. The doctor's sewing it up now but she'll be OK. Kathy's fine. The problem is, in defending themselves, they messed the four guys up pretty bad. Now the police have arrested them for assault. I was hoping you could help me."

"Let me get this straight. Your girls beat up the four guys who attacked them?"

"Kathy and Carla are both instructors at a karate school."

Mr. Avery started laughing in the phone. "I bet those guys will think twice before jumping the next poor defenseless girl they meet." He became more serious now. "I would like to help you but I really can't. I could recommend another attorney. She is very good and she has experience in criminal defense."

"If you don't mind telling me," Rae Ann asked, "why can't you do it?"

"I really don't want to go into that right now," he said sounding very evasive.

"Is it because of what we are?" Her voice was rising.

"I really can not go into it right now. I'm sorry I just can't represent you right now."

"I see! You don't want to ruin your practice defending a couple of Monos." Rae Ann's voice was loud and clear. People in the waiting area were staring at her.

"Please, that is not the problem," explained the attorney.

"Well, then, what the hell is?" demanded Rae Ann.

There was a pause on the line. "I just accepted a retainer from your husband to start divorce proceedings."

Rae Ann went silent. "I'm sorry. I didn't mean what I said." Her words came out in a whisper.

"Call this number. I'm sure she can help you out." The attorney gave her the phone number.

"I'm sorry," is all Rae Ann could say and hung up the phone. The new attorney did agree to take her case. She agreed to go to the police station to meet with Kathy while Rae Ann stayed with Carla.

When Rae Ann went back in the room, the nurse had just finished bandaging Carla's side and the policeman was still in his corner sulking. Rae Ann approached the policeman, "Why is it that no one seems to be interested in my girls' side of the story."

"That ain't the way it is. Look, when she goes downtown we'll get her statement."

"In the mean time, is there a policeman standing guard with each of the four men who attacked her?"

The policeman started to speak then stopped, took his hat off and rubbed his head. "No. There is not a policeman guarding the four men."

"I see, so because my children are monoecious, that makes them less honest than the four hoodlums in the other rooms." Rae stood with her arms crossed staring the policeman in the eyes.

Finally he said "OK, I'll request an officer be assigned to watch the boys too, at least until I get orders from the station. Is that what you want?"

"Yes," Rae Ann smiled, "that's a start." She turned and went to Carla.

The hospital held Carla for an hour to be certain she was not having a reaction to the medication. Rae Ann helped her daughter into the required wheelchair for the ride out of the hospital. The policeman stepped in front of the wheelchair and pulled out a set of handcuffs.

"I'm not going to try to escape, I promise," Carla said groggily.

"That may be, but it's the rules. Just like you, I have my set of rules I have to follow. I can cuff your hands in front though, it doesn't have to be behind your back."

Carla held out her hands and the cuffs were put on. Rae Ann handed Carla a jacket to fold over her hands to conceal the handcuffs, then pushed her down the hall to the exit, the policeman walking along side.

As the electric doors opened they were greeted by a dozen reporters and camera men from every local newspaper and TV station. Monoecions turning violent and attacking the peaceful general population was big news and they all wanted a piece of it. The reporters surged forward and started shouting questions as the policeman tried to clear a path to the waiting patrol car. "Is she being arrested in connection with the assault on the four boys?"

"We are only taking her in for questioning right now. Please move out of the way." The policeman pushed a man with a camera out of the way of the car door.

A newspaper reporter called "Can you confirm Kathy and Carla Baird as the two prime suspects?" The policeman ignored him and opened the car door. A woman reporter standing directly behind Rae Ann yelled "What's the condition to the four victims?"

"You'll have to ask the hospital staff that question."

Rae Ann turned face to face with the reporter. "My daughters were the victims, not the four punks in there who attacked them." She turned back to Carla to help her into the car.

"Right," the reporter said, "that's why she's being hauled off to the police station." Several reporters started laughing.

Rae Ann looked down and noticed the female reporter's open toed shoes as they all jostled for position. As Carla got in the back seat, several photographers pushed in to get a better picture. Rae Ann allowed herself to be pushed off balance. She stepped back to recover, placing her heel with precision on the reporter's exposed toes, making sure to apply all the force she could muster. The reporter let out a scream and the policeman whirled around to see the cause of the commotion.

Rae Ann lifted her heel off the woman's damaged toes. "Oh, excuse me. I was knocked off balance by your camera man in all this crush. Please accept my apology." She smiled sweetly at the reporter.

The reporter responded with "You bitch, you broke my foot!" and then regained her professional composure despite the pain.

"I'll be right behind you," Rae Ann told Carla as the door closed. She headed for her car and followed the patrol car to the station.

The reporter finished her tape for the evening news standing on one foot. When the camera man gave her the wrap signal, she limped inside the hospital door Carla had just come out.

The story was the lead in for the six o'clock news. "Four local men are in the hospital tonight after reportedly being attacked by two Monoecions. Two suspects, Kathy and Carla Baird, were apprehended at Lakeland Memorial Hospital where Carla Baird sought treatment for an injury allegedly received in the assault. This was the same hospital at which the four men were receiving care for their injuries. The two suspects are instructors at a karate school, Bruce Kasey's Tae Kwon Do Training Center. The four men said they were talking by the side of the road when the two Monoecions ran by. One of the men made a comment and the Monoecions allegedly attacked them. Matt Proctor, nineteen, suffered a concussion, Tom Hillard received cartilage damage to the throat. Keith Underwood has three fractured vertebra in his neck and Rex Seiler suffered a dislocated knee and a broken leg. The assault took place about a block west of the Baird's residence on Hoover road. Carla Baird was admitted for a cut on the side. She was treated and released into police custody."

The national news ran it at eleven without bothering to delve too deeply into the facts. They ignored the indicators that this story was questionable. They only cared that they would lose viewer shares if they were the only network not running the story.

The detective in charge of investigating the assault started once again. "We don't have a case. These four guys can't get their story straight. Their statements don't match even on the basics. The two girls on ..."

"Monos damn it. They're not girls," the chief growled.

"Yes sir. The two Monoecions' stories match perfectly. Plus we have the telephone report."

"Screw the telephone report. Just because their mother called in a report that her children were attacked doesn't mean it happened that way."

The detective shook his head. "I'm not talking about that telephone call. Look, about five minutes after it aired on the eleven o'clock news, a woman who lives in the neighborhood called to say she was driving by when it happened and she claims to have seen the men attack Carla Baird, not the other way around."

"Have you checked to see if she a Mono too?"

"Yes, I have," replied the frustrated detective. "She has three sons to testify for her. Now may I release them before we get sued for false arrest?"

"Yes," the night chief conceded, "get them out of my God damned station! I don't want them smelling it up."

"And what do we do about the four men?" the detective asked.

"Not a thing for right now. I don't see sufficient evidence to arrest them yet." The Chief's face had turned a glowing red. He turned to the window and looked out over the parking lot, nearly empty at this late hour. "Go on. You got what you wanted now get out of here."

The detective hurriedly left the room. It wasn't a good idea to be near the chief when he had been shot down in flames. Carla's and Kathy's lawyer was waiting for him.

"Well, do my clients get released?"

"Yes, I've discussed it with the chief and we've decided to release them for now."

"For now?! How about the four men?" asked the attorney.

"Insufficient evidence, counselor," replied the detective.

"I'm not going to tell their mother that. And if you value your life, I advise you don't tell her that either. Maybe if you get her kids out here right now, she might forget to ask."

"Look, I'm on your side but there is only so much I can do." The detective shrugged his shoulders and left to get Carla and Kathy.

The Baird's attorney looked at her watch, twelve twenty-five. At least they didn't have to spend the full night in jail.

Chapter 17

Monday, August 12

It was Senator Fenton's time to speak and he planned to use it to full effect. "Today is a day that will go down in infamy," he intoned in his best FDR voice. "We have been attacked no less than we were on December seventh, nineteen forty-one. Plotted, planned and executed by an opponent far more dangerous than the Japanese. This opponent wishes to defeat not just one country but the entire human race.

"What I have heard here today, from my esteemed colleagues, has been deep concern expressed for the human rights for those people involved and I agree one hundred percent! Let the record show that I support Human Rights! Let the record also show that the Monoecions are not humans!" A loud murmur traveled through the Senate. Fenton held up his hands to quiet the voices. "Let's look at what is required for any animal to be of the same species. It must be able to reproduce another animal of the same kind as the parents. When a human man and woman mate, the offspring are male and female children who grow up to become men and women like their parents. Thus they are of the same species. When a Monoecion and a human male mate, they produce a monoecious offspring. They are incapable of producing a male or female human offspring. Now when a Monoecion and a human female mate, a practice that is too disturbing to imagine but is a recorded practice among these creatures, still a Monoecion offspring is produced. They are incapable of producing a human offspring, either male or female. The offspring of a Monoecion mating with anything will not produce a human offspring. Thus, Monoecions are not human. They are not in the species Homo sapiens.

"So as far as I can see, the question of rights for Monoecions is yet to be defined. They are clearly not human so the question is whether they are protected under laws meant for human beings. I think that question has not been answered under current law. Do they have *any* human rights? Not under the laws as they are written now. Special laws are required to define their rights under the law and until such laws are written and passed by this legislature, their rights are undefined.

"I know I have colleagues who think it's a crime to treat these creatures like the family dog. Well I've got this to say to them, when was the last time Fido plotted to destroy your family? They say we should freely embrace this new life form on the planet earth, that they mean us no harm and only wish to live their lives in peace. Tell that to the four men in Macon, Georgia, who were viciously attacked by two highly trained Monoecion warriors just yesterday. The FBI has uncovered numerous instances of monoecion involvement in falsifying coroner's reports, squelching research inquiries concerning female births and falsely reporting male births to monoecion families. And this is just the tip of the iceberg. These creatures are out to destroy us and they will not stop as long as there is a human being alive in this world.

It is documented in the journal of one Dr. Irene Moore. This journal lays out the plan, the methods, and the subterfuge to be used to destroy mankind. I for one refuse to idly stand by and let it happen.

"Senator Turner and I are proposing a bill to immediately deal with the problem in a fair and impartial way. If these creatures wish to join the human race and live out their lives in peace as they claim, all they have to do is be sterilized so they can bear or father no more offspring. If this is done they will regain citizenship in the human race and all rights thereof. If they do not wish to be sterilized, then they will be considered undesirable aliens and be removed from the country. If they do not leave, they will be arrested and sterilized or deported, by force if need be."

The Senator spoke for fifteen minutes, explaining the basic structure of the bill. Many of the fine points were still being worked out, such as custody of minor children when the father could not be identified or was a Monoecion. Property ownership was ill defined but voting rights were clearly described. There were none. Penalties for violation were set at deportation if a country could be found to accept the refugees or involuntary sterilization if no country could be found in ninety days. The cost of the operations were to be passed on to the Monoecions when they could afford it. If not, then it would be paid for by selling any property confiscated from Monoecions in violation of the law. "The American taxpayer should not have to foot the bill of this war." Fenton knew this would not be an easy sell. There was a growing opposition to the hard line approach to dealing with the problem but the smear campaign against the individual Monoecions who were receiving media attention was holding its own. If it appeared that a Monoecion was getting any sympathetic press, his team of mudslingers went to work dredging up accusations of sexual infidelity, child abuse, drugs, anything to tarnish the image. He couldn't afford to have any of these creatures to be viewed as virtuous. That would delay the decisions long enough for Congress to water the bill down to the point of being ineffective.

"The world is looking to us to lead it out of this crisis and this plan provides that leadership. Thank you."

There was the sound of one or two people clapping in the silence, then a few more joined in. That encouraged more until Gordon realized that over half the Senate was on it's feet applauding. This was encouraging. The real test will be when the polls started coming in. He would know in a few hours if it was fanfare or folly. Thank the Lord for CSPAN and Fox, he thought.

Senators Fenton and Turner sat at the conference table along with their aides going through their options. They had been arguing for over an hour about how to proceed. "You can't just ignore the fact that we don't have enough votes in the house to pass this bill," Todd Lindell repeated one more time to Fenton. "As much as we would like to believe a little more arm twisting will get us over the top, it won't."

"So what you suggest is to throw in the towel. Let the bastards water down the bill until it's worthless," Fenton growled.

"No," said Senator Turner. "Look, I've been talking with several of the more moderate members of the house, ours and theirs. I think we have a solution that will draw enough support to pass while keeping the basic bill intact. We provide one more option for the Monos, a reservation."

"What, like the Indians?"

"In many ways, yes," said Senator Turner. "Just listen for a moment and let me lay it out for you. We provide in the bill three options for the Monoecions, one is to get the operation and rejoin society as a normal human being. Two, leave the country to somewhere else that will accept them. So far, no country has come forward to volunteer. Three is to move to the reservation.

"I think that we will all agree that number one will be the most popular option. It allows them to lead a normal life with their friends and old jobs and in most cases, no one but their immediate family will know that they had the surgery or that they were Monoecion.

"The second option is the cause of all the resistance in the house. No country that won't require sterilization themselves has committed to accepting the Monoecion refugees. No one is convinced that this is really a valid option.

"Option three provides a way out for the Monoecions who refuse to be sterilized. There are several military bases that are or have been shut down to reduce the defense budget. We select one with sufficient federal land and turn it into a reservation for the holdouts. If you have ever toured any of those sites, you know that this is no gift. The land is mostly worthless, we have no one who wants to purchase the land and much of it is contaminated to some extent. This not only provides an out for the Monoecions but also provides an out for the more squeamish Congressmen."

"I don't like it," said Fenton. "We don't cure the disease. A tumor is allowed to remain in the body of the patient. How can we be sure it stays in remission? What happens when the public starts to forget about them and they start to quietly slip out and rejoin society?"

"When the public starts forgetting about them is when we start squeezing. We find ways of applying pressure, making life unpleasant to the point where only a handful haven't chosen sterilization. These remnants will be viewed as fanatics by the rest of the world. Then we can surgically remove the tumor and no one will object to the loss of a few dangerous radicals."

"Will this get us enough votes to make it through the House?" asked Fenton.

"I've been double checking his figures," said Lindell. "With this change, it looks like the bill will pass with room to spare. It will also guarantee us a clear majority in the Senate. More important, with the change, we should be able to fight off any attempts to amend any riders to it."

"I want to make it clear that I still don't like it," said Senator Fenton "but it's better than letting one of the other pansy-ass bills go through. Let's get to work. How soon can we have wording ready for the addition?"

Turner smiled. "How's the first cut at four this afternoon sound? I had my staff on it all night last night."

Fenton smiled back. "No disrespect to your staff Henry, but your boys are probably tired by now. I'll have mine ready to start proofing what you have after lunch. We don't want to miss anything." Fenton turned to Lindell. "I want a list of suitable sites on my desk tonight. Don't forget the main criteria, this place needs to be hell on earth."

The atmosphere at the Landis household had been tense during the Senate hearing but Becky Lovett attributed it to the stress of the constant questioning by the authorities. Then the snide comments started from Robert's mother. Nothing that was really obvious, just little things like how the house was so crowded with everyone there and questions as to how long Becky planned to stay. Then the sniping became more serious with Mrs. Landis commenting on the "damning evidence coming out of the investigations" and how "people like that shouldn't be allowed to raise children." The jabs always came when no one else was within earshot and were always designed such that they could be construed as innocent if taken without the tone of voice with which they were delivered. There never was a friendship between the mothers. After all, they rarely had the opportunity to see each other but it had always been cordial. Now Mrs. Landis was making it clear that she did not approve of what her son had married or the family it came from.

A few days after testifying before the Senate, Becky was sitting with the girls, telling them about their "great grandfather" Irene. The girls had not been told about their rather unique family tree until a few days before and they were bursting with questions. Becky was doing the best she could to answer them when Mrs. Landis burst into the room. "I do not think it is proper to fill these impressionable minds with stories of women having sex together. What are you trying to do, turn them into abominations like your parents?"

Becky was taken completely by surprise by the sudden attack. "No I'm not. These girls need to know where they came from and what the facts are, not what's fed to the world by the media."

"The facts are quite clear I'm afraid. I'm going to protect my grandchildren from being corrupted by this Monoecion propaganda if it's the last thing I do."

Becky felt her anger growing faster than she could control it. "The truth rarely damages the listener, the absence of truth often does. These girls will not be harmed by hearing that Irene Moore had sexual relations with Carol Jacobs and produced their grandmother, me. Nor will they be harmed by knowing that Irene and Carol had a caring, loving relationship until their death. But you wouldn't understand that since you never had one." Mrs. Landis' mouth opened and closed but no words came out. "How many did the last divorce make, your third?"

Robert heard the raised voices all the way in the study and rushed in to see what was going on. "Rebecca! Mother! What the hell is going on in here?!"

"Did you hear what that woman said to me?" sputtered Robert's mother.

"Yes, I did. And the children are listening to you two scream at each other like six-year olds and I'm not putting up with it." Robert stood like a school principle on the playground separating unruly children.

"I'm sorry Robert," Becky said. "I was wrong to say these things about your mother in front of the children. I was only trying to explain things to them about my parents, about being Monoecion."

"I think that is for Christine and me to do, not you. You've screwed up their lives enough already." Robert felt the anger in his words but could do nothing to soften them. Becky left for home the next day.

Thursday, August 15

Alicia sat at her desk, trying to decide how to test the water. She was always at odds with Zak, her cubical mate, over politics. They agreed on most of the goals but they usually disagreed on how to get there. "Look at this crap," she said throwing the front page of the newspaper on Zak's desk. "I thought they gave up mandatory sterilization and race extermination with Hitler."

"What's the big deal?" asked Zak. "They're not killing anyone. They're just trying to stop the spread of a dangerous hereditary disease. We put people into asylums for TB back in the twenties. There are states experimenting with it again now for the people who don't follow up on their medicine. This is just as humane, if not more."

"First, this isn't a disease," replied Alicia, "it's not even a defect technically. It should be considered a race trait just like skin color or eye shape. No one will catch this, unlike TB."

"Oh yes they will, every child born to one. If you knew you had AIDs, would you have a child if you knew you would give the disease to it?"

"Of course not because AIDs is a fatal disease. This is not a fatal disease. The child will grow up to live a normal life like everyone else." Alicia had to play a cautious game and not come across too pro-Monoecious. But then, disagreeing with Zak had become a tradition. "Our major differences are over the concept of disease versus race."

Zak looked exasperated. "How can you not call this a disease? If it's not eliminated, men will cease to exist. We will be bred out of existence."

Alicia knew she had to lighten up or suspicions would be raised. "At least no one would have to deal with male egos any more."

"That's true," said Zak "but the highway system would turn into a parking lot of women talking on their cell phones and touching up their makeup in the rear view mirror."

Alicia blew Zak a big raspberry. "Let's get to work, we can solve the rest of the world's problems at lunch." Alicia had a hard time concentrating on work. The bill proposed by Fenton had been debated all week but the changes had been minimal other than the addition of the reservation concept. The two other bills proposed to be more moderate approaches to the problem had been shot down without ever having a chance to come to a vote. The fact that this one looked as if it was coming to a vote meant that Fenton and Turner felt they had enough support to pass it. The president had announced that he would veto any bill that did not deal fairly with the human rights issues but no one seemed to know what exactly that meant. What was known was that his popularity nose-dived seven points after making that announcement. Alicia was sure if it meant the end of his reelection hopes, the veto wouldn't happen.

Alicia didn't get out of work until after seven o'clock that night. On the way home she wandered the radio dial looking for anything worth listening to but finally gave up and selected an old Stevie Ray Vaughn album from the MP3 menu. "That man played the blues too good to be white," she said to the empty car. She let her worries fade into the background as she concentrated on the sweet sound of the Stratocaster riffs. Halfway through the album she was home. She sat in the car long enough to finish off one of her favorite cuts and headed in the house.

"Hi Scooch Butt, how's my rug rat today?" Alicia chirped to Jessica who smiled and threw a soggy Raggedy Ann doll out of her playpen.

Marci came around the corner. "Where the hell have you been?! I've been worried sick." Alicia's blank stare just made Marci angrier. "Have you ever heard of the telephone? It's a great new invention that would have kept me from losing my mind!"

"I did call you! I called about five but there was no answer so I left a message. Did you check it?"

Marci suddenly felt very stupid. "I just ran outside for a few minutes. I never thought that you might have called in that short of time. I called the office after you were an hour late and got your voice mail."

Alicia walked over to the answering machine that sat buried under yesterday's newspaper on the desk. She slid the paper aside to display the blinking light. Marci chewed her lower lip and looked sheepish. Alicia pressed the play button and her voice came out loud and clear, "Hi, just calling to let you know that I'm going to be late tonight. We need to complete the testing before the client shows up tomorrow. I should be home by seven thirty or eight. I'll be in the lab so if you need me, call me at extension four thirty-three." At the end was a whispered "Love ya."

"Oops." Marci hesitated for a moment. "Well, how was I to know you were going to call the moment I left the house?"

"You could have thrown out yesterday's paper so you could see the answering machine light, that might have helped," Alicia replied in a slightly irritated voice.

"Um, I love you," Marci said meekly.

Alicia dropped her stuff on the dining room table. "Love you too, I just hope you didn't get the kids worked up. Anything left to eat?"

Marci suddenly remembered what had been so important only moments ago before Alicia arrived home. "The vote, where's the remote?!" and she began frantically searching the living room.

"What are you talking about?" Alicia asked puzzled.

"I'm trying to find the TV remote control," Marci said as if that answered everything. There it is!" She grabbed it off the stereo and turned on the TV, turning the channel to CSPAN. "The house is holding the vote on the bill tonight, right now."

"Already? The paper said this morning that they didn't expect a vote until next week."

"The paper was wrong." The picture faded in to display a view of the podium and a portion of the House of Representatives floor with business going on as usual. In the picture corners were two boxes tallying up the vote, currently at one hundred thirty-seven for to one hundred eleven against.

"This isn't a good sign. They wouldn't have pushed up the vote if they weren't sure of the outcome." Alicia had forgotten about dinner. She kicked off her shoes and sat down on the couch, curling her legs under her. She picked up a throw pillow and clutched it to her stomach, a habit she had whenever she was nervous.

"We've still got a chance, the vote's close so far." Marci sat on the couch next to Alicia and snuggled her head onto her lap. She knew Alicia was right but she just couldn't accept it without a fight. Alicia's fingers played idly in Marci's hair as they watched the votes mount and their hopes fade. The vote ended two hundred forty-eight to one hundred seventy-seven. The remaining ten either abstained or were not present for the vote. There's still the Senate vote," said Marci. "It's not over yet."

"Don't kid yourself," Alicia said with a slight tremble in her lower lip. "This was supposed to be the close vote. It will be passed in the Senate and signed by the President by the end of the week. Soon we will be fugitives for real. Just another endangered species to be hunted to extinction. The Supreme Court is our last chance. If they don't act it will be all over."

Marci squeezed Alicia's hand. "Please don't stop believing we will make it. I don't think I can go on hoping if you've given up."

Alicia squeezed back and whispered "I haven't given up. Not yet." She wasn't positive of who she was trying to convince.

Fenton was pleased with the House vote. The margin far exceeded expectations. He was already hard at work on the implementation phase. "We can't let this look like the Gestapo round up or we lose all the support we've gained so far. We need the voting public to look at this as a piece of minor corrective surgery, a chance for the Monoecions to lead a normal life."

"Don't forget that we're not out of the woods yet," Todd Lindell reminded Senator Fenton. "The ACLU is throwing a fit. They are masters at tying things up in court and you can bet they are already hard at work on this one. They will let it get all the way through and signed, ready to be enacted before they strike. That way the delay will be maximized."

"I've already received assurances that we will have fast track access to the Supreme Court if a lower court issues a restraining order. The court will be able to overturn it within a week, two tops."

The Senator abruptly changed courses. "How about the medical procedures? We need that set of guidelines ready by the time of the signing and they need to be clear. I don't want any loopholes in this one."

"The draft copy is already being reviewed by the team of legal medical specialists." Todd opened his notes and scanned the page. "The final should be available for first review in two days. The sticky questions concern dealing with people at high risk to any surgical procedure; at what age is the procedure no longer necessary; can we use menopause as the cut off, and if so, is the menopause test accurate enough to be risk free of tampering. There is a major concern of the time and expense of the surgery. If it were as simple with Monoecions as it is with men, it would be cheap but with Monos we have to remove the testicles and the ovaries to do the whole job. That's not as easy or as quick, which translates to expensive. Then we have to deal with the hormonal drug treatment especially with younger women." Lindell closed his notebook. He spoke with concern in his voice. "What we are having problems figuring out is how to sell this to the Monoecions. The preliminary interviews are showing a much higher resistance to the surgery than expected."

"I think it's a given that they won't flock out of the woodwork volunteering for the surgery, penalty or not. I think it will change when they find out that they will be found by the FBI. When they learn that it's much more pleasant to come forward on their own than have the police hauling them away in handcuffs from their job, the trickle of volunteers will become a flood. How many has the FBI identified to date."

Todd again searched his notes. "As of this morning they have logged seventy-two thousand, eight hundred and actually confirmed four thousand plus. That's with almost fifty percent of the Bureau devoted to the project working six to seven days a week."

"That's not fast enough." The Senator leaned forward across his desk. "The bitches can breed faster than that. We need a simple, cheap, accurate test and we need it quick." Fenton leaned back in his chair. "We will need a public service campaign to air on prime time. We'll need stars, people the Monos will trust putting our message across." The Senator jerked up in his chair. "My God, I know exactly who we need." A broad smile came across his face. "Who would make the perfect spokesperson for our cause?"

I hate these stupid little guessing games he plays, thought Todd. "I don't know, a woman star, the president's wife... I don't know."

"I do. Just imagine a sincere, heartfelt message from the one person they truly trust, Christine Landis."

Todd's looked at Fenton in disbelief. "You are out of your frigging mind. That woman hates your guts. She would rather run naked through the streets than do anything to help you!"

"That's just because she hasn't been convinced yet. What does she want most out of this world? She wants her world to return to normal. She wants her kids to go to school without being called names. In short, she wants her old life back. If we can make her believe we can deliver that to her, she just may defect to our side." Fenton thought for a moment. "But in the meantime, see what you can do to find a double for her, someone that looks and sounds so close that no one but her mother will question it."

Things were beginning to settle into a routine for Christine's mother, Becky, now that she was back in Kalamazoo. The public, and thus the press, was finally beginning to tire of her and the various investigative agencies had slowed their visits to one every few days instead of several a day. There was a sudden flurry of activity after the house passed the bill but only for a day. She patiently explained to the newsman interviewing her that even though she was too old to bare a child, she wasn't too old to father one. Because of the wide range of ages capable of fathering a child, this law being passed would affect all Monoecions no matter the age.

She wondered what obscure aspect they had forgot to ask her about now as she moved across the living room to answer the door. She expected the FBI or NBC news but she did not expect to see Gloria Wilkins standing on her front steps. Becky recognized her immediately and went cold inside. Becky didn't speak. She just stood in the half open doorway and gave Gloria a stony stare.

Gloria looked up from her feet at the sound of the door opening. She saw Becky's features change from resigned to ice as she was recognized. The silence lasted for several seconds until Gloria had to speak for fear of Becky closing the door and leaving her there on the stoop, her words unsaid. "I'm sorry for everything that has happened. I didn't understand, Charlie didn't understand." Becky remained silent. "I don't expect you to forgive us, I just want you to know that we are good people. We did not mean to harm you or your family." Mrs. Lovett said nothing to acknowledge Gloria's words. Her body remained totally motionless in the door way. Gloria stood there for many long seconds and finally said "Thank you for listening to what I had to say." She turned and started down the steps.

"Why did you come to tell me this?" asked Becky.

Gloria turned and examined the mannequin face staring at her. There was emotion there, hiding in the shadows, fear and anger. "I wanted you to understand why we did what we did. Charlie and I are good people. We weren't out to get your family or to cause you harm. We thought we were doing what was right."

"Well, I don't understand. You did this thing and you didn't have the decency to come to me and ask if it was true, to ask if you had your facts straight. If you had, I would have explained it all to you." Becky's frustration began to flow in her words. "It would have done me no good to try to keep any secrets then, the world would know about us anyway. But just maybe we would have been portrayed as only people who are different, of another race, a genetic mutation, trying to live in peace, instead of monsters trying to destroy the human race. If you had known how people would have reacted to us, you might have decided not to go public at all."

"We were afraid of you. We were afraid of what you might do if you knew that we discovered your secrets. After all, we were only two people against the millions of your people. We were afraid that we would be murdered if you found out we knew, you know, better that two humans should die than all of you be exposed. We thought we had to go public to protect ourselves," Gloria pleaded. "That's what Charlie thought anyway," she added, embarrassed to admit that she hadn't stopped her husband.

"And you didn't think we were murderers?"

Gloria paused before she answered the question. "No. I didn't think we should go public but Charlie thought we should. We were afraid to be the only ones to know this."

Becky stepped on to the porch, finally moving out from the doorway, her features beginning to soften. Becky hated to admit it to herself but she could understand a little of how Gloria felt. "It could have been handled differently." The sternness in her voice faded somewhat.

"I know that now. But, at the time, our minds were clouded by the excitement of unraveling the mystery, like being Sherlock Holmes." Gloria paused for a few seconds thinking of the real reason for her embarrassment. "Greed played a major role, too."

"The Nation's View pays well I hear." Gloria nodded her head. Becky looked over at the neighbors who staring at them, trying to see what was going on at the freak's house. "We can't stand out here and discuss it all day," said Becky. "Why don't you come inside? I think there's some coffee left." Gloria accepted.

Chapter 18

Monday, August 19

Christine sat at her desk sorting through the stacks of mail, trying to make sure a bill didn't get lost in the heap of letters from admirers and detractors. She opened up a letter with a typed address and no return address. She was quite sure of what it was by the way it was addressed. In large letters written with a red crayon was "Landis you bitch. You will die in 24 hours. Have a nice last day." She slid it back in the envelope and added it to the death threat pile.

She calmly opened another. Chances are this wouldn't be violent, she thought, it has a return address written in a feminine hand. As it turned out it was very friendly. It was a woman in New York who wanted to have her baby. She dropped it in the crank pile. "Where do these people come from?" she asked herself.

The next letter tore at her heart. It was from a Monoecion who had told her husband the truth about herself. He had beat her and thrown her out of the house with nothing but the clothes on her back. She couldn't get any money because her husband had moved all the money to new accounts that were in his name only. He wouldn't even let her see her two kids. She told the police and social services but they said there was nothing they could do. "Please Mrs. Landis, you are a lawyer, please tell me what I can do?"

Christine bowed her head and fought back the tears of frustration. "I don't know, why do they keep asking me?" she whispered to herself. She sat up, wiped her eyes, took a few deep breaths, placed the letter in the keeper pile and opened the next.

Todd Lindell arrived at the Landis home late in the morning. Both Christine and Robert were there as he had requested. He had already warned the FBI that all conversations in the house between himself and the Landis Family were to be secret. If any of these were leaked to the media like some others had been, the perpetrator would not just be fired but would be crucified. He also arranged to listen in on what they had to say after he left. He started out with the usual small talk about their home and family, how things were going for Robert at work and the like. He told them that the Senate version of the Monoecion Correction Bill would pass this morning. He explained that since it was so similar to the House version it would be signed into law by tomorrow, Wednesday at the latest. Todd then started getting down to business. "The reason I'm here is to ask you to help yourself and your people. We need a spokesperson to explain the options in a series of public service announcements."

"So what does that have to do with us?" asked Robert.

Lindell cleared his throat. "We would like Mrs. Landis to be our spokesperson."

"If that was the purpose of your visit then I'm sorry that you have wasted your time. I'm not interested." Christine remained calm but firm.

"Please don't make a quick decision on this, Mrs. Landis. Allow me to explain the whole package and show you the benefits of what I'm suggesting." Christine didn't stop him so Lindell continued. "Your performance in the congressional hearings earned you a lot of points with the Monoecion population. From the feedback that we have received, they feel that you are someone they can trust. We want them to identify with our spokesperson and listen to the message that we are trying to get out."

"And just what is that message Mr. Lindell?" interrupted Christine.

"The scripts for the announcements are still in the rough draft stage," Lindell explained. "The gist of it is to encourage the surgical option which would allow the person to regain their old life quickly and in many cases, without having to reveal their condition to friends or employers."

Christine's next question threw him off balance. "Mr. Lindell, who do you work for?"

He looked at her a little baffled. "The United States Government."

"So do I. I mean exactly what and who do you work for?"

"I'm head of Office Operations for Senator Gordon Fenton. What does that matter?" he asked cautiously.

"Oh, nothing really. I just wanted to know who had just been elected god when I wasn't looking." Christine gave a cynical laugh and continued "You have a lot of damned gall to even show your face here. Then you set a new world record by asking me to assist you and your over-inflated boss to mutilate innocent women and children."

"Now Mrs. Landis, I think that may be a bit drastic of a term for a corrective surgical procedure," Todd said in a soothing tone.

"To remove a malignant tumor is a corrective surgical procedure. To remove a part of a person's body that God put there, just because you think he was wrong, is mutilation!"

Yeah, thought Todd, this is going just about as I expected. He tried to lead the debate in a new direction. "Look, Mrs. Landis, we are prepared to offer you complete amnesty from all prosecution for any crimes real or imagined committed before today. No more investigations will be started or continue."

"Well that's real kind of you since I haven't committed any crimes. Even with all your henchmen digging for dirt, you can't convict me of spitting on the sidewalk so it's real damn nice that you will quit accusing me of crimes I didn't commit." Christine put every bit of contempt she could muster into her voice.

"Mrs. Landis, I'm not here to discuss the investigation in your alleged treasonous acts, I'm here to offer you a chance to clear your name and to return your family life back to normal." Lindell changed to his second path of attack. "Mr. Landis, this also includes you. Any questionable activities you have been involved in are water under the bridge," Todd paused and looked slyly at Robert, "even that United Technologies stock deal." He watched Robert's face carefully for any reaction. He was rewarded as surprise ran across Robert's eyes before he regained his composure.

"There was nothing illegal about that deal," he finally blurted out like a kid on the playground saying "the same to you" when he couldn't come up with a return insult.

Todd returned his attention to Christine. "We are looking for someone to go on TV and explain the options to the Monoecion population in a language they can understand. We don't care if you support the government position or not, we just want you to explain it to your people."

"I'm sorry! I'm not going to be your spokesperson for an atrocity. You'll have to find someone else to advertise your brutality on TV. The only way you'll ever get me in the hospital is kicking and screaming, that I promise you."

"You don't have to go." Todd did his best to put sympathy in his voice. "All we ask of you is to sign an agreement to have no more children."

"You think I would go on television and tell other people to go have this surgery without having the guts to do it myself?! And if I did become pregnant again?" she asked.

"We would request the accidental pregnancy be terminated. I think it's the best you can expect. Christine, your people need your leadership right now to ease the way for them."

"When did I become the leader of the Monoecions?" Christine was up pacing the floor. "I didn't get elected, no one put me in charge, and even if they did, I sure as hell wouldn't get up in front of them and lie."

"You became the de facto leader when you represented them in front of Congress, at least as far as the government is concerned. And we're not asking you to lie to them, Christine, we are asking you to tell them the truth."

"Your version of the truth of course. And my kids? What happens to them? Do they go through your little shop of horrors?" Christine was beginning to lose control and Robert could see it. He started to move closer to her.

"They are of childbearing age," Todd said. "You can understand that they must have the corrective surgery just like any other Monoecion."

"Get the hell out of my house!" Christine yelled. She lunged forward and grabbed his tie and shirt, pulling him out of his chair. "And I mean now!"

Christine's attack caught Todd by surprise. He thought he was beginning to wear her down but now she exploded with violence. He pushed her arms away as Robert came to his rescue. "I'm sorry, Mrs. Landis, I didn't mean to upset you. I know you have been under a lot of stress." Her eyes looked like those of a wild animal, caught in a cage for the first time.

"Get out of my house you bastard!" she screamed.

Robert held her trying to separate her from Lindell. "I think you had better go now, please."

"I'm leaving," Lindell said as he moved towards the door. "Please think about what I've said." He opened the door and slid out. Todd went to his car and called the Senator to tell him what had happened. He felt good, it had gone much better than he expected. Robert wanted out, he wanted an end to the situation and now he had a way to do it. If Robert started talking to Christine about the offer then Todd could count on his support. Christine on the other hand had reacted as trapped. If she felt powerless and trapped, she might start to consider the idea herself. Then her husband's encouragement would put her over the edge. Yes, he thought, it had gone much better than planned.

Christine slipped down out of Robert's arms, sat on the floor and cried. Robert looked up to see his girls peeking in the living room from the hall. He looked back down at his wife without a gesture. The girls took that as approval and they came in and huddled around their mother, holding her, soothing her until she stopped crying.

Robert felt like the odd man out at a couples party. He couldn't conceive of what was happening inside their heads right now and it made him lonely. Four out of five people who lived in this house could share things that he couldn't and there was no way for him to learn how. He began to feel the bitterness of being alone. Christine was the reason for his current condition. All she seemed to care about was avoiding a simple operation so she wouldn't look bad in the eyes of a bunch of Monoecions she didn't even know. Robert went into the kitchen, partly to get away from the scene of them huddled together on the floor, partly to hide the shame and anger that was starting to grow inside him.

After the kids went to bed, Robert raised the subject with Christine while they sat in the family room. "You've already made up your mind?"

Christine's face was devoid of all emotion. "About what?"

"Don't start playing games with me. I'm on your side, remember. You know what I'm talking about."

"You think I should take them up on it?" Her voice was completely flat.

Robert tried to keep his voice calm and quiet. "I don't know, that's something you have to decide. I'm just letting you know that I'm here to act as a sounding board or anything else you want. Just please don't shut me out."

"Do you want me to prostitute myself, condone what I think is wrong just so I can get out of a jam?"

"No," Robert told her, "I just want you to take a long hard look inside yourself and make sure that those high moral ideals you hold so dear aren't just plain selfishness, fear and prejudice on your part. Then I want you to think about what all of this is doing to our family and the fact that your kids can't go outside without a bodyguard. And think about that stack of death threats that are overflowing your desk."

"Do you really think that they can give us our old life back?" Christine gave a humorless laugh. "No wonder Wall Street is always such a mess. Economists will believe anything they're told. Well I've got a news flash for you, Bobby. There is no magic bullet for this monster."

Robert hated it when she called him Bobby and she knew it. He struggled to keep this from turning into a brawl. "I didn't say they could give us our old life back, but maybe, just maybe, we could make a new start. It's going to be pretty damned tough to take care of our kids if you're in one federal pen for treason and I'm in another for insider trading. Then Uncle Sam will have our kids and he'll do what he damn well pleases. If the Feds want to take you down, they will do it. And if they can't find any real evidence, they'll just make some up."

"They want to cut open my girls and take their future out of them. You don't understand what our link means to us, what it feels like. I want to be a grandmother. I want to feel my grandchildren being born like my mother did."

"And you think I don't want grandchildren? I want them too, but the lives of the children I already have is a damned sight more important to me than the lives of grandchildren who only exist in dreams." Robert paused to look at Christine. She seemed to be made of stone. She just stared into space. "They can adopt when they grow up, you can have your grandchildren, but for heavens sake, give them a chance to grow up."

"You don't understand," Christine said softly. "And there's no way I can explain it to you." She seemed to awake from a secret sleep. "I'll think about it, I really will," she said and left the room. Robert wondered who this woman was. She seemed to resemble the woman he married less every day.

Tuesday, August 20

The next afternoon Christine started walking, she really didn't care where, she just needed to walk away, away from the letters, away from the house, away from the neighborhood that was smothering her in it's contempt. The FBI tail car held it's respectful distance but always remained in sight. After eight blocks, she started into the transition community, smaller ranch style homes, a business here and there. By twelve blocks, the houses had thinned, replaced by gas stations and apartment buildings.

Christine entered a convenience store - deli and poured herself a cup of coffee. As she approached the counter she decided to act on the desire that had been eating at her since the public revelation. "Give me a pack of Benson and Hedges." The instant the words came out of her mouth, she hated herself for her weakness but she still picked up the pack. "I need some matches."

"Five cents," said the Indian clerk as he tossed the matches on the counter.

She went to one of the two small tables and tore open the pack. It had been a year and a half since she had a cigarette but now she wanted one so bad she couldn't stand it. The clerk gave her a dirty look and tilted his head towards the no smoking sign. Christine ignored him and pulled a cigarette from the pack and lit it, inhaling deeply. The shock to her lungs caused her to start coughing, blowing smoke through her nose, which was also unprepared for the onslaught. After a few moments of uncontrolled coughing, she regained control.

The clerk called out to her in broken English "Hey lady, you quit the smoking and maybe it not kill you."

"You miss the point," Christine said more to herself than to the clerk, "if I start again, maybe it will." She sat sipping her coffee and chain-smoked five cigarettes. Her self-loathing surged to the surface with each match she struck, fading into the background noise of her mind as she sucked the smoke into her lungs. Damn, she thought, what if someone who knew her came in and saw her. She had made such a big deal about quitting months ago and now here she sat puffing like a smokestack. She imagined how she looked to the outside world, her hair was a mess, and wearing the same sweats she had on yesterday. 'The picture of the successful lady attorney', she mocked herself.

She was halfway through the fifth cigarette when she felt her guts start to twist and her throat constrict, revolting at the idea of operating in reverse. She got up and stumbled for the bathroom feeling like she was in the nightmare where you are being chased and your feet are made of lead. In slow motion she made it across the tilting floor finally making her way to the door marked "Ladies." Below it hung a sign that read "Out of Order." Without pausing she opened the door marked "Men," lunged inside and puked in the sink. After several convulsions, her stomach started to settle down. She ran some water, washing most of the sludge down the sink drain, then cupping the cold water in her hands, splashed it on her face.

She stood there for several minutes, regaining her strength, wondering how she had gotten where she was. Just a few weeks ago, life had been so good, kids on the honor roll, the job was satisfying, and Robert was there for her. Now all that seemed so long ago. Now she was in the men's room of a convenience store hurling her lunch into the sink. This thought brought her back. She cleaned the sink as best she could and left the restroom, trying to look inconspicuous on her still weak legs.

The clerk called after her "Hey lady, you not mess up my bathroom?!"

Christine gave a noncommittal grunt and went back on the street for the long walk home. She was a block away from the store when she remembered the pack of cigarettes still sitting on the table where she left them. She was struck with a strong desire to go back and get them but knew she didn't have the strength.

Trying to concentrate on the task of walking home, she struggled to block out all the images that kept forcing themselves into her brain, her youngest girl's tears at being called names at Sunday School, the constant questions and investigations, the death threats. She was still seven blocks from home when she caught her toe on a raised slab of the sidewalk and fell heavily to the ground. She tried to catch herself on the way down, scraping her hands on the rough concrete.

She lay there on the sidewalk, her hair covering her face, trying to soothe her burning hands when she heard the voice. "Mrs. Landis, are you OK?" The voice was kind, filled with concern. "Are you all right? Do you need a doctor?"

Yeah, she thought sarcastically, is Kevorkian available. "I'm OK, I just tripped. I'm sorry." She pushed the hair out of her eyes and looked up at the man bending down over her. She recognized him immediately, one of the FBI agents assigned to follow her every move. "I'll be all right. Go on back to your car before you break some government rule for contact with a suspect."

The agent seemed a bit confused as to what he should do next. "Would you like a ride home?" He seemed almost embarrassed in his tone of voice. "We could drop you off a little ways back from the house so no one would see you riding with us."

Christine looked down at her hands, little drops of blood were forming in the scrapes; tiny chunks of stone were embedded in the skin. She realized she didn't have the energy to make it home. "Sure, if it's OK, I could use it. I'll try not to bleed on your upholstery."

The agent helped her up and signaled to the car, still parked half a block back. He pulled out a handkerchief and wordlessly gave it to Christine to use on her hands. The car pulled up next to them and he gently guided her to it, supporting her like a person, not controlling her like a criminal. He opened the passenger side front door and held it for her. She looked at him quizzically. "Suspects get out the back door of a police car. I thought you might be more comfortable sitting in the front seat."

"Thank you," Christine said "I appreciate that." No other words were said as they drove her home. "Just pull in the drive, let the damned neighbors think what they want." The blue Ford Crown Victoria stopped in the driveway and the agent jumped out and opened the door for Christine who was trying to operate the sunken door handle with her damaged hands. "Thanks again."

"No big thing," he said. Then, as if remembering what his mother told him, he added "You're welcome."

As Christine walked away from the car she overheard a voice from inside the car saying "Christ Jack! That was really dumb. You're going to get reamed for that one."

"If I have to get reamed out for being human, then I'll just have to get reamed," was the reply. Christine smiled as she followed the walk to her front door. It made her feel good to know there were still some real people in the agency.

Robert met her at the door and asked her what was going on. She explained that she had fallen while walking and they had been kind enough to give her a lift home. Robert told her to go in and clean her scrapes and to gargle while she was at it, her breath smelled like a cigar store. A wave of self-hatred rolled over her for being weak. She went to the bathroom, shoulders drooping like a child who had just been caught doing something terrible. She hardly spoke the rest of the day. Her thoughts reeled back and forth as if they were small boats battered in rough seas. She didn't go to bed that night. It wouldn't have mattered, she couldn't sleep anyway.

Chapter 19

Wednesday, August 21

When Robert came downstairs at six AM to check on Christine, she was sitting on the couch holding a cup of coffee. On the coffee table were three piles of letters, the first were typical crank letters, lots of hot air and little substance. The second stack of letters were much more serious. Each one threatened her life, any one of which would have triggered a police investigation if she weren't a Monoecion. This pile didn't scare her half as much as the third pile. This pile was serious death threats just like the second pile, but the targets were her family, not just Christine. She could take putting herself in harms way, but she couldn't do it to her kids. She looked up as Robert came in the room. "What are you doing up at this hour?" she asked him.

"That's a good question. Probably the same reason you're still up. Is there any more coffee left?"

"Yes, but it won't do you any good, it's decaf. Staying awake hasn't been my problem."

"Making any headway?" he asked.

"Yes, I've made up my mind at least a dozen times, each time realizing I couldn't do it and going back to undecided within ten minutes." Her frustration came through in her voice. "Choice one, I can cut off my leg, or as a second choice, I can cut off my arm. None of the choices allow me to keep both. Only in this case the stakes can be a lot higher than an arm or leg. It could very well be my life, or yours or the girls."

"No one can make the decision for you. And by not deciding you are making the decision. A month from now you can't suddenly conclude it was a good deal and decide to take it."

"I know that. I just made up my mind again when I saw you come through that door." Christine sat quietly as he watched her, waiting to hear her decision. "I'll call Mr. Lindell and tell him I'll do it his way." Christine could see in Robert's face that he was happy with the decision. But if Robert was so sure that this was the right decision, why did she have this nagging feeling that she had her chance to do the right thing and just blew it.

"Give him a call and accept. I'm sure there's someone there to answer the phones or else leave him a message."

"Not at this hour," she said. "The government shuts down at night just like everybody else. Besides, I want to make sure that I don't change my mind in an hour."

"That's the point. You'll go through a case of buyer's remorse, convince yourself it's a bad idea and change your mind. You've been doing it all night."

"I'll have to take that chance. I want one more thing from him before I agree. I want the girls to be left alone until they turn eighteen so they can decide for themselves. I can't make this decision for them. If he agrees to that, it's a deal."

Robert thought it over. "I think he'll go for it but don't you think that's putting a tough decision on the kids at that age. I think it would be kinder to make it for them. They may be upset with us now, but they'll get over it quickly. If you leave the choice until then, they will think about it for years before trying to decide and years after wondering if they made the right decision."

"I understand what you're saying but you don't understand what this means to us. You are just going to have to trust me on this. They must be the ones to make the decision."

At seven Christine called the number Todd Lindell had given her. She was so surprised when he answered the phone at that hour that she stumbled over her words. She explained what the deal was and that the girls would not be penalized until they turned eighteen and made up their minds. Todd said that he didn't think he could make that deal, that it would be unfair to the others involved. Christine told him fine, no deal and hung up. Thirty minutes later Todd called back and accepted the deal.

Lindell had seen the Senator happy before but today he was the cat who ate the canary. "She accepted with no other conditions?" Fenton asked.

"She said she would have to review the exact content of the messages along with her demand of delaying any action on her children until they turn eighteen."

"Excellent!" Fenton tittered. "I want the video team in production within a week. Is the copy ready yet?"

"We have four public announcements roughed out but they still lack the details. We need the procedures finalized before Mrs. Landis can go on TV and explain what they are." Todd was getting frustrated. This is Washington for Christ's sake. Nothing gets done in a week. "That will take at least a month to get through the committee. I don't see any way to start filming in a week."

"Don't sweat the committee approval. Let me take care of that." Fenton again giggled like a child who was about to burst in his attempts to hold his excitement in check. "I want the text of the announcements on my desk before dinner. We need to act just as fast as we can to get Mrs. Landis on video tape. She could change her mind in a week. Once we have her signature on the dotted line and her face on the screen, I don't care if the bitch changes her mind. Matter of fact, I hope she does cause then the deal will be null and void and we can put her in prison where she belongs. Just like we discussed yesterday, we will set up a phone bank with an 800 number to be displayed in the public service announcements."

"Right," affirmed Lindell. "There will be one for Monoecions to call and a separate one for the reporting of illegal activity, noncompliance and so on."

Fenton added "We need to record each conversation and track each number as they call in so if they get cold feet when it comes down to giving a name and address we still have something to go on. The FBI will be supplied an updated list daily for development of the complete family tree. AT&T should be able to get you required phone numbers reserved by tomorrow afternoon with installation done within a week if you can get them the details of the building by 9:00 AM tomorrow. Do we have a building selected yet?"

"No Senator, we have three suitable spaces available, all of which could be occupied within seven working days but only at a premium price for the contractors." It was only 9:30 in the morning but Lindell was already exhausted. It didn't help to be spending his time with this lunatic. Fenton of all people should understand that you can't make things happen this quickly in Washington no matter how much power you think you have. Fenton's bill had passed by Congress and been signed by the President. The Commission to Oversee Monoecion Affairs was formed and empowered all in record time, but at a cost. Staff had been working seven days a week, sleeping in their offices until they were dead on their feet. Political favors had been promised and arms twisted. To top it all off, it was beginning to look as if it was all to no avail; Senator Fenton had to play second fiddle. The directorship of the commission was given to the Honorable Senator Perryman from Ohio, a moderate who seemed in no hurry to implement any action plan until it had been thoroughly evaluated. He wanted environmental impact studies of the possible reservation sites and economic plans before one was selected. An independent review of the medical guidelines by a board yet to be selected was also required. Just selecting the board would take at least a month. Who knew how long the review would take. Fenton's mad rush to start video production of the public service announcements and phone bank arrangements were useless without approval of the commission director. "Do you want me to prepare a formal presentation to the director for selection?"

"No, I don't think a formal presentation is necessary, just pick the best one and get the details to the director ASAP so we can get things under way," said Fenton. "There's one more thing I need you to take care of this morning."

Just what I need thought Lindell, one more thing for the morning. "Senator, you have given me quite a load already. Is it something I have to do personally?"

"Oh no, just delegate it to one of the staff. Have them send some flowers from me to my old friend Senator Perryman at the intensive care unit at Walter Reed. Express my wishes for a quick recovery from that massive stroke he had early this morning."

Todd Lindell stopped writing in his notebook and looked at Senator Fenton with dawning comprehension. "Senator Perryman had a stroke?"

"Just about an hour ago. Have the card signed from me, *Acting* Director of COMA." Fenton smiled broadly.

Lindell smiled back. "I'll get right on these assignments Senator." He's a damned cat, thought Lindell, throw him out the window and the bastard will land on his feet and walk back in.

Thursday, August 22

The FBI courier cooled his heels in the waiting room outside Fenton's office. The main thrust of the FBI's investigation was to identify every living Monoecion on the planet. The only way that this could be accomplished was to track each family back to ensure that all the branches were accounted for. What they really needed was the base of the Monoecion family tree, the first Monoecion. Finally after forty-five minutes of waiting, he was ushered into Fenton's office. "Good news, sir. We believe we have located the first Monoecion." He produced a file folder from his briefcase and placed it on the Senator's desk.

"Oh really," said the Senator, a trace of sarcasm in his voice. "How can you be sure?"

"As far as we can verify, no members of the family were taken in or adopted. The woman had natural brothers but she had only female offspring as did all of her offspring. She was born in 1719 which would match with Dr. Irene Moore's estimates from her journal." The FBI agent seemed very pleased with himself.

"Very good." The Senator picked up the envelope but didn't open it. "Does anyone else know about our Rachel Delings?"

"No sir, not yet..." The agent stopped in mid-sentence and suddenly looked very worried. He had not told the woman's name to the Senator.

Fenton picked up a remote control and turned on a television that sat neatly in a corner cabinet. As the screen faded in, a voice clearly spoke "...ide sources claim that the FBI has tracked down what is thought to be the first Monoecion. Rachel Delings appears to be at the root of the family tree of Dr. Irene Moore. It's not known if Rachel was Monoecion, but it appears quite certain that all of her children were." The Senator pressed the power button and the screen went blank. The FBI man shifted his weight from one foot to the other nervously.

"Imagine my surprise when I turned on the TV to scan the late breaking news, I find out that as head of the COMA," Fenton stood for emphasis and slammed his fist on his desk, "I'm the last fucking man in the free world to find out this news!" The FBI man visibly winced at the impact. "I want you to go back to your boss and inform him that I want the man who leaked that story to be crucified. And if he can't find the informant, I'll crucify him!" Fenton's face was beet red. "Do I make myself clear?!"

"Yes Senator," the agent replied in measured tones. "I'll give him the message." The agent turned and made a speedy getaway from the Senator's office.

Fenton buzzed Lindell. "I've got the information from the FBI, let's hope that at least some of it is accurate. Is the press conference set?"

"One hour in the briefing room."

"Get in here and we'll finish the opening statement." Well, thought Fenton, we have the tap root, now all we have to do is pull.

Todd Lindell came by that afternoon with a binding contract for Christine to sign. It took her only a quick glance to reject it. It was very specific in the duties that she was to perform but gave the government complete control of the content of the "announcements" with no right of refusal for Christine if she objected to the content.

"This is garbage and you know it," she railed. "How can you expect me to sign a contract like this and not even provide me the scripts."

"You didn't asked me to provide them," he replied. "If I knew you wanted to see them, I would have brought them."

"Bring them. And eliminate all the sections on artistic control. It's simple, if I don't approve of the final product, it doesn't play. Keep it simple."

"So what's to keep you from disliking everything we put in front of you?" grumbled Lindell. "We do have a message to get out."

"If we can't come to an agreement on the content and format for a minimum of five spots, either party has the right to cancel the deal with no repercussions." Lindell left in a foul mood. He didn't have time to deal with this crap.

"What are you trying to do, scuttle the whole deal?" Robert asked after Lindell left.

"No, I'm trying to get a fair deal! I'm not going to sign anything until I have in writing exactly what I get and exactly what I have to do to get it. The way that contract was worded, they could make me say anything they wanted and if I backed out, we would be liable for every expense incurred in the production of the video. That could easily be half a million dollars in a week."

"OK. Just be a little more cooperative. At least show that you are willing to work with them."

The nagging feeling in the pit of her stomach was growing. She called Ben and told him about the contract. He agreed with her and told her to be sure and not sign anything until he could look it over. She went in the bedroom and really prayed for the first time in many years. It was a prayer very similar to the one spoke on the Mount of Olives two thousand years ago. Christine asked, "Why me?" and then asked God to guide her in her actions, to help her do what was right. When she finished, she felt a little more in control but still had no idea as to what to do next.

Friday, August 23

Charlie had not had a good day. The roof trusses that were promised to show up at seven AM hadn't arrived until almost noon. That meant he paid a crew for a half-day for doing little make-work jobs instead of getting the house dried in as planned.

But Charlie knew the late delivery wasn't the real cause of his anger. He had lost control when a new guy in the crew found out that Charlie was the one that had discovered the Monos and told the media. The guy was really impressed that he was THE Charlie Wilkins and wanted to shake his hand for saving the Human Race. Charlie told him it was no big deal and to get his ass back to work, even though Charlie knew there was nothing for him to do until the trusses arrived. Then the guy made the comment to one of the other workmen, loud enough for all to hear, "I wonder what it would be like to fry one of the bitches knowing her whole family was feeling her burn too?" Dousing Monoecions with gasoline and lighting them on fire had been reported more than once on the evening news.

That's when Charlie lost it. He threw his note pad to the ground and grabbed the guy. "You want to know what it would be like to fry in front of your family? Well why don't we find out? We'll get your mama, your wife and your kids all collected here to watch and we can fry your butt right here. What do you say?"

The workman's eye grew too large to fit his face. His mouth opened and closed but nothing came out. Finally he got over his shock at the sudden attack. "What the fuck, man, I just asked a question, that's all. You don't need to be so touchy."

"Yeah, well I don't happen to enjoy the thought of watching somebody being burned alive, no matter who they are. I'm funny that way. Now if you get into that sort of thing, that's a little too strange for me, so why don't you pack up your tools and get off my job site."

The workman looked to the other men for support. They all averted their eyes and went back to what they were doing. "Look, I didn't mean anything by it." Charlie said nothing. "I really need this job, OK. I'll keep my comments to myself from now on."

Just then Charlie saw the truck coming up the road with the load of trusses. He knew he couldn't afford to be shorthanded and still finish the job on time. "Get your ass back to work and watch your mouth." Charlie walked out to the street to guide the truck in.

Now he was home but he still didn't feel any better. He sat in his recliner with a can of beer trying to shake the frustrations of the day. He had told Gloria what had happened and she told him that he got so mad because he felt responsible for what was happening. That just pissed him off even more. "I'm not responsible for what other people do!"

"I didn't say you were," Gloria explained. "I said you felt responsible. There is a difference."

He came in the den with his beer to sulk. The only reason he took the beer was to irritate Gloria. She had been harping on him because of his gut and one of the things he said he would give up was his second beer in the evening. Now she had gone off to the bedroom just to make him feel guilty, he was sure. He cycled through the channels, looking for something to numb his mind. No matter how hard he tried, the image from last night's eleven o'clock news kept creeping back, an image of a mother and child's blackened bodies intertwined. "I didn't do it," he said to no one. "It's not my fault."

Thursday, August 29

The video taping of the "Public Service Announcements" had already begun. As Fenton had requested, Lindell had hired an actress double to play the part of Christine Landis for the initial taping while the final scripts were prepared. They told her truthfully that it was for a set of preliminary tests that would be used to determine the most effective message and that she was not meant to be the one on camera for the actual announcements. What wasn't told was that if the deal went sour with Christine Landis, they planned to use these tapes as the real thing.

Fenton laid out his plans. "If all goes as planned, then Christine Landis will make the production tape and we have gained little with these test shots. But, if she backs out, we already have these test tapes so we use them rather than spending the public's hard earned money to redo the same film with another actress. We can't help it if the woman in the advertisement happens to resembles Mrs. Landis and that most of the Monoecion public thinks it is Mrs. Landis." Fenton had thought out everything. "If Landis backs out, we first air the announcements when she is occupied elsewhere, out of contact with the press, new hospital tests or even incarceration for some good cause. We created these films as a test and then the Mono backed out of the deal. Our intentions were honorable and forthright. By the time Landis finds out and raises a stink we will have a list of names and addresses that will keep the FBI working nights for a long time to come. With a little pull we can keep the news on page three of the papers and off the network news." Fenton did not like to leave things to chance.

The actress had her hair cut, styled and dyed to match. She was shorter and a bit thinner than Christine but that wasn't visible on camera. Wardrobe supplied exact matches to the suits Christine wore in her televised appearances in front of Congress, right down to the jewelry, watch and reading glasses.

The actress sat for hours on end viewing all of the available videotape, practicing her movements and voice, trying to capture each element perfectly. She had never worked on a government production of a public service announcement but it seemed odd to have a Senator's aide buzzing all over the place, checking on each detail himself. She thought the arrangements were a bit extreme for just a test shot. "But hey, this is the federal government," the director said. "When did they ever make sense?"

Her practice was going quite well however there was one part that would really sell the job; try as she might, she just couldn't seem to get it right. The director was talking to Todd Lindell when she called him over for another attempt. "Mr. Spalding, is this better?" She took a couple of deep breaths and started "Hi, I'm Christine Landis and I'd like to talk to all the Monoecions and their families who are watching." She then gave a broad smile.

"You're getting closer but I doubt you'll ever match the original. You can keep trying but I don't think you can get it much better."

"Wow," said Lindell. "How can you get much closer than that. The voice and the movements were almost perfect. What was wrong with it?"

"The one thing that nobody else could match. Let me show you." The director rewound the VCR the actress was using and pressed play. "It's coming up... in just a second... There! Did you see that smile. That look of pure innocence. That woman could murder ten people in the middle of a crowd of witnesses, go to court and smile like that at the jury and claim she was innocent and walk away a free woman." Unknown to them they were looking at Christine during her link with Jasmine.

"Yeah, I see what you mean," said Lindell.

"And she's looking at you, into you. If you're sitting on your couch watching her, you know she can look right through the camera into your living room and see you munching your popcorn." The director ran his hands through his hair, folding his hands at the back of his neck. "You can't fake that," said the director as he dropped his hands to his sides, "you can come close but you'll never get it right. I think we better skip it rather than get it wrong."

"What surprised me was how well she picked up her cues. She made that camera change perfectly," added the actress.

Lindell's ears perked up. "What do you mean cues?" he asked the actress.

"The camera change, where she went from looking in one camera to looking in the next as the active shot changed." She rewound the tape again and ran it one more time in slow motion. "See how she is looking right into the camera and now the active camera changes and she switches her look with it. She didn't jump the gun and start early like most people do. She waits for the switch allowing the new shot to catch her in profile and then she swings her gaze to it. Perfect timing."

"You mean she was told what camera was transmitting?" asked Lindell.

"Sure, she had to have been, or else she was watching it on a monitor. It's too perfect to be an accident," the director replied. "I didn't realize that Congress used stagehands to keep them looking good when on camera."

"We don't, that's the problem. The cameras, do they have a red light on the front or something that tells you that they are the active camera?"

"No, normally not. All that is usually decided by the director in the control room. He gives orders to the cameramen on the floor as to how he wants each one positioned, the zoom and so on but he controls which one is actually feeding the network. The cameraman rarely knows the instant the shot changes unless the director tells him and this timing was much too smooth for that. This is typical of a planned shot where the actor knows when the camera is changing."

"So you're telling me that the director was in on this and was feeding information to Mrs. Landis during the Senate hearing?"

"I can't say that for sure," the director said back peddling as best he could. "Even though it's unlikely, it could still be coincidence."

"Yeah, right." Todd realized that he had a conspiracy involving some CNN employees and possibly more. He had to get this to Fenton and he didn't want this director telling all his friends in the business to cover their asses. "In other words there's not enough here to know for sure. Too bad." He directed his attention back to the actress trying to keep the talk light. "Do you think you can get that smile?"

"I'll do my best," she said, "but that's a tough one."

Lindell graciously extricated himself out of the conversation and slipped out to call the Senator.

"You're sure of this?" asked Fenton.

"She got the cue from somebody. It's obvious when you know what to look for. We need to get the FBI on this one quick before any more time passes. It's has to be someone inside the crew for that telecast, probably the director."

"She could of had a receiver and was getting direction from someone watching the broadcast." Fenton doubted that she had time to set this up without someone catching her in the act. They had wire taps, microphones and at least two agents on her at all times.

"No way," said Lindell. "Get the tape and watch it. Someone watching and trying to tell her from the outside couldn't have directed her that quick. This had to be prior warning."

"Or maybe she knew it by reading the directors mind. Maybe their powers are much greater than they have revealed." Damn, thought Fenton, wouldn't that open up a nice can of worms. That would mean they knew of every plan while it was being made.

"Why stop there?" asked Lindell. "What if she put the idea in the directors mind? It's all possible but it doesn't match with what we know so far. Right now, I think I'd lean towards the director or cameraman being in on it."

"The FBI needs this information ASAP! Head over to the FBI building now. I want some answers as soon as we can get them. Don't call this in, do it person to person in case they are monitoring our phone calls. If they are learning what's going on with their telepathy, I want to know about it." Fenton hung up the phone. If they have moles in the networks, they probably have them in the phone company too he thought. They could be listening to everything coming in and going out of this office. He made a note to have the phone security checked just to be on the safe side.

Chapter 20

Friday, September 6

Todd Lindell arrived at Christine's home at 9:30 in the morning accompanied by a staff attorney with a rewrite of the agreement. Ben Davis was waiting with her to review the terms and conditions, and advise her on her options. No one else was home. She wanted it that way but she wasn't really sure why. She tried to convince herself it was to avoid distractions but she knew deep down that she was ashamed of herself for doing this, and didn't want any spectators to her humiliation.

"I think this revision addresses all of your previous concerns with the last one. Under this contract, we could not use any partial segment of the taped footage in another announcement without your permission. You will not be bound to do any additional announcements outside the four we have planned currently and I have the scripts with me for you to read. We retain the right to edit and modify them as long as it does not change the basic content or moral message from the original. In other words, we want to be able to fix a mistake in the grammar with out getting lawyers involved." Both Ben and Christine gave him a look with a raised eyebrow. "No offense, I'm a lawyer too you know."

Christine and Ben studied the document in silence for a few minutes. "May I have the scripts?" ask Christine. Todd gave a copy of the scripts to each of them and they again took a few minutes to scan them for changes from the originals they had received the night before. "Could you excuse us for a few minutes, Mr. Lindell, I'd like to discuss a couple of items with Mr. Davis in private."

"Certainly," Todd said rising from his chair, "We'll just step outside for as long as you need."

"No need. Ben and I will step out back. I need some fresh air anyway." Ben followed Christine through the kitchen and out onto her patio deck.

"Is there a problem? Have they changed something?" asked Ben.

"No, nothing like that. I just want this ache in my stomach to go away." Christine looked down at her feet, too self-conscious to look him in the eye. "Did you take care of that other item for me?"

"I was truly hoping you wouldn't do this to me. This goes against everything I stand for."

"I'm sorry Ben. I shouldn't have asked you to do it. It's OK." Christine leaned on the railing gazed over her back yard.

"Oh hell!" said Ben. He reached in his pocket and produced a pack of cigarettes. He slapped them on the rail and said "Don't ever ask me to do this again."

"You're a saint Ben!" Christine's hands were shaking as she opened the pack. "Don't leave all these. I'll smoke them all and puke all over my back yard." She took one cigarette out of the pack and started to hand it back, thought again and took another out. "For after the signing. Shit. I don't have a..."

"Match?" asked Ben holding out a book of paper matches.

"Thanks. Tell me Ben, why didn't I marry you?"

"That's easy, I'm old enough to be your father and my wife wouldn't allow it. Now if the question was why didn't you have an affair with me, the answer wouldn't be quite as easy."

"I know you, the answer would have been the same. Would you go in and tell the Senator's pit bull that I'll be there in a little while. I'd like to be alone for just a few moments." Ben nodded and went back in the house. Christine lit a match and watched it burn halfway down before lighting her cigarette. She was more cautious this time, inhaling slowly to avoid a coughing fit. Christine tried to clear everything from her mind, to focus on the one simple pleasure of sucking this noxious, poisonous fog into her lungs. Nothing at all but the joy of a nicotine buzz.

"What are you doing?" a child's voice inside her mind asked.

Christine felt like she had been caught drowning the neighbor's cat. Her shame and embarrassment surged from the hole that she had been trying to bury it in and flooded her soul.

Jasmine recoiled at the negative emotional onslaught. "I'm sorry, Christine. I'm sorry. Please don't feel this way. I'll go away so you won't cry."

Christine could feel Jasmine's emotional tears falling on her like a thunderstorm. "It's OK, Jasmine. It's not your fault I feel this way." Christine struggled to find that emotional hug that was so easy to give before. Now, the harder she tried, the more it eluded her. She begged Jasmine not to leave her. The two of them struggled to soothe the damage that had been done to each other in that split second. After what seemed an eternity, their emotions calmed and she felt the first tug at her heart of that warm hug. Christine started the long process of explaining why she felt so bad about what she was about to do.

"You won't be like us anymore if you have the operation?"

"I don't know, this has never been done to us before."

"Will I still be able to visit you?" Jasmine asked.

"I truly don't know honey. I don't want this to happen but I have to make a choice and both of them are bad."

"I understand," said Jasmine. "My mommy explained it all to me. You shouldn't feel bad about making a choice that's difficult because there is always a best choice. Even if you have to choose one of two bad things, one is less bad than the other so it is the best choice."

"Your mommy should be very proud of you. You are a very wonderful girl, and your mommy must be very smart to be able to teach you so well."

"Oh she is." Christine could feel Jasmine's pride. "She told me to come to her if I ever have to decide like this. Maybe she can help you. I'll ask her."

With that, Jasmine was gone and Christine was back to the real world. She looked down at her cigarette, still burning in her fingers. It didn't seem so important any more. She flicked it out into the yard. God, how Robert hated it when I did that, she thought. Only now she didn't really care as much as she used to.

Ben looked out the window to check on Christine. She stood like a statue, not moving a muscle, never even taking a drag on that damned cigarette. Ever since his little brother died of lung cancer, he was a one man vigilante group when it came to smoking and Christine knew it. She had to be having a rough time to even think of asking him to bring her a pack of cigarettes. He saw her quickly look around, like a student who was daydreaming in class suddenly snapping out of it. He was happy to see her ditch the cigarette but she didn't turn to come in. She just moved down the rail a couple of steps and continued to gaze into the distance. Lindell called from the living room, asking if Christine was OK. As if he gives a shit, thought Ben. Why doesn't he ask what he really wants to know, is she ready to sign on the dotted line so he can go back to his boss with his trophy. "She's fine, she's just not ready yet. She'll be back in a few minutes. Give her a chance to study the documents without distraction." Only she wasn't even looking at the documents, now she was a statue again, staring off into space.

Jasmine came running out of her room so excited she could hardly speak. "Mama, mamacomere!"

That's me, thought Marci, Mama Come Here. Some day I will get my name changed legally and then there won't be any question. "Shhh. A little quieter please. What do you want?"

"You gotta help, mama! Kissteen needs you."

"Who needs me? I can't understand you. Slow down honey and say one word at a time."

Jasmine was frustrated. "Kissteen 'andis. The lady like us on TV. She wants you to help her." Jasmine began to question her mother's superior intelligence. She didn't get it at all. Finally the light came on over Marci's head.

"Christine, Christine Landis? The woman on TV when the men were all asking her questions?"

"Yes!" Jasmine screamed. "Please mama, she needs help. Will you help her?"

Marci felt the very real anxiety coming from her daughter. This was real, at least to Jasmine it was. Marci wondered if it was something on TV. Maybe she's been arrested. "I can try, honey. What's wrong? What can I do?"

Jasmine grabbed her mom's hand and pulled her into her room. "Sit on my bed and talk to her."

Marci looked at her daughter, not understanding what she wanted her to do. "I can't talk to her, she's not here."

"Noooo! Sit on my bed in my travel spot." Jasmine patted the bed near the middle.

Marci sat down. "What do you mean, your travel spot?" she asked a little concerned.

"This is where I go visit," she said matter-of-factly and she sat next to her mom. A second later Marci's head exploded.

The trip was instantaneous. Marci felt her mind as a maze. She saw down paths and corridors of her past and saw possibilities she never imagined. Then she ran into the stranger and fear overwhelmed her.

"Mommy, this is Christine, you don't have to be afraid," soothed Jasmine.

Christine felt relieved when Jasmine returned. She was afraid that Jasmine wouldn't be back for days and she so needed the focused concentration that a conversation with Jasmine provided. What Christine was not prepared for was the extra presence, Marci. Christine recognized her right away from the imprint left by Jasmine. "My God, Jasmine," said Christine, "you can link up more than one person at a time. This is amazing!"

Marci was in shock. "Jasmine, how did you do this?! What's happening to me?"

Jasmine could still feel her fear. "It's OK, mommy, just say 'One Bright Day in the Middle of the Night' and you won't be scared anymore."

Marci wondered if this was what it felt like to be insane. It wasn't at all unpleasant once you got past the initial shock. "One bright day in the middle of the night..." Marci recited the nonsense poem and she was pleasantly surprised to find she did feel better.

"I like that very much. I'm afraid we haven't been properly introduced. I'm Christine Landis." Christine opened her mind, giving Marci little peeks inside but being much more guarded than she had been with Jasmine. Christine was surprised by Marci's reaction of shock and fear when they first touched. "Did you know your daughter could do this?"

"I had no idea. She connected Alicia and I once before but only for a split second, nothing like this. I'm Marci, Jasmine's mother as I'm sure you already know. How did you just show yourself to me?"

"I don't really know. Every time Jasmine visits me, I just try things. Jasmine, give your mommy a hug and have her hug you back. Maybe that will help her understand."

"OK." Even though the hug was directed at Marci, it overflowed to Christine who directed it back to Jasmine and on to Marci. If the FBI agent who was assigned to watch Christine through the telephoto lens of his camera would have been watching instead of talking to his partner, he would of seen the smile that was giving the actress so much trouble.

"Jasmine told me you were in trouble. What can I do to help?"

Christine again felt her shame at what she was about to do. "I doubt that there is much you can do." She slowly opened up her soul to this stranger she met seconds ago. As she did, she felt her mind surging into high gear, operating in ways she hadn't experienced with Jasmine. It was as if each additional mind squared her mental powers.

"Oh please be careful," Marci begged, "I don't know how some of this will affect Jasmine."

Jasmine's response came, feeling much older than her years, "I'm all right. Please, mommy, help Christine."

Christine lost herself in the intricate workings of this alien mind that she was now only a small part of. As if someone turned on a light in a dark room, she now saw the path that could safely carry her through the obstacles that lay ahead. Nothing was certain, but now at least she can see a way. "Thank you, Jasmine, and you too, Marci. I wish I could express what this means to me." She then found out she could since words were no longer in the way. There was a silent goodbye and a promise to return. Christine found herself on her deck, her mind alone but with a plan for the first time in weeks. It was a bit fuzzy where moments ago it was clear, but she knew what she must do. But first was another matter to attend to. She reached in her pocket and pulled out the second cigarette that Ben had given her. She looked at it for a moment with contempt then ground it to fragments in her hand. Brushing the chaff from her hands she turned on her heel and strode in the house.

"Mr. Lindell, I'm sorry to keep you waiting," she said with authority of someone who was in control of the situation. Ben looked up at her, startled by the change in her manner. She gave him a sly smile. "Do you have the contract?"

Todd produced the contract and slid it towards her on the coffee table. "Right here. Now if you'll sign it right here..." he said indicating with his pen.

Christine remained standing. "No, I don't think so."

Todd jerked his head up so fast it hurt his neck. "What?"

"I'll make this as clear as I possibly can. No. If I am to take responsibility as the government appointed leader of the Monoecions, I better start acting the part. I can't do that if I am no longer a Monoecion. I'm sure you can find a more suitable person to fulfill your need of a spokesperson. What we do need to talk about is the reservation. Has the site been selected yet?"

Lindell was flustered. The bitch had made a fool of him. "You can't do this. We had a deal!"

"You offered me a deal, Mr. Lindell. I never accepted the deal. Is that not correct, Councilor?" she said nodding at Ben.

"That is correct." Thank God she's back, thought Ben. I thought I lost her.

"Now, are you prepared to discuss the reservation site?"

Todd stood up in a huff. "Hell no I'm not ready to talk about the site. Do you know what you are throwing away?"

"No, but I know what I'm keeping. How is tomorrow at two o'clock?"

She's gone mad Lindell thought. "For what?"

"To talk about the reservation site. Are you paying attention?" asked Christine.

"No... I don't know..." Lindell growled grabbing his documents. How the hell was he going to explain this to Fenton. "I'll call you."

"By this afternoon please, I'll be waiting. Now, please excuse me, I have a lot of work to do." Christine showed Lindell and his assistant to the door.

"You're going to regret this, Mrs. Landis," fumed Lindell.

"I doubt it but that's a chance I have to take." Christine closed the door on Lindell.

After they left, Ben looked up at Christine over the tops of his glasses and said "As your attorney, I must advise you that this course of action is not the safest choice you could have made. As your friend, I must tell you that seeing Lindell leave with his tail between his legs like a whipped puppy was the finest thing I've seen in years."

"I decided it was time to quit playing it safe and start playing it honest. I'm sorry to tell you that I will no longer require your services as my attorney."

"Oh? Are you seeing another attorney on the side?" asked Ben.

"No, I just can't afford you. I'm going to need every dime I can scrape up to help the Monoecions I get letters from every day, most in much worse shape than I'm in. That has to be my first priority."

Ben's smile faded a bit as he stood. "I would be proud to donate the vast fortune I have acquired by representing you, all thirty-seven dollars, to the cause. Consider your bill paid in full. But seriously now, be careful. These are very powerful men you are antagonizing and their bite is much worse than their bark."

Christine gave Ben a hug and a quiet "Thank you."

Lindell burst into the Senator's office mad as hell. The time it took to drive back to the office only allowed his anger to fester rather than abate. "That fucking bitch!"

Fenton didn't even look up from his paperwork. "She turned it down," he said calmly.

Lindell stopped in mid-step like a comic book character, then slowly put his foot down. "Yeah, she turned it down." Lindell waited for the Fenton's rage, sure that this was just the calm before the storm.

"Is the taping of the 'test' shots done yet?" asked Fenton, finally looking up. His face remained calm, almost serene.

"I'm not sure. They should be. They were going to finish this morning." Todd was confused. He expected the Senator to be screaming by now but he didn't even flinch. "What gives?"

"You really expected her to go through with it?" Lindell didn't answer. He sagged slightly like an inflatable doll with a slow leak. Fenton continued. "I knew she wouldn't go through with it from the beginning. That's why I was pushing the double. We had to have her film in the can before it was known that the Landis bitch changed her mind, otherwise our story wouldn't hold up."

"If you were so damned sure, why didn't you let me in on it?" Todd dropped into a chair.

"I thought the reaction would be more authentic this way. What did she have to say?"

"She wants to meet me tomorrow to go over the plans for the reservation and check the site selection. She said the government has selected her as the leader of the Monos so she's going to do just that. What a bunch of horse shit."

Fenton leaned back in his chair, hands clasp behind his head, and smiled. "That's perfect. She's playing right into our hands. How long until we can be ready to man the phone bank and run the public service announcements?"

"That's still at least a week away. By the time we get the film copied and distributed to the stations, time slots arranged, I'd guess nine days." Todd still wasn't sure of what Fenton had in mind.

"Our first choice for the reservation is the Hastings Army Training Center in northern Nevada, right?" Todd nodded in agreement. "I believe that base has been closed for some time now, a couple of years."

"It was one of the first to be closed by the last round of budget cuts," confirmed Todd.

"I doubt there are any working phones or televisions on that base." The Senator smiled at Todd. "If a representative for the Monos was to tour the site for say a week, doing a thorough job of checking it out, she would be completely out of touch with civilization."

"Especially if we arrange a security blackout so there won't be any publicity of the proposed site," added Lindell.

"Very good. Start arrangements as soon as the broadcast dates are set. Now for God's sake, don't let site selection out to the public or the security blackout will be obvious bullshit." Fenton added "If all goes well, in two weeks we will have the names and addresses of seventy percent of the Monos in the United States."

Robert returned a couple hours after Lindell and his assistant left. He entered cautiously expecting to find Christine in her usual state, frustrated and depressed. What he heard was one side of a heated argument.

"I don't care what your sheriff told you to do. That, my boy, is illegal search and seizure." Christine held the phone on her shoulder while making notes on the legal pad in front of her. Surrounding her were the piles of letters that she had been keeping but hadn't known why. "The constitution has not been revoked, at least not yet, so I advise you find Mrs. Heinlein today and return her belongings before you folks end up on the receiving end of a lawsuit." Christine saw Robert come in the study and smiled at him. She mouthed "Just a second," and went back to her phone call. "You have my number. I want confirmation today." She hung up the phone and said, "Hi sailor, been in port long?"

"You're in a good mood. Everything go well today?"

"Yes, I think it went as well as could be expected." She picked up another letter off the keeper stack.

"So when do you start filming?" Robert asked.

"Filming? Oh, for Fenton. Never, I turned him down."

Robert exclaimed "You what?"

"I turned him down. I just couldn't become a prostitute for any amount." Christine continued reading the letter in her hand.

"What's going on here? You told me that you were going to accept. We agreed that it was the right thing to do. Then you tell me you didn't want me here for the final negotiations so I leave, only to come back and find out you blew the deal! You never intended to sign, did you? You just wanted me out of the house so you could dump the deal without interference!"

Christine kept her voice level and calm. "Let's get a few things straight. One, I didn't blow the deal, I blew off the deal. They accepted everything I had asked for and were willing to sign on the dotted line. Second, you decided it was a good deal. I still wasn't completely convinced but I thought you were thinking straighter than I was at the time. Third, I wanted you gone because I was too ashamed to have anyone I cared about witness me signing that document. It was at the last possible moment that I decided I wasn't going to sign. When the offer was first made, you told me it was my decision. Well, I made it. I'm sorry if you don't like but it's still my decision. Get over it."

Robert lost his temper at that point. "That is the most selfish thing I've ever heard! To hell with your family! To hell with what it does to their lives! You're too self-righteous to give in enough to reach a compromise. It's your way or none at all."

"I had to make a decision for my people, not just my family."

"Your people!" Robert scoffed. "You're going to sacrifice our one chance at a normal life together for a bunch of people you don't even know!"

"You'd be surprised to know how well I know them," she said quietly.

"What the hell does that mean?" he demanded.

Christine paused for a moment, remembering that the house had ears, all of them attached to the FBI. "You haven't read the letters from them. You haven't felt their pain and anguish."

"They haven't felt ours! You haven't felt mine!"

"My sisters have felt my anguish while I wrestled with this decision, and they felt my joy when I made the right choice." Christine suddenly changed directions. "Do you remember our undergraduate days back in college? Remember the campus radicals and all their slogans?" Robert looked at Christine with uncommitted eyes. "There was one I never understood until now. 'If you're not part of the solution, then you are part of the problem.' I've decided to become part of the solution. You're just going to have to make up your mind which side you're on."

"You've lost your mind." With that, Robert turned and marched out of the room.

"No," she said as she picked up the next letter, "I just found it again."

Alicia returned home about six-thirty. She had to correct a drawing foul-up at the office that kept her late. Since she was already late, she stopped off at the music store for a new set of guitar strings for her old Gibson L6. When she came in the front door, she saw Marci sitting in the middle of the floor with her headphones on, eyes closed, rocking back and forth with the music.

Try as she might, Alicia could not resist the tempting target. She quietly put her things down at the door and tiptoed over to Marci, sitting down ever so carefully squarely in front of her. Alicia cradled her chin in her hands, put a silly grin on her face and waited. It didn't take long. Seconds later, Marci's eyes fluttered open, caught a glimpse of a face only inches from hers and screamed loud enough to raise the dead. She instinctively tried to push herself away when her brain finally registered who the face belonged to. By this time Alicia had already begun to giggle madly.

"You jerk! Are you trying to give me a heart attack?"

Alicia continued to roll on the floor, unable to control herself. "I'm sorry but I couldn't resist. I didn't realize..." She had to pause to wipe the tears of laughter from her eyes. "I didn't realize it would scare you so bad. But your face..."

Marci's fear had turned to anger. "Stop it! Why did you do that to me? You know I hate it when you scare me."

Alicia's laughter was tapering off as she realized how scared Marci was. Jasmine had felt the jolt of fear and came running into the living room. Marci's scream had scared Jessica who was now crying, adding to the chaos. Alicia got up and went to get Jessica.

Marci called Jasmine over and gave her a hug. "It's OK, baby. Alicia was just trying to be funny and it scared me. I'm all right."

"That was mean 'licia!" Jasmine commanded. "You 'pologize." She gave Alicia a stern look, doing her best mommy impression.

Alicia was just getting Jessica calmed down, putting all the good feelings she could into soothing her. "I'm sorry. I really am. I didn't think about how much it would scare you all. Please, will you forgive me?"

Jasmine turned to Marci and waited. "Apology accepted," said Marci. "Please, don't ever do that again. Not after what happened today."

Alicia felt a tingle of fear. "What happened today?" she asked with apprehension.

Jasmine spoke up before Marci had a chance. "I took mommy visiting."

"Oh really. And who did you visit?"

"We visited Christine Landis," said Marci, her voice trembling a bit.

"She was in town?" asked Alicia excitedly. Damn, she thought, Marci should know better than exposing us like that.

"No!" said Jasmine in a tone of voice that showed her impatience in dealing with her slowwitted parent, "in there!" Jasmine pointed towards her room.

Alicia looked at Marci with questioning eyes. Marci got up and took Jessica from Alicia. "Jasmine, could you keep an eye on the baby for a few minutes? I need to talk to Alicia." Jasmine nodded as Marci led Alicia to their bed room. There Marci described what had happened to her.

Alicia was floored. "You mean she just hooked all three of you together? Like the time you ran out of gas and she connected you and me?"

"Yes, but so much more. You know how time seems to slow down when you are in a crisis situation?"

"Oh yes. I sure do." Alicia knew exactly what Marci was talking about. She had been in an automobile accident when she was in college, someone had pulled out in front of her from a cross street. Time seemed to slow to a crawl, allowing her to examine every possible evasive maneuver in the fraction of a second before the impact. It made no difference as to the final results but she had always remembered that feeling of time in slow motion.

"Take that and multiply it by a hundred. It's like finding the turbo button for your brain. I mean, one second I'm sitting on Jasmine's bed and the next I'm five hundred miles away discussing ethics with Christine Landis. And the scary part was that Jasmine was right in there with us understanding the whole exchange."

Alicia was excited and she showed it. She was trying to figure out how it was done just like normal humans try to understand normal Monoecion telepathy. "But she's not related, at least not recently. I can almost understand how she connected the two of us, but how did she do the two of you?"

"How should I know how she does it? I'm beginning to understand how the rest of the world views us. My own daughter scares me with the things she can do."

"And she's done this before?"

"Not with me but Christine told me that Jasmine has been visiting her on a regular basis. The first time was during the Senate hearings on TV." A little shiver ran through Marci. "It was so matter-of-fact. She just took me 'visiting' as she put it."

"We have two choices as to what caused this ability in Jasmine," said Alicia. "It could be because we are both Monoecion, like we talked about before. Or it could be a freak occurrence, an extension of our normal telepathy that will just happen every once in a while to anyone. If it's the first cause then we'll know within two years. By then Jessica will be Jasmine's age."

"If that's the case, we'll know earlier than that. You were the oldest. Didn't you teach your little sisters all your bad habits at an early age? I know I did everything at a younger age than my oldest sister."

"Yes but I didn't teach them to walk at an early age. I think this will be more like walking than teaching them how to spit with style."

"You taught your little sisters how to spit?" said Marci with a grimace on her face. "That's gross."

"Yeah, I know. Mom thought so too. That's why I did it, to irritate her. Can Jasmine do it any time she wants to? Do you think she could connect us, right here?" asked Alicia.

"I don't know. It sure seems she can. She didn't have any trouble connecting Mrs. Landis and me a little while ago." Marci hesitated. She didn't want to disappoint Alicia but she hadn't recovered fully from the earlier experience yet. "I'm not sure I want to try just yet. It really scared me."

"Please, for me. I want to see what this is all about."

Marci was scared, not so much by the thought of experiencing the connection again, but of what Alicia might see inside of her. She didn't want to take a chance on losing Alicia's love because of what she was really like inside. It never occurred to her that she might learn something about Alicia that would shatter her love. She was sure that nothing could do that. At times though, Marci went through periods of low self esteem, unable to understand why Alicia gave her love to Marci so completely. She had seen the doubts inside Christine when it came to Robert and she was afraid she might see those same doubts in Alicia. "I'm scared," she whispered.

"What is it that scares you? Does Jasmine scare you?"

"No, not that kind of scared. Do you remember when we first started seeing each other." Alicia nodded. "That time when your parents were gone to the movies and I stopped over."

"The first time we made love? I remember," said Alicia a bit puzzled. "It was wonderful."

"It's not so much the first time we really made love, we had kissed and caressed each other before. It was standing in front of you, with the lights on and taking my clothes off. I was so afraid that you wouldn't like what you saw that I shook all over."

"I remember," said Alicia, "you told me you were cold."

"I was petrified. I took off everything and you could see me all together for the first time, flaws and all. That's the way I feel now. Only it's not my body that you will see now but my soul, and I'm afraid of what you'll think when you see me really naked for the first time." Tears were forming in her eyes, filling her lower eyelid until it could hold no more. A single drop tumbled down her cheek leaving a glistening trail.

Alicia wrapped her arms around Marci and gently laid her back on the bed. She kissed Marci with all the love she could give. "I love you naked, you're beautiful, and I'm sure your soul will thrill me just as much. I'm the one who should be scared of what you'll see. Sometimes I'm not sure I have a soul. You are my whole life and I'll take you just the way you are, warts and all."

Marci hugged Alicia so hard it took her breath away. She smiled at Alicia with red eyes and said "I think I can do it now. Why don't you check on Jessica and make sure she's OK. Then have Jasmine come in so we can talk to her."

A few minutes later they all sat together on the bed. "Mommy told me how you took her to visit your friend Christine and I wondered if you could bring mommy and I together so I can see what she means."

"But you and mommy are together. You're right here." Jasmine hadn't thought of using this talent for anything other than communicating over a distance. "Do you want me to get Kissteen too?"

"No honey, we don't need Christine do we? Mommy just wants to show Alicia what it is like when you connect us. Do we have to be apart?" Marci asked.

Jasmine thought for a moment. "Uh-uh. You don't have to be 'part. You sit there," she patted the bed beside her and Marci moved over, "and you sit there and I sit here."

After a few seconds Alicia wondered how long it took. "What do we do now?"

Jasmine looked up at Marci. "Now, mommy?"

Marci nodded and felt her brain jump to light-speed. For a moment Marci had the uncomfortable sensation of looking down a hall of mirrors, seeing herself through Alicia's eyes who was seeing Marci through her eyes who was seeing herself through.... to infinity. Marci thought to close her eyes to stop the loop but her mind corrected the image long before the physical command could be followed. She felt Alicia there, lost in wonder of what was happening to her mind. Jasmine freely floated amongst them, an old pro with the two novices, giving advice and encouragement.

Marci saw how Jasmine pictured herself, not as a child but as an inexperienced adult. She felt how much Jasmine understood already and it concerned her. Was Jasmine learning about life too quickly? Could she cope with all the feelings and knowledge rushing into her. Marci felt the reassuring hug and the smiling "I'm OK, mommy."

Alicia kept back, reaching out a little at a time, feeling the water. "My God! This is unbelievable," She seemed to be operating on two planes simultaneously. Her personal mind seemed to be acting as a controller, adjusting how much of herself she put into the group mind. The group mind had a life of its own. Alicia could exert some control but so could everyone else. It also seemed to dart off all on it's own at unexpected times. Slowly Alicia became bolder, showing more of herself.

Marci physically reached out and touched Alicia's cheek. The sensation sent chills through all their bodies at once. For what seemed minutes, Alicia and Marci touched each others hair and face. The sexual excitement exploded from each contact. "We can't do this with Jasmine here," Marci felt herself pleading but unable to take her finger tips from Alicia's lips. Alicia felt the same desire for control and started to pull herself back.

"It's OK. You can be alone for a while," said Jasmine as Marci and Alicia felt her slowly, shyly pull away, "I understand."

Alicia was hesitant. "This isn't right with Jasmine here."

Their combined mind spoke to them. "We're just touching, caressing, loving. This is not a bad thing to teach our child." Alicia opened herself up to Marci, giving back every sensation as Marci's fingers brushed her lips. Jasmine sat on the bed next to them, eyes closed. She appeared to be meditating. Alicia's fingers caressed down Marci's neck, over her shoulder and down her chest. Every touch seemed to be electric, sending slow motion shudders through their bodies. When Alicia's finger tips touched the nipple of Marci's breast through the thin fabric of her blouse, they experienced a mental climax more intense than any ever felt during physical love makings. They both sucked in a ragged breath as time stood still and the intensity of their love seemed to burst into an all consuming flame. As the feeling faded, neither had any concept as to how long it had lasted.

Finally they felt Jasmine returning. "When I grow up, I want to love someone as much as you do." She said it to both of them at the same time. Marci and Alicia hugged their daughter as they slid back to the real world.

Chapter 21

Daniel Nash wasn't an idealist, he knew what his job was. It was to sell newspapers. Reporting the news was just a sideline. He had never had a problem with that before now. Always before, the story would affect a person or maybe a family for a short time, maybe cause someone to lose their job. The worst was when he revealed some starlet's affair with a rich business man and the guy's wife committed suicide. But hey, that was the guy's fault for messing around on the side, it wasn't Danny Nash's problem.

This story was different. He couldn't pull his eyes off the screen where the TV news camera showed the police cutting down the three charred bodies of a mother and her two daughters. They had been tied to a fence with barbed wire, doused with gasoline and set on fire. Their only crime was that they had a genetic mutation that Daniel Nash sensationalized in his articles. Now every story he heard of an assault or murder of a Monoecion was like fingernails being pulled down a chalkboard. Danny knew that it was his story that had laid the foundation for all of this and it made him sick to his stomach. He forced himself to watch as men unwrapped the wire from around the bodies, pulling chunks of flesh away with it where the victims had struggled to free themselves before the flames finally killed them.

The public never saw this part of the tape. The network news only showed a shot of the emergency staff carrying the bodybags to the ambulance. Danny thanked his buddy at the network for letting him view the raw footage and told him he may want a few prints later for an article. His buddy asked him how well these pictures would go with shots of bikini clad babes showing off their silicone jobs. Danny had to admit he had no idea how he was going to pull it off.

He had decided some time back that this story could be worked from both angles. His first article was an exaggeration of the facts and he knew it. True, it was all supportable from the documents and investigation, just in case it ended up in court, but it was still an exaggeration. If Danny could show that this was a cover-up to protect themselves from extermination, not to eliminate the human race, he could swing the fervor in a whole new direction. He could turn this into another Trail of Tears, Custer massacring the Indians instead of the other way around. All he needed was a story good enough to pull the swing vote. After all, the Nation's View was perfectly happy to print both sides of a scandal, as long as it sold copies at the news stand.

He drove across town and wandered the subdivision for a few minutes before finding the address. He parked his rental car in the driveway, pulled his note pad from the rear seat and walked up to the door. He saw two men parked in a car down the street take a sudden interest in him. He turned towards them giving them a profile and head on shot for their files. "Smile," he said to himself, "you're on candid camera." Nash stepped up and rang the bell.

Christine looked over the man at her front door and decided he didn't look like much of a threat. She opened her door a few inches. "Can I help you?"

"Mrs. Landis? I believe you can. I'm a reporter and I'd like to see if I can help you tell your real story to the world. May I talk to you for a few minutes?"

"Do you want to know what was published the last time I granted an interview to a reporter who gave me that line? I read that I had admitted to having contact with beings from outer space. Sorry, not interested." Christine closed the door.

"Wait!" Daniel shouted. He rang the doorbell again.

After a second the door opened again. "Look, I'm not interested. Now go away before I signal to my personal bodyguards over there and they escort you off my property," she said tilting her head in the direction of the two FBI agents sitting in car parked in the street.

"Please, I think people might listen to my article."

"Why is that?"

"We haven't been introduced. I'm Daniel Nash." He smiled and held out his hand.

Christine recognized the name immediately. "Oh, you're that nice reporter who wrote all those filthy lies about us without bothering to check their accuracy. And now you want to straighten it all out with a new set of distortions. How nice to meet you. Please excuse me for a moment." She stepped back, slammed the door with a loud bang and screamed "He's got a gun!"

It took a fraction of a second for the situation to sink in. Daniel looked over his shoulder in time to see two burly FBI men jumping out of their car with guns drawn. Daniel dropped his note pad and stuck his hands in the air. He started yelling "I'm unarmed, I'm unarmed!" From inside the house he could just make out Christine Landis laughing her head off.

Saturday, September 7

The first member of Christine's start-up team, as she called them, was a real surprise. She was on the phone trying to find medical help for a Monoecion who was refused admittance to a hospital in St. Louis when Ben Davis stopped by. He patiently waited while she finished her conversation and then sat her down for a critique. "You can't do this the way you are doing it," he said.

"What are you talking about? Can't do what?"

"Start a nation. Like it or not, you are the leader of the Monoecion Nation and you are going to have to act like it. You can't solve each person's problem by yourself. You need to deal with the top issues and organization and you need to deal with it now. Pull a staff together and delegate. Right now you need someone to monitor the legal aspects of the laws being passed and be the watchdog on the government. I'd be proud to fill that position if you want me."

"I don't know what to say," said Christine. "Of course I want you for the job but can you get away to do it?"

"I notified the firm that I'm taking a leave of absence. As of this morning, I'm all yours. Now, who else do you have?"

"No one yet. Give me a chance," said Christine. "I just decided to accept this role three days ago!"

"Three days wasted," said Ben. "Let's get a staff built. Who do you need and what have you got to choose from?"

"Well, the first thing we have to do is evaluate a reservation site. That's a task I know nothing about." Christine thought for a moment. "What I need is someone with an engineering background." Christine started digging through a stack of mail. "I know it's in here," she muttered. "Yes!" She held a letter from Robin Willey who had written asking for advice on a job discrimination case with the engineering firm who fired her. She was a mechanical engineer with nine years of experience, the last five with an architectural and engineering firm. The firm fired her when they found out she was a Monoecion. The company claimed it was because of job performance and had nothing at all to do with her "problem."

"Perfect," said Ben. "Now call her, check her out and see if she will fit in. If she sounds good then tell her to get her tail up here and help you. She won't win a job discrimination case anyway, she may as well help you build a new nation."

"Just like that," said Christine, "out of the blue, say 'hey, your suit is a lost cause so come here and work for another lost cause.'"

"Honesty is the best policy," replied Ben.

"Show's what you know," said Christine as she picked up the phone. At first Robin was reluctant when Christine asked her to come to Washington but her husband convinced her to go for it. Robin realized that she and her family would end up on the reservation since she had no intention of having the required surgery. She figured it would be better to be one of the organizers than one of the huddled masses that would be shipped in. Two days after she received Christine's call, she was in DC at work on the site inspection procedures.

Wednesday, September 11

Dorothy Joyner, a business administration type who had done volunteer work in several local and state election campaigns, filled the bill for the economics advisor. She was trying to keep her head above water doing independent consulting after she and her whole department were laid off. The firm she had worked for supplied services to major Department of Defense contractors who were affected by the latest round of defense department cuts. Dorothy called Christine offering her services, just wanting to help in whatever way possible. Dorothy knew that Christine had become the focal point of the resistance movement to the government's sterilization program because of the media coverage she had received. She hadn't expected Christine to put her to work the instant she called. Christine asked her to create an information clearing house that Monoecions could contact for the latest updates, sort of a web based hot line to counter what Fenton was planning in the public service announcements.

Christine had just hung up the phone when she received a call from Todd Lindell. "Hello, Mrs. Landis. I need to talk with you concerning the reservation site. Do you have a few minutes?"

"Of course. Did you want to meet at your office?" asked Christine.

"No, that won't be necessary. I think we can cover this over the phone. Are you interested in touring one of the reservation sites?"

Christine was suspicious. It was exactly what she asked for and it seemed far too easy to get. "Is this the current front runner?"

"At this point in time it is," answered Lindell.

"Is it just me or can the rest of my staff come along?" asked Christine.

"We would like to limit it to six people." Lindell knew her staff numbered three and he wanted everyone there. "There are also a few requirements. First, there will be a complete news blackout. That means you and your staff will not be available for comment while on site or be able to call out to anyone. Second, you will prepare a preliminary review of the site and submit it to COMA within one week of your arrival."

"Will we have complete access to the site and all buildings?" asked Christine.

"Absolutely," confirmed Lindell. "Now there are many states who are already saying 'not in my back yard' so you cannot reveal the purpose of this trip to anyone outside your staff and immediate family. We don't want a leak that will make this process any more difficult than it already is."

Christine agreed to the conditions and set the departure for early Saturday morning. She then called Dorothy Joyner back and asked if she could go to the proposed reservation site in three days. Dorothy agreed and arrangements were made to get together for a planning session on Friday.

Even though they would have to keep the site a secret until it was officially announced by COMA, Christine jumped at the chance to speed the process along. She wanted the site open now as a refugee center to protect Monoecions who were in danger. Murder and assault of Monoecions had become so common, it was hardly newsworthy. Christine was convinced the sooner the reservation was opened, the more lives that could be saved.

The rules were strict, there was to be no communication to the outside world while they were on site. They would be flown there on military transport but would not be told where they had been until the site was announced to the general public. Christine started making plans with her team. Robin and Dorothy could make it but Ben had promised his wife a weekend away in New England. He apologized but said he couldn't disappoint his wife.

Christine thought this would be an excellent opportunity to get to know each other and to lay plans for the future. There was one task assigned to everyone. Christine pulled out a piece of paper and wrote a simple question. "How do we communicate without letting Uncle Sam know everything we talk about?" She then spoke out loud. "We all need to think about this one. Until we find a solution, this business is going to be very difficult." Robin and Ben nodded in agreement.

Robert disliked the whole mess. It seemed that the phone was in use sixteen hours a day. There was a steady flow of people coming and going at all hours, the living room and study were converted into offices, even the media was welcome. Robert had tried his best to get the family back into a routine, keep it ordinary to discourage the media and now Christine was trying to stir them up again.

All the while, the Feds were taking a great interest in Robert's past business dealings, especially the United Technologies stock transaction. When he tried to talk to Christine about it, she was always too busy to listen. Robert began to feel that she was leaving him on his own, that she thought her problems were more important than his. It had been the subject of a major blowup on Wednesday night which put him in a foul mood to have to sit through one more session with investigators on Thursday morning. As the investigators left his office Todd Lindell arrived. "I was just on my way to lunch. Can we meet back here in an hour?" asked Robert. "I really need a break for a few minutes."

"Sure," said Todd. "No problem. But I've got a better idea. Why don't you let me buy you lunch and we can talk then?"

The tone of voice that Lindell used made it clear that Robert was expected to agree. "OK. Up for Italian?" asked Robert. "There's a good one down the block. In walking distance and it beats fighting the traffic." Robert wanted to establish some control by picking the place to eat, plus it was expensive. If the government was going to ruin his lunch, they were going to pay.

"Your call. Lead the way." After they were out of the building and on their way down the sidewalk, Lindell started the required small talk, the introduction to any negotiation, asking about the kids.

When Lindell asked how Christine's efforts were coming in her new role as leader of the Monoecions, Robert had a hard time hiding his irritation. "Oh, she's going to town. She has three people on staff already and she's trying to set a new record for time on the phone."

Todd picked up on the anger and smiled to himself. After they were seated and had their drinks delivered, Lindell got down to business. "Senator Fenton told me that you were having a few problems with the Securities Exchange Commission investigation and thought that maybe I could help you out."

"Oh, I see. And what form would this help take?"

"I'm sure the commission will be glad to clear a man who has evidence that there was no wrong doing. Especially a man who was cooperating with the ongoing FBI investigation of the Monoecion activities." Todd picked up his drink and took a sip. "I think we could make those investigators disappear in no time. It's only fair. This mess certainly wasn't your fault. Hell, she didn't even tell you until she was forced to."

Robert sat with his hands wrapped around his drink. "And just what would I have to do to be considered a cooperative innocent bystander?"

"That's the easy part, just have a lunch with me every once in a while, answer some simple questions that we could get the answers to ourselves if we tried hard enough. You'd just be saving the taxpayer a few dollars."

"When do I have to make a decision?"

This could be a touchy point. They needed Robert on their side by Saturday when the first Public Service Announcement was aired. "We really need that answer soon. If the investigation into your financial deals yields solid evidence of wrongdoing, even the Senator can't help you. As long as nothing is proven yet, we can still act. Think about it but make it quick."

During lunch, the conversation went back to the things that Robert missed so much, things that used to be so important to him. They talked about football, cars, and the legs on the waitress serving the other table. All the while, Robert's mind kept returning back to the offer.

After they finished eating, Lindell paid the check and said "Well, are you ready?"

Robert replied "Yes, I think I am."

The FBI agent tried his best to explain his position to Senator Fenton and Todd Lindell. He had been trying to do so for fifteen minutes. "I know you disagree with the investigation results but the facts remain. We have thoroughly checked out the director, the cameramen, and anyone else who had the slightest chance of passing any information concerning the camera shots to Mrs. Landis. We are convinced that none of them are involved."

"What did your experts say about it after watching the tape?" asked Fenton.

"They were all convinced that she was cued on the camera change and that it was unlikely that the smile and camera tracking was a coincidence," he said with frustration. "But those same experts also agreed that no one in the CNN crew was involved and that no one else could have given the cue because of the timing."

"Then what do you suggest happened?"

"Senator, that's what we have been asking ourselves all day. We don't have an answer for you. One explanation we have come up with is the possibility of Mrs. Landis wearing a radio receiver on her body that could be used to send her inaudible signals, like Morse code. It could be hidden in her watch or somewhere on her body. Someone watching the broadcast from outside the building could signal her at the proper moment."

Fenton leaned forward and ask in a low conspiratorial whisper "Did you and your partner come up with any other possibilities?"

The FBI man looked uncomfortable. "Yes, we did. We thought that if their telepathy was more accurate than they let on, then that could have been used."

"Is there some reason that you weren't going to mention this hypothesis?" asked the Senator.

"Yes sir. We have no evidence to indicate it to be worthy of serious consideration."

"Thank you," said the Senator. "I trust I will get a copy of the report and any follow-up that becomes available. If there is nothing else, you may go." The agent left the office but Todd stayed. "Well, what do you think?" the Senator asked Lindell.

"I think she was cued. I'm sure of it. I just don't know how she was cued."

"And the telepathy theory?"

"Senator, I think it's the most probable of the options."

Fenton sat quietly for a moment, lost in thought. "You know what that would mean? People who could communicate over any distance with no equipment necessary. A spy could pass every piece of information and never take a chance of being caught."

"They can be caught, just like all spies can be caught," said Lindell. "You simply bait the trap with the right information and wait for it to show up at the other end of the pipeline. If we isolate these Monos and they find out about the 'announcements', we have our proof."

"And speaking of isolating, how are our negotiations going with Robert Landis?"

Todd nodded. "I think we can count on his support. The only problem I have now is that Ben Davis and his wife were planning a weekend getaway and told Christine he wouldn't be able to make the party."

"I don't like that. Davis is far too sharp to have wandering around free next week. He knows how to use the media and won't hesitate to call in old favors for the coverage. We need him on the trip to the reservation."

"Don't worry," Todd said. "We have the situation in hand. He should be on the plane Saturday morning."

"Just in case, make sure Harry is kept up to date and has a contingency plan together."

Todd felt a cold chill with the mention of that name. He squirmed in his chair a bit. "OK. I'll brief him."

The Reservation

Chapter 22

Friday, September 13

Friday morning Ben came in Christine's front door at the usual 8:00 AM. The house had become "the office" in everyone's mind and was treated as such. Ben would simply walk in, sit down in one of the makeshift work areas and start in. This morning he went straight for the boss. "Need some more company on your trip?"

"Don't tell me that you backed out on your sweet wife. You, sir, are a wife abuser and as such will not be allowed to accompany us." Christine was half-serious. She did not want Ben to become so involved as to ignore his family obligations, although she could never see Ben doing that.

Ben crossed the room and slipped her a note. "It's nothing like that, I promise you. The hotel that we were booked in called yesterday evening to confirm that we were still coming. When we said yes, they explained that because of an error, they overbooked this weekend and offered us an extra night's stay at no additional charge if we could reschedule. And you know Rosemary, the bargain hunter queen. She accepted on the spot."

Christine picked up Ben's note from the pile of letters on her desk. They were positive the house was bugged for sound but they doubted that it was wired with cameras. Just the same, when they were playing to the microphone they took extra precautions. Ben's note read

This stinks to high heaven. This is a setup. They want the whole team together next week. Any idea why? Plane crash to get rid of us all at once maybe. That would be too obvious and we don't have enough organization yet to be a threat. Maybe they want to detain us, but they don't need to have us all together to do that. They could arrest me in New Hampshire as well as here or at the reservation. I can't figure it out.

Christine kept her poker face on. "Well, since it's with the understanding that you'll spend an extra day vacationing with your wife, and soon, I guess it's OK if you want to go with us. Myself, I think she's trying to get rid of you permanently by sending you off with three women to spend a week at an undisclosed location. Sounds like she's putting together grounds for a divorce case." She wrote a few lines on the back of his note

"Not a chance," said Ben. "No one else would put up with her cold feet in bed at night. I'll call 'Fido' and make the arrangements." Fido had become Todd Lindell's nickname among the team.

"When you have a chance, check out this letter. We might be able to help if we can still reach her." Christine handed the letter and note to Ben who went to his work area and started his morning ritual.

While preparing his coffee, he looked at Christine's comments on the back of his original note.

I don't like it. I think you need to find a good excuse to stay away from us. This trip could prove fatal. Then again we may be overestimating our importance and this is nothing but a coincidence. Seems most likely they are trying to contain us for some purpose, keep us out of public contact. Is something new being introduced in Congress?

Ben wished he knew the answer. All he knew right now was that the government wanted them all to be together on Saturday morning and he was going to make damned sure it didn't happen.

It was noon when Dorothy Joyner arrived in a small silver Mazda. As she approached the house she saw the car parked down the street. She went past the driveway and stopped, pushed the transmission in reverse and quickly backed up the driveway, stopping with her bumper inches away from the garage door.

Robin heard the car pull in the drive and looked out the window. "That's odd," she said. "Someone just backed up your drive."

"I think I know who it is. I'm expecting a visitor after lunch."

Dorothy got out of her car, grabbed a briefcase from the back seat and came to the front door where Robin waited. "Hello, I'm here to see Mrs. Landis." She handed her business card to Robin as she shook her hand.

Robin motioned her inside. "You can leave your things here for the moment. I'll take you in."

Dorothy made no motion to put her case down. "If you don't mind, I'd rather keep my things with me."

Ben stood and joined Robin. "We need to check your bag then. There's been a number of death threats. Do you mind?"

"No, I understand. She opened her case and Ben began to inspect the contents.

Christine stepped into the room. "Don't bother Ben. She's all right." Ben gave Christine a concerned look over his shoulder. "Care to explain why you parked you car that way in the drive? I believe my friends think it's for a fast getaway."

Dorothy looked a bit embarrassed. "I'm sorry, I didn't mean to alarm you. I figured that if I parked that way, the Feds outside wouldn't be able to identify me with my license plate. I thought I'd be here for a while and it would irritate the hell out of them not knowing for sure who I was."

"What's to keep them from creeping up and getting your vehicle ID number off your dash?"

"Oh, no," said Dorothy with a sly smile. "I shoved a rag up there before I got here. I checked it when I got out, can't see a thing. They'll just have to wait until I leave."

Christine held her hand out to Dorothy. "Hi. I'm Christine Landis. I knew there was something special about you when we talked." Christine gave her a quick orientation. As she spoke, she wrote notes to fill in the gaps of the conversation. She showed her the file system while writing a note.

We are sure the entire building is bugged. Don't let it bother you, just don't say anything you don't want the FBI to hear. We communicate all important information by hand written note in small print so cameras can't pick it up. We then burn all the notes at the end of the day in the fireplace and flush the ashes. All the important files are kept in encrypted form on the hard drive of my computer.

The four of them sat at the "conference" table, Christine's dining room table to organize their strategy for the site evaluation. "I doubt we will have much say in the approval process unless the site is totally ridiculous, like a nuclear waste dump. Most Americans think the commission is doing a fine job according to the latest poll, so unless the site is stupid we will probably have to accept it. The first thing we will need to check is the existing buildings. Robin, that is going to be your job."

"We are going to need five types of facilities to start with, housing, medical, offices, educational, and manufacturing. The list is in order of importance as the refugees come in. I'll be checking the structural integrity of the buildings, fire safety, insulation, etc., as best I can by myself." Robin looked at her list. "What I'm most concerned with is the condition of the HVAC equipment."

Ben and Christine looked at Robin with blank faces. "What is HVAC?" asked Ben.

"Oh, sorry. Heating, ventilation and air conditioning. That's the most likely equipment to be damaged, that and the electrical wiring. Since we don't know the last occupants of the buildings or how long they've been empty, or even if they are empty, I can't plan much past this." Robin was nervous about the task she had in front of her. She knew she was completely unqualified to do the job correctly but Christine had told her that she was eminently more qualified than anyone else on the team. "I'll also need to check out the waste treatment and water sources. I checked a few books out of the library to bone up on the areas I'm weakest in. I'll do my best."

Dorothy spoke up. "How are the people coming to the facility, will they be brought in at a reasonable rate or will we have a population of two million next week?"

"We have no idea," said Christine. "Don't plan on any favors but do plan on bureaucratic red tape. That will slow things down most of all. I want the reservation open as soon as possible to accept refugees, Monoecions in danger. After that we can only hope that the flow is one we can handle." Christine lowered her voice and became deadly serious. "We may find we're the only ones in the reservation. I'm sure the government will make the sterilization process as attractive as it can and make life in the reservation as hard as it dares."

"What are we going to do for our own organization?" asked Dorothy. "What is our government going to be?"

"A dictatorship for right now." Dorothy gave Christine a shocked look. "This is the way it is. The US government has decided that I am the spokesperson for the

Monoecions and that is that. Until we have enough people in the reservation to hold elections, I'm in charge. This can change at the drop of a hat if the government changes its mind. I wasn't thrilled about it myself."

"So where do we start?" asked Ben.

"Has anyone here ever started a government before?" Christine looked around the table going from face to face. "I didn't think so. Let's start by bringing up an idea and let everyone throw rocks at it. I'll start. I think we need to organize this like a business. We can't afford dead weight at the top so it needs to be flat with as little management as possible. We would have a chairman of the board and up to ten board members. After that, I think it gets unwieldy."

"It sounds good but the population won't be employees," injected Dorothy. "The management staff will have no direct authority over the people."

"The government has no direct authority over its people beyond what the people grant," said Robin. "The people will follow as long as they know they can change the leadership if they don't like it. They'll all be Americans, used to democracy and elections, not a mob."

"Maybe," said Ben, "but they will be coming out of comfortable middle-class homes for most of them and they may find themselves in a barbed wire fenced tent city. They are going to give you very little time to make things better. Just look at what happened inside Russia when it came to economic reform. The people supported their leadership at the start but they expected results. When it didn't come fast enough, support evaporated like the morning fog."

"Chances are that I will not be successful in creating the Garden of Eden out of what ever hellhole they put us in," said Christine. That means that I, and all of my cabinet, will probably be drummed out of office in disgrace inside the first year. Are you all still sure you want to throw your lot in with me?"

"I'm in," said Robin.

Ben nodded. "Me too but I don't count. I'll be on the outside as your lobbyist. I won't have to take the heat you folks will."

Dorothy looked around the table. "I've only been here for two hours but I like what I see. It beats the hell out of sitting at home worrying. Count me in."

"Congratulations, you all now qualify as certifiably insane. Now let's get to work and design a nation."

On the way home, Ben stopped off at a convenience store to use the phone. He called the lodge in New Hampshire where he had his reservations. "Hamilton's Inn. How can I help you?"

"I was looking for a room for this weekend, a little peace and quiet now that the color tourists have left. Have anything available?"

The clerk was apologetic. "No, I'm afraid not. We're booked solid through the weekend." Ben began to think that maybe he was jumping at shadows. The desk clerk added "We had rooms up until yesterday but there's some corporate shindig going on and they rented every room in the place for the weekend."

"Bingo," Ben muttered under his breath.

"What was that sir?" asked the clerk.

"Oh, nothing," said Ben. "Is there another inn you would recommend that has space available?"

"Sure. I just checked a few minutes ago at the Carriage Road Inn. They have several rooms available. Would you like their number?"

Ben took down the number and made a reservation there in his wife's maiden name. With his cover story complete, Ben headed for home.

Saturday, September 14

The plan was for them to meet at the airport at 8:30 in the morning. Considering traffic on a Saturday morning would be light, Christine probably wouldn't leave until around 7:15. Ben called her at 7:00 o'clock sharp. His wife already had the bags packed and stacked by the front door for their weekend in New Hampshire. "I thought about it last night on the way home and I decided to try to find a place for this weekend. And I am proud to report I was successful. I found a room at a nice little inn not too far from our regular lodgings so I won't be able to join you. I hope it's not a major problem for you."

Christine played her part well. "No, I understand Ben. You were primed and ready. I knew you were really disappointed yesterday when you told me you weren't going on your trip. I'm glad it worked out for you."

"I'll be back Monday night so it won't be until Tuesday when I get to the office," said Ben.

"Don't worry about the office. I'll try to call you if I can but they made it clear that secrecy was the first order of business. Have a good weekend and I'll see you in about a week."

"Good luck, Christine." There was a very worried overtone in Ben's voice.

"Watch your backside Counselor," Christine replied. Both were sure that one of them was in mortal danger. The line went dead. Ben picked up the bags and said "Let's go, Rosy, we need to move fast if we're going to catch that flight." They got in the car, heading to the airport by the most direct route; all the time watching his rear view mirror trying to identify the tail that he was sure was following them. The traffic slowed to a crawl when they were a mile back from the airport exit. Ben could just see the car with the two plainclothes police that had been following at a safe distance several car lengths back in his rear view mirror. They had tried to move in closer but the traffic had gone bumper to bumper and blocked them off. Ben toyed with the idea of losing them and driving to New England just to irritate them but decided against it. He stuck with his original plan and took the airport exit after inching his way past the automotive carnage that was the cause of the slow down.

He parked in a long term lot and took his time collecting his bags. He saw the familiar car pull in the lot as he and his wife made their way toward the terminal building. If his flight was on time they would be in Boston in an hour and a quarter and then on to New Hampshire. As they sat at the gate, Ben noticed one of the two men keeping an eye on them. He figured the other was on the phone making arrangements to have the tail picked up on the other end of the flight. As usual the flight was delayed and they arrived an hour late, by which time Hertz had rented it's last fullsize car. Instead, they gave Ben a Lincoln Town Car. He expressed his disappointment but decided to suffer through with it.

Christine tried to call Mr. Lindell seconds after Ben had called her. Unfortunately he didn't pick up on his office number or his cell. She would have liked to have heard his voice to gauge his reaction to the news that Ben wouldn't be coming with them. As it was now, Lindell would know long before Christine could get to him.

She sat down with her girls and gave them a last few parting words as all mothers do when they leave home. She just wished she felt more confident that she was coming home. Something was brewing and it irritated her to have no idea what it was. She ran through the list of chores one more time in the hopes that when she came home in a week she would find at least half of them done to her satisfaction. One at a time, she gave each a hug and a kiss.

Robert sat in the kitchen, sipping a cup of coffee. He had tried to talk her into staying home, just say "to hell with the whole thing" and stay home. When Christine said she couldn't, the same old argument broke out again. Now she came in and sat at the table across from him.

Robert put on a worn smile. "Have a good trip. Do what you have to do and come home."

"If I do what I have to do, that place will need to become my home, at least until the human race regains its sanity."

"Or you regain yours," he replied with more than a hint of sarcasm. "Go on. The girls will be OK here. I'll see you in a week." He leaned over and kissed her on the cheek like he would have kissed a corpse, turning away as soon as he had done it.

Christine stood and gave him a formal, "Goodbye." She picked up her bags and went out to the car where Dorothy and Robin were waiting. She couldn't get over the terrible feeling of loss that clung to her like the smell of smoke to a sweater.

Dorothy started her car and they headed to Andrews Air Force base where Lindell was waiting for them. The drive was uneventful at this time in the morning. No self respecting government bureaucrat would be on the road before eight AM on a Saturday. Christine rode shotgun supposedly to direct Dorothy who was unfamiliar with Washington's roads but mostly Christine sat silently and stared out her window. Dorothy made several attempts to draw Christine into a conversation with little success. She did manage to get basic directions but that was the extent of the communication. Once she got on the Capitol Beltway going in the right direction, Dorothy followed the signs to the front gate of the base. A sentry in his little hut greeted them and asked them their business. Dorothy identified the people in the car and explained they were here to meet Todd Lindell.

The sentry checked his clipboard. "I have here that there is to be a fourth, a Benjamin Davis. Will he be arriving in a separate vehicle?"

Christine leaned across and explained "Ben won't make this trip. He just called me this morning to cancel."

"OK then, just pull over to the side and there will be an escort by in a minute to lead you to the parking area." The sentry motioned them to a row of parking spaces near the visitors center.

After a few minutes wait, a van arrived with a military driver and Todd Lindell in the front passenger seat. He hopped out of the van and came over to the car. "All set to go?"

"Yes we are," answered Christine. "What do we do with the car?"

"Just follow us and we'll guide you to the reserved parking area. Then you can put your things in the van and the driver will take us to the plane." Todd looked around the inside of the car. "Where's Mr. Davis?"

Christine seemed to get more irritated than usual dealing with Lindell. "He couldn't make it, he decided to go off for the weekend with his wife after all. He found another inn with space available. He called this morning."

Lindell put a frown on his face. "That's too bad. I think he could have added significantly to your team's efforts." He seemed to brighten a bit. "Shall we go?"

"How long are we going to have to keep up this charade?" Christine's frustration came through loud and clear. "I'm really getting tired of this crap."

Lindell looked genuinely surprised. "I'm sorry, I don't understand the question."

"Enough! I know that within five minutes of Ben calling me this morning, you were informed that he wouldn't be on this trip. We know our phones are tapped. We know our house is bugged. Why don't you just cut the crap."

Todd snickered, shaking his head. "You have a great imagination. Obviously you consider your conversations much more important than we do." He stood up straight and headed back to the van. "Follow us please."

The van led them to a parking lot where they left the car. The women loaded their bags into the van, noticing that the van driver didn't lift a finger to help, not even open the back door. They then drove across the base to a complex of hangers and stopped next to a Gulf Stream jet. Two enlisted men and two officers waited by the open door of the plane. "All aboard," called out Lindell. "Just carry your bags over to the door and they will be loaded in the baggage compartment for you."

He led them over to the officers who introduced themselves as their guides for the tour of the reservation. "I'm Captain Murray and this is Lieutenant Ackermann. We will do our best to show you around and answer your questions concerning the site."

Christine introduced Robin and Dorothy. "When will we learn of the site location?"

"Not until we get there. Everything will be explained in detail then but please do not discuss it until then," said Captain Murray sternly.

Christine noticed that Lindell carried no bags to the plane. "Aren't you coming along?"

"No, I'm afraid my schedule won't allow it. I'm sure Captain Murray will be able to provide everything you need." Lindell turned his back to the women and waved to the officers. "Have a good trip. The Senator will need a full report on your return. Goodbye, gentlemen." He then walked back to the waiting van without another word.

"Shall we board?" Captain Murray motioned to the open door. Christine sat across from Robin, Dorothy sat behind Christine. The seats did not seem to match the airplane. Most of the small corporate size jets that Christine had been on were equipped with a bit more plush interiors. These seats appeared to be straight out of a short haul commuter airliner.

As they boarded, they were relieved of all of their carryon items for inspection. The inspection also included the usual wanding except the wand looked different than the ones they were used to seeing at the security gates in commercial airports. It seemed to beep at every piece of metal and electronics they had. In the end, the only items they were allowed to carry onboard were a pen and notepad. After they fastened their seat belts, Lieutenant Ackermann asked them for their watches. "I'm sure you ladies would never consider hiding any fancy electronic gadgets in these but we need to be on the safe side." They removed their watches and gave them to him as the plane taxied out to the runway. "Thank you. Now sit back and relax. It's going to be a long flight. I hope you brought a book because there is no in-flight movie." He smiled and went back to his seat.

The Lieutenant was right. It was a long and uneventful flight. The sky was overcast much of the way and even when it wasn't, Christine could only tell they were moving west. She spent the first hour speaking with Robin and Dorothy, trying to lay plans for their week but the noise level deterred extended conversations. It didn't take long for two of them to drop off to sleep for lack of anything else to do. Only Dorothy stayed awake, reading a political science text book to try to get a grasp on what they were doing. Nation building was not in her previous job description.

After what seemed to be days in the uncomfortable seats, the Lieutenant again returned to the back of the plane. This time he carried three sack lunches. "I'm sorry our lunch service is a little short of elegance but hopefully it will keep you alive until we can get to the reservation site. There the food will be worse." He laughed but knew he was probably being more truthful than he wanted to be. "I hope Cokes are all right, we don't have any coffee." They all nodded sleepily and gratefully accepted the lunches. He returned a minute later with three cans of Coke.

"How much longer?" asked Robin.

"Lunch and a short nap should do it. We are about two-thirds of the way." He moved back to the front seat next to the Captain. He was a little optimistic on his estimate. It required the reading of two magazines to go along with the nap before they were ready to land. Once again he came back, this time requesting that they close their window covers.

"Are you going to blindfold us when we land too?" asked Christine.

"No, it's just that many buildings have signs on their roofs that could be used for identification." He made a closing motion with his fingers. Christine pushed the blind down with flair. He nodded his approval and moved on closing all the windows at the unoccupied seats.

The experience of coming in to land without a height reference was very unsettling. Every dip of a wing felt like a death spiral. When the wheels finally did touch the asphalt, Robin screamed right along with the tires. She looked sheepishly around the plane but Christine and Dorothy just returned supportive smiles. Without a reference for her eyes, the landing had left Christine feeling nauseous. She focused on a point on the seat in front of her while the plane taxied for many minutes. They could clearly hear other traffic taking off and landing.

Captain Murray turned and addressed them. "The ground crews here have been instructed not to talk to you. Do not take offense if they seem abrupt, they have been given specific orders and this trip is top secret until the site is announced. So please do not talk to them, just follow instructions. We will be moving from the plane to a helicopter for the last leg of the journey. While in the helicopter, please do not identify yourselves, or the fact that you are Monoecions, to the pilot or copilot." Actually, the crews had been leaked a cover story to explain the secret movements. They were convinced that they were carrying a topnotch team of language experts to act as translators at a secret trade meeting with the Ukrainians.

The plane came to a stop and the engines wound down. The plane vibrated slightly as someone opened the baggage compartment and removed the luggage but no one made a move to open the exit door. The air quickly became foul in the cramped passenger compartment, made worse by the claustrophobic effect of the closed windows. Just when Christine thought she couldn't stand it anymore, the door opened and fresh air and sunshine flowed into the plane. As the occupants crouched out of the plane, they were escorted by ground personal directly to the waiting helicopter.

"This isn't fair," said Dorothy. "I just want to walk around for a minute and stretch my legs."

"Sorry, ma'am. Orders." He firmly helped her into the chopper's open door.

The windows of the helicopter were covered with fabric obstructing the view of the outside world other than a limited view forward over the pilot's shoulder. As soon as they were all on board, the rotor cranked up and the door was closed. Once again they were airborne, skimming across the countryside to the, as yet, undisclosed site. "How long do we have to ride in this thing?" shouted Christine over the whap-whap-whap of the rotors.

"Not too long now," replied Captain Murray.

"I hope not, I can't take much more of this." If the seats on the plane were uncomfortable, these were out of Dante's Inferno. There was no way to sit on the hard bench seats without pain. She began to seriously consider staying at the reservation just to avoid the trip home. The "not too long" turned into an hour that seemed determined to last forever.

Finally the helicopter began its approach with all three Monoecions straining to catch a glimpse of what would become their new home. As the helicopter turned, they caught flashes of mountains and sparse forest in the distance. As the ground grew near, great clouds of dust swirled around the chopper, blinding them completely. Christine marveled that the pilot could maintain control as the craft made gentle contact with the ground and the rotor disengaged. After a minute, the dust began to clear and two enlisted men opened the door from the outside and helped everyone out. Once the passengers were clear, the pilot revved up the motor and took off. The helicopter was on the ground less than five minutes.

Christine shielded her face from the swirling dust as the helicopter climbed away. Again she waited as the breeze carried the dust away in a twisting cloud. In front of her was a small airport with a single runway. The helicopter had landed on the taxiway in front of two hangars. Off to her left was a short cement block control tower, a single story building with a glassed in room on top. Surrounding them were layered hills of yellow, orange and brown. Multicolored stone outcroppings jutted from the ground. The overall effect was quite beautiful and quite desolate.

This is when her body made it's wishes known in no uncertain terms. It had been hinting for the last forty-five minutes but had given up on being subtle. Christine motioned to one of the enlisted men, "Excuse me, but I really need a restroom."

"Yes, ma'am. There are facilities at the main base. We'll be there in about ten minutes," replied the corporal. He motioned for the private to collect the bags and load them in the van.

Christine tapped him on the shoulder. "No, I'm afraid you don't understand. I need a restroom. Is there anything available here."

"Oh." His face took on a thoughtful cast. "The hangars are locked up and I didn't bring the keys..." then his face brightened, "but I do have the keys to the control building. It has running water." He looked over at the Captain with the unspoken question. The Captain nodded his head not bothering to hide his feelings of disdain for her obvious weakness. "Follow me," said the corporal and he strode off towards the control tower.

Robin fell in step along with Christine. "If you don't mind, I'll join you in this expedition."

"Not at all, Stanley. Please do."

Robin gave Christine a strange look. "Stanley?"

"Stanley and Livingstone. They explored Africa in the eighteen hundreds. Didn't they teach you anything other than engineering at that school?"

"They tried their damnedest to but it just didn't seem to stick."

They walked in silence to the building. The corporal climbed the three steps to the landing, sorted through his keys and unlocked the door. There were no windows on the ground floor but light poured in from the open stairs leading to the control room above. The building appeared to be square, about twenty-five foot on a side. He stepped inside and turned on the lights, looking around the floor carefully. "Use caution when you enter buildings that haven't been opened for a while. They have the bad habit of collecting unwanted wildlife, if you know what I mean."

Christine and Robin immediately joined him in scanning the floor. Christine wasn't sure that she still had to go as bad as she earlier thought. "What kind of wildlife are you referring to?"

"Oh, the usual. Mostly centipedes and scorpions but sometimes a rattler will find its way in." The lower floor was one big room with four doors against the back wall. Two were equipment closets, the third was marked MEN and the fourth WOMEN. The corporal, satisfied that nothing was out of order in the main room, opened the bathroom door and flipped on the light. Christine and Robin stayed close to the exit in case a fast getaway was called for. The corporal stepped back out after a few moments. "The room looks clear," and motioned to the door.

"Thank you," said Christine and strode in with all the confidence she could muster. Once inside the tiny bathroom with the door closed, Christine performed her own search of the premises. Satisfied that he was right, she relieved herself in the single stool. When she came out, Robin went in. "I assume there were many more men than women on the base," Christine observed when Robin returned. "We will probably have an excess availability of urinals. That could be one of our first exports." They laughed and left the room, turning out the lights on their way. The corporal led the way back to the waiting van.

They loaded up and set off for the main base, three miles away. The captain remained reserved along the way. When Christine asked him a question regarding the facility, he explained that everything would be explained when they reached the compound. Everyone rode in silence, patiently waiting. As the van crested a small rise, the base was visible below. There was a collection of what appeared to be apartment buildings along the road and then a few hundred yards up was the main concentration of buildings.

The van pulled up to a stop in front of one of the barracks and everyone climbed out. Captain Murray cleared his throat and said, "Welcome to Hastings Army Training Center. I'm authorized to tell you anything you need to know to evaluate the site and begin your plans for it's conversion to the Monoecion reservation. If you will bear with me for a few minutes, I will give a quick overview of the facility.

"The base is approximately seventy square miles in a rectangle ten miles east and west by seven miles north and south. We are currently at the main base, located about a mile from the west boundary of the base, which has all the housing, administration, clinic, and so on. We just came from the airstrip three miles south east of here. Just north of here about two miles is the original weather station. East of here about three miles is the artillery repair and storage facility.

"To give you a little history of the base, it was first started as a weather station back in 1938. It was used for those purposes until the beginning of World War II when it was used as an artillery range. The first repair facility was built close to the current site east of here. The base became a permanent training center in the sixties and seventies with the building of the facilities where we are currently standing. The base tripled its size by 1983 when the airstrip was added and it was used for a practice range for helicopter gun ships working in concert with standard field artillery units. The base was closed about two years ago and is now just operated by a security staff until the government decides what to do with it. Obviously, the government has decided what to do with it. That's why you folks are here.

"What I suggest is that we start with a short walking tour of the main base today before it gets too dark, have dinner, then get you an office set up so that tomorrow morning you will be ready to get started. So, if you would like to stow your things and take a few minutes to get cleaned up and put on your walking shoes, we'll reconvene in twenty minutes right here." With that, he turned and walked off, Lieutenant Ackermann being drawn along in his wake.

The two enlisted men started to pick up the bags that were piled on the ground by the van. "I think you will find the barracks quite comfortable," said the corporal. "It was vacated last month so it didn't take much to clean it up. We told them it would be a lot easier to open up one of the base housing units instead of a building designed to house forty people but you know the army. That would have made too much sense."

"I'm sure we will be just fine. Thank you, gentlemen, for your assistance." Christine picked up her own bags. Robin and Dorothy followed suit. The corporal led them into the barracks, showed them where to store their things, pointed out the bathroom and showers, and excused himself.

Christine flopped down on her bunk exhausted. Robin sat down on the bunk next to her. "Do you get the impression that our Captain Murray has a broomstick shoved up his ass?"

Christine leaned up on an elbow and gave Robin a surprised "What?"

Robin was flustered for a second. "Sorry. Old habits die hard. I grew up in these places. My father was a career officer. To the rest of the world that phrase translates to Captain Murray is a bit too formal with us don't you think?"

Christine dropped back down on her back. "I didn't realize you had a military upbringing. And to answer your original question, yes, it does seem our Captain Murray has a broomstick shoved up his ass." They all giggled like girls at a slumber party. It seemed to help relieve some of the tension. Christine unzipped a bag and pulled out her brand new hiking boots, purchased for this trip, and started lacing them on. "I hope we don't have to cover too much ground today. After all those hours crammed into an airplane seat, my legs are so cramped I can hardly walk."

Robin had already finished tying up her well worn boots. She stood and started a series of stretching exercises. "Stand up and do a few of these," she said between stretches. "It will get your muscles loosened up so you won't cramp. Come on, I'll show you how."

"My God. Not only is she an army brat but she's a health freak too. We may have to rethink your appointment to the board if we keep uncovering this kind of information. By looking at your figure you probably shun cream-filled donuts."

"Guilty as charged, Madam Justice," intoned Robin. "Actually, my downfall is a fresh bagel smothered with cream cheese."

"Ah ha!" said Dorothy. "So you are human. I was beginning to wonder." The three of them did a few stretches and Robin ran in place for three minutes. They then went out to meet up with their tour guides who had already arrived.

"Where exactly are we, Captain Murray?" asked Christine.

"We are in Nevada, Mrs. Landis, fifty miles west of Elko." He pulled out a map and showed them the location on the map.

"What's the elevation here?" asked Robin.

"Just over a mile. Fifty-six hundred something I believe."

"So the nights are quite cold here, even at this time of the year," said Christine. "I take it we should carry a jacket with us."

"It wouldn't be a bad idea. Why don't you grab one now and we will get the show on the road."

While they got their jackets, Christine said "We are going to have to be able to handle winter weather in thirty days. They start a flow of refugees in here over the next two months and with a bad winter, this place will be hell."

"I think that's the plan," said Dorothy, "but what can we do, say we want a site in a southern California because the climate is better?"

"As we check this place over, keep notes on how we handle cold and snow. If the army can do it on this base, so can we. That is, as long as we can limit the flow of people." Christine led the group out and they began their tour. There were rows of barracks on the road. "How many men could be stationed here at one time?"

Lieutenant Ackermann answered that question. "At its peak, twenty thousand men were stationed here at one time but for the last years before the base closed there were less than five thousand."

"How much land is available for expansion outside the current site?" asked Dorothy.

"Why would any land be required outside this site?" the Captain asked. "I don't think any expansion would be necessary according to the figures we were given. The last estimates from COMA put your population at half what was originally estimated by your doctor Moore. That combined with the estimates that only one percent is expected to move here instead of having the corrective procedures, which places your peak population at forty thousand, less than 600 people per square mile as an end population."

"Let me explain to you what is really going to happen here." Christine ticked down the list of the most important points. "First, I accept the number of eight million for the total Monoecion population in the United States. That is probably quite accurate. Second, the estimate that only one percent will choose the reservation is off by a factor of fifty in our poll. Now even if we are off by a factor of five, we will still have ten percent. That's four hundred thousand, not forty. Third, they are not coming alone. Many will be bringing a spouse with them. That will add another fifty thousand. Can you fit two cities the size of Las Vegas in this camp? I don't think so. I don't think my figures are more accurate than yours but both cases are possible. That is why we are asking the question."

"To answer your question, Mrs. Landis, the government owns the land on all four sides of this base. What they intend to do with it is not known to me at this time so can we keep our discussions to this particular piece of land, please." Captain Murray could not hide his feelings of contempt for these creatures. As far as he was concerned, setting this land aside for them was enough. Put up a fence and turn it into a cage where they can fight out their own future. He didn't want to spend his tax dollars to support a bunch of freaks out to destroy mankind. "Now on this end of the compound are the support services. There is a waste treatment facility, a power substation , diesel backup generators and water storage." He shielded his eyes to the sinking sun. "Those buildings to the west are the base recreation facilities."

"What is the gallons per day rating on the waste treatment facility?" asked Robin.

"We will have to look that up and get back to you," said Captain Murray.

Lieutenant Ackermann flipped through his notebook for a few seconds. "Actually, it's rated at two hundred fifty thousand gallons per day maximum. I have all the utility ratings collected here if you'd like them. I assumed these would be the first figures you would need."

Robin noticed that Captain Murray was gritting his teeth but he said nothing. She guessed that the Lieutenant would catch hell later for being a smart ass and showing up his captain. "Is the water potable?"

"Not out of the waste treatment plant directly but it can be used for irrigation. Now if it were fed back into the water treatment system, it may meet federal specification, I'm not sure." Ackermann closed his notes and smiled confidently. It was then that he caught a glimpse of Murray's grim face and removed the smile from his own.

Robin made notes on the map that Lieutenant Ackermann had supplied to her earlier. "So those buildings over there are the entertainment end of town?" she asked pointing out the buildings that had been identified earlier.

"Yes, you could put it that way," said Ackermann. "That building is the theater, that one is the gym. Those were the base exchanges and commissary. And those buildings were the clubs."

"How much of the equipment is still intact?" asked Christine.

"Anything that is semi-permanent is still in place. The gas tanks and stoves are still in the mess kitchen but the movie projectors aren't in the theater. The phone wiring is still in place but the phones are all gone except the ones necessary for the security staff." Murray led the way as they walked on a little further back toward the center of the base.

The sun was just beginning to touch the horizon and the temperature was already dropping. "We are coming into the control center of the base. The police station is on this side. There are ten cells, each capable of holding four prisoners. The clinic is on the right. It's actually a small hospital. There are two operating rooms and space for twenty beds." Captain Murray stopped in front of the largest building on the base. "This is the HQ building and communications center. After we have something to eat, we will get you some office space. Is anyone hungry?"

"Starving," said Christine. The rest voiced their agreement.

"Well, follow me. There's a small lunch room/kitchen in here and one of the enlisted men was going to see what they could come up with." Captain Murray led them into the HQ building, through the reception area and down a hall. The odor of food greeted them as they approached the kitchen. "I'm afraid we will be getting the same food that the security personal get here, a poor imitation of TV dinners. But we do have a good supply of fresh fruit and juice. I also hear there is a good stock of Miller in the fridge."

The corporal they had met earlier had five dinners, heated, waiting on the counter when they came in the room. "Just grab one when you see what you like, or can stomach. To help choke it down, there's beer and soft drinks in the refrigerator over there."

They filed by, collected their dinner and silverware, and sat down at one of the tables in the lunch room. Christine and Dorothy selected a beer but Robin had a diet Coke. Dorothy snorted in disgust. "What's with you, girl? Do you live just to make us look bad?" Robin just smiled and ate her dinner.

"When will the site selection be announced?" asked Christine.

"The commission would like a written report from you by Thursday. If all goes well after that then it will be announced by Saturday, a week from today. Then you will be allowed to reestablish contact with the outside world. Until then, make the best use of your time here at the base."

After they finished eating, Lieutenant Ackermann took them to the offices that had been set aside for them. The three offices were all side by side, each with a window facing the main road in the front of the building. "I hope these will be satisfactory. There's an internal phone system and if you need any supplies, just ask."

"These are great," said Christine, "but there is one thing we do need. I would like one room where we can setup and work together. The individual offices are fine when we need to get off by ourselves to be able to think but most of the time we need each other in the same room. Basically, we need a war room."

"I know exactly what you mean. You get cut off when each person is in a separate office. Follow me." Ackermann lead her to a large office area that had a few folding tables setup against the walls. "How is this?"

"Perfect," said Christine. "It's close to the other offices and it is big enough for all three of us to setup without sitting on each other's lap. This will do fine."

"OK then, I'll leave you to get organized. If you need anything, just ask. You know where we're at. Breakfast is in the same lunchroom, 7:00 AM. See you then." Ackermann headed down the hall towards the office he had staked out for the duration.

Christine, Dorothy, and Robin set up their computers and supplies in the "war room" and planned the next day's activities. They decided on their basic schedule; morning for site investigation; regroup and short planning session after lunch followed by more site investigation until dinner; type up results after dinner; plan the next day until they can't stay awake. Repeat until they run out of time.

Ben pulled the big boat of a car onto Interstate 93 North and set the cruise control at seventy when the traffic thinned enough to use it. He and his wife played a game of pin the tail on the car. It was easy to play. They each picked out a car that they thought was their FBI tail. If that car pulled off or disappeared then the other person received a point. Ben was playing well. He was still on his original car but Rosemary was on her third by the time they were halfway to the inn at Glendale. When they arrived at the inn, the car that Ben had selected way back in Boston slowly cruised by looking for a place to park on the country road. "Next time," said Rosemary, "I get to chose first. That was the car I wanted."

Ben laughed and pulled the bags from the trunk. Their room had a sliding glass door opening onto a balcony overlooking Lake Winnipesaukee. "It's beautiful," she said. "I think I like this room more than our old one." Ever since the last of the kids had moved out, they made a habit of coming here every year for a weekend in the fall to get away from all the chaos of Washington. Having a long weekend away from the stress of the office helped settle and prepare them for the coming holidays. Only this year was different. The government had made it different.

Ben couldn't hide his concern. "I just wish I knew what they were up to. There has to be a reason they were so all fired up on having me at the reservation site with Christine and the others." He tried to shake it off. "My dear, I spy a rowboat for hire on the dock. Would you care to accompany me on a relaxing float?"

"I'd love to." Rosemary put on her sweater and picked up Ben's jacket.

"I won't need that," Ben said.

"That's what you say every time. Then when you get tired of rowing and stop for a while, you take a chill. I know you better than you think old man."

Ben conceded defeat. "Yeah, I do seem to remember that from last year."

"And the year before that and the year before that and..." They walked out to the dock, hand in hand.

Chapter 23

Sunday, September 15

Ben woke first the next morning. The sunshine was streaming in the windows, illuminating the dust particles which were performing an intricate ballet in the eddy currents of air. Ben lay for many minutes watching the dance, as fascinated as he had been as a child. Finally he could resist nature's call no more and put his feet to the floor. He quietly slipped into the bathroom and closed the door. Halfway through his shower, a set of cold hands made contact with his rib cage. "Good heavens woman. Don't do that!" he chastised.

"I'm sorry. I didn't mean to scare you," Rose apologized.

"You didn't scare me. I heard you come in. It's just that your hands are like ice. Are you trying to freeze me to death?"

"Give me a minute and I'll warm you up." She stepped into the shower and gave him a kiss that kept her promise. Ben finished up in the shower first and stepped out to dry off. Rosemary washed her hair, thinking how wonderful it would feel when Ben dried it. She loved the feeling of him playing with her hair. She listened to his electric razor as she worked her fingers through her hair, creating swirls of lather. Ben was already out of the bathroom by the time she rinsed off and stepped out. She brushed her teeth, imagining him turning the bed back and plugging in the hair dryer, and waiting for her, brush in hand, to send her to head massage heaven. When she opened the bathroom door, he was sitting on the end of the bed, towel still wrapped around his middle, remote control in hand. "What are you watching?" Her fantasy sharply shattered.

"I'm just checking the CNN headlines for any news of plane crashes or the like." Ben heard the disappointment in her voice. "It will just take a minute. Something like that would be in the headlines. Why don't you get out the hair dryer and your brush and I'll dry your hair as soon as the lead stories are over."

Rosemary understood. He was worried about his friends. She looked around for a nearby outlet and plugged in the hair dryer. True to his word, Ben turned off the set after the lead stories. If he had watched for another ten minutes, he would have heard that the government's public service announcements directed at Monoecions had started today. But by that time Ben was already caressing Rosemary's hair, sending tingles through her body with his expert brush and dryer work.

Later they went out for brunch and a walk along the beach. The weather was magnificent, light breezes and sunshine. When they ran out of beach, they walked the store fronts to see if there was anything new in the line of tourist traps. After checking out the usual antique shops and a stop at the candy factory they went back to the inn. Ben was feeling better than he had in a long time. Rosemary's peace and loving company healed him to his soul.

"Where do you want to eat dinner?" Ben stretched out on the bed as his wife freshened up in the bathroom. "Do you want Italian or Greek?"

"Are you sure I shouldn't dye my hair?" asked Rosemary as she poked her head out the bathroom door. "I mean, it sounded so noble when I was forty-two and had three gray hairs to say I'd never dye it. Now at fifty-two, it makes me look so much like my mother."

Ben looked up at his wife. "I'm confused here. Just what does gray hair and dye have to do with Italian restaurants, or any other kind for that matter?"

"That's easy. Don't you know how to follow a conversation? You asked about going out to a nice restaurant. This naturally made me think about dressing up and looking pretty for you even though you wouldn't notice. That caused me to look in the mirror and realize that the thing I have most in common with my mother is our hair color. Which in turn, prompted me to ask you about coloring my hair. Come on Ben, keep up."

"I'm sorry dear, sometimes I'm a little slow." Ben picked up the remote control. "At the risk of sounding redundant, do you want Italian or Greek?"

"That's easy dear, Chinese. There is a new one in Laconia that the woman at the front desk said was fantastic."

Ben muttered something under his breath that even he didn't understand and clicked on the TV and muted it. The TV was no longer on CNN, it was on the local CBS station. Obviously the maid was keeping up with her soaps as she went from room to room today. Being too lazy to find the channel guide that was somewhere in the room, he started flipping through the channels looking for CNN and at the same time looking for anything else that might be entertaining. He went through the whole loop once without finding it. He started another loop only faster. He was already past the station when the image sunk in enough to make him pause. He turned back to the station and there was Christine. Ben fumbled for the mute button, finally getting the sound back on.

"...call the number below. There will be trained people to assist you. Remember, it's not just for you, it's for all mankind." The image changed to a family eating at Pizza Hut.

Christine had a hard time adjusting to the time change. She woke up at five AM and struggled to return to sleep until six when she finally gave up. She got out of bed quietly and slipped into the shower room. The look and smell of the room took her back to high school gym class. It took a few minutes before the water warmed up enough to step into the stream but once it had, she savored the feeling of the hot water splashing over her body. She had to admit to herself that she was also a bit self-conscious about using a communal shower. The thought of taking a shower with a dozen other people was not a pleasant one but she would have to get used to it. It was going to be cramped living by the time the first ten thousand Monoecions moved in.

"Couldn't sleep?"

Christine jumped, startled by the intruder's voice. Robin came in the shower room and hung her towel on the rack. "I didn't see you coming," said Christine.

Robin smiled. "That's OK. My husband says I can be pretty scary in the mornings sometimes." Robin had her dark blond hair tied back in a pony tail. She walked naked across the shower room, soap and wash cloth in hand, and turned on a shower.

Christine noticed how Robin was at peace with her body. There was none of the nervous embarrassment that had surged through Christine when Robin came in. Her first thought was "if I had a body like that, I wouldn't be embarrassed either," but she knew that wasn't true. Christine knew she would feel the same way no matter how she looked. She carefully positioned her body trying to expose herself as little as possible. Christine stole quick glances at Robin as she washed her legs and shoulders, rivulets of soap foam waterfalling off her breast and streaming down her thighs. Robin's eyes caught Christine's as she looked at the younger woman. Suddenly Christine felt like she was six years old and had been caught with her hand in the cookie jar. She dropped her gaze in embarrassment, turned off the shower and hurried out of the shower room.

As she dried herself in the outer room, Robin came out. "I'm sorry," said Christine. "I didn't mean to offend you. I guess showering with a group will take some getting used to."

"No sweat," said Robin with a warm smile. "I grew up with it, living in temporary housing units on base, phys ed in school, that kind of stuff. I still spend a lot of time in a locker room environment at the gym where I work out. It's just a little tougher for some to get used to it than others. After a while, you don't even notice it."

Christine appreciated her understanding. At six-thirty they roused Dorothy. "Up and at 'em. We have a full day today." Dorothy pulled her pillow over her head and curled into a fetal position.

Robin picked up a piece of pipe and winked at Christine. She gave the bunk a half dozen loud raps and shouted "Out of bed, private!" Dorothy rolled out of the bunk onto the floor. Robin had the grin of a eight-year old. "God, I've always wanted to do that."

Dorothy glared at her from the floor. "Just wait, you little twerp. I'm going to fill your combat boots with scrambled eggs."

Christine took control of the situation. "Now children. Behave yourselves or I'll put you on latrine duty for the rest of your lives." Dorothy's pillow caught Christine squarely in the face.

After a hearty breakfast of something with the taste and texture of cardboard covered with syrup combined with greasy sausages, they got down to business. Robin started a building by building inspection of the barracks and apartments. These would provide the initial housing as the Reservation started up. It wouldn't take long to outgrow them but they were a start.

Dorothy went on a tour of the buildings suitable for manufacturing. If the reservation was to be successful, they had to have an income. The three possible income producing activities were manufacturing, agriculture, and intellectual property. Christine felt that intellectual property and services were the best bet for the short term but did not rule out specialty manufacturing.

Christine went to look at the land that could be used for crops and cattle. There was very little acreage that could support cultivation. There was a little more that could support cattle or sheep. It was obvious that they were not going to be self-sufficient when it came to food production. It might provide a way to keep people busy. Boredom would be one of their greatest enemies, especially for the young people.

Christine's guide was to be the Captain and a new enlisted man she hadn't seen before. They took a jeep and drove west, bypassing the weather station until the return trip. They had driven about five miles when they came to the old artillery repair facility. The land was covered with a tough grass brush, suitable for cattle and sheep but little else.

They parked at the nearest repair building and got out to look around. The two repair sheds looked like small aircraft hangars. Twelve foot barn style doors covered the front. The inside consisted of one main repair area taking up almost the entire building plus a few small office-type rooms at one end. The floor was concrete with three trenches in it, much like a gas station. The other repair building was the same layout as the first. There were two smaller sheds flanking the repair buildings.

"What about pollution on this site? Are there any areas that cannot be used for habitation?" asked Christine.

Captain Murray pulled out a map of the site and pointed to a marked off area. "This was the artillery range while the base was operational. Within that area, there may be high concentrations of lead and some chemicals used in projectiles. Nothing that couldn't be cleaned up though. My main concern would be for any unexploded shells that weren't found in the initial sweep when the base was closed."

"Great. So we have live bombs for neighbors?"

"There may be a few," said Murray, "but not many. Our boys do a pretty good job of cleanup." They got back in the jeep and followed the road east. After they passed a fork in the road, Captain Murray said "The artillery range is off on our right. It continues for about three miles."

The artillery range looked about the same as everything they had seen so far, rock outcroppings, scrub grass and brush but at a rise Christine got a glimpse of a stream in a little valley off to the north. "I'd like to see that area please," she said pointing down into the valley.

Captain Murray stopped the jeep and stood up to get a better look down into the valley. "It would be safer to go back to the fork and take the trail back. Going cross-country can get pretty rough and I don't want to get stranded out here."

"No problem as long as we get there." She had caught a glimpse of the best piece of land on the reservation. The stream cut across the northeast corner of the reservation feeding the little valley a supply of life giving water. When they reached it an hour later, Christine was overjoyed at the abundance of plant life growing along the banks. With careful irrigation, Christine thought she had found their best bet for agriculture.

It was not Christine in that government commercial. Ben knew that but the woman sure looked like Christine. The voice was off and the movements weren't quite right but it was a good imitation. Damn, he thought, the phone number at the bottom of the screen! As hard as he tried, he couldn't remember what it was. Ben turned up the TV and turned on the heater, anything he could think of to make noise to drown out his voice. He went in the bathroom, held his index finger to his lips and turned on the shower. He cupped his hands around his wife's ear and whispered "I think I know what their game is now." Rosemary motioned him to go on. "They are using a double for Christine Landis in a TV commercial to get the Monoecions to call in and identify themselves. I could tell it wasn't Christine but I doubt that anyone who isn't family would know."

"What are you going to do?" she whispered back.

"I don't know yet. First, I have to actually see the whole commercial and call the phone number. I only caught the very end of one so I can't be sure. We need to stay here long enough for me to catch it again on TV." Rosemary nodded and Ben started shutting down the noise makers. He again muted the TV and sat on the bed, remote in hand and started cycling through the channels.

As he watched the channels flip by, he worked through his options. Today was Sunday and he knew he would have little luck stirring things up. He needed to make this a controversy. The government was intentionally using a double as a tool to entrap the Monoecions. Ben felt sure he could make a case of it, timing the release with Christine's trip to the reservation, but he couldn't come up with a single law that had been broken unless they identified the person as Christine. Ben doubted if Fenton was that stupid. This was a sting operation. It was intended to bring in the few which would lead to the many. If just one Monoecion in ten called in and gave their name and address or called from their own phone, the FBI would be able to track down the rest of the relatives in a matter of hours. The government could have ninety percent of the Monoecions identified in a week without raising a sweat.

Suddenly, Christine's face was on the screen. He turned off the mute and moved closer to the set.

"...here to discuss a very serious problem, a genetic disease that if left unchecked could destroy mankind. The Monoecious trait is passed from parent to child and is one hundred percent dominant. That means if you have this genetic disease, your children will too.

"But this cycle can be broken by a simple surgical procedure. The operation is quick and safe. It can be done as an outpatient procedure and the recovery time is no more than you would expect from a case of the flu.

"As I am sure you know, you are required by law to report to your local authorities if you are monoecious. Your movements can be restricted and some rights that you have always taken for granted can be denied. This does not have to be the case. All it takes is a simple corrective surgical procedure to regain your old life.

"If you choose to have the corrective procedure, your name will be kept in the strictest confidence. Your employer or friends need never know. It's quick and easy.

"If you would like more information concerning this surgical procedure or have any other questions concerning the government policies regarding Monoecions, just call the number on your screen. That's 1-800-555-MONO. We are waiting to help you. Remember, it's not just for you, it's for all mankind."

Damn, thought Ben, they did a good job. Anyone who had seen Christine in the Senate hearings and on the news would swear that it was her in the commercial. What he needed to do was make this a big enough issue that it makes the news so everyone would know it wasn't Christine. He didn't know what he could do tonight but he had to try to do something.

Ben motioned to his wife to come in the bathroom. He again turned on the shower to cover his voice. "I need to get to Boston," he whispered in her ear.

"I'm coming with you," she whispered back.

"Please, I need you to do what we discussed on the drive down. Get a cab to drive you to your cousin's and call Gerald like I explained. Tell him to meet me at seven o'clock at the Shell station near his place. He'll know the one I mean. Tell him to wear tan pants like these." Ben indicated his own. "I want to dump my tail so I have a little more time with the reporters before the government damage control team arrives. Can you do that for me?"

Rosemary nodded. "I love you. Now be careful and don't drive too fast."

"I love you too. I'll be OK." Ben grabbed his shaver and toothbrush and put them in his pocket. He didn't want to look like he was checking out so he left his bag there. He picked up his bright blue wind breaker on his way out the door and put it on over his red flannel shirt. Once in the car he put on his tweed cap, sunglasses and started the car.

The man in the lobby noticed Ben leaving and signaled to his partner. They followed at a safe distance trying to figure out where he was going. They had never put a listening device in his room. They were only told to keep track of him and report any movements that seemed unusual. They didn't report in until Ben hit I-93 southbound with no indication that he was stopping soon.

Ben watched the time carefully. He adjusted his speed down slightly to keep from arriving in Boston too early. He also kept a close eye on the car following him. He had several opportunities to lose them but it was never a sure thing. He didn't want to let them know that he was trying to lose them until they had no chance to recover. The drive continued to be uneventful as he reached his exit north of Boston. Ben checked his tail as he pulled onto Montvale Avenue going west. They were still firmly in place. He pulled into a filling station, parked out front and went inside.

The two FBI men in the tailing car pulled into a parking lot next door and waited. "He's been in there quite a while," said one of them. "I'm going to take a look. I don't want to lose him just because he walked away and left his car here."

As the agent was getting out of the car a semi pulled into the station lot blocking their view. "Shit. Pull over there where we can see."

"I can't yet. Some idiot has me blocked," said his partner, indicating a pickup truck behind him waiting to pull out on the street.

"Pull up there as soon as you can, I'm getting on the other side of that truck."

A scruffy looking man in the long coat loitered at the corner of the gas station watching Ben's car. He moved into position, waiting for the driver to come out. At last he saw the owner come out the door. He paced his walk to meet the owner just as he reached the car. From beneath his grimy coat, he produced a sawed-off shotgun. "Gimme the keys, old man!" he growled.

The agent rounded the truck on foot just as he heard the shotgun blast. He instinctively reached for his gun and cautiously looked around the truck. A dirty looking man in a long coat was getting into Ben's car. "Freeze! Federal Officer!" yelled the agent. The man stuck the shotgun out the window and fired on the agent. The agent jumped back behind the truck for cover. He leaned back out and placed three shots into the fleeing Town Car as it screamed onto the street. On the ground lay a crumpled form in a bright blue wind breaker.

As soon as he heard the first shot, the agent behind the wheel laid on the horn and backed up, narrowly missing the pickup. As the other shots rang out, he pulled around the pickup and rolled up and over the curb, forcing his way onto the street. The pickup chose that moment to try to get out his way by pulling out into the traffic but only succeeded in blocking him again. "Get that piece of shit out of the way!" screamed the frustrated agent as the Town Car sped down the street.

The agent on foot waved his partner on as he went by, finally free of the meddlesome pickup. When he arrived at the body, people were coming from the store to see what had happened. "Call 911," he shouted to them. He looked down at the crumpled mass on pavement. Half of the head was missing. The shotgun blast had entered at the chin and exited from the back of the head. The blast had removed much of the victim's face and the top of his head. What was left of the skull was mostly empty. "No hurry on the ambulance," he said to no one in particular. He pulled out his hand-held radio. "Do you have him in sight?"

"No," his partner called back disgusted. "He's cut off on one of the side streets. I'm going to cruise the back streets and see if he pops up."

"Yeah, give it a try. I'll stay here and wait for the police. Be back here in ten minutes if you can't find him." He shoved his radio back into his pocket. "Damn!" he said and kicked the curb. It hurt like hell. He saw a man leaning down over the remnants of a tweed cap. "Hey you. Leave that alone and get your ass back in the store. I want statements from all of you as soon as the police arrive." He pulled out his cell phone punched the speed dial. "This is Batson. Somebody just murdered Ben Davis."

Tom listened a moment. "Yeah, I'm sure he's dead. Somebody blew half his head off. Trust me, he's dead. We're in Boston. We left his wife up at the inn in New Hampshire. Could you see if you can get someone to notify her and get her down here?" Again Tom listened to the voice on the other end, said goodbye and hung up. He knew how this was going to look on his record. "Damn!" he said again only this time he refrained from kicking anything.

Alicia's mother called Sunday afternoon to see how things were going, check on the grandchildren and mention how surprised she was to see that Monoecion who testified before the Senate in those government commercials. "I never thought I'd see her mouthing that propaganda. If you didn't know better, you would never know she was talking about sterilization. She makes it sound like something noble like a bone marrow transplant."

"Who are you talking about?" asked Alicia. "What woman?"

"You know, that one who was in the Justice Department that they were trying to pin all that stuff on."

"Christine Landis?" It couldn't be her but she was the only one Alicia could think of.

"Yes, that's her. She didn't come across as the type to buckle under."

"No mom, that's not possible. She turned them down. She said she wasn't going to do it. Hold on just a second." Alicia called to Marci and told her to pick up the other phone in the bedroom, explaining what her mother had just told her. "Now mom, you're sure it was her?"

"They didn't put her name on the screen but it sure looked like her. I've seen two different commercials so far today. Turn on the TV and check it out."

Marci said "I just can't believe it was her. She was so dead set against it. It doesn't sound right. Maybe she's being forced into it."

"You two talk as if you know her. Have you met her?" asked Alicia's mother.

Marci thought about telling the truth but she didn't want to do it over the phone. "We met her secondhand. I need to explain in person. I'm going to turn on the TV and start looking for it. Bye." Marci hung up the phone and went to the living room and started scanning the channels looking for the film clip while Alicia finished up with her mom.

It took over an hour of channel surfing to find it. Alicia and Marci were both shocked by what they saw. "Is it really her?" asked Alicia. She hadn't seen her as much as Marci had and she had never connected with her.

"I don't know. It sure looks like her. But she would never do this. I've seen inside of her. You know what I'm talking about. I was inside her and I know she couldn't do this." Marci clutched a pillow to herself and buried her chin in it as she thought. "So what do we do?"

"Call her up and ask her," said Alicia.

"Jasmine?"

Alicia nodded. "We don't dare use the phone. She said she was sure it was bugged. It's the only way."

Marci, Alicia and Jasmine sat together again on the bed. "We need to talk with Christine and see what is happening," Marci explained to Jasmine. "We think the government might be forcing her to do something against her will and that could be bad. Do you think you could connect us again so we could ask her?"

Jasmine nodded. "Uh-huh. Can we go to McDonalds today?"

Alicia wondered if Jasmine was bargaining or if she just thought of food now. "We can go after we help Christine. OK?"

Jasmine smiled and nodded once again. "OK. Did you want to go visit too?" Jasmine asked Alicia.

"If I can. Can you take both of us at the same time?"

Jasmine's front teeth bit over her bottom lip in a mischievous smile. Then she nodded her head one more time, this time more slowly for effect. In the next instant they were jerked into another plane.

"Jasmine, you might want to work on the entry a little bit. Even when you are expecting it, it's kind of rough."

"I'm sorry Alicia."

"Hello Jasmine, hello Marci," came the greeting. "I'm Christine Landis, you must be Alicia. Jasmine has told me much about you."

Alicia still wasn't used to connecting and was startled by the speed of Christine's arrival. She felt the surge of information roll over her, the type of things you would tell people when you first meet only this was the equivalent of hours of conversation. Alicia carefully reached out a part of herself to Christine and she felt it being accepted.

Marci broke in. "We need to talk to you. Are you in a position to do that?"

"For a quick second. I'm in the middle of a conversation with one of my staff and I don't want them to know about your daughter's ability yet."

"This won't take long." Marci showed Christine her mental images of the commercial they had seen. "Was that you?"

"No, of course it wasn't! But now I see their game and how it was to work. They wanted us all together here at the reservation site so no one would be available to raise a stink with the media over using a double of me to put across their message. Ben Davis stayed behind. Could you call him? He's at an inn in New Hampshire with his wife. I doubt the phone is tapped but if they want to, they could find the source of the call with little difficulty. You better use a pay phone if you can find one. Don't use a phone that can be traced back to you."

"Sure," replied Marci. "What do you want us to tell him?" A flood of information filled them. "Whoa! We'll be on the phone for hours to tell him all this."

"Don't worry. Ben already knows most of it. I just wanted you to know some background information. Just tell him to activate the call-in network we were starting to build. If we can just get enough people to call in and complain, the media will do the rest."

"We will get the message to him. I'm glad it wasn't you in the commercial," said Marci.

"I'm sorry I must leave you so soon. I so need this contact with your daughter. It allows me to focus clearly on the problems at hand. I hope you consider coming to join us at the reservation as soon as possible. We will need you, and the time left to stay undetected is dropping to days instead of months."

"We'll talk about it and let you know," said Alicia.

"Goodbye, Jasmine. Visit me again soon and I will make time just for you." A hug passed all around and the connection was gone.

Alicia grabbed one of Jasmine's crayons and scrawled the phone number on the back of one of Jasmine's books. Jasmine's eyes grew large as her mouth fell open. She jumped up and yelled "No! Mommy says don't color on books! That's my book!"

"I'm sorry, honey," soothed Alicia. "I will clean it off in just a second. I had to write it down before I forgot it." Alicia took the book out to the kitchen to transfer the number to a piece of note paper.

Jasmine sat back down on her bed and she started to sniffle. "It's OK, Jasmine. 'Licia will clean up your book, good as new," said Marci.

"I don't care," she said, kicking her heels against the bed frame. "Why do people hate us?"

Marci now understood what the tears were about. "We scare them, baby. They don't understand how our telepathy works and that frightens them."

"And we always have babies like us, not like them," Jasmine said.

"That's right. All our babies are Monoecions. The other people can only be a mommy or a daddy all their lives but we can be either one. They are afraid that there won't be any people like them left in the future if they don't control us."

"Is that why you and Alicia are scared of me, because you don't know how I can put people together?"

Marci stopped, frozen in time. Fear gripped her but it was a fear that all mothers understand, the fear of hurting their child by saying the wrong words. "We aren't afraid of you baby. We don't understand how you can do the things you do, and sometimes it's these things that scare us. But it's the things that you can do, not you, that scare us. We love you and worry that you will grow up too fast, learning about so many things while you are still so young. You understand things that I didn't until I was an adult."

"I'm OK, mommy," Jasmine said in a voice much older than her years. She looked up and saw Alicia standing in the doorway smiling at her. "Family hug?" she asked with arms outstretched.

"Family hug," said Marci as she bent down to pick up Jasmine. "But it can't truly be a family hug without your little sister."

Jasmine tilted her head to one side. "OK, almost family hug." The three of then squeezed together. "Can we go to McDonalds now?"

"Sure we can," said Alicia. "We'll go up to Cedar Bluff and make the call from the convenience store then hit MickyDees. I'll get Jessica, you get a sweater on this one," Alicia said to Marci while grabbing for Jasmine's nose. Jasmine covered it with both hands, blocking the assault. "You're getting too quick for me, hot rod. I can never get that nose any more."

When they made it to the convenience store, there was someone on the phone. Alicia went in the store, got five dollars in change and came back to the car to wait. The woman on the phone finished one call and started another. After another ten minutes, Jasmine and Jessica were both getting restless when the woman finally hung up and gave them a dirty look. "She must have heard you call her a long-winded old bag," said Marci.

"If the truth hurts, I'm sorry." Alicia went to the phone and dialed. When the desk clerk answered, Alicia asked for Ben Davis and waited while the phone rang what seemed forever.

Finally the clerk picked up again. "There is no answer in the room. Can I give him a message?"

"Yes, tell him it's a message from Pugsly." Christine and Ben had arranged that code name if she could get a message to him. He used to call her that back when she worked for him years before. "Tell him to check out the public service announcements that started on TV today and to activate the phone network to complain about the impostor. Make sure he gets this as soon as possible."

"Consider it done."

Alicia came back to the car. "Everybody ready for those French fries?" Jasmine's cheer was deafening.

Christine came back to the conversation with only a slight hesitation. The connection with Jasmine lasted only a couple of seconds. Christine and Dorothy were discussing the need to break the mind set of the people who would be pouring into the reservation in the very near future. "We need to break their perception that this is a refugee camp. There is nothing temporary about the move. They are going to have to understand that this is a life sentence. If we manage a parole sometime in the future, great, but for now the attitude has to be that they are coming here never to leave. To make this palatable we must have an economic plan that is workable."

Dorothy handed a thumb drive to Christine. "This is what I have so far. As we discussed earlier, manufacturing is the heart of any economy. We can handle most anything in light manufacturing but the real problem will be the high cost of machinery. Our primary limitations will be money and water."

"We still have to overcome the public attitude that we are evil," said Christine. "Our best chance is to build an economy from the inside out. We need to produce for our own needs as much as we can. We also need the small business people moving in to bring their business with them." They spent several hours examining their options with the available buildings and then moved on to the next critical task.

Services had to be available from the instant that people start arriving. Fire, police, hospital, trash, phone, housing commission all had to be organized and staffed.

Dorothy leaned back in her chair and pulled her hair into a knot behind her head. "The government is going to do everything in its power to make this a ghetto, someplace to get out of. They will try their best to make us a welfare case that the public will get tired of quickly. We both know what will follow that."

"What are our options?" said Christine. "Move into the trap they've laid for us and try to beat the government at its own game, or fight with delaying tactics in Washington in hopes a better choice will come along? Outside the reservation we are targets, each one of us with a big bullseye painted on our back. One hell of a choice." Christine moved back to the economics of the reservation. "The people coming in here will have some money to invest. I think they will understand that an investment will be necessary to create jobs, but that won't be enough to get things going in the front end. We are going to need government loans to survive in the short term."

Dorothy didn't think that was practical. "You really think the government will offer us loans? They are the ones that want us to fail."

"No. COMA wants us to fail. Congress just wants us contained and out of the way without costing the taxpayer any more money than it has to. If we can show Congress that we can become self sufficient rather than being a drain on the welfare system we just may have an ally."

Christine's mind kept drifting back to the message she received from Jasmine. She wanted to let the others in on the information but there was no way to explain how she knew. She just prayed that Ben was being careful. Christine changed gears on Dorothy. "We need to start the survey on office space available for service industry jobs. Do you think you could be ready to start tomorrow morning?"

"I'll try but I've hardly scratched the surface on the manufacturing space study yet."

Christine nodded. "Do your best but time is the one thing we don't have. Do what you can and move on to the next task. I won't keep you any longer." Dorothy left the office to return to her work while Christine prepared for a tour of the mess facilities on the main base.

At the inn, Mrs. Davis had just finished loading the bags in the cab and she came inside to settle up the bill. The clerk said he was sorry they had to check out early and gave her the message for her husband. Rosemary thanked him and left. In the cab she read the note. The message must be from Christine but she couldn't figure out how she knew.

At her cousin's house, she called her husband's old friend Gerald and gave him the message on where to meet Ben and what time. The rest of the day was spent visiting with the family until an afternoon phone call interrupted it.

"Listen to me carefully. I don't know how to break this gently." Ben's voice was on the edge of panic. "Gerald has been murdered but I think I was the target."

"Murdered! How?"

"Shot. He met me at the gas station like we agreed. He had parked his car in the lot next door. When I got there, we talked for a few minutes and I gave him my hat and coat. He put them on and went out to get in my car to lead the two Feds on a merry chase while I went to meet with my media contacts." Ben's voice began to crack. "That's when a man came out of nowhere. I looked out just in time to see him pull out a gun and point it at Gerald. Gerald grabbed for the gun and the guy shot him in the head."

"Oh my God!" cried Rosemary. "Are you all right?"

"In all the commotion, I slipped away and took his car out of there. I'm across town at a truck stop."

Rosemary twisted her hair in her fingers as she always did when she was nervous. "Poor Emily," she said referring to Gerald's wife. "Does she know yet?"

"I don't know. I haven't called her yet but the police probably have by now. It's all my fault. I got Gerald involved in all this. If it wasn't for me, he'd still be alive."

"Are you sure they were trying to kill you or was it just a robbery that went bad?" Rosemary heard the anguish in Ben's voice and it tore at her.

"It was a setup, it had to be. I mean, two FBI men have been following me for days. They are parked only a hundred yards away yet this guy has time to shoot Gerald, get the keys off the ground, start the car and drive away. Then a few seconds later, one of the agents runs up on foot. By the time the other shows up in the car, the murderer is long gone. It was a setup, I'm sure." For the last thirty minutes, Ben had been running scared, unable to think straight. Talking to Rosemary was beginning to calm him down. "The problem is what do I do now?"

"Go to the local police and tell them what you saw. They had nothing to do with it. No one will be able to touch you there. They can't get to you in a police station."

Ben thought about it for a moment. "No. The Feds can arrange anything they want. They can get me detained with no access to the outside for days." Ben's mind had been running in circles since it happened. "But I still have to do it sometime."

"Go ahead with your plan to see the media people then go to the police," Rosemary suggested. "That will give you some protection having your side of the story out."

"Yeah, I thought about that too. I just wish I had some hard proof instead of circumstantial evidence. It probably is the best choice. I'm going to hit the news people and then go to the local police. Don't believe it if you hear of my death by natural causes. I'm not ready to go yet."

Rosemary was worried about Ben. What if he was right? "Be careful. I'll call Emily and break the news if the police haven't. I love you."

"Love you too." The line went dead.

Fenton received the call at home. He never liked having his Sunday disturbed because it was rarely good news. This turned out to be no exception. "What do you mean Ben Davis is dead? Give me some details." The desk jockey at the FBI fed him the details that were available at the time. Fenton hit the roof. So you mean that your two agents assigned to watch this man not only did not prevent his murder but didn't even witness it!? Even though it was done in broad daylight in the parking lot of a gas station?!"

"I'm sorry, Senator, but I don't have the information available to explain what happened."

"I want updates as they are available. I want updates no less than every hour even it there is nothing additional to report," said Fenton and slammed the phone down.

He picked the phone up again and dialed Lindell. "Ben Davis has been murdered. I want to make sure that I get all the details as soon as they're available."

"Who did it?" asked Lindell.

"Who knows, probably some nut angry about him supporting the Monos. Witnesses say it looked like a robbery but I doubt that." Fenton gave Lindell detailed instructions on how to handle the press. "Call me if you run into any snags. We meet tomorrow morning, first thing, to discuss if any further action is required."

Agent Batson and his partner stayed at the scene as ordered, overseeing the police investigation, watching procedures, and making sure no one screwed up. After the photographer shot all the film he needed, and the lab boys were done, the ambulance crew moved the body to the waiting ambulance. Batson was reviewing the samples taken by the lab crew when the police detective approached him.

"Did you say this guy's name was Ben Davis?" asked the police detective.

"Yeah. A DC lawyer representing the Monoecions in Washington," replied Batson.

"Then can you explain why the driver's license in his wallet says his name is Gerald Watson?" The detective handed him the wallet.

The agent looked the license over. "A fake? He might have been planning to make a break to lose us and needed and ID just in case he got stopped."

"Nope. Already checked. It's real. And the guy we just hauled away matches it to a tee. I think you gentlemen are mistaken as to the identification of the body and your Ben Davis is wandering around the city someplace."

Agent Batson looked worried. "Shit! Have you called this guy's phone number to confirm if he's there or not?"

"Just got off the phone with his wife. She said he left the house about and hour ago. She said he was going to meet an old friend who needed a hand, a guy by the name of Ben Davis." Batson jerked his head up and locked eyes with the detective. "You know what else she said? She said she already knew of the untimely demise of her husband. It seems that Mrs. Davis had already called her and told her all about it. She said that Ben Davis witnessed the whole thing and he's convinced that it was a hit with the cooperation of the Feds."

"That's a bunch of BS!" Batson yelled.

"Sure it is," said the detective, "but the public isn't always quite so understanding. As of right now, you folks are restricted from access to the evidence and the site until I'm told otherwise by my superiors. I respectfully request you to move back away from the scene and wait over there until I have a chance to get detailed statements."

"What about Ben Davis?"

"We have been informed that he will be making arrangements to talk to us shortly after he feels better about his safety. Now get over there and take your partner with you."

By the time that Fenton and Lindell arrived at the office, they had the news that Ben Davis was alive. They immediately went into damage control mode. "Davis wants to put this across as an attempt on his life by the Feds," said Lindell. "We need to play on that. He has no evidence to back that up so we can play him as a paranoid radical. Hell, he's already thrown his lot in with the most despised beings on the earth. He's just trying to turn the good guys into the scapegoats."

"Sounds good so far. Are you sure that we had nothing to do with this incident?" asked Fenton.

"Not that I've been able to find out," said Lindell. "It looks like a typical carjacking where the driver resisted and paid the price. We need to come out and show our sympathy at his loss of a friend and the effect that it is having on his reasoning. If we show that his reasoning is impaired, then the media will have little interest in what he has to say about the public service announcements being a plot."

"This may be a blessing in disguise," mussed Fenton. "We already told the media about the reasoning behind using the Landis double in the announcements. It was buried in the press releases yesterday announcing the start of the campaign. No one said a word about it except a page six mention in the newspaper today. If we show that Davis is unbalanced by reason of his recent grief, they won't dwell on his real message that the announcements are really a government sting operation to get names and addresses of every Monoecion in America."

"That will turn this into local news, not national." Lindell picked up the phone to start calling his press corps contacts. "By the time we're done, he'll be lucky to get a mention on the evening news in Boston."

Marci and Alicia flipped through the channels, looking for any mention of the Christine Landis look alike story. CNN carried nothing and the eleven o'clock news came and went without a mention.

Alicia laid down the remote control. "There should have been something by now. I just wish there was some way of being sure he got the message. Maybe we should contact Christine Landis again."

"Not tonight," said Marci. "Our phone system has already been put to bed and I don't want to wake her. This is rough enough on her. Why don't you call Mr. Davis at the hotel again tomorrow morning on your way to work? If he's still there, you should be able to catch him for sure at that time of the morning."

"It's worth a try. I'll call you from work and let you know. Then you can contact Christine if you need to."

"Maybe it isn't considered big enough to make the news," said Marci. "I guess we'll know tomorrow."

As Marci and Alicia went to bed, the FBI had finished up with the desk clerk at the inn and faxed the report to the DC office. Jack and his partner read over the reports and paid special attention to the copy of the note delivered to Rosemary Davis. "Do a search on our database for the name Pugsly. I'll search the case notes."

A few minutes later his partner came over with a one page printout. "Six matches but none that look like they have anything to do with the Monoecions. You get anything yet?"

Jack had a much slower task. He was searching the entire transcripts of every interview and note taken on the case for any word that came close to matching. He finally hit pay dirt. "Look at this. In an interview with a secretary who worked in the office with Ben Davis and Christine Landis. She referred to Landis as Pugsly. She said she got that from Davis who occasionally used it. We were told that Christine Landis was under security silence at eight AM Saturday morning, right?" asked Jack.

"That's what we were told," said the other agent.

"And the public service announcements weren't made general knowledge until Saturday afternoon. The public didn't see them until Sunday, late morning. So, if the Pugsly in the message is Christine Landis and she truly is cut off from all contact at the reservation site, there is no way for her to know about the commercials other than telepathy."

"I don't know," said the second agent. "I know they told us to watch for signs that they had more abilities than they let on but I still find it hard to believe they can read minds. There has to be a better explanation."

"There is also no way for her to get instructions out of the reservation other than telepathy," said Jack. "I'd sure like to talk to the person who placed this call. I want to know what the message really means. Find out where this call originated and if possible, who made it."

"I'll do my best," yawned his partner.

"What else did you have to do on a Sunday night?"

"Nothing, Jack, nothing at all."

Chapter 24

Monday, September 16

Alicia pulled into the convenience store at six thirty-five AM and again went in and got change for the phone. She went back outside to the pay phone and dialed. A sleepy clerk answered the phone.

"May I have Ben Davis' room, please?" asked Alicia.

The clerk's brain immediately froze. This was the call he was to be on the lookout for but he couldn't remember what he was supposed to do, he fumbled for what to say. "No, I'm afraid he checked out yesterday." That blew it, he thought, she will end the conversation right here if I don't say something else. "Yeah, they were planning to stay until today but they checked out early with all that went on."

"What do you mean, all that went on?"

"Oh, some friend of his got murdered in Boston yesterday," said the clerk trying to control his voice.

"I'm sorry to hear that. I left a message for him yesterday afternoon. Do you know if he got it?"

"Yes ma'am. At least I gave it to his wife, I assume she gave it to him. In all the excitement it might have gotten lost in the shuffle. They left some things in the room so I'm sure they will be calling back. Do you want me to give him another message if he does?"

Alicia thought for a moment. Something didn't sound right in the clerk's voice. "No, that's OK. I'll catch him at the office. Thanks." Alicia hung up the phone.

She got in the car and drove to work. On the way she thought of how the clerk's voice sounded. He was anxious, she was sure of it. That was the last call she was going to make, it might have been one too many already. After she arrived at work, she looked around for an empty office so she could call Marci and tell her what happened. Since she shared an area with three other engineers, private conversations were impossible. She walked the hall, looking for an empty office. There was usually someone out of town on business. Today was no exception. Alicia slipped into a vacant project manager's office and closed the door. When Marci answered, Alicia explained what had happened during her attempted phone call to Ben Davis.

"Hold on, the computer is up. I can Google it. It has to be on the news feeds," said Marci.

"No! No good. It wouldn't surprise me if they are tracking the web searches. That can be tracked straight back to our computer. Go to one of the news feeds like CNN and see if they have anything on it. But remember, don't search for the name. Just scan through the articles until you find something. Call me if you do."

"OK. You do the same if you find something. Check your voice mail." A few minutes later Marci had the article up reading the details. As an extra bonus she also found a mention of the Christine lookalike being used for the public service announcements. Neither appeared to be a lead story, buried well down in the national news.

Marci and Jasmine sat together on the couch where they could keep an eye on Jessica. Marci had told Alicia to be alone at exactly ten o'clock and they would "pick her up" for a visit with Christine to pass on everything they had found out. She figured it would be more effective to include Alicia than trying to transfer information to her verbally later.

At first, Alicia thought of a bathroom stall but she just couldn't bring herself to "visit" someone from there so she again searched out a vacant office, closed the door and picked up the phone. She thought of putting a piece of scotch tape over the hook switch so it wouldn't connect to the switchboard but knew it would be her luck to have someone call that extension while she was supposedly in there using it. She called Marci instead.

The visit began as usual. Alicia felt her mind leap to light speed and she felt Jasmine and Marci. An instant later she felt Christine join them. Alicia started by telling them all about the two phone calls and the voice inflection of the inn clerk that made her nervous in this morning's call.

Marci then opened her knowledge from the Boston Globe newspaper report as to what had happened to Ben and his friend. The feeling of deep remorse and sorrow almost overwhelmed them. At a very tender age, Jasmine learned what it was like to lose a friend. Christine had met Gerald but was not close to him like Ben was.

Now the anger started to build. The government had done this. They had attempted to murder her close friend. Instead, they had succeeded in murdering an innocent bystander. This phase passed quickly as their joint mind probed the facts that were known and made guesses on what wasn't known. The only possible conclusion was that the murder was a simple act of random violence. Ben was wrong. The government had many reasons not to murder him and very few to murder him. He was too close to the problem to see clearly. But this knowledge did not eliminate her anger. The death of Ben's friend was still the fault of the government. If the government hadn't been trying to manipulate them, Ben wouldn't have been where he was and the murder never would have happened.

"Don't attempt any more communication with Ben. It's getting too dangerous to expose yourself any further." Christine knew that Jasmine was the most important person in their race right now and that she must be kept safe at all cost. Each of them contributed as much of themselves as they dared to the "Mind," as they named the union of their mental capacities, and felt it's power grow. It explored what their next actions should be and why. Alicia was shocked to find that logic had only minor sway over the reasoning. There seemed to be a natural order, a feeling of correctness to a decision that held far more importance than conscious reasoning. The first conclusion should have been obvious, they must stop feeding outside information to Christine. Every new fact she collected from the outside increased her chance of unconsciously giving themselves away, exposing Jasmine's abilities to the government.

The Mind also touched on the immediate problems of each individual. Christine now could see a clear plan of action for opening the reservation. Alicia figured out a new approach to solve a software problem that had been plaguing her at work for the last week. Marci came to terms with her fears in dealing with Jasmine, and Jasmine learned that it was OK to still be a child even when so many people needed her. Each held the Mind in awe, feeling a little like they were having an audience with God, except they knew where this one was created and that it was far from infallible.

With the business out of the way, the four of them were free to enjoy each other's company for a while, learning about each other, building a trust that each would learn to lean upon. But the time was shortened because Christine had to rejoin the others. Jasmine also let them know that she was tired and they reluctantly said their good-byes and set the time for their next meeting in two days. Jasmine said she would be all rested by then. The world returned to their lives.

At a little after nine o'clock, two agents from the Knoxville FBI office came in the convenience store and asked who was on duty at the time of yesterday's phone call. They were collecting the person's name, phone number and address when they received a call from the office telling them about the call made that morning. "Were you on duty this morning at six forty?"

"Yes," said the clerk, "I've been here since five-thirty."

"Did you notice a woman make a call this morning at that time from the phone outside?"

"Yeah, sure did. She came in and got change for the call. I recognized her. She's been in here before but I don't know her name. She's tall, dark brown hair, medium length, you know, down to her shoulders, nice figure. I'd say she was in her late twenties to early thirties."

"So she's a local?" asked the agent.

"Yeah, I think so. I'm pretty sure I've seen her in here before, maybe once a week. She fills her car here I think. What's this all about? She looks like a nice woman. She doesn't look the type that would be messed up in the wrong kind of things, if you know what I mean."

"They rarely do," replied the agent. "Do you have security cameras here that would have a picture of her this morning?"

"Normally yes but it's been broken for a while now. The manager said it is supposed to be back tomorrow. I'm afraid all we have are silent alarms."

"Could you come down after your shift and spend a little time with our artist to get a drawing of this woman? It shouldn't take long."

"OK," said the clerk. "I could be down about one thirty. Is that all right?"

"Great. Here's our number. If you see this woman again, give us a call right away. If you can, get a license plate number, or anything else that might be helpful in identifying her. We just want to question her. We have no reason to believe that she is dangerous so please don't overreact. We don't want to spook her into running. Just call us and let us handle it." The clerk nodded dumbly.

Alicia came home for lunch, she needed to be with her family for a while to regain her equilibrium. After lunch, Marci dropped Alicia off at work and ran over to Wal-Mart to pick up a few things. Jessica squirmed in her seat in the shopping cart, wanting to be held. Jasmine trailed along behind mom pointing out each sight of interest. Between lunging to grab Jessica as she attempted to crawl out of the cart and putting back the fifty items that Jasmine pulled off the shelves, Marci completed her fifteen minute of shopping in only forty-five minutes

Then came the gauntlet, the checkout lanes. She looked for the shortest line. There was no such thing. Another ten minutes was spent diverting her children's attention from the candy and trinkets that line the way to the counter.

As her eyes passed over the rag magazines on the shelf, she momentarily felt that queasy feeling she had experienced when the first article exploded her world. Marci was surprised. Only two of the magazines had headlines about Monoecions and they were both smaller backup stories. The only problem was that now the stories were in Time and People instead of the rag mags. They were a daily occurrence in the newspaper. Monoecion bashing had been raised to a new level of acceptance. A respected magazine would carry an article expressing their horror at the murders and attacks on individual Monoecions while in another article they would expose some supposed plot of the Monoecions to control a local government because one was on the city council. It seemed to take less evidence by the day to suspect a conspiracy if a Monoecion was involved.

Marci was already feeling irritated by the time she finally got to the car and strapped the kids in. She started the car, backed out of the parking space and glanced at the dash as she pulled away. "God Damn It!" The gas gauge was on empty.

Jasmine gave her the look. "That's bad words," she said.

"Those are bad words," corrected Marci, "and you bet your butt they are. Alicia gave us the car with an empty gas tank and didn't even warn me. If I didn't look down, we would be pushing this damn...darn thing home instead of driving it." Marci pulled out of the lot and picked her way through the traffic. She took the back roads to Cedar Bluff and pulled into the Weigel's Market. She told the girls to be good and got out to fill the tank. After pumping her gas, she went inside and decided to get some milk while she was there.

There were two people behind the counter talking as they took care of the customers. Marci caught a snatch of the conversation as she headed toward the milk cooler. "...down there now with a police artist..." Marci thought about the neighborhood violence now moving into her area. It's not safe to raise children anywhere. Marci searched the bottom shelves for the yellow capped skim milk jugs and pulled a gallon from the cooler. She looked out at the kids in the car to make sure they were behaving and got in line at the counter. "...glad it was him and not me. I don't think being questioned by the FBI is the kind of excitement I want in my life." The clerk doing all the talking looked at Marci. "Is that all?"

Marci realized something was not right. The FBI doesn't investigate corner market holdups. "Uh, yes... No, there was gas on pump..." Marci couldn't get her brain to function.

The clerk calmly cycled through the gas pumps on her meter. "Thirty-five twenty-five?"

"Yeah, that's it," Marci said thoughtfully. "Sounds like you had some excitement here. Was it a robbery or something?"

"No, nothing like that. They were just looking for someone who made a phone call from the pay phone this morning. Probably a credit card scam or something. The morning clerk just left to go downtown and help with an artist sketch."

"Oh, so the clerk didn't recognize her or anything?" Marci caught herself as she said it. Good heavens, girl, how can you be so stupid. The clerk didn't say if it was a man or woman.

The clerk never batted an eyelash. "No, he didn't. He thought he had seen her in here before but that was it."

Marci's heart raced as her hands seemed to lose their connection to her brain. She fumbled her debit card as she ran it through the reader. She looked over her shoulder at the car and saw Jasmine looking intently back at her. Marci sent a reassuring calm to the kids and returned her attention to the clerk. The clerk gave her a cheery thanks. Marci quietly slipped out to her car, trying to look as inconspicuous as possible.

As soon as Marci opened the car door, Jasmine asked "What's wrong, mommy?"

Marci took a few deep breaths to calm herself down before answering. "It's OK, honey. Mommy just got a little scare but it's over. We just need to get home and I'll be OK."

Just then there was a rap on her window. Marci jerked and a gasp escaped her lips. The clerk stood out side her window, a jug of milk in her hand. "Ma'am, you forgot your milk!"

"Oh, thank you," said Marci as she rolled down the window. "I wouldn't have noticed that until I got home. Thank you very much." She took the milk from the woman's hands and set it on the floor.

"Sorry, I didn't mean to scare you. Have a nice day." She waved and walked back to the store.

"Let's go home before I lose it completely." Marci started the car and pulled into the flow of traffic, her mind was relieved to be forced to think about something as mundane as stoplights and dodging idiots in Volvos. She debated all the way home about calling Alicia at work or waiting until she picked her up from work. She thought about connecting to her with Jasmine but didn't want her little girl any more upset than she already was. She decided to wait until they could discuss it face to face.

Marci could tell that Jasmine suspected that mommy was more upset than she was letting on. Jasmine sat in the seat next to Marci, her thumb clamped firmly between her lips. Marci and Alicia had been trying to break her of sucking her thumb and had succeeded in getting her to stop in their presence. Marci brushed Jasmine's cheek, a gentle reminder. Jasmine just turned her face away and continued sucking her thumb. Marci didn't press the issue.

The remainder of the afternoon crept by. Marci kept looking out the window, half expecting to see someone looking back from a parked car or clump of bushes. Several times she thought she saw cars slow down as they went by the apartment building. Twice, there were cars with men sitting in them parked across the lot. The first time she thought she recognized the driver as a tenant. Another man came out from an apartment and they drove away. The second instance scared her much more. The car was the traditional 'Feds' dark four door, right out of the movies. Marci didn't recognize the car or the driver. After about forty-five minutes, he started the car and drove away.

Marci's jitters had put the children on edge, manifesting itself as two foul tempered and irritable kids. She finally decided that her paranoia was playing on her and that she had to do something to take her mind off it. "Hey Jazz! I've got an idea, how about a picnic in the park?"

Jasmine's eyes lit up. "Will you push me on the swings?" Jasmine loved the swings and the "Fort," with the rope bridge.

"I sure will. And if you help, we could make some deviled eggs real quick." That was the clincher, deviled eggs were Jasmine's favorite picnic food. The kitchen became a flurry of activity, keeping Marci too busy to think of what she had to say to Alicia. That would come later when they could talk privately with Jasmine off on the playground. Marci pulled out a paper grocery bag to act as a substitute picnic basket. She always meant to buy one but never justified it in her budget when a paper bag did so well. Small hands helped her load their feast, chicken sandwiches for herself and Alicia, PB&J and pudding cups for Jasmine and Jessica. A thermos of milk, a bottle of Coke and of course, the Tupperware container with the prized eggs topped off the bag. Marci lugged the clothes bag and grocery sack to the car. She came back for the kids, locking the apartment door behind her.

As an after thought, she opened the door and carefully put one strand of her hair in the door where she could check for it on their return. At least I learned something from those Ian Flemming books of dad's, she thought.

Alicia came out of the office talking to Zak about the latest management fiasco, the planned move of their department from one end of the building to the other, dreading all the disruption it was going to cause. Zak smiled and waved at Jasmine who pretended to be shy and covered her face. "It looks like the troops came for you. See you tomorrow." He waved to Marci and walked off towards his car.

Alicia said "See you," and climbed into the car.

"Licia, we're going on a picnic," Jasmine squealed excitedly.

"We are? And who says we are going on a picnic?"

"Mommy and I do, that's who." Jasmine pointed to the bag of food on the floor behind Marci's seat. "See, we made sam-itches an' eggs an' everything."

"Oh! I see." Alicia looked over at Marci. "And whose idea was this?"

"Jasmine talked me into it," Marci lied in a stage conspirator's whisper.

"Uh-uh," Jasmine shook her head. "It was mommy's idea."

"Shhhhh. We don't want Alicia to know that," said Marci.

Jasmine looked confused. "But she already knows."

"Well, now she does." Marci moved her attention back to Alicia. "And yes we are going on a picnic. The food is in the back and ..."

Alicia interrupted "I wish I had know about this, I might have worn something a little more appropriate than heels and a dress."

"Already taken care of. There are shorts, a top and tennies in the trunk. You can change at the park." Marci hoped Alicia could read her expression and the tone of her voice. "We need the time together." It was quick and then it was gone, replaced by a forced smile. "And I made your favorite, road kill stew with asparagus tips."

Alicia heard the tension in the voice and saw how the eyes did not match the words. "Sounds great but we had that last time." She reached over and gave Marci's hand a squeeze. Marci gave a weak smile in return. Alicia could feel Marci relax a little. Something wasn't right but she would just have to wait to find out what.

At the park, Alicia grabbed her clothes from the trunk and went to the bathroom to change while Marci spread the blanket and unpacked the car. Alicia unzipped her dress and pulled it over her head. She hung it carefully on the hook on the stall door. She pulled down her panty hose and slipped on her shorts and baggy T shirt. As an after thought, she unhooked her bra and pulled it out through the sleeve. I've worked all day, I'm tired, and I'm going to be comfortable, she thought to herself. If somebody doesn't like it - tough! In college she had rarely worn a bra but since becoming gainfully employed, she had become much more conservative in her dress habits. She couldn't remember the last time she had been in public sans bra. Even though Marci did it all the time, Alicia was always uncomfortable at the thought of running into someone from work. This will shock Marci, thought Alicia, she doesn't think I've still got it in me. She collected her clothes under her arm and joined Marci. Marci never even noticed.

"Where's Jazz?" Alicia asked.

Marci pointed over at the "fort." "I told her she could play for a few minutes before dinner. It will give us a chance to talk." The edge in her voice made it obvious that she had very little control left. Alicia said nothing, just waited for Marci to continue. Marci swallowed hard, like taking a foul tasting medicine. "The FBI is looking for us." Marci watched Alicia's eyes as a dozen emotions flew across them. Alicia's mouth started to work but nothing came out right away. "They don't know who we are yet, at least I don't think they do."

"What do you mean the FBI is looking for us?" Alicia sputtered. Then shaking her head she said "I know what you mean, how do you know they are looking for us?"

Marci described everything that had happened that afternoon in as much detail as possible. Alicia listened intently, interrupting constantly with questions, most of which Marci couldn't answer. "That's all I know!" blurted out Marci, frustrated by the questions. "I was scared out of my mind so I'm afraid I didn't hang around to ask a lot of questions myself. And I'm not going back for more specifics."

"OK, OK. I understand. I'm just trying to learn all I can." Alicia saw that Marci's eyes were red and glistening. A single tear escaped and tried to flee down her cheek. "Are you all right?"

Marci assaulted the tear with a violent swipe of her palm. "No! I'm not all right!" Marci noticed Alicia looking out over the playground. She followed her gaze and saw Jasmine staring back at them. Marci took several deep breaths trying to calm her emotions with little success. Marci's voice softened to nearly a whisper. "We need to get out of here."

"What? Get out of here, the park?" asked Alicia not comprehending.

"No! Here, Knoxville. We need to move away from here as soon as we can. It won't take long for the FBI to track us down. All it would take is an artist sketch taken to all the apartment complexes in the area and we're caught."

"But we haven't broken any laws." Alicia had to make Marci see reason. "They can't do anything to us. So we made a phone call. So what?"

"We're god damned Monos! We don't have to break any laws. We have no rights. We can be held as long as they see fit and there is nothing we can do about it. And if we're held for questioning, what happens to Jasmine and Jessica? They end up in the care of the State."

Alicia tried to calm Marci. "They can't do that. Mom and dad would take care of the kids. And they can't hold us forever."

"We have no *human* rights, remember? They can hold us as long as they want and do anything they want with the kids. And do you think Jasmine is smart enough to keep her secret from an experienced interrogator? Once they find out about her talent, we'll never see her again." There were no tears in Marci's eyes now, only grim determination. "Our little girl can read minds. She can tie people together on opposite sides of the world with no radio, no mistakes in translation. Do you have any idea what her ability is worth to the federal government?"

"Where will we go? What do we live on? We can't just pack the car and leave. That will raise all kinds of questions that I'm sure will lead the FBI right to us."

Marci tried hard to keep her frustration from coming through in her voice. Alicia always became defensive when she felt Marci was talking down to her. "No, that's not what I'm suggesting. We have to create a cover story that won't arouse any suspicion. We can tell them you have accepted a job with a small start-up firm outside St. Louis and you need to start right away so you are only giving one week notice and using up your other week of vacation. We have a moving sale and sell what we can, also make sure the neighbors get the same story. In reality, we head to the reservation and join up with Christine as soon as we can."

"Wait a minute, the reservation isn't open yet. Christ, the site isn't even announced yet."

Marci rocked her head in her hands. "I know that but it will be open soon. Until then, you keep your head down. The less you're out, the less chance we have of anyone recognizing you. You go to work and come home, that's all. I'll take care of all the shopping and anything that requires going out. As soon as the reservation opens up, we go out."

Alicia understood the truth of what Marci said but she still didn't want to accept it. "What do we do after we get there? We still need to make a living."

"I don't know. I don't have all the answers. We work with Christine and do what we can to help build a world our kids can grow up in."

Alicia said "It's going to be tough on the kids, and on us."

"Not as tough as what will happen to them if the government gets a hold of them."

Alicia wanted to hold Marci in her arms, to comfort her, to make it all better. But she knew that she dared not touch her that way in public. People were already looking over at them, attracted by their intense discussion. Even if they couldn't be heard, the emotional heat of the discourse was obvious to anyone watching. Alicia thought about how it would be in the reservation, how she could hold Marci's hand in public, touch her cheek, kiss her lips, without people staring at them in shock. "The reservation will have some advantages." Alicia long fingers slyly caressed Marci's hand. Marci lifted her face and for the first time in hours, smiled without the cloud of fear behind her eyes.

Chapter 25

Thursday, September 19

Fenton paced around his desk, he thought better when he moved. Even when on the telephone, he preferred to use the speaker so he could walk freely and use his hands. But mostly if he was stifled, forced to wait for an outcome, then the real need to pace came out.

The first few hours of the public service campaign were a rousing success with calls almost matching his projections. People wanted to know about this "new surgical procedure" and where and how they could get it. By the end of the day however, things had changed. People were asking if the woman on the commercial really was Christine Landis. The operators had been carefully trained to handle the question, never exactly confirming or denying. Callers also wanted to know how the new surgical procedure differed from sterilization. In the last three hours of the first day, twenty percent more asked about relocation to the reservation than asked about the surgery. With each succeeding day, the ratio fell. The report on the NPR news program Monday morning had tried to accuse him of underhanded tactics but careful damage control on CNN had helped soften that.

The campaign had not been a total loss, he reassured himself. The FBI had picked up thousands of names so far, each could lead to tens of thousands more. Fenton idly opened the cover of the large volume on his desk. It was neatly labeled Monoecion Family Tree Vol. 1. When they had started a few short weeks ago, there were only a few pages. It was now up to eight large volumes not including the cross references and indexes. He was sure that it would double in size in the next two weeks with the new information being processed. But even with all the manpower devoted to the job, there were hundreds of dead ends, branches ending in the single word UNKNOWN. And, the investigation into the activities of Ben Davis on Saturday had yielded some possible evidence of further telepathic powers.

The evaluation report was due from the Landis group at the reservation by the end of the day, not that it mattered. The decision had already been made by the committee with the support of the President and, after a few well placed promises about future federal spending, the Governor of Nevada.

Lindell came in with a none too pleased look on his face. He pulled a graph from the folder he was carrying and tossed it on Fenton's desk. "The blip last night was only an aberration. It's gone right back to most of the calls centering on reservation information."

"I expected as much, but I hoped it was a turning point." The Senator noticed that Lindell was bothered by something and it wasn't like him to not come right out and say it. "You look worried Todd. What is it?"

Lindell didn't answer right away as he formulated his reply. "We are making the site announcement in the morning, right?" He didn't wait for Fenton to answer and continued on. "With the way response has been coming in, you and I both know that site will be insufficient to house them. What will the rest of the committee say to the site six months from now when it becomes obvious that we blew it?"

"It's not a problem. By then the Monos will be so disenchanted with their reservation and Ms. Landis that they will be leaving by droves to get the surgery and rejoin society. I'm sure that, initially, there will be a great rush on the available space in the reservation and there will have to be limits put on the number allowed to enter. But, I predict that the flow in will be half the flow out in six months. People think with their wallets. Once they realize that entry into the reservation is a life sentence to poverty, the net direction of flow will cease to be a problem."

Christine, Robin and Dorothy sat around the table in the war room reviewing their preliminary findings. "Well," said Christine, "it appears that this facility is woefully inadequate. There is nowhere near enough housing, even by our most conservative estimates. The housing that is here is sub-standard with serious flaws in the plumbing, electrical, heating and air conditioning systems. Water and waste treatment will only handle twenty percent of the expected load in the first year." Christine took off her glasses and put them on the table while rubbing her eyes with her other hand. There was a nervous silence around the table. "In other words, it's better than we expected. Is that the picture?"

Robin nodded. "The buildings are fundamentally sound, that's about all you can say for them. There's just not enough of them or the infrastructure to go with them."

"We'll be limited in what we can use for commercial and industrial space," said Dorothy. "Most of the buildings will have to be converted for use as group housing."

"No they won't." Christine said it so harshly, it surprised Robin and Dorothy. "We can live in tents but we'll have a hell of a time working in them. If we have to, we will live in our factories but they will remain first and foremost factories. Otherwise, we will have no income to build real homes and we will always be refugees." Christine's voice had a hard edge to it that she didn't recognize as her own. "The choices that we make now must be completely rooted in the future, not in the present. I'm not interested in being forced into the same trap as the American Indians of the eighteen hundreds. I plan on winning this war by beating them at their own game and that will take sacrifices on everyone's part."

There was a long pause as each looked from one to the other. Now was the time for decisions and Robin was the first to make hers. "When do we move in?"

Christine smiled, her whole body seemed to soften. "You tell me. When can we move in?"

"I think we can do it in three weeks. There's a lot of preparation that must be done, most of it will be easier to do in Washington than it would be from here. We will need to start screening people to come in the first wave. We need electricians, carpenters, engineers and managers to start this place up. Anybody with building trades experience."

"We will also need general laborers to provide the support functions like cooking, cleaning, and child care," said Christine.

Dorothy spoke up. "We shouldn't take families with small children in the opening crew. It will take up vital resources we can put to better use."

Christine thought of Jasmine. "No. There will be two criteria right from the start to determine order of admittance, skills we need and need of protection. If a person has the skills we need, I don't care if she has six kids, we will take her. And I refuse to deny admittance to someone in danger. We will find a way." And there is one child we need here more than any of us, thought Christine.

Dorothy sat back at the rebuff by Christine. "I was only suggesting that if we have a choice between two people with similar skills and one has children ..."

"We will take them both. I don't think we will have an excess of suitable candidates, I think we will have a definite lack of them." Christine could tell Dorothy was irritated that her idea was shot down but she would have to get over it. There wasn't time for prima donna treatment here. "We need to finish our evaluation tonight and have it ready to FAX to Washington by seven PM. I'll write up a cover page summarizing our concerns about this site if you two can finish off your detail reports."

"Mine will be ready," said Dorothy coolly.

"Mine too," said Robin. "Do you think our evaluation will be considered?"

Christine gave a short sarcastic laugh. "I'm sure the Honorable Senator Fenton will give careful consideration to our evaluation of this site before he ignores it and rams this place down our throat. My concern now is how fast we can get it open for the general population."

"It would speed things up if we could get a press conference set up to publicize the talents we need." Robin asked "Did anyone else send in resumes of sorts looking to help?"

"You mean besides yourself? You were the closest thing I had to an expert so I picked you. There are probably less than a dozen qualified people that I know of in our database. Robin, get the web site updated to give a list of the skills we need and a method of applying for the first wave. Make sure we keep the disclaimer on the entry page that if you are trying to keep your identity a secret, you just blew it. I'm sure the feds haven't stopped recording every hit on our web site. We can appeal to some of the more balanced news organizations to spread the news but if we can't get the press to publish what we need in the media we will just have to advertise."

"I can see the ad now," said Dorothy. "Monoecions Wanted: Construction and engineering types. Hard work, no pay, no benefits. Needed to build your own prison. It will go over big."

Robin became very serious. "Do you think anyone will answer the ad? I mean for real. Are we really doing this for someone other than ourselves or are we just fighting windmills?"

"There is only one way to find out," said Christine. "I'll need to center my efforts on raising operating capitol and dealing with Fenton and his committee. I think I can move my operations here within two or three weeks. There are humans out there who think we are getting a raw deal and are willing to help." Christine was surprised at how easily she had made the transition from considering herself human to viewing herself as Monoecion. The term "Human" had rolled easily off her tongue meaning "them", the beings who were not the same as her. She wondered if this was how the prejudice would start inside her, growing into an us versus them hate. She knew she would have to be on her guard to prevent it from taking root. "We need funds for equipment, public relations, food, legal aid for Monoecions in trouble, everything. I'll try to keep Fenton from interfering with your work in setting this place up." Christine looked from Robin to Dorothy and back. "When do the two of you want to move in?"

Robin spoke up first. "I'd like to be back within a week of our return to DC. I think I can do a more effective job out here where I can check things myself. That is as long as we have effective communications."

Both Christine and Robin looked at Dorothy. "Ah... I'm not sure. I think I need to coordinate closely with you," she said, nodding at Christine. "If I'm going to be expected to create an economy in this place, I'm going to need access to the money people for some serious fund raising. It's going to take some time before I can move my operation out here."

Christine felt the resistance in Dorothy's voice. It was obvious that she did not look forward to moving from her nice comfortable home to this dusty wilderness. "You won't have it. Fenton will be pushing us out here, and if he doesn't, I will. If we wish to maintain any creditability with the people we're supposed to be leading, we will need to be here with them."

Christine was evaluating her heads of staff as she spoke. Robin was young and energetic, she had that "I can do anything if I try hard enough" attitude that is the sole property of the young and inexperienced. It would be a great asset in getting things done but it would also be a liability when it came to realistic schedules. It's a shame, Christine thought, how quickly the world beats that attitude out of you. Dorothy, on the other hand, was a realist. Her view of the world was much more cynical and self-controlled. What concerned Christine was that at times, it appeared to be self-serving also. "We'll need to limit the initial number to a few thousand to get the reservation started. It's going to resemble a Girl Scout camp more than a home for the first few months."

Dorothy interrupted Christine. "One of the first things we will need is a bank, or better yet, a credit union. As people move in, they will need somewhere to put the money they brought with them. At the same time, we will need startup capitol for businesses inside the reservation."

"Excellent," said Christine. "That will help jump start the inside economy and build the jobs base. Start looking into how to do that as soon as you can. And try to recruit some experienced people when we get back. Do your best on this one, our bank will have to be squeaky clean for the people to trust it considering there probably won't be any federal guarantees on the deposits."

Robin raised her hand, looking a bit like a school girl asking for permission to be excused. Christine looked over at her and nodded. "I know we will have to limit the number of people coming in at first to those with special talents, or those in physical danger, but how do we turn the others away?"

"We don't," said Christine. "We must make them understand that we are only delaying their entry as long as absolutely necessary. I don't want anyone feeling that they were rejected. That could be used against us by the media to encourage them to switch to the government's *simple corrective surgical procedure* over moving to our little paradise."

"Is that what they are calling it?" asked Robin. "What a bunch of government double speak. Why don't they just call it what it is, mass sterilization or genocide?"

"This sounds much nicer." A cold chill ran through Christine. Where had she picked up the phrase "simple corrective surgical procedure?" She couldn't remember if it was in the script she was given or if she received it from her last connection with Jasmine and Marci. Shit, she thought, If that wasn't in my script, I just screwed up big time. She quickly changed the subject. "Let's get back on track and finish this report so we can get on to the more important task of planning the move." She silently prayed that the FBI would miss her slip. They almost did.

Chapter 26

Friday, September 20

Robert had been waiting in the reception area for fifteen minutes. He was beginning to feel uncomfortable, it had given him too much time to think of what he was doing. He didn't like the feeling that he was sneaking around and lying to Christine. He hadn't actually done anything or told the committee anything they didn't already know but he knew sometime they were going to ask him to do just that. He was still undecided as to what he would do when they did ask.

Todd stuck his head out of his office. "Robert, good to see you. Come on in. I hope you weren't kept waiting long. I got stuck on a critical phone call and couldn't get loose."

"Yeah," Robert replied in a flat voice. "It wasn't that long." Robert rose and sullenly crossed the room to Lindell's office. After closing the door behind himself, he cut the formalities. "Why did you want to see me?"

Todd smiled and kept his friendly face on, the one reserved for irritated lobbyists. "Just wanted to touch base with you and see if there was anything we could do for you. We realize that you are in a difficult position."

"Difficult is not the word for it." Robert ran his fingers through his hair. "I am going to try to convince my wife to give this up. I want assurances from you people that you will leave us alone if I can convince her to come back to her family and rejoin the human race."

"She won't do it." Todd could see Robert visibly wince when he said it. "I can tell you right now that she is making plans to return to the reservation in no more than two weeks after her return to Washington."

"Then it's over." Robert nervously worked the end of his tie in his fingers. "I'll be divorcing her when she leaves me and the children." He looked up at Lindell with questioning glance. "There's no way she can take the girls is there?"

"No, absolutely none," Todd reassured him, "but are you sure that's what you want to do? We both know that the court's have already set a precedence in the favor of the human fathers. You would automatically be awarded full custody but think of it this way, if you stuck with her for a few months, moved out to the reservation with her, you might be able to convince her to give it up and come back to the real world. Once she deals with the frustrations and problems, she might be more amenable to chucking the whole thing and having the surgery and joining the human race again."

"But what about my home? If I move out to the reservation, it will have to be sold and I don't want to lose it."

"Not to worry. We already have it set up. When you put it on the market, you will get a good offer from an average looking couple. It will be a fair offer, accept it. When you return from the reservation, you can have your home back, just the way you left it." Lindell moved around his desk to get closer and more intimate with Robert. "Even if Christine doesn't come around, the house will be yours for you and your daughters. Your job will be there too, or one like it. I know how tough this will be on you and the kids and we want to do everything we can to help. All we ask is that you try to convince Christine of the error of her ways."

"And I'm sure that would add clout to your sterilization campaign to have the leader of the Monoecions to come over to your side." Robert was no fool. He knew the political stakes. Fenton had his eye on the presidency and a successful handling of the Monoecion problem would almost guarantee his election.

"We wouldn't need her to make any statements. Just the fact that she chose the government supported route for herself and her children will be all we need to turn the tide, to solve this problem for all time."

Both men were quiet for a long moment, Robert thinking over what had been said, Todd confident that he had made the sale. "I'll need some time to think it over."

"Time is limited. Christine will be back tomorrow and I think she is expecting a confrontation with you on her return. Just think about it, you don't even have to give us a response. Just put your house up for sale and move with her." Todd saw Robert nod his head noticed his eyes were focused out in space, outside the confines of the office, and wondered what he saw.

When Robert returned home from work, Ben's car was in the drive. He hadn't seen Ben since Christine had left for the reservation a week before. Inside, he found Ben sorting through the pile of mail that had arrived. "Hello. You're back. I was beginning to wonder if they locked you up and threw away the key."

Ben looked up from his work. "No, it's tough to keep a lawyer in jail for long. We just keep slithering loose." Ben didn't dislike Robert, he just wished that Robert would support his wife more. It seemed he had fought her every decision. Ben also knew that Christine's decisions had made life very tough for Robert and the kids. "They just questioned me hours on end and let me go. They keep saying that the murder was just a random act of violence and that someday, pieces of my car will show in some chop shop raid."

"And you don't believe them?"

"Let's just say that I have my doubts..... No, I'll say a lot more than that. It was a setup. They planned to kill me just because I didn't go to the reservation with the others."

The outburst surprised Robert. He didn't know Ben that well, not like Christine did but he never thought of Ben as one to make wild accusations. "Why would they want to kill you? That doesn't make sense."

"It makes perfect sense. It was no coincidence that the media blitz to get Monoecions registered to be sterilized began the day after Christine and the others were sequestered at the 'Top Secret' reservation where they couldn't be reached for comment. It was also no coincidence that the actress doing the commercials looked and sounded exactly like Christine. They didn't want anyone making a big stink about it until they got what they wanted, a name, address, and phone number on every Monoecion who called in."

"I don't know Ben." Robert couldn't believe what he was hearing, at least he didn't want to. "If that was the case, what about me. I knew it wasn't Christine. No one tried to kill me."

Ben lowered his voice. "I didn't see your face on the 6 o'clock news raising a ruckus over it either."

Robert turned his back on Ben. Does he know I've been talking with Lindell and Fenton? "It wouldn't have mattered. I called to protest, was put on hold and ignored. There was nothing I could do about it." Robert had done exactly that, just to make sure that the call would be on record but he had been careful not to push it. He filed his protest with the secretary at the commission and ended it there. Robert turned back to Ben. "They explained it all the day after the announcements started, you know, already had the tapes, saving the taxpayers money and so on. We were beat before we started."

"At least some of us were."

Robert bristled "What's that supposed to mean?"

"Just that some of us try harder than others." Ben returned his attention back to the stack of mail on the desk.

Chapter 27

Thursday, September 26

Rae Ann sat at the table with her lawyer. Amy Faltner had stuck with her even though Rae Ann told her she wouldn't be able to pay her for quite some time for the legal services already rendered. Rae Ann's husband, Randy, sat at his table looking straight ahead, hardly acknowledging her existence, as his lawyer finished his argument to the judge. It was bad enough that he had filed for divorce without even a word to her but he wouldn't even take the time to say hello, good bye or drop dead. Rae Ann had tried to talk to him but he never talked back. He wasn't mean about it, he just refused to discuss anything. Randy would just sit there and listen to her until she got tired of talking and wait for her to walk away.

His past treatment of her had almost driven her crazy but now she was in shock. Even though her lawyer had warned her, she couldn't believe what she was hearing. His lawyer was just finishing up.

"Because of the circumstances, I do not believe my client deserves a divorce. We feel nothing short of an annulment is called for in this case."

Rae Ann burned in her chair. An annulment, not a divorce but an annulment. The bastard didn't want to get rid of her; he wanted to erase her from his existence. He wanted to pretend that their entire life together never happened.

Amy Faltner rose to her feet. She was irritated because she hadn't thought of this line of action. "Your Honor, I object to the Council's request. I believe an annulment would only be proper if no children are involved. Mrs. Baird has two, fathered by Mr. Baird. I think that fact alone should rule out this line of action."

Randy Baird's attorney interceded before the judge had a chance to respond. "Your Honor, that applies to human offspring. The only offspring from this union are monoecious and thus should not be considered during these proceedings."

The judge rocked back in his black leather chair weighing the conflicting arguments. "Can you prove that the children are Monoecious?"

"Yes sir, I can," the attorney replied. He picked up an envelope from his table and carried it up to the bench. "Enclosed are two medical records, the first showing that the two offspring are identical twins. The second is a hospital report confirming Carla Baird is indeed monoecious."

Rae Ann heard Carla begin to cry. Carla was sitting with her sister in the gallery behind her mother and she just couldn't take it any more. Carla rose quickly and hurried out of the courtroom. Kathy followed her out, pausing at the door just long enough to catch her father's eye and give him the finger. The judge called out to the bailiff, "Keep those two out of my courtroom. I will not tolerate that kind of behavior!"

Ms. Faltner started to speak but a tug on her arm distracted her. Rae Ann simply said "Give it to him."

Amy bent down and spoke in a hushed voice. "You don't understand. A divorce is completely different from an annulment. In an annulment, you will have no right to child support or property claims. I can't even get him to pay off your debts, nothing."

"I don't care. Sit down and let's get this over with. I came here ready to give him a divorce. I see no reason why I would want it on record that I was ever married to that slime ball. Besides, even if I was awarded any money, he just wouldn't pay it. I'm tired. Let's get it over with."

Amy nodded her understanding. She approached the bench. The annulment was concluded within an hour.

Monday, September 30

Alicia asked her department manager if he had time to talk for a moment. He answered "No problem. What do you need?" Alicia handed him her letter of resignation. He kept looking back and forth between Alicia's face and her letter trying to determine if it was legitimate. There had been a rash of practical jokes going on in the office and he wasn't sure if he was being had. Alicia wasn't cracking a smile so he decided he better take it seriously. "Has there been a problem I didn't know about?"

Alicia shrugged her shoulders. "No, it's not that. I really hate to do this to you but I've been offered an opportunity to work with an old friend from college at a start up company in Salt Lake. I know it's a big risk but I'll either get rich or go broke and I want to play guts ball once before I get too old to try. I hope you understand."

Her boss looked her in the eye. Something seemed to be bothering her about this. "Are you sure about this. Are there any problems here that are bothering you? I don't want to lose you because of some conflict here."

Alicia felt like shit. She liked him as a boss. He had always been straight with her and she hated lying to him. But she knew she couldn't tell him the truth. "It's nothing like that. Don't be so nice when I tell you I'm leaving right in the middle of an eight-month project. I feel rotten enough but it has to be now. They need me by the end of next week or it goes to someone else."

"I'm being nice while I try to talk you into staying. Once I'm convinced you won't, then I become a slave driver. I need to get four months of work out of you in a week and a half. I can be a real pain in the ass when I try."

"You don't have to try, it always came natural since I've known you," Alicia chided him.

"Thanks, I know that was straight from the heart. We will miss you. Have you already announced this to the office and I'm the last to know?"

Alicia shook her head. "No one knows. I can't believe I actually kept it to myself for the last two weeks while I negotiated with them."

He asked her "If you could, hold off telling anyone outside the department until I release a memo. I'll have it out by lunch. I don't want anyone else getting any ideas."

Alicia thanked him and walked back to her cubicle. The whole office looked different. She used to call it the sweatshop from hell. God, how she would miss this place. The work had been hard, the demands extreme but it was balanced by the respect she had achieved and the quality of the people with whom she had shared the past five years. They had achieved a record of on time and under budget projects envied by every office in the corporation. She entered her area and sat down at her desk. She began to think about what she had gotten herself into.

"We need to get that factory acceptance test run-through done by the end of the day if we're going to make schedule," Zak told her as he dug through the stack of papers on his desk. Alicia didn't respond. He looked over at her as she stared off into the distance. "Hey, space cadet." No response. "Earth to Alicia! Hello, anyone home?"

She snapped out of it. "Oh, sorry. I was lost there for a second but I'm back now." She opened the file drawer and pulled out a folder and handed it to Zak. "FAT test."

Zak eyed her suspiciously. "How did you do that?"

"I put things away so I can find them again. You should try it sometime."

"Nah, too radical a concept for this office. It could have all sorts of negative repercussions."

"Zak, can you keep a secret?" asked Alicia in a low voice. He paused, thinking hard. "You only have to keep it till lunch."

"In that case then I think I can handle it. What good gossip have you got?"

"I turned in my resignation this morning. I'm moving to Salt Lake City, Utah." Zak's eyes got big. She had been working on this project with Zak for months and she knew this would not go over big.

"You're not kidding are you?" he asked hoping against hope that he was wrong. Alicia gave him an 'I'm sorry' look back. "Damn. I mean... you know, so what's the deal?"

"Well, I got an offer I couldn't refuse so I didn't refuse it. It's with an old friend on the ground floor of a start up company." Zak looked like he still didn't believe it. She tried to reassure him on the project. "Henry knows what we're doing on this and he knows this software package almost as well as I do. He can be up to speed by the time I leave with no schedule impact."

"Yes, but the client will notice. You and I have led the last three projects for them and they have a comfort zone with us. They don't know Henry. Well, they know him but they don't know his work. I'm going to have to start over again with him." Zak seemed to grow embarrassed as the silence stretched out.

"I'll miss you too, Zak. I've enjoyed our work together. Most of all I'll miss our political discussions. I'll need to find another stone hearted conservative to argue with."

"You air head liberals are all the same," he responded good naturedly, "always looking for a fight. Is there anything I can do?"

"Now that you've offered, what I really need is some help loading the truck next week. Do you think I could talk you into helping with the heavy stuff? Marci and I can get the small stuff ourselves."

Zak nodded. "Sure, you can count on me. I'm sure Ron will be there too."

Alicia looked at the test procedure in Zak's hand. "We better get back to it if we want to pull this off on schedule." Alicia tried to concentrate but her heart was no longer in it.

Tuesday, October 8

Macon had been good to Rae Ann since she moved there as a newlywed twenty years ago. But now things were different. Old friends wouldn't acknowledge her on the street. Businesses she had used for years now made it clear they no longer desired her patronage. She had been relieved of her position at the insurance office because of "poor performance" and excessive time off (one full day and one afternoon off dealing with charges against her daughters that were later dropped). Rae Ann knew it was all bull but she refused to work where she wasn't wanted. It had taken her two weeks to find another job as a waitress at a Big Boy restaurant across town next to the interstate.

Kathy and Carla had been let go from their part-time jobs at the Taekwondo school because of the "incident." The owner of the school had been quite apologetic but he felt it was the only thing he could do if he wanted to stay in business in that town. He told them that he would try to find them some work on the side as private tutors but it never materialized. Kathy did manage to get some hours through a professor on campus, but the work was erratic.

Rae Ann was feeling the money crunch limiting her options at every turn. Now she sat behind the wheel of her old green Chevy, steam rolling out from under the hood, trying to nurse it to the service station two blocks from work. "You damned old piece of junk!" she swore out loud. "Why now?" Through the haze of steam she saw the BP sign and crept in the drive, shutting off the overheated engine. Grabbing her purse, she ran inside to find a mechanic. She glanced at her watch, ten to four. "Damn." She had to be at work by four for the dinner shift. She was never going to make it.

The station manager followed her out to her car, popped the hood and only took a minute to render an opinion. "It's your water pump. See how it's dripping there from the belt?" he said pointing to a pulley. "It won't cost much but I'm all booked up for the rest of the day. I could get to it tomorrow morning."

"What do you mean by not much?" Rae Ann asked suspiciously.

"It should be less than two hundred. Just depends on the price of the pump. That engine is pretty good to work on so the labor will only be about seventy-five."

It was better than what she feared but it would still cut into what she had managed to save up. "Is there a cheaper way?"

"I could get you a rebuilt pump. That would save you about forty bucks but I can only warrant that for thirty days instead of a year."

"Shit," she cursed under her breath. "Excuse my French but this hasn't been my week. I live across town and this isn't exactly where I want my car. Is it safe to drive to a station closer to home?"

"I wouldn't advise it. It could be done but only drive a few blocks at a time and then let it cool twenty minutes." He waited a few moments, shifting his weight from foot to foot, anxious to get back to the job waiting on the rack.

"Does the bus run by here?" asked Rae Ann.

"Yeah. There's a stop up here at the corner," he said motioning back in the direction she came from.

"Well," she sighed, "go ahead and fix it. Use the rebuilt part. I need to save every dime I can." They went inside to settle the paperwork and then Rae Ann walked the last two blocks to work.

As usual, her boss was in a bad mood and Rae Ann arriving late didn't improve it. Even after she explained that it was car trouble and offering to have her boss call the station to confirm, the abuse continued. "Listen Rae Ann, I've had about all I care to take from you. If you screw up one more time, you're history. Do I make myself clear?"

"Perfectly," responded Rae Ann coolly. I've had my ass chewed by better than you, you old bag she wanted to say, but for now she needed this job. "I'd like to get to work now." The manager turned her back so Rae Ann assumed the conversation was over.

Halfway through her shift, Rae Ann began to get the feeling that things were not right tonight. At first she thought it was because she had received such a chewing out from her boss but no one would say more than two words to her. Even the bus boys ignored her to the point that she started cleaning her own tables. She also noticed that her tips were half of what they usually were. She already knew how the hostess could control your income. If the best customers were sent to another section and you only got the deadbeats, your income could be cut in half. She had learned the golden rule in the first week on the job, keep the hostess happy or you don't get any gold.

At break, she stepped out back where one of the other girls stood smoking a cigarette and sipping a coke. Immediately, the girl snubbed out her butt in the ashtray and started back inside. "What the hell is going on?" Rae Ann asked her.

The girl looked at her blankly, "What do you mean?"

"What do you mean what do I mean? We have always been on good terms since I've started here but now as soon as I show up, you're gone. Nobody will bus my tables and I couldn't get a decent customer if I gave them tips." Rae Ann kept her voice low but she held it firm. "What is going on?"

The other waitress continued inside trying to ignore Rae Ann who had followed her. She suddenly whirled around to face Rae Ann. "You want to know what's wrong? How about I don't like being lied to," she said irritatedly.

"I've never lied to you."

"Oh yeah. You never told me you were a Mono. That's the same thing."

Rae Ann didn't flinch. So that was it, probably some customer had identified her to the management. Rae Ann made no attempt to deny it. "What was I supposed to do? Stand up and announce it to everybody at the employee meeting. Maybe I should paint a big sign on my bumper, Mono On Board! You didn't have any problems talking with me yesterday. I'm the same person I was then, so what's the difference?"

The other waitress scowled at her. "Today I know the truth about you. Why didn't you just tell me before...."

"Before you started being friendly to me? Did I ruin your perception of us? You just can't take the fact that we're not monsters or what?"

The manager rounded the corner and marched up to them. "Would you two quiet down! You're upsetting the customers. Your break's over. Get back to work." The two women started to move back towards the dining room. "Not you, Baird, go to my office."

"Why? Are you in a rush to fire me?" Rae Ann spit out.

"You bet I am and I'll be glad to be shed of you. I don't like your kind stinking this place up. Get your stuff and get out. I'll have your check tomorrow afternoon."

Rae Ann had visions of slam dunking her boss's face in the trash can but thought better of it. That would only give them another story to spread in the news proving how violent Monos are. "I'll be back for it tomorrow," was all she said.

Rae Ann sat on the bus thinking. It had been a hell of a day, her car, then her boss, now no job. She was thumbing her way through the newspaper that was left on the seat in front of her, working her way to the want ads, when a small article caught her eye. It told that Christine Landis was collecting Monoecions with construction backgrounds to help get the reservation ready to accept the general Monoecion population. Hell, she thought, I can swing a hammer. She had helped her husband remodel two houses and one was a complete gutting and rebuilding. Anything would be better than staying here waiting to be slowly strangled out of existence. The thought of surgery had come and gone in a flash. Rae Ann was not going to give anyone the satisfaction of seeing her give up, even though she had no intention of having any more children. The thought of Nevada kept rolling around her mind. She had never been to Nevada. The farthest west she had been was at her uncle's place in Mississippi.

By the time she arrived at her stop, she had made up her mind. They were going. She knew it wasn't going to be easy but she never had been afraid of hard work. There was something soul cleansing about hard physical work. She just wanted to be where she wouldn't get fired for what she was, where she could help build something positive and not fear for the lives of her children.

The long walk from the bus stop to her house gave her time to think about how she was going to break it to the girls. A block away from home Rae Ann noticed a passing car suddenly slow down after it passed her. It picked up speed again and turned the corner leaving her with an uneasy feeling in her stomach. When she was in sight of the house, she heard the car coming from behind and looked over her shoulder just in time to see someone lean out the window. It took half a second for the thought to register, I'm going to be shot. She recovered her mental balance and dived behind a tree and braced herself for the burst of gunfire as the car roared past. Instead she heard the wet thud of eggs exploding around her and the screams of laughter coming from the receding automobile. Rae Ann got up immediately and brushed herself off. She was not going to give them the satisfaction of seeing her crawling on the ground. The eggs had missed and the only damage was torn hose and a scrape on her elbow. She marched to her front door.

Carla was in the living room watching TV when she heard Kathy ask "What are you doing home early?" followed by a gasp and, "What happened to you?" She ran out, fearing the worst.

Rae Ann stood in the kitchen looking at the dirty smears on her waitress uniform. "Don't worry about it. Some young punks tried to hit me with some eggs. I dodged them but I had to slide to do it." She didn't mention that her first thoughts were of bullets, not eggs. "As to why I home early, I got canned."

"What happened," asked Carla.

"Just what I knew would happen eventually. Someone who knew me must have spotted me working there and told the manager that I'm a Monoecion. All she did then was use anything as an excuse to fire me." Rae Ann went over to the kitchen sink, pulled out a fresh dish cloth and started to wash off her elbow to get a clear view of her scrape. "Sit down here both of you. I have something we need to discuss." This wasn't the way she had planned to break the move to the girls but it would have to do. "On the way home tonight on the bus... Oh yeah, the car is in the shop with a shot water pump in case you're wondering. Anyway, I saw this article." She laid it on the table between the girls.

"Is the car OK?" asked Carla concerned.

"Yes, it will be fine. I pick it up tomorrow afternoon. Thanks for showing almost as much concern for me as you do for the car. I feel my status is elevated now." Rae Ann tapped the newspaper with her finger, returning their attention to the article.

The girls huddled over it, each trying to get in better position to read it. "What about it?" asked Kathy suspiciously.

"I think we should go." Rae Ann paused, waiting for a reaction.

Carla stayed quiet, not knowing yet what to think. Kathy burst out with, "Why? Just because some kids threw a few eggs at you. They were probably cruising the neighborhood throwing eggs at anyone they could find."

"No, that's not it. I made up my mind before that even happened. We can't stay here if we can't work. Do you know how hard I had to look to get this crappy job only to have it taken away just because I'm a Mono. And those kids you mentioned yelled 'Mono bitch' at me as they drove past. They knew exactly who I was. What happened to the punks who attacked Carla? Nothing. Do you want to wait around for them to finish the job."

"You already made up your mind and that's it? Don't we have a say in this? After all, it is only a little matter of our lives."

Rae Ann was surprised at the strong resistance that Kathy had against the reservation. When they had discussed it before, Carla had seemed supportive and Kathy was non-committal. Now there was a violence to her opposition. "I have only decided that I want to go now. What each of you do is up to you. You are both adults and can make up your own minds but I was hoping to keep this family together a little longer."

"There are other alternatives. We can move to where they don't know us."

"What are you saying, go underground?" Rae Ann looked at Kathy with her you don't have a brain in your head look. "I'm not interested in living the rest of my life as a fugitive. If you're caught there is a minimum sentence of six years and sterilization. Sorry, that's not my first choice."

"We could have the surgery." Kathy's words came defiantly. Carla's eyes jerked up off the page and looked at her mother, waiting for the explosion. It was no secret how her mother felt about that subject.

"You want some intern to cut you open and remove your chance of producing a child? Just because someone else can't accept you for what you are, you are willing to give up a family you haven't yet created for them?" Rae Ann wanted her words to cut, to draw blood and inflict pain. She knew why but she could never bring herself to share it with her children. The abortion she had when she was fifteen years old had imprinted her emotions for all time. The feeling of loss had followed her wherever she went. Her father had forced her to do it, claiming that her life would be ruined if she had the child at her young age. And even though the fetus was only seven weeks old, she still felt it die in her soul, felt the newly forming connection suddenly disappear. While she was still a child herself, she felt what it was like to lose a child in that special way that only a Monoecion could. It had nearly driven her mad. Now she felt driven to prevent her children from ever making the same mistake.

"No," said Kathy, nearly in tears, "that's not what I want. I don't know what I want. I don't want to have to choose."

"We are going to have to choose because we are being forced to. In a few months we will be required to make a choice and I've already made up my mind so why wait around?" Rae Ann's voice became gentle, showing the love she honestly felt for her daughters. "The connection I have with you two is a beautiful thing and I want you both to have it with your children. I don't want you to give up the possibility of having it and I'm tired of fighting the bigots around here. I want to go where our kind is in the majority for once."

Carla had been quiet during the exchange but now she spoke up. "I want to stay together if we can." She had already decided to go with her mom. She knew that there was no way to change her mom's mind once it was made up. There was a hint of pleading in her voice as she addressed Kathy. "Look, it's no big deal. If we don't like it we can leave. The choice doesn't have to be permanent if you don't want it to be." Carla looked at her sister's face. "Please, let's stay together a little longer."

"I'm going to hate it," Kathy said quietly.

Rae Ann put her arms around her daughters and hugged them close to her. "Only if you decide to. It's up to you how you feel about it. Just give it a chance." Rae Ann knew that the biggest fear was the unknown. She was sure that once Kathy was there, her fears would be dispelled and she would become comfortable with the place. "Thank you. I need you girls to stick with me for now, to keep this family in one piece. Now, start packing. I want to be out of here as soon as we can arrange it. And pack light! I don't want you two sitting in my lap the whole way."

That night, Kathy confided in Carla. "I'm scared."

Carla was surprised. She had never known her sister to be scared of anything in her life. "Scared of what?"

"I'm scared of being the outcast there. I mean, how mom feels here, I'm going to feel there."

Now Carla was confused. "Why would you be an outcast there. They are all going to be like us."

"That's the point. There won't be any men, at least not many, and any that are there will already be taken." Kathy was having a hard time talking about this with her sister. They had rarely talked about sex before and it was a lot more complicated now. "Do you remember when mom talked to us and told us about our condition?"

"Yeah. You mean when we were fourteen?"

"Yes. She warned us about having feelings for girls and warned us not to act on those feelings. I never had to worry about it. I've never had the slightest attraction to a girl but I sure like the feel of a man close beside me. I'm going to feel like the only straight person at a gay liberation rally."

Carla couldn't say the same. She had found herself attracted to a girl on more than one occasion but she had always resisted it. "There's bound to be more there who feel the way you do."

"That just makes it worse. If a stray guy does get in the place, there will be a thousand girls throwing themselves at him. I'm not pretty enough to compete on that scale."

Carla gave a weak smile. "Give it a try with us, just for a little while to see what it's like. If you don't like it after a few months, then head out. Hell, I may go with you. It would help mom to have us all together when we start out."

Kathy nodded. "I'm going, I just wanted you to know how I feel. I don't want to hurt mom, I just don't think it's for me." They said good night but sleep was still a long way off.

Wednesday, October 9

Rae Ann got the girls up bright and early the next day to start sorting through their possessions once again. When they moved into this cracker box of a house she forced the girls to only bring what they needed. Now they would be forced to cut much deeper. Her car could haul a small trailer but not much else so they had to reduce their belongings to the bare minimum. Everything else would be sold by a friend who would send her the money. At ten AM she got a call from the garage telling her the belt also need to be replaced to the tune of forty dollars. Rae Ann told them to use the old one. It only needed to get her to Nevada and after that she didn't care. The mechanic said it was fine by him but he couldn't guarantee how long it would last.

Rae Ann's plan was ambitious. She would take the bus and pick up her car, her check and a trailer in that order. That night they would pack everything up and take off by six the next morning. With all three of them taking turns driving, they should make the reservation in three days. The only problem was she had no idea what she would do after she got there. She shoved that thought to the back of her mind.

When she arrived to pick up her car, the mechanic popped the hood and showed her the belt. "See that notch right there. It's been damaged by something. I don't trust it and I wanted you to see it before you left out of here."

Rae Ann tried to look knowledgeable and peered into the engine compartment. "Yeah, it looks bad but I just can't afford to replace it. Do you think it will get me to Las Vegas?" she asked, not wanting to say where she was really going.

"I don't know if it will get you across the street, but then again it may last ten thousand miles. There's just no way to tell for sure. You driving all that way in this car?"

"Leaving tomorrow morning."

"Just a minute. Let me check out back." With that he disappeared through a backdoor and returned a few minutes later, grinning, holding his prize. "I found another one. It's not much better shape than the one you have now but if yours gives out on the road, it would sure help to have a spare."

"Thanks, how much?"

"Nothing. Just keep it," said the mechanic.

Rae Ann smiled at him, touched by his genuine concern but then her face clouded over. "I appreciate your kindness but you don't know who you're giving it to. You see I'm..."

"I know who and what you are. I recognized you from the news when your kids were attacked. Take it. I hope you have good luck out there." He held the used belt out to Rae Ann.

She took the belt from him gently, as if it was precious, because it was. This was the first kindness she had received from a stranger who recognized her. "Thank you," was all she could say. She went inside to pay the bill and get her keys.

Rae Ann's experience picking up her check brought her back to the real world. The manager made her sit out front for thirty minutes before she could be bothered to get Rae Ann's check. Then she was ordered to go back to the manager's office to sign a reprimand report before she could get the check. The manager finally produced the check from her desk drawer and gave it to Rae Ann.

With her cash in hand, she could finally execute the plan that had been shaping in her mind all morning. Rae Ann began to speak in a slow and deliberate tone. "You know, the government just loves to tell lies." The manager looked at her quizzically, confused as to what she was getting at. "They told everybody that this Mono crap is a genetic disease that can only be passed on from mother to child, and you know, that's just a bold face lie."

"What are you talking about?" said the manager eyeing her suspiciously.

Rae Ann leaned close to her and whispered "Well, you see it's this way." With that, Rae Ann grabbed the manager's hair and pulled her head back, planting a wet kiss on her lips, thrusting her tongue in her mouth for an instant before the other woman could react and pull away.

"What the hell are you....."

"This disease can also be passed on by the exchange of bodily fluids... like saliva." Rae Ann smiled a big mocking smile. Her manager was turning white and making little squeaking sounds. "Don't worry, it will be months before you start noticing that girls look pretty good. Bye, bye." Rae Ann turned and walked out of the office, then stopped and leaned back in. "Yesterday I spit in your tea. That little kiss wasn't because I found you attractive, it was just insurance to make sure that the disease took. Ta-ta." Even though everything she said in the office was pure bullshit, she knew that it would have the desired effect. That woman is a worrier, smiled Rae Ann to herself as she walked to her car, and even though everyone reassures her, it will still drive her crazy for weeks not knowing for sure. It wasn't enough but it was something.

She picked up a small trailer at U-Haul and headed home. On her return, the real work began. The instructions she had received from her call for information said to come packed for barracks living. She looked at the huge pile of things each of her daughters had selected to take along and had a fit. She ordered them to cut it to the bone with little results. She then ordered them to cut the pile in half. To the remainder, she added her pile of necessities. They loaded the car and trailer and looked at the little space they had left. Rae Ann allowed each in turn to add an item until she felt the load was at maximum. It was late when they finished.

Rae Ann had tried to prepare herself for how hard it was going to be to pack her life into a small cube of space but her heart still ached as she looked at the things she had to leave behind. The things that hurt the most were the keepsakes, toys that belonged to the girls when they were little that Rae Ann was keeping for the future grandchildren, the bed her grandmother was born in, but most of all the memories that were attached to every piece left behind.

They sat down long enough to devour a delivered pizza and then packed road food so it could be easily tossed in the cooler in the morning. After making sure that everything was secured, they fell exhausted into bed.

Thursday, October 10

At six AM, the alarm buzzed but Rae Ann was already up, making one last breakfast before the trip. They did their best to clean out whatever was left in the refrigerator, either by eating it or putting in the cooler for later. By seven, Rae Ann stood at the backdoor, knob in hand. The girls were already out but she hesitated. When she closed that door, there was no turning back. "Are you sure you have everything?"

"That's the second time you've asked. Yes, we're sure." Carla could see that her mom was having a hard time with this, she could feel it inside her. The fear and indecision were too strong to mask. She walked over to her mom and put an arm around her. "We're ready, let's go."

"I hope we are because we're not coming back." She pulled the door shut. The drive up 75 North was uneventful. They stopped for lunch at the rest stop south of Chattanooga. After a short stretch, they loaded back up and picked up Interstate 24 West for Nashville with Kathy behind the wheel. After a couple of hours, Rae Ann again took the wheel explaining that she didn't want the girls to drive with a trailer through a major city. She completed the loop around the south side of Nashville and had just entered I-40 westbound for Memphis when the truck behind her started honking and flashing it's lights. The next thing she knew, it sounded like her engine was disassembling itself under the hood.

Chapter 28

The days had gone by quickly with all there was to do. Marci found a renter to take over their lease. The apartment was a sea of boxes awash in Styrofoam peanuts and crumpled newspaper. Jasmine kept them in contact with Christine every couple of days, keeping them informed about the status of the reservation. Christine told them that Robin was already there and would be expecting them. Alicia had sent in a resume so Christine had an excuse to single them out for special attention because of Alicia's skill set. It had been a constant stream of fast food and pack until you drop activity. Everyone was feeling the stress of overload, especially the children. The lack of regular hours was making Jasmine cranky and Jessica demanded to be held continuously.

Moving day arrived with dark clouds and threatening gusts. Alicia picked up the Ryder truck as early as the rental lot opened to allow maximum time to load before the predicted afternoon rains. Even though the truck wasn't huge, it was still much bigger than anything Alicia had ever driven. The man behind the counter eyed her suspiciously. "Lady, have you ever driven a truck like this?" he asked.

"Sure, I used to drive my dad's truck on the farm," she lied, "but it's been awhile. Go over everything again in detail to remind me." The man briefed her carefully on the operation and watched with concern as she drove unsteadily off the lot. He wasn't worried about the woman behind the wheel as much as he was worried about getting his truck back in one piece.

It was still early when Alicia arrived back at the apartment. Zak and a few others from the office were already there hauling boxes down the stairs and piling them on the sidewalk. Alicia backed the truck up to the curb and set the brake.

"It's about time you got here. Where's the beer you promised?" yelled Zak.

Alicia jumped out of the truck. "Quiet! Some of the people who live here actually like to sleep late if you don't mind. Also, you know the first rule of using free labor, never break out the beer until the job is complete."

"If that's the way it's going to be then lets get to it. I came over here thirsty."

Alicia gave Zak a face. "You mean you could drink a beer at eight in the morning and like it? You're sicker than I thought."

"Actually, no I couldn't, not any more but it sounds macho," Zak laughed. "When I was in college I had beer and corn flakes for breakfast and loved it. Of course I usually hadn't gone to bed the night before."

"I wondered what happened to all your brain cells. They died a tortured death in a dorm room." Alicia allowed herself to get serious for a moment. "Thanks for coming to help. I don't know what we would have done without your help."

Zak refused to get suckered into being serious this early in the morning. "We haven't done much yet and we won't if we just keep standing around insulting each other. Let's get it done." By the time Alicia's father arrived an hour later, the truck was half-full. In another hour the apartment was empty except for some cleaning supplies.

Zak hung around after the rest of the crowd had evaporated into what was left of the morning. He waited until Alicia's dad and Marci were busy elsewhere and cornered Alicia as she was closing the truck's pull down door. "Look, there has been something bothering me and I wanted to talk to you alone."

Alicia sensed a somber edge to Zak's mood and instinctively tried to put some distance between them. "I need to get the truck moved so people can get in and out of here. It will just take a minute." She slapped the latch closed and started for the driver's side door.

Zak hurried in front of her to intercept. "Could you leave it here for just a minute more, I've got something I need to ask you."

"It should be moved..." She could tell it was important to Zak so against her better judgment, she conceded. "But no one has complained yet. What do you want?"

Zak paused for a moment, too embarrassed to ask the question he had come for. "I know that you're aware of the talk that's circulated around the office about you..."

"No, what talk?" Alicia asked with obvious anger in her voice. "You mean that crap about me being gay because I wouldn't date those guys from the office?"

"Not that." Zak looked down at his shoes. Butterflies danced in his stomach as he tried to regain his composure. He hated confrontation and he didn't want this conversation to become one. "Look, I don't want to upset you but I couldn't help but notice that you resisted in giving me a phone number where you could be reached at your new job. When you gave it to me the day before yesterday, I tried calling it." Zak thought he saw Alicia twitch. "It's not in service. I also noted that where you're going is awful close to where the Monoecion reservation is and wondered if there was some connection."

Alicia was worried. If Zak suspected, then how many others also suspected. The safest way out was flat denial. She had practiced it over and over in her head for months. "So you are asking me if I'm a Mono. Is that it?"

"I'm not trying to judge you, I just want you to be honest with me. We have worked together closely for four years and I'd just like to know the truth."

Alicia's anger and frustration came out in her voice. "No, I'm afraid the office gossips will just have to get along without me. I'm not a butch lesbo on the loose or a genetic freak. I'm sorry to disappoint you but I'm going out west to take a new job with an old friend and that is all there is to it. I must have messed up when I wrote down the phone number."

"OK," said Zak in a tone that revealed his lack in sincerity.

"I like guys but I don't date men I work with." Most of Alicia's anger was focused inward but it projected itself into her words. She hated the lie, she hated the foul taste it left in her mouth to say it to a good friend but she was afraid to use the truth. All she could think about was the FBI linking her to the phone at the convenience store. "Why don't you just accept what I say and go away?"

Zak was surprised by the anger in her words. "I'm sorry. I didn't mean to upset you. I accept what you say." He didn't have any choice other than accept it but he didn't totally believe it. "Have a good life. Maybe I'll see you around." Zak turned and walked to his car, parked across the lot.

The first rain drops started dropping as Alicia watched him walk away. Her emotions were raging like a storm inside her. 'He is one of the most decent human beings I've ever known and I just lied to him straight in the face. He's not the enemy.' He got in his car and closed the door, never looking back. Alicia ran across the lot shouting "Zak, wait a minute! Zak, hold it!"

Zak rolled down his window. "Yeah?" He did little to hide his irritation.

"You said you wanted the truth. Well, sometimes the truth isn't as easy as it looks." The rain pelted Alicia face, hiding the tears that were now starting on their own paths down her cheeks. "The truth is that I can't tell you what you want to hear. There is just too much at stake and too many people involved for me to do anything. I hope you understand."

"It's OK," said Zak. "I didn't have a right to ask that question."

"I'll give you a call as soon as I can answer it." She bent down and kissed him on the cheek. "Thanks for helping." Alicia turned and ran for the truck. She didn't dare stay and talk any more.

They finished cleaning, returned the keys, and hit the road. The drive to Nashville was spent getting the girls used to the limited space in the cab. Jasmine curled her nose and complained about the smell. She wanted to ride in the back with her toys and couldn't understand why mommy objected. The rain stopped and the skies gradually cleared. Marci read a story over the roar of the engine and finally Jasmine and Jessica fell asleep. Unfortunately, Jasmine woke just as they entered the thick of it around Nashville. They circled the Music City and were back westbound on I-24 in fifty five minutes. Traffic was beginning to thin as they continued west and Alicia was starting to consider letting Marci take the wheel. It wasn't that she thought Marci wasn't capable, Alicia just didn't like riding in any vehicle with anyone else driving. She just didn't want to give up control so early.

"Look," said Marci gesturing with her hands, "the traffic is as thin as it's going to get. Unless you plan to drive all the way to Nevada, it's time for me to give it a try."

Alicia looked at her with suspicion. "The next rest stop, we'll switch. That will give the fireball here "Alicia ruffled Jasmine's hair, "a chance to wear off some energy and we can stretch."

"Fair enough. But if you start getting tired before that just pull off." Just then Marci caught sight of the rest area sign. "Perfect timing! One mile... What's that?!" Marci pointed to the car in front of them pulling a trailer. Black whiffs of smoke came from under the hood. Alicia flashed her lights and honked the horn to alert the driver in front of them as she stepped on the brakes, giving more room between the two vehicles. Chunks of something black came flying out from under the car. Almost instantly the brake lights came on and the car started to pull off onto the shoulder.

"Pull over and stop," said Marci.

"I don't want to try to pull this thing back into traffic without a merge lane," replied Alicia while slowing down the truck.

"The traffic isn't that bad. Pull over," she said firmly. "They might need a ride to the rest area to use the phone." Alicia knew when to give in so she put on the emergency flashers and pulled off coming to a stop about fifty yards past the disabled car. Marci said "I'm going back and check with them. Keep an eye on the girls."

Alicia looked down at Jessica curled up asleep on a pile of blankets on the floor. "Hold it. I don't want you to go back there by yourself. We're coming with you. Jessica can stay here and sleep."

"I want to go too," cried Jasmine.

"Don't worry," said Alicia, "you have to go. I don't trust you in here all by yourself." Alicia helped Jasmine down out of the truck into Marci's arms. "These cars are going fast. You stay away from the road and hold onto mommy's hand. Do you hear me?"

Jasmine nodded her head "Uh-huh."

Alicia closed the passenger side door as quietly as possible, gave one last check on Jessica and climbed out the driver's side. Together they approached the car behind them. Three women stood around the front of the car, one of them opening the hood. Garbled voices could be heard then one clear word came through, "Damn!" Marci looked over at Alicia a bit nervously as the got closer. The older woman was obviously irritated. "I knew it. I knew as much as I knew the sun would come up in the morning. Damn!" she repeated as she walked away from the car. That was when she noticed Jasmine between Alicia and Marci. "Oh! I'm sorry, please excuse my language."

"Hello, is there anything we can help you with?" asked Marci.

"How are you at changing drive belts?" called back Rae Ann Baird to the approaching strangers.

"Not too bad," replied Alicia "if I have the right tools and a spare belt."

"The belt I've got but I'm fresh out of tools. We've only been on the road a few hours and this happens." Rae Ann's frustration was impossible to hide. The twins tried to hide their embarrassment at their mother's language. "I must apologize for my French but I'm so mad at myself I could just spit. The mechanic told me the belt needed to be changed but I figured he was just trying to gouge me for few more bucks so I told him to forget it. How do you like that, so many are crooks and I get the honest one."

Alicia looked under the hood. "It looks pretty straight forward. We could give you a ride to the rest area up ahead and you could call a mechanic. I'm sure he could put in on right here with no problem. As a matter of fact, you could drive it up to the rest area with no problem, you can see it from here."

"Yeah, that's what I thought," said Rae Ann. "I just don't want to run it any longer than absolutely necessary."

"We may even be able to find someone with a wrench and a pry bar to do the job." Alicia noticed Rae Ann's two daughters talking off to the side of the car in hushed voices and then start giggling.

Rae Ann felt a tingle like a little chill run through her body. She couldn't identify it because she had never felt anything quite like it before. It was there, and just as quick, it was gone.

"Mommy," Jasmine tugged on Marci's sleeve.

"Just a minute, sweetie. We're trying to work something out."

"Mom," called Kathy, "come here for a minute. We have an idea we want to discuss." There was a note of conspiracy in her voice.

"Oh lord, they've been thinking again. This could be dangerous." Rae Ann walked over to her daughters. Alicia and Marci could overhear snatches of the conversation. It appeared that Kathy and Carla wanted to do something that Rae Ann was not in favor of.

"Mommy?" Jasmine tugged once again on Marci's sleeve.

Marci listened to scraps of the exchange between the woman and the young ladies. "Please. It would be fun to try and it would save us time and money."

"And what am I supposed to do, walk?"

Marci absently said to Jasmine "Yes, what is it, honey?" Jasmine curled her finger, beckoning Marci to come down to her. Marci leaned her ear down to Jasmine.

Jasmine cupped her hands and whispered in her mother's ear "They're like us. They're Monoecion too!"

Marci's first reaction was to quiet her daughter so they wouldn't be overheard. She placed a finger over Jasmine's lips and whispered "Quiet now. We'll talk about it later."

"It's OK mommy, they really are like us," Jasmine whispered back. "I checked."

"What do you mean you checked?" asked Marci filled with concern. "No, hush, we'll talk later when we're alone." Marci's tone made it clear that there was to be no more discussion. Jasmine nodded and held her tongue. Alicia heard some of the exchange and gave Marci a questioning glance. Marci shook her head and whispered "I don't know. As soon as I can, I'll find out."

"We don't know these people," Rae Ann explained to her daughters "and I'm not letting you two out of my sight up there by yourselves while I catch up on foot."

Alicia called out "Do you want a ride up to the rest area?"

Rae Ann came back over to Alicia. "That's what my girls had in mind. My daughters have come up with a hair brained scheme to get the car fixed for free but they said that I couldn't ride with them if it was going to work."

"Sure," offered Marci, "come on up. We need to go back and check on my littlest anyway." Alicia gave a concerned glance at Marci.

"Are you sure it's all right," asked Rae Ann picking up on Alicia's tension.

"No problem," said Marci as she glared Alicia into submission.

Rae Ann turned back to her girls. "OK, but if I see the slightest hint of trouble, I'm coming in like the Marines. Got it?"

"Don't worry, mom. We'll be fine," assured Kathy.

As the four of them walked back to the truck Jasmine spoke up. "Hi, my name's Jasmine."

"How do you do, Jasmine, I'm Rae Ann," she replied as she held out her hand.

Jasmine shook Rae Ann's hand and added "My little sister's sleepin' in the truck."

"At least we hope so," added Alicia. She climbed up on the running board and peeked in. "Yep, still dead to the world." Alicia carefully opened the door and climbed in. Marci climbed in after and held Jasmine on her lap while Rae Ann followed, closing the door.

"My daughters," Rae Ann said, "told me to give them five minutes. They decided that two sweet young things pulling into a rest area with car problems would get quicker attention without their mother standing beside them. They're probably right but I'm not sure that it's the kind of attention I want them to have."

"You're probably right," laughed Marci.

In the car, Kathy and Carla quickly put on a little make up and glossed their lips. Kathy rolled up the pant legs of her shorts making them as short as she could get them. She pulled out her blouse, unbuttoned it and tied it up exposing as much as she dared. Then she buttoned just enough to cover her bra.

Carla pulled out her Tee shirt and started to tie it up. "Darn, I can't do that. It exposes my scar and I don't think that will to attract many guys."

Kathy looked at her sister thoughtfully. "OK, lose the bra."

"What?!"

"Trust me," Kathy said. "Take it off. Come on, we don't have much time."

Carla reluctantly unhooked it and pulled it out her sleeve. "Mom will kill me."

"No she won't. Now turn around and let me pull your shirt tight." Kathy tucked Carla's shirt in the back of her jeans making the baggy Tee shirt look like one a size too small. "Perfect. We're ready to go." Kathy honked her horn two quick beeps to signal her mom to move out. After the truck pulled away, Kathy started the car and followed.

Alicia pulled into the section marked for trucks and cars with trailers and parked in the first available slot. She watched as Kathy drove on past and parked farther down close by two semis. Marci said "I'm taking Jasmine to the bathroom. Check Jessica to see if she needs to be changed."

"OK," Alicia replied. "I want to stay here for a minute and see how those girls fare getting their car fixed." Marci slid out of the truck with Jasmine in tow.

"Thanks for the lift. I can watch over them from over... My God," exclaimed Rae Ann, "Do you see her? She doesn't even have her shoes on."

Kathy had hopped out of the car and was standing in front of it looking at the grill. "How do you open this thing?" she shouted to Carla who had slid over into the driver's seat.

"There's a latch thingie under there somewhere," Carla replied.

"Yeah, but you have to pull something first don't you?"

Carla was amazed. If she didn't know it was her sister out there she would swear it was one of the campus airheads who made their grades on their backs rather than in the class room. "Yeah, I think so." Carla acted like she was searching and then pulled the hood release. "Found it!" Carla yipped. Kathy tried to lift up the hood but the safety latch still kept it from opening. "You have to undo that thingie now."

"Oh yeah." Kathy made a production bending over looking for the release. The hood released and Kathy held it open and looked inside. "It won't stay up."

"You're over doing the airhead act," hissed Carla. "We want to attract guys, not scare them away." Carla got out of the car. "Use the rod to hold it up, dopey." Carla grabbed the support rod and put it in the hole.

"I just wanted you out here with me," Kathy whispered to Carla. "I didn't want to face these guys by myself while you sit nice and snug in the car." Kathy motioned over her shoulder. Carla looked up and saw three men approaching from two different trucks.

"Why don't you stay here and watch," offered Alicia. "You'll be closer in case they need you."

"Thanks," said Rae Ann. "I appreciate this."

Marci looked around to make sure they were out of earshot of everyone. "Now, honey, tell mommy again. You think that they are Monoecion?"

"Uh-huh," Jasmine nodded. "I checked and they are."

"How did you check? You didn't connect with them did you?" Marci was scared. She was afraid that Jasmine didn't understand the danger of connecting with strangers, even if they were Monoecions.

"I didn't connect, I know better. I just se'ed if I could," she explained.

"How did you do that? Can you tell me?"

Jasmine shook her head. She didn't have words that could express it. Suddenly her face brightened. "I can show you!"

Marci felt her mind do the now familiar jump and freely joined with Jasmine's mind.

"I can't explain it but I can show you how it feels," explained Jasmine. "I'll do it to that person over there," indicating a woman leading a small boy down the sidewalk. Marci felt the probe reach out, like a hand reaching out in the darkness. The sensation was one of missing, like the hand not making contact with anything but air. There was something there, but like a vapor, it was impossible to grasp. "Now we can do it to her," said Jasmine indicating Carla. "Don't think anything while we do it so she doesn't know who it is." This time the hand reached out and touched a solid object. Instantly, Jasmine released the grip. "See, mommy, they are Monoecions. I checked them all, they're all like us."

Marci understood. "I know it frustrates you sometimes to be thought of as a little girl but you still are one. You know things that no child you age has ever known because you can learn from the experiences of the ones you connect to but you are still only five years old. You must learn from your own experiences and that requires time. We don't know where the holes in your experience are so we can't always trust what you think is right. Do you understand?" Jasmine let her mother know that she understood. "Let's bring Alicia in with us to let her know and we can decide what to do. OK?"

"OK," agreed Jasmine and instantly, Alicia was with them.

"Thanks for the warning," Alicia greeted them sarcastically. "I was right in the middle of a conversation. I hope I can keep this all straight." Marci and Jasmine explained what had happened and how. "So the question is do we reveal ourselves to them and hope for the best. I say let's do it. I'm tired of being alone. We need to take a chance and it's obvious that they are heading the same way we are."

Marci and Jasmine agreed. Marci was firm on one point. "I do not want you to connect with them though. Do you understand? It's too dangerous to reveal your gift to anyone." Jasmine indicated she understood. Jasmine said good-bye and they all jumped back to reality.

Rae Ann looked slack jawed at her daughters performance. "My God, do you believe that? I can't believe what I'm seeing." Within seconds, three men had come to the aid of the damsels in distress. Tool sets seemed to appear from nowhere and work was proceeding rapidly, not all of it directed at the car. "Did we have that kind of power when we were that age?"

"I never looked that good when I was that age," said Alicia.

"It's not how good they look that bothers me, it's how easily they play the game. I'd like to know how they've been spending their evenings. Where did they learn how to do this?"

"They learn it early nowadays." Alicia allowed a short pause in the conversation. "I was wondering if you had any experience in the construction or engineering fields?"

Rae Ann looked at her suspiciously. "A little bit. Why do you ask?"

Alicia tried to approach the topic as delicately as possible. "Well, I hope you don't mind me asking but I've been putting things together. I guess first it would be best to tell you that I'm a Monoecion. So is Marci and her kids. We're heading for the new reservation in Nevada and I was wondering if you are too."

Rae Ann was not sure how to respond. She would truly love some traveling companions but she didn't want to take a chance with someone who would reveal themselves so freely. "What would make you think I am?"

"You're a woman on the road heading west with two daughters. Wherever you're moving, you don't need much furniture, that little trailer wouldn't hold much. That would match up with the barracks life style we are going to live with for a while." Alicia couldn't come up any other logical reasons but she sensed that she hadn't sold the other woman on trusting her. "I also have a gut feel. If I'm wrong, I apologize. If I'm not, I'd truly enjoy your company on the trip out. I think there is safety in numbers while we're on the road."

Rae Ann wasn't sure what to say. She was afraid to reveal herself so quickly. She looked back to her daughters, buying time to think. The men had just finished putting the belt on the car and one of them planted his hand on Kathy's rear and gave it a squeeze. "Just a second. I think it's time for a mother to intervene." Rae Ann jumped out of the truck and headed for the group surrounding her daughters.

Alicia checked the emergency brake and gave the cab a quick check to make sure Jessica couldn't get into trouble if left alone for a moment. She jumped out of the truck and hurried to catch up.

Kathy had pushed the man's hand off her and was nervously looking at Carla for an idea as to how to break this off now that the job was done. "Well thanks guys. We really appreciate the help you've given us."

"Well ladies, we would appreciate it if you would join us in our cab. Have you ever seen the insides of one of these? It's really nice," the trucker smiled. The man tried to guide Carla in the direction of his truck.

"Kathy! Carla! Assume defensive positions!" Rae Ann yelled. The girls instantly moved clear of the men and assumed a defensive stance facing Rae Ann. The men looked curiously at this strange woman approaching them. Rae Ann bowed to Kathy, then to Carla. The girls returned the bow. Rae Ann hurled herself at Carla like a woman possessed, raining rapid fire blows at her.

Carla blocked and parried each thrust but not without difficulty. Carla didn't have a clue as to what her mother was up to. Without a pause, Rae Ann rotated and kicked high at Kathy who easily countered by dropping low and sweeping, going for Rae Ann's supporting foot. Rae Ann jumped that and backed off. The men stood back trying to fathom what was going on. "Not bad girls," Rae Ann laughed. "Not bad at all. Are you girls heading to the Martial Arts Nationals in St. Louis too?"

Kathy and Carla looked at each other not sure of how they were supposed to respond. Finally Kathy caught on. "We have to. We're the defending champions in team competition," answered Kathy. "How are you doing coach?"

"Pretty good since I saw you last," Rae Ann signaled back to Alicia. "I'd like to introduce you to the two best Karate students I ever had. This is Kathy and Carla Baird."

Alicia realized that Rae Ann didn't know what her name was so she jumped in with "Hi. I'm Alicia. You looked real good just now. You don't see many good karate demonstrations at rest areas."

Rae Ann asked "Can I buy you two a coke. I'd like to catch up on what you've been doing the last year."

The girls looked at each other and shrugged. "Sure, as long as you promise not to compete against us."

The men began to sense that their fish had sliped the hook. "Hey," one of them called. "I thought you were coming with us to see the cab." He gave them a broad smile.

"We'd like to but we haven't seen our old coach in forever and we just want to get caught up on old times. You understand." Kathy stepped over and kissed the man on the cheek. "Thanks a lot for the help with the car. You guys are real sweethearts." The man mumbled something unintelligible and spit on the ground. The women walked off talking and laughing like old friends reunited. When they were out of hearing range of the truckers, Carla hugged her mom. "That was brilliant mom. We didn't have to break any legs and we still got out with our virtue."

"Speaking of virtue young lady, where the hell is your bra?!" demanded Rae Ann.

"I told you I'd catch it for that," Carla mumbled to Kathy.

Kathy kept looking over her shoulder. "You know, the tall one is kinda cute in a red neck sort of way."

"Forget it, girl. I'm not going to have my daughter cruising cross-country with a crowd like that." Rae Ann looked over at Alicia and smiled. "You did well at thinking on your feet. I'd like to take you up on that suggestion you posed earlier."

"Girls, we're going to team up with these folks for the drive to our destination. It turns out that we're both going to the same place, and I believe for the same reasons."

"The very same reason," agreed Alicia. She saw a look of concern on Kathy and Carla's faces. They never expected their mother to be so open about their situation.

Jasmine came running up and latched on Alicia's leg. Marci followed holding a groggy Jessica over her shoulder. The sour look on Jessica's face showed her disapproval at being left all alone. "Come here, baby," Alicia cooed. Did you wake up and no one was there? Are you mad at me?"

Marci passed her over to Alicia as the twins crowded around to be introduced to Jessica. "I was over playing with Jasmine when I saw you heading for the car so I came and got her."

Alicia introduced everyone but found she couldn't remember which of the twins was which. Alicia then explained that they had decided to join forces for the drive. "Why don't we split up some and get to know each other. I've served my time behind the wheel for a while. Marci will be driving the truck. Anyone want to ride up top?"

"Sure," said Rae Ann. "I'd love to get away from those two for a while. There's nothing worse than traveling with two teenagers. It will be nice to have some mature company, like your Jessica here." Kathy and Carla stuck their tongues out at their mother. "I told you they were immature," said Rae Ann.

"Can Jasmine ride with us?" asked Kathy. "She is so cute." Jasmine grinned at Kathy.

"Sure, as long as you have room for me," said Alicia. They all talked for a few more minutes, getting comfortable with the idea of being together for several days of hard driving. "Hit the bathroom, kids. It's a long way to St. Louis," announced Alicia. A few minutes later they were on the road.

The miles passed easily as the two families got to know each other. In the truck cab, Rae Ann played with Jessica while the twins had fun with Jasmine. She seemed to know so much for such a little girl. They were impressed when they found out that Alicia played guitar in a blues band in college. Alicia was impressed that Rae Ann had really been the twin's karate instructor and that they had won several major competitions. They stopped for fuel in Paducah and let Jasmine run off some more energy. Fatigue was starting to show on them all but they had set a goal for the night of reaching St. Louis. They decided to cut the stop short and push on hoping to at least get close. After nearly three more hours on the road, they pulled into a cheap motel twenty miles short of St. Louis.

Chapter 29

Friday, October 11

It was after ten o'clock but everyone was either too wound up or just too tired to fall asleep. The first day's drive had left them stiff and sore. Waking to the thought of three more days driving did little to encourage a cheerful attitude. The plan had been to wake up at six and be on the road by six-thirty in the morning. Despite their best intentions, they were forty-five minutes late getting started which put them in the thick of the morning rush hour traffic. The day went down hill from there. Construction on the interstate slowed traffic to a crawl and they didn't start to make time until ten o'clock.

Jessica decided to start fussing early and continuously. Alicia had lost all patience and was contemplating flagging down Marci to trade places when Carla asked if she could give it a try. "Sometimes just a change of people will be enough." Carla pulled the car off on the shoulder and traded places with Alicia. Jessica quieted considerably in Carla's arms and finally accepted being returned to the car seat.

The weather was magnificent, warm sun and blue skies tried to lift the gloom from their emotions with little success. Jasmine had read all her books a dozen times and had lost interest in following their progress on the map. The flat landscape of Kansas gave little break to the monotony. Even the sight of two hot air balloons floating over the highway was met by a yawn. "When are we going to stop?" was asked every five minutes with Marci's answer always met with a sigh or whine.

The crossing of the state line into Colorado was met by cheering in both vehicles. They all looked forward to seeing the Rockies but that would have to wait until tomorrow. After nearly eight hundred miles, Alicia turned into a motel on I-70. Even Stevie Ray Vaughan cranked on her headphones couldn't keep her awake any longer. Rae Ann followed her in without protest.

Saturday, October 12

Breakfast was eaten in the major metropolis of Limon. The temperature was much cooler than they had experienced so far. Frost covered the windshield and the weatherman told of a major storm system approaching by nightfall. Snow flurries and temperatures below freezing were expected in the mountains.

"The map says it's only six hundred miles to Salt Lake City," said Rae Ann. "What it doesn't tell you is that it's all straight up and down. I've driven this before and it's going to take some extra time to cover. I know you troops are tired but we need one more good hard day of driving. Just think of it, tonight we stay in a motel but the next we spend at our new home."

Carla wrapped her arms around her mom. "I know a pep talk when I hear one. What you're trying to say is that if we don't get on the stick, we are going to be stuck in a hotel room, sleeping in warm beds and watching cable TV for two days until the weather clears instead of getting blisters on our butts from the car seat."

"Not quite. What I'm trying to say is that we have enough money for one more night in a motel. The next night will be spent sleeping in the car and eating crackers. It's your choice."

"As much fun as that sounds," said Kathy, "I guess we better hit the road."

Alicia took Rae Ann aside. "If you are short on cash, we can help you out. We're in this together."

"Thanks, I'll keep it in mind but I think we're OK for now. Sometimes the girls just need a little motivation, if you know what I mean."

Since it was Saturday, the Denver traffic was minimal. They had been driving together so long it had become automatic. That's why neither one noticed when they became separated. Marci just looked up ahead and said "Where did they go?"

"Who?" asked Kathy dreamily.

"Your mother, your sister, my spouse, my little girl... you know, those other people we've been traveling with."

Kathy became more alert now. "They were just up ahead a few minutes ago."

"I'm afraid I was caught daydreaming. When was the last time you saw them?" asked Marci.

"I'm not sure. It might have been fifteen minutes or more ago." Kathy sounded a little worried.

"Shit," said Marci under her breath. If Jasmine was with her she could have connected to Alicia to find out where she was but now Marci would have to wait for Jasmine to contact her, and she didn't relish the idea of that initial jolt of the connection as she rounded a curve with a five hundred foot drop off next to her.

"Should we stop?" asked Kathy. "Maybe we passed them."

What if they are both asleep, thought Marci, we could be out of contact for hours. "No. I think they're up ahead of us. We'll catch them soon." Marci tried to sound confident. "But just in case, does you mom have a cell phone? Alicia had to turn her company phone in when she quit so I'm the only one with a phone."

"No, I'm afraid we don't have one. After my dad... after we moved out, we didn't have much money so we cut everything to save money."

"Don't worry, we'll catch them soon" Marci said with more confidence than she really had.

Kathy relaxed a little and then seemed lost in thought. "Do you mind if I ask you something?"

"Go ahead," said Marci.

"You called Alicia your spouse. Are you really married?"

"Last I knew we still were." Marci saw that Kathy was embarrassed at asking the question. "The state and the courts may not agree but we never paid much mind to them. We rented a hall at a church with the help of a gay rights organization on campus and had a minister assist. At the time, Alicia's parents fought it but at least her mom understood. It took her dad a lot longer to come around and accept me as a member of the family."

"Did they attend the wedding?" Kathy asked.

"No. My mom was the only family member there. It was mostly just friends from college. But we surprised them. Eight years and two kids later and we are still going strong."

"If you don't mind telling me, how did you have the kids?" queried Kathy.

"The usual way, at a hospital," laughed Marci.

"I didn't mean..." Kathy stopped, too embarrassed to rephrase the question.

"I know. I was just having some fun with you." Marci noticed that being separated from the others helped draw Kathy out of her shell. "We looked at the whole situation and decided together who was going to be mommy and who was going to be daddy. Then I collected the sperm from Alicia and she..." Marci searched for the right word to describe the action but couldn't find one. "You know, delivered it to me."

"You mean you knew you had both sex organs?" Kathy was excited to know someone who had actually fathered a child. "We didn't know we had dual sex until it came out in the papers."

"That seems to be true of a good percentage of the population," explained Marci. "We only knew because my grandmother knew another Monoecion who knew Doctor Moore."

Kathy's curiosity seemed satisfied. "So what do we do about the other half of the group?"

"Beats me."

Just then Marci felt the familiar presence and the question "Where are you?"

Marci told Jasmine to connect to Alicia so she could see what mile marker they were at but found out she was asleep. It seems that Carla just noticed that they were missing and they were talking about waking her. Marci guided her to look at the road and spot the first mile marker.

"You're about five miles ahead of me. Wake Alicia and have her stop at the next rest area. We will be just a few minutes behind you. You got that?" Jasmine assured her that she understood. "If you don't know what to do, just come to me." Jasmine made it known that she could handle it and was disappointed at Alicia's apparent lack of confidence, then she was gone.

"Oh, I'm sure that they will stop and wait for us at the next rest area. Alicia and I talked about that some time ago. We will just keep driving until we get to one." Kathy seemed to accept it and wasn't surprised when they found them waiting twenty miles up the road at a rest area.

They took a break, donning their sweaters and coats against the dropping temperatures. The twins played with Jasmine, running and chasing like they were her age. "My girls have fallen in love with Jasmine," said Rae Ann. "I haven't seen them pay so much attention to a little kid in a long time."

"I've noticed," responded Marci. "And it's really appreciated. They have made the trip so much more enjoyable for her. I hate to think of how this drive would have been without them."

"She's cute as a bug's ear and she's so smart. It's hard to believe that she's only five. She is very mature for her age. I think she really can relate to my girls and that is what endears her to them."

The words tugged at Marci's heart. It was her greatest fear that Jasmine was growing up too quick because of all the time she spent connected with adults and the problems she had to deal with. "Yes, she understands a lot for a little girl. In times like this you have to grow up quick, too quick." Marci watched silently as Kathy and Carla took turns giving Jasmine helicopter rides, swinging her around and around.

The temperature continued to drop and the snow flurries began. The forecast was for scattered light snow showers throughout the afternoon with some accumulation to come only in the higher elevations starting in the early evening. They kept driving. They pushed hard through most of Wyoming, stopping only a few minutes to take pictures at the continental divide. "It's all downhill from here," proclaimed Alicia.

"There may be more truth to that than we would like," commented Rae Ann.

The snow began to get heavier as the afternoon turned to evening but it never got bad enough to slow them down. They pulled into Salt Lake City ahead of schedule. At the motel Marci announced "Since this will probably be our last night out in the big city for quite a while, I propose that we go out to a nice restaurant and live it up just a little. My treat."

"It sounds great," said Rae Ann "but I can help cover it."

"Don't worry about it," Alicia said. "It's a gift from us to you. If you hadn't stuck with us you would already be there by now. Traveling with two little kids and a lumbering truck does not make for high speed travel." Rae Ann and the twins graciously accepted.

Sunday, October 13
They slept in until eight, a glorious luxury, and woke to frost covered windshields. The high was supposed to hit 45 degrees but that sounded freezing to the trio from Macon. Marci and Alicia were a little more used to the cold temperatures but it felt more like December than October. They all knew it was going to get much colder before it got warmer. They all had butterflies in their stomachs as the drove the last couple hundred miles of interstate. Soon they would be at the reservation, living a life they couldn't fully imagine, facing hardships but in a safe environment, without fear for their lives. Hope intermingled with fear, sorrow for what they were giving up touched with excitement for what they were about to build.

The exit from the interstate put them on a blacktop state road heading north. The two-lane highway was fine but high winds had blown sand over it, obscuring pieces of it for twenty yards at a time. At least there were tire tracks showing it had been traveled recently. Alicia guessed they were still thirty miles from the reservation when she spotted a pickup truck and trailer pulled about ten yards off the road. A woman was standing by the truck waving at them as they approached.

Rae Ann immediately slowed the car and looked to pull off the road next to the car. Marci looked at the woman and pickup with suspicion. She couldn't put her finger on it but something wasn't quite right. The area was flat, you could hardly distinguish the road from the landscape. Alicia pulled in behind Rae Ann's car and set the brake. She rolled down the windows and told Jasmine to stay put and not to touch anything. "There can be snakes out there and I don't want you walking around until I know. And I need you to watch over Jessica, you can look right down there and see her in the back seat of the car, OK?" Jasmine promised she would keep an eye on her. Alicia climbed down and joined Marci.

Carla went over with her mother and sister as they greeted the woman. Rae Ann called out "Hello, you need some help?"

"It quit on me and I can't get it started," she replied back with the slightest quiver in her voice.

Marci and Alicia were on the passenger side of the truck by now. Alicia started over towards the woman's pickup but Marci grabber her arm and gently stopped her. "Stay here," she whispered looking down at the ground. Alicia gave her a questioning glance. "I don't know why, just stay here with me." Marci stepped back against the reassuring feel of the truck.

As Rae Ann and the twins approached the pickup, the woman turned and opened the driver's side door. Three men jumped out from behind the pickup holding guns. "Freeze right where you're at or I swear we'll shoot you down like the animals you are!" yelled a man with a full beard.

Fear raced through them all, feeding on each other and threatening to overwhelm them. Marci and Alicia fought for control, trying to stem the terror building in Jasmine. The woman pulled out a pistol from under the seat and pointed it directly at Marci. "You two get over here away from that truck. Come on! Move it!"

Rae Ann watched as Alicia and Marci slowly shuffled out in the space between the vehicles. She had trained all her life for a situation like this and now that it was here there was little she could do. You can't dodge a bullet. To take out a person with a gun, you must first get close enough to strike. To get close enough to strike, you must move. To move visibly is to become a target. You must move so slowly that no motion is visible. Rae Ann looked from one daughter to the next, trying to reassure them and remind them of the rules they needed to follow if they were going to survive. Their attackers were stationed around them, each with a clear field for fire and all out of striking distance.

The man with the beard started talking again. "We are here to give you and your kind a message. That message is that we don't want you here. The government may be naive enough to think that you are all going to quietly go on this reservation and mind your own business and never come out but we know better. The solution to the problem is when all of your kind are dead! Only then will the God-fearing people be safe again."

Alicia thought about the loaded colt revolver rigged under the driver's seat. That was one gun against four and at this point, she didn't stand a chance. She would be gunned down before she could get near it. She thought about the little single shot derringer her father had given her, tucked in her right boot. If she could get it pointed at one of them at close range then she might be able to get a Mexican standoff. She thought the men might back down if they thought one of them would get killed. The problem was getting it out without drawing attention to herself.

The leader signaled the younger man who then approached Carla. "Damn, I really hate to mess this one up. She looks too good to be a Mono."

Carla positioned herself, ready to take him out when he tried to lay a hand on her. Then she caught her mother's eye. It was obvious that she didn't want Carla to act yet but she couldn't figure out what to do, so she did nothing.

"This ain't no beauty contest, this is our very existence we're dealing with. Do it," shouted the bearded man. The younger man said under his breath, "We'll get together later when we're through with the others." He then backhanded Carla across the face knocking her backwards a step.

The leader was obviously displeased. "Good Lord, Kyle! We're not playing patty cake with these whores. We are here to send a message that will be read loud and clear by all who want to follow them here." He stepped forward, grabbed Alicia by the hair and jerked her back next to the pickup. Holding his shotgun in his left hand, he made a fist and slugged Alicia in the face. Blood and saliva flew from her mouth as Alicia spun and staggered back, managing to stay on her feet by clutching the trailer behind the pickup.

Marci screamed "Stop it! Why are you doing this?!"

"Shut up and listen and you might find out." He again approached Alicia.

Jasmine, kneeling on the seat of the truck, watched out the open window. She had felt the fear coming out of her parents and added her own to it. When she saw the man strike Carla, she started crying even though she tried not to. When the bearded man hit Alicia she lost all control. She screamed at the top of her lungs. Her mind ran like a wounded animal, touching down in Alicia, Marci, Carla, and finally Christine Landis. Jasmine had no control as she leaped from person to person, never staying long enough to make a cohesive connection, just screaming her mortal fear and flying on to the next.

Jasmine's leap into Alicia's brain acted to shake her back to focus for a split second. She tried to calm Jasmine but the connection was gone before she could react. Alicia concentrated on her right hand, making a fist. When the man approached her a second time she swung as hard as she could, just aiming for the man's face.

The man saw the blow on its way and jerked his head back. Alicia's fist glanced off his cheekbone, most of its force spent on empty air. "You filthy bitch," he swore and let go a hard right to her stomach. Alicia sucked for air as she doubled over clutching her midsection. Still holding his gun in his left hand, he gripped her hair in his right and swung her around him in a wide one hundred eighty degree arc.

Alicia tried to lift her left arm to protect herself but it did little to soften the impact as she was slammed into the side of the trailer. Blackness enveloped her. Marci lunged forward screaming, "Leave her alone!" Marci grabbed his hair as he tried to duck out of the way. He tried pushing her away but she held tight pulling his head toward the ground. He pointed the gun barrel at her and shoved it into her chest breaking a rib and her hold on his hair. She fell to the ground still crying, "Leave her alone!"

He placed the muzzle inches from Marci's head. "One more fool move like that and I'll blow your head off!"

Back in Washington DC, Christine didn't know what hit her. Jasmine's entrance into her consciousness was so violent she jerked in her chair. Ben was across the room on the phone but she saw him look up at her. Christine knew immediately that it was Jasmine and that something was very wrong. The pure panic that overtook her blocked out all other rational thought. Images of people, of the truck, of Marci and Alicia lying on the ground flew threw her head like a demented dream sequence viewed under a strobe light. Christine cradled her head in her hands and tried to get a grip on herself and her mind and then... Jasmine was gone.

Through the fog Christine heard Ben ask, "Are you all right?"

Christine's voice quivered as she answered "I'm OK, just a little tired. I must have got a chill." Ben eyed her with concern. 'What do I do now?' she thought. One thing she was sure of was that Jasmine and her parents were in trouble. She looked at her watch. They should be arriving at the reservation about now so she assumed they must be close. The image of Marci and Alicia lying in the dirt and a man standing over them holding a gun was clear but for some reason she was sure they were still alive. And Jasmine was in the truck on the side of a road. She picked up the phone and dialed the direct number to Robin at the reservation. She hoped that she was making the right decision but there was no way to tell. If only Jasmine would come back, maybe she could calm her and find out what was happening. This was going to be dangerous but she had to do it.

"This is Willey," Robin answered.

"This is Christine. Did you ever get those patrols to the main road started like I asked you?" she demanded.

"What?" Robin had no idea what Christine was talking about. "I'm sorry, I don't follow...."

"Listen up. We have construction workers showing up now every day and we already had one assault, not to mention how poorly the road is marked. Now I told you to have that road patrolled by our people with a cell phone to keep an eye on things and help guide them in. I want someone out there on the road to the interstate in the next fifteen minutes. Have you got that?!"

Robin realized that something was very wrong, they had never talked of patrolling the route to the state highway. Hell, they didn't have a spare person on the site for stuff like that. But Christine would not have talked that way on an open line without reason. "I'll have one out there in five if I can. I'm sorry for the delay, there is just so much to do here it must have slipped my mind."

"I understand but this is important. Get on it right now. If you can't get it out in fifteen minutes, call me with a reason." Christine hung up the phone. It's going to take a real stretch for the government to accept it as a coincidence that Christine decided to start the patrols the same moment that one of the families was attacked. She bowed her head and prayed.

Jasmine stood in the seat and screamed. Her high shrill screech pierced the stillness. Her mind found no solace in its quick travels so now all it could do was scream in terror. Kathy followed her mother's signals and carefully edged closer to the woman holding the pistol. Carla was still next to the youngest man. Rae Ann tried to get in position for a lunge at the remaining man who still stood too far away to be in striking distance. She couldn't give her intentions away yet. They needed surprise, they needed the leader out of the way for a few seconds more.

"Shut that kid up," barked the leader looking up at the truck window. "She's getting on my nerves with all that screaming."

Alicia swam slowly back to consciousness. She tasted the blood in her mouth and forced open a bruised eyelid. She could see Marci lying on the ground letting out gasping sobs. The gun barrel was only inches from her head.

"Shut that kid up I said."

He's going to kill her! He's going to kill my baby! Alicia tried to reach down with her left arm. The pain shot through her bringing on a wave of nausea. She vomited in the sand, lying on her side barely able to lift her head away. The man looked at her in disgust and returned his attention to Marci. Alicia inched her right hand to her boot, slipping her fingers inside, feeling for the grip of the derringer. Her fingers found the checkered grip as she thought of what Dirty Harry would say in this situation. She was sure she needed something witty when she blew him away but she couldn't come up with the energy to open her mouth. She pulled out the small gun cocking it on the way up, aimed and shot. A large black cloud of smoke enveloped her and her target.

The man heard the hammer cock. It's a sound that gets your attention. He whirled his head around just in time to see Alicia's hand tighten on the grip. He jumped back as fire sprayed from the barrel. The impact hit him adding its velocity to his backward lurch. The round lead ball entered under his right arm and exited through his back after flattening itself on his shoulder blade, chipping off a piece of the bone along the way. His own gun was flung away with the jerk of his arm in response to the pain. He hit the ground and rolled yelling, "I'm hit! I'm hit!"

When Carla saw Alicia fire the gun she knew this was their chance. She didn't wait for a signal from her mother as she took out the man next to her with a blow to the throat. She kicked the gun away as he tumbled backwards.

The woman also saw what was happening, turned and shot at the smoke cloud just as Kathy lunged at her knocking her down. Kathy accomplished her primary goal of disrupting her aim but the woman still held the gun as she rolled away.

The last man standing saw Kathy's charge. He whirled and fired from the hip. The shot ripped into Kathy's rib cage as she lunged toward the woman with the pistol. He didn't see Rae Ann coming until she hit him with all the animal rage she had ever felt. Rae Ann took him down with two rapid-fire kicks, one to the head and one to the body. As he dropped to his knees, she grabbed his hair in one hand and pummeled his face with the other. The first blow crushed his nose, the second landed squarely on his right eye. That was when she heard the woman's voice and looked up to see her holding her pistol to Kathy's head screaming, "Stop it or she's dead! I mean it! Stop or I blow her brains all over this place!"

Kathy clutched her side trying to stop the flow of blood soaking her coat as the woman stood, cocked the hammer, and pressed the barrel to Kathy's temple. Rae Ann let go of the man's hair and stepped back. He dropped face first in the sand. The woman didn't seem to know what to do next. "Help them into the back of the truck, right now! Move!" she commanded nodding her head at her incapacitated companions.

Carla looked to her mother. She was sure she could take her if her mom could cause a distraction. "Do what she says," Rae Ann said firmly to Carla. "I'm not taking any chances with your lives." Carla pulled the still choking man up by the back of his coat and guided him to the pickup keeping him between her and the woman with the pistol in case she needed a shield.

Rae Ann dropped the tailgate and helped Carla load him. "Don't try anything, it's too big a chance," she whispered to Carla. The two of them picked up the unconscious man and shoved him in the truck bed like a sack of feed.

"Be careful!" shouted the woman, "Or I'll do the same for this one." Kathy groaned as the gun barrel was pressed harder against her head. "Get him too," the woman ordered nodding her head toward the leader who was still on the ground whimpering. Marci was just staggering to her feet as Carla and Rae Ann jerked the man to his feet and dragged him to the open tailgate.

Marci bent down over Alicia. "Are you OK?"

"I think my arm is broken," she mumbled through swollen lips.

Pain surged through Marci's chest as she tried to help Alicia away from the pickup trailer. She gritted her teeth and pulled Alicia up. They leaned on each other as they hobbled towards their truck.

The woman released Kathy and pointed the gun at Carla. "Stay back. We didn't come here to kill anybody but I will if you do something stupid. Just stay back and let us get out of here." She fumbled for her keys and looked down at the ignition.

Carla looked at her mother, expecting her to act but saw that she was staring at Kathy who was lying on the ground shivering. Rae Ann knew if she tried anything it would only delay getting aid for her daughter. She stood quietly with her fists clenched. "Hurry up damn it," she cursed under her breath. After what seemed an eternity, the pickup started and pulled away, heading back in the direction of the state highway.

Rae Ann ran to Kathy, opened her coat and gasped. The wound was bad. The shotgun blast that hit her had likely damaged several organs. Kathy was slipping deeper into shock as she lost more blood. "We need to get her to a hospital. We've got to go back to Elko now!"

Marci had come up after sitting Alicia down at the truck. She looked over Rae Ann's shoulder at the hole in Kathy's side. "She'll never survive the two hours it will take to get back to Elko. Get her in the car." Marci tried to run back to the truck but the pain was too much. She walked as fast as she could. Jasmine had crawled down out of the truck to Alicia who was trying to calm her as much as possible. "Jasmine! Kathy is hurt real bad and we need your help. You need to be a real big girl right now. Can you do that?"

"Jasmine rubbed the tears from her eyes and said, "I'll try."

"You have to link us up right now, Alicia, you, me, and Christine." Jasmine just looked at her with wide eyes. "Come on, honey, right away. We need to....." Thank God, breathed Marci as she felt her mind slide into Jasmine's. Seconds later she was limping back to the car, clutching her own side.

Carla was in the back seat with Kathy's head in her lap. Rae Ann pulled little Jessica out of the car to pass her to Marci, assuming that she was coming to get her. "Here, we'll meet you at the hospital in Elko."

"No! That will take too long. We are only fifteen minutes from the reservation gate. There's a good surgeon there and we can get a helicopter to pick her up." Marci took Jessica from Rae Ann and got in the passenger side front seat.

"How do you know? There might not be a doctor at the reservation. We have to go back to Elko." Rae Ann got behind the wheel.

"We don't have time to argue. We just checked with Christine Landis and there is a topnotch doctor there. I know you won't be able to understand this but you must believe me." Marci leaned out the car door and shouted back to Alicia and Jasmine who were waiting by the truck. "Jasmine! Show her!" Marci suddenly felt Rae Ann's fear and anguish as if it were her own. Then she felt her awe and wonder. "Yes, it is for real. I know it's hard to accept but we just connected to Christine Landis a few moments ago just like this and she assured me that the doctor was there. Now lets get going. There's a car on the way to guide us."

The connection evaporated. Rae Ann stared at Marci. "You just got inside my head. How did you do that?"

"Does it matter? Get going!"

Rae Ann snapped out of it and pulled out onto the road, tires squealing as they struck pavement. "How is she doing?"

"Not good, mom. She's breathing really shallow and I can hardly feel a pulse," answered Carla. A shiver ran through Kathy's body as Carla pressed harder on the blanket she was using as a pressure bandage.

"I don't want to die." Kathy's words were barely a whisper.

Tears filled Carla's eyes. "You're not going to die, you can't die. You're my older sister and you wouldn't let me go through life without someone to fight with." Carla squeezed Kathy's hand and gave her a forced smile.

A jeep approached and Marci hoped that it was the vehicle that Christine told her to watch for. "Flash your lights and wave them down," Marci commanded. Rae Ann obeyed. The jeep stopped and rolled down its window. "Are you the ones from the reservation?" yelled Marci across the car.

"Yes, why?" the woman behind the wheel asked hesitantly.

"My daughter's been shot. Do you have a doctor there?" pleaded Rae Ann.

"Sure do. I'll call while we go. Follow us!" The jeep pulled a U turn in the road and sped off with Rae Ann in hot pursuit.

"How did you know that they were from the reservation?" asked Rae Ann.

"When my daughter connected me to Christine Landis, she told me she had sent out help to look for us. With so little traffic on this road, I figured it had to be them." Marci could see that Rae Ann was starting to understand Jasmine's abilities.

Alicia had promised to wait for help to arrive but changed her mind. Jasmine helped her into the truck and she did her best to keep up with Rae Ann. Unfortunately, driving that big truck with only one good arm was tougher than she thought it would be. Alicia was also afraid of passing out and she wanted to be going slow enough to stop if she felt lightheaded. They soon lost sight of the car and trailer.

"Is Kathy going to die?" asked Jasmine.

Alicia didn't answer right away but Jasmine waited quietly for the response. Jasmine exhibited much more patience than the average five year old. "I don't know if she will, no one knows for sure except God."

"Do you think she will die?" Jasmine wanted an answer.

Alicia hadn't seen the wound herself but she knew from the short connection with Marci that it was a long shot for her to make it to the reservation. Alicia had always tried to be honest with Jasmine and she didn't want to make this an exception. "If she is hurt as bad as I think she is, I'm afraid she will."

"But I don't want her to die," whined Jasmine changing back into a five year old.

"I'm sorry, baby, but it's not up to us." Alicia didn't catch herself until it had slipped out. Jasmine hated to have anyone call her baby. She considered herself past that but this time she said nothing. Jasmine just scrunched herself into the corner and put her thumb in her mouth, eyes fixed in space. Alicia decided to let her be for the time being.

Kathy wondered if this was what it was like to die. Everything became sharp and clear. Her pain eased somewhat and she could see outside the car even though she had her eyes closed. But the view wasn't right, she could see the truck not the car. That's when the other presence in her mind said "Don't be afraid, it's just me, Jasmine." Kathy was sure she was just hallucinating from the loss of blood. If it was real she would have been joined by her mother or her sister, not some child who wasn't related. "Would you like me to get your sister?" asked the voice in her head. "I can if you want." Yeah, I really would. Maybe then I wouldn't be so scared. "OK. I'll get her." Well, at least my hallucination is a cooperative one. Kathy's mind leaped another level as she felt a new presence, one so very familiar yet so very different than she imagined. She instantly recognized her sister but at the same time she realized she had never really known her sister.

Kathy had accepted what was happening to her mind easily because she thought it was the onset of death. For Carla it wasn't so simple. It took Jasmine quite some time to explain to her what was happening and get her over her fear of exposing herself. When she realized she was truly one with her sister, she finally accepted it and thanked Jasmine for bringing them together. Together, they examined Kathy's condition. The conclusion was obvious. Kathy was going to die. Her liver, kidneys and part of her stomach were gone. Even if the organs were not totally destroyed, she was rapidly bleeding to death and would be gone in five minutes. The medical center was still ten minutes away. Kathy started the difficult process of saying good-bye to her sister. Jasmine hesitantly asked a question they didn't fully understand, "Can't you share?"

Rae Ann knew that Kathy was still alive because she could still feel her. She had experienced the link being broken when her grandmother died and she would never forget it. She had felt her daughter's fear drop over the last few minutes but she wasn't sure if that was a good sign or not. "How is her pulse now? We're almost there."

Carla wasn't sure how to answer the question. "Mom, we need to talk to you about that." Carla was afraid to tell her mother what they had done but it couldn't wait. "Kathy is OK but her pulse stopped a little while ago."

Marci turned in her seat. "Is she breathing? Do you know CPR?"

"She's not dead," said Carla. After a pause she added "She's in me."

"What are you talking about? Who's in you?" Rae Ann saw the gate to the compound up ahead.

"I... I don't know how to explain this but Jasmine..." Carla heard Marci gasp. She began again "Jasmine came to us and we had an idea. We could see that Kathy was going to die if we did nothing so Jasmine helped her move out of her body and into mine."

"Oh my God!" Marci was as scared as she had ever been in her life. What had she created?

"You're talking crazy," said Rae Ann. The jeep in front of them stopped at the front gate. A few seconds later it lurched forward, an arm reaching out the window signaling them to follow. "Kathy has to be alive. I can still feel her. Check her pulse again."

"I am still alive. I just happen to be in Carla's body now."

A chill ran through Rae Ann's spine. She had always been able to tell her daughters apart when they spoke to her. There was no question in her mind that Kathy had just spoke to her. She looked back over her shoulder and could see the still, blood soaked form of Kathy lying in the seat. She then glanced into Carla's face and saw Kathy looking back at her. Rae Ann recovered control of the car just in time to avoid hitting a building. She swerved left and came to a stop next to the jeep.

Robin and the doctor were waiting at the door. They ran out, opened the car door, gently pulled Kathy's body onto the stretcher and rushed her inside. Rae Ann followed behind them.

Carla didn't move at first. Marci collected Jessica and stood outside the car. "Are you coming?" she asked Carla.

Carla took a deep breath. "Yeah. It's difficult to see yourself die and then look at the body afterwards." She pulled herself out of the car. Again she paused. "It's difficult to make decisions when it's all decided by committee."

"There's actually two of you sharing your body?" Marci asked with a quivering voice.

"Our body," corrected Carla. "Oh yes. We are still very much separate. I hope we did the right thing back there."

"Can you change it?" asked Marci.

"Jasmine didn't think so. We're pretty sure it is permanent."

Marci noticed Carla's method of referring to herself as we. "Then I think you better learn to live with it." Marci took Carla's arm and guided her in the building. Carla didn't resist.

Inside, Marci saw Rae Ann coming towards them from the other end of a long hall. "She's down here!" Marci and Carla hurried down the hall and rounded the corner, joining Rae Ann who was watching through the window as the doctor leaned over Kathy's body. The doctor straightened and looked at Rae Ann. Rae Ann knew what the look meant, the doctor was confirming that the connection was gone. The problem was that it was still there, just as it always had been. Tears started streaming down Rae Ann's face as she turned and walked away from the door.

Carla watched the doctor cover the body with a sheet then went and touched her mother lightly on the shoulder. "We're OK, mom. We really are both here."

"I know that. That's what scares me, I'm not sure who you really are. Are you Kathy, or Carla, or some mix of the two? I don't know what to think." Rae Ann turned and embraced her daughters. "I'm glad you are both still here, I'm just trying to cope with what has happened."

"Trust us, mom, so are we."

Marci started back out to the front door to wait for Alicia when she realized how bad her side hurt. She chose to ease herself down into a nearby chair and wait instead. Jessica, who had been quiet until then, began to fuss. Carla came over and took the child up in her arms and started to rock her. "Don't worry. We won't say anything to anyone about what has happened," Carla assured Marci. "We understand what it would mean if her abilities became public knowledge."

Robin came out the doors to the emergency room and approached Rae Ann. "I'm sorry. There was nothing that you or the doctor could have done. The injuries were just too great. Are there others who are injured?" Rae Ann nodded toward Marci.

"Alicia should be here any minute, she was driving a truck behind us. I told her not to risk driving but she ignored me as usual. I think her arm is broken and she may have a concussion. I took a heavy blow to the side. I may have a broken rib or two." Marci pealed back her coat exposing a bloody stain on her shirt.

"Your friend made it to the gate and someone is driving her over. Come on back and let the doctor take a look at you." Robin ushered Marci through the double doors. "I'm sorry for what has happened. We are trying to get the authorities to move as quickly as possible to get the people who did this."

"And you think anything will be done even if they are caught?" asked Marci bitterly.

Robin didn't answer.

Chapter 30

Monday, October 14

Christine and Ben Davis sat in the interrogation room at the FBI headquarters, waiting for what seemed forever. "What are they doing? They haul me down here, put me in this room and then nothing."

"You know the drill," soothed Ben. "Your imagination is worse than anything they have on you. The longer you wait the more time you have to stew. They're trying to make you nervous in hopes that you'll make a mistake. Just keep your cool and stick to the truth. You can't make a mistake with that."

But Christine knew that there was a little girl whose life depended on her not telling them the whole truth. "I know Ben. I just didn't fully understand how effective the waiting was." She took a deep breath and tried to focus her mind on what she would say. She was sure of the topic.

The door opened and two men and a woman came into the room. Christine immediately recognized both men. One had questioned her before; the other had been the friendly agent who had given her the ride back to her house when she had fallen on the sidewalk. "Hello again, Mrs. Landis. Nice to see you again." Christine smiled and nodded in his direction.

The other agent, an older man with graying hair, spoke up as he sat down at the table "I hope this meeting isn't too inconvenient for you."

Christine's smile faded to her business face. "I'm sure it really doesn't matter if it is. Can we get on with it so I can get back to work? You have already wasted most of my day."

The older agent tried to put all the sincerity he could muster into his voice. "Surely you can spare a few hours to increase the understanding between our two races?" When Christine did not respond the agent picked up a folder he had carried in with him. "Yes, you have been busy haven't you. Organizing the reservation startup has kept you hopping."

"Yes it has. Is that why you wanted me here, for a status report?"

"No, that's for the bureaucrats. My interest is a little more in the details area. You placed a call yesterday afternoon to your assistant, a Mrs. Willey. Is that correct?"

"I call her several times a day, just as she calls me."

"Yes, that's right. And each of those calls typically cover several subjects I'm sure and take several minutes to complete." The older agent threw down a log of her phone calls. Christine ignored it. "I'm not asking about your average phone call. No, I'm referring to a specific call." The agent paused. "And you know what call I'm talking about don't you?"

"Sorry," said Christine flatly. "I'm not clairvoyant. You are going to have to be more specific. I spend my life on the phone. If you told me the content of the call then maybe I could help you."

The agent dropped back in his chair, his expression never changing. "You know damned well what call I'm talking about. The call you placed about the people who were attacked on the road to the reservation, Mrs. Baird, her daughters, Ms. Inman and Ms. McBride."

"I'm afraid you're confused. Robin called me to tell me that they had been attacked, I didn't call her." Christine's voice was even, giving away little emotion. "And one of Mrs. Baird's daughters was killed in that attack. What have you done to capture her murderers?"

The agent ignored the question. "No, Mrs. Landis, before Mrs. Willey called you about the assault, you called her about getting someone out to patrol the roads to the reservation. As far as we can ascertain, you placed that call at the exact moment that the group was being attacked. Can you explain that?"

"Just lucky I guess." Christine offered no further comment.

"Just lucky? You must be the luckiest person alive to hit that one. Maybe you should be buying lottery tickets with luck like that." The agent kept his eyes on Christine's face. "During the phone conversation you made the comment that you had already told Mrs. Willey to put out patrols. Just exactly when did you tell her to do this?"

Christine thought for a moment, "I'm not sure. I'm guessing it was during one of our planning sessions but I don't remember when."

The older agent walked around the table and leaned on the table over Christine. "Was it over the phone, did you write a memo, did you whisper it in her ear or what?"

"I don't remember." Christine paused and added "For that matter, I could have intended to tell her and never actually done it. It wouldn't be the first time."

"When? Do you remember when you told her?"

Christine could feel herself starting to perspire. She could feel his stale breath in her face. "I don't remember."

"Damn! Is having a bad memory part of being a Mono? Because our men just talked to Mrs. Willey at the reservation and you know what? She can't remember either. Now ain't that odd?" He stood and turned to face the woman agent. "Does anyone else here think this is odd? What do you think, Susan?"

The woman stared into Christine's eyes, probing, never blinking. "I think she's lying. I don't think she ever talked to Willey about this. I think her telepathic powers are a lot better than she's told us. She knew that those Monos were being attacked and wanted to send help. This is just an attempt to cover up her knowledge." The woman agent paused a practiced amount of time. "Isn't that right, Christine?"

"You can think anything you want but it doesn't make it true. I think you're building a case on one piece of circumstantial evidence." Christine had to convince them that this was all an innocent coincidence. "For all I know I may be more of a psychic than even I know. I just knew that it was important to get the patrols started and I called right then to get them started. Was it because of some subliminal ability or was it pure coincidence? I have no more idea than you do. We have all played a hunch and had it pan out. Whether it is because of dumb luck or picking up on cosmic signals, who knows. I'm going with dumb luck."

The gray haired agent jumped in again. "Oh you knew all right. But maybe it wasn't telepathic ability. Maybe you knew because you planned the whole thing to bring sympathy to your side against the reservation. Some nice grotesque mass murder to sway the public to your cause."

"My God!" exclaimed Christine coming out of her seat. "Where the hell have you been! I could think up nothing more grotesque than what has been done to my people already. How do you get more brutal than nailing them to trees and then burning them alive? If the public hasn't been aroused by that, what could I possibly come up with that could be worse?"

"True," drawled the lead interrogator "but there hasn't been a major incident since we have identified and arrested suspects in nearly every one of the high profile attacks. Maybe you were running a little thin on sympathy headlines and figured you needed a public relations lift."

"Also true," countered Christine. "Several of the perpetrators have been arrested. How many of them have been prosecuted?"

"The wheels of justice turn slowly. You should know that better than anyone."

"And how about the disappearances?" Christine tried to gain the initiative. "Now they know that all they have to do is hide the body and there are no questions asked. We know when a family member has been murdered. We feel it happen."

"Possibly," injected the agent who had helped her get home. "But disappearances are under the jurisdiction of the local authorities, especially when we find Monos that have been 'murdered' turning up in hiding." Before Christine could respond he added "Now I think we need to discuss your use of the term 'simple corrective surgical procedure' while you were at the reservation the first time. Could you explain where you heard that phrase?"

Christine felt a tremor move through her body. She had forgotten about saying that. "I'm afraid I don't know what you mean," she replied, her voice not as firm as she wanted it.

The agent knew he struck a nerve. "You used that term in a staff meeting while you were at the reservation, under a complete communications blackout. That term was only used in the commercials shown after you entered the reservation. Was that also some subliminal coincidence too?"

"I'm sure it was in one of my scripts or I overheard it at the visit to the studio before I changed my mind about doing the taping."

"No, sorry. I checked. That spot wasn't written until after you changed your mind."

Christine had regained her composure. "Maybe the spot wasn't written but it doesn't mean that the term was never used in my presence."

The agent just looked in her eyes with a confident smile. "I don't think so. I think we were closer to the mark a minute ago. Do you care to reconsider your comments? Also, I'm sure that you know what it means if we find that you lied to Congress under oath."

The interrogation went on for another two hours but always came back to the same two points, over and over. Ben finally brought it to a head when he thought

Christine had all she could take. "Do you know that this is the flimsiest case I've ever seen." Ben knew what they had and he knew it wasn't nearly enough. They had wanted to scare Christine into revealing more that they could use and it had failed. "If I went to a judge and said I had been recording every word this woman said for the last months and because of these two instances I plan to prove that she can read minds, I would be laughed out of chambers. I believe that this interview is over." He stood and offered his hand to Christine. Instinctively she took it and stood also.

The lead interrogator looked at his two agents and then back to Christine. "Remember, 'in truth there is power' and we know the truth. It's only a matter of time, Mrs. Landis, and you will be looking at the world from behind bars. And you should know the life expectancy of a Mono in the prison system. Have a nice day." He then nodded in the direction of the door. It opened to let them out.

On the drive back to Christine's house, Ben silently mulled over what had been presented by the FBI. He had seen Christine when she made the phone call, she had been near panic at first. He could feel her nervousness for the next hour and a half until she received the next call from Robin letting her know what had happened. He had also seen her relief even as she was told of the one death. Someone very important was in that group of people and Christine was very worried about them. Ben felt a little jealous of being left out of the loop on this. He couldn't help but feel that he wasn't completely trusted. After they arrived back at her house, Ben jotted a short question in shorthand. "It's true isn't it?"

Christine looked at the note and then back to Ben, no emotion showed on her face. She gently kissed Ben on the cheek and went to the fireplace to burn the note. There are some things that are better if you don't know, she thought to herself. She sat and watched the flames consume the scrap of paper. Nothing more was said of the incident.

Fenton was not pleased. Lindell did his best to put a positive spin on it. "They are not stupid, they knew we were fishing. There was nowhere near enough evidence to prove our suspicions but I think it will have one desired effect. The FBI boys take us more seriously now. I think that they are convinced."

Fenton jabbed his finger in the direction of the White House. "It damned well better make an impact on them. The Attorney General is making noises about how much this is all costing the taxpayers and is suggesting cutting back the staff for the investigations. Hell, they're almost breeding faster than we can sterilize them as it is." Fenton rifled through his in box. "Where are the figures for today? I haven't seen them yet."

Lindell opened his brief case. "I'm sure you got a copy but here's mine." He handed them over to Fenton. "Our numbers choosing sterilization have remained steady but the number choosing the reservation have gone down slightly. The undecided have gone up."

"One percent!" Fenton threw the report in the trashcan. "The undecided is up one lousy percent. The ones choosing the reservation still outnumber us two to one. We need some drastic changes. They need to see what life is going to be like in that hole. That will change some minds but quick."

Lindell tried to caution the Senator. "We need to be cautious with that approach. That can play right into the hands of the Monos who are saying we are trying to recreate the Nazi concentration camps. Remember that the President depends on some swing votes from the liberal side of the aisle to get things done. He will talk tough on this one but will appease the liberals when it comes to living conditions."

"There are no liberals on this issue!" Fenton shouted. "There's just those who want to preserve the human race and those who don't give a damn. I want that reservation filled to capacity in thirty days. Then you'll see those number change, you can bet your ass on it."

Tuesday, October 15

Christine's mother stood at her daughter's door the next morning. "Close your mouth and come with me for a ride."

"Ah... OK. What are you doing here and where are we going?" Christine was dumbfounded by her mother's sudden arrival.

"Does it matter? Listen to your mother and do as she says. We'll be back in a few minutes." Becky led Christine to her car and they got in. "We need to talk and this seemed to be the only way to do it."

"Careful mother. They could have the car bugged."

"Not very likely. They had no idea I was coming or what car rental company I would choose. And I picked it out off the lot where I could see it. I'm quite sure it is safe."

Christine relaxed a bit but the message still concerned her. "So what was so important that you had to fly all the way here to tell me. Oh, turn right at the next light. It's a nice street, not much traffic."

As Becky made the turn, she started the explanation. "A millionaire wishes to donate his time and money to the reservation. He is a contractor and has been in the building trade for nearly thirty years. He is willing to help build new housing and renovate what is there if he can be of service."

Christine still didn't understand why her mother was there. "It sounds great. Why didn't you have him just call me. We could have worked all this out over the phone."

"He wants to remain anonymous, at least for the time being, from everyone but you."

"Yeah, I can understand. Keeps from having his home firebombed and business ruined by the nut cases out there." Christine knew just how he felt. If only there was a way to do the same for herself.

"You can put it that way. Only in this instance, we are the nut cases he is worried about. His name is Charles Wilkens."

"What!" Christine's yell nearly caused her mother to swerve off the road. "What are you saying? The bastard who lied to you and put us in the national press wants to join us? How cute! And he expects us to just forgive and forget?"

"No, he doesn't," replied Becky, "that is why he wants to remain anonymous. Look, I've been talking with his wife almost since it was published. She's a good woman. And her husband is not a bad man, he just misunderstood."

"That was a hell of a misunderstanding," Christine spat.

"All he wants is a chance to repay a little of what he feels he owes us."

"Mother, have you lost your mind? This is probably just a stunt to get a little more publicity. Why should I trust him?"

"Because I trust him." There were advantages to being the mother. Children could rarely resist when it came to a request from mom. "Christine, please give him a chance. Just for me."

Christine continued to ride in silence for another block. "What if the people on the reservation find out who he is? I can't be held responsible for what would happen. And not just to him. My leadership would be as good as over. Those people wouldn't follow me across the street for a cup of coffee if they found out I accepted money from him." Christine began to think of the other options. "Then again, we may be able to use this. It would be great political mileage to be able to show the man who started all this coming out on our side."

"No, that's out of the question. The Feds have already gotten wind of this and have promised that he will pay for the rest of his life if they see his face on national TV supporting our cause." Becky knew that she was not making this easy for her daughter. "Please just let him do what he does best, build. He wants you to take the money and do whatever you think best."

Christine felt her resolve weakening. She never could say no to her mother. But, in this case she couldn't say yes either. "Look, if a man shows up at the reservation with skills in the building trades, I doubt that he would be turned away. But understand this, I will not be responsible for what happens to him and I will disavow any knowledge of him being there. Do you understand?"

Becky just said, "Thank you. You will receive a donation in a few days via my bank in Kalamazoo. I'm sure you can take care of it."

"Better have it transferred out to our bank in Nevada," Christine said. "We finally found one to handle us out there. We're closing up shop here this week. The plans are that I'm flying out there tomorrow unless the government stops me but I can't see why they would want to. I'm sorry that this messes up your visit but I had no idea you were coming."

"That's no problem. I wasn't planning on staying long." Becky tapped her airline ticket, "I have a flight out tomorrow morning. I just came by to talk to you about Gloria and Charlie and to see the girls. How are they?"

Christine and her mother dropped back into their roles of mother and grandmother. Before they realized it they had spent over an hour talking about the children and what was happening with the rest of the family. Christine looked at her watch. "Oh no. We've got to get back or Ben will be out searching for me and Robert will be ticked off about our lunch date."

Chapter 31

Wednesday, October 16

Robin met Christine at the front gate just after two in the afternoon. A state trooper had driven Christine from the airport because of the recent attacks on the road to the reservation. "Welcome home boss," greeted Robin. "Nice to have you here. Where's Dorothy?"

"She's still back in DC taking care of some money matters. She should be here in a week or so." Christine was worried about her choice of Dorothy. She wasn't sure what it was but something deep inside kept eating away at her confidence. She certainly couldn't complain about her performance. Dorothy worked like a dog and her ideas were excellent. At times she would disagree with Christine's decisions but she didn't want a bunch of yes people following blindly into the abyss. Christine pulled her bags from the trunk of the cruiser.

"Let me get those for you," offered Robin.

"That's all right. I've got these. Grab my briefcase and computer from the back seat." Christine felt alone, cut off from the real world. Robert had convinced her to let the girls stay until the house sold and then come with him. She knew that it made sense not to have the girls here for the first month or so but she missed them already. They were the anchor that she held on to when the storms hit. No matter how bad things got she could go to them for a hug and a chat and life didn't seem quite so impossible to cope with. "Are the people who were attacked available? I'd like to talk to them as soon as possible."

"Sure. Mrs. Baird and her daughter are at the office. We made arrangements to bury her other daughter this afternoon. There were no caskets so I had a simple one made. We started a small cemetery just outside the main compound like you asked." Robin set the briefcase and computer in the back of her jeep.

Christine put her bags in and dropped into the passenger seat. "It's a lousy way to start my administration here, presiding over our first funeral." Robin was quiet as she drove Christine to the office.

Robin parked at the front door and they carried in the bags. "I set you up a room off your office to use for now as you requested. There's not much to it, a bed, a dresser and small table but that pretty well fills the space available."

"It will be all I need for right now." Christine asked "Is there a phone? I want to call Robert and let him know I made it OK."

"Yes, we have pretty good communications. We have a husband and wife team that used to work IT and communication for a fortune 500 company. They have us up and running over most of the reservation. Nothing fancy but it works." Robin opened the door to Christine's room. "Here it is. Your office is next door and the bathroom is down the hall on the right. I doubt you'll have much use for the urinals but there is a shower that works. Oh!" Robin jumped when she saw the figure standing in the doorway. She regained her composure when she recognized her. "Mrs. Landis, this is Rae Ann Baird." Rae Ann stood in the doorway with her arms folded across her chest, her jaw set.

Christine stepped forward with her hand outstretched. "Hello Mrs. Baird. I'm truly sorry to hear about your daughter." Christine saw a young woman in the hall behind Rae Ann. "If there is anything I can do...."

Rae Ann made no move to take Christine's hand. "Yes, there is something you can do, you can tell me what is being done to find the people who murdered my daughter."

Christine held her hand out for another few seconds and then let it fall to her side. "Mrs. Baird, the first thing you will have to understand is how much authority I have outside the confines of this reservation. That is a big fat zero. The only thing I or any of us can do about a crime that happens outside these fences is to pester the local authorities and hope they have to decency to do their jobs."

"That really sucks." Tears stared to form in Rae Ann's eyes. "That will be real comforting as I put my little girl in the ground today. Thanks for all your help." Rae Ann turned on her heels and disappeared down the hall.

Christine bit her lower lip as she watched Rae Ann depart. "I'm sorry," she said hoarsely.

The young woman who was in the hall slipped in the door. "You'll have to excuse my mother. She's just really upset right now."

Christine was impressed by this girl's emotional control. "I know, it's OK. I just wish there was more that I could do."

"I'm Carla Baird," she said as she offered her hand. As Christine took it Carla said "We just wanted you to know that we are all right." Carla motioned down to her hands with her eyes. Christine followed her gaze to Carla's open palm. On it was written "Jasmine will explain." Carla smiled an understanding smile and left the room to catch up with her mother.

Christine turned back to Robin. "I'd like to leave this till later," she said motioning to her bags. "Is the other family here?"

"I'll check and see if I can find them. They were at the cemetery making sure everything was ready."

"Can you run me out there?" Christine asked. "I'd like to meet them before the service."

Robin agreed and drove her to the makeshift cemetery a half a mile outside the compound. As they approached, Robin saw them setting flowers near the newly dug grave. "There they are. The short one is Marci McBride and the taller one to the left is Alicia Inman." Robin peered through the dirty windshield. "Oh, it looks like their little girl is there too."

Christine saw a head pop up from behind the pile of dirt next to the grave. Her heart fluttered in her chest. I'm finally going to meet her face to face. "I see her!" Christine turned to Robin. "Thanks for the ride. I can handle it from here. I'll just walk back."

"OK. Did you want me to introduce you?"

Christine smiled. "No, I don't think so. I can handle it." Robin watched as Christine climbed the small hill and shook hands with the two women. What really amazed her was the way the little girl ran up to Christine and jumped into her arms, just like she had known her forever. Robin put the jeep in reverse and backed out.

Christine looked at Alicia's bruised face, her left arm in a cast and a sling. "How are you?"

Alicia smiled through swollen lips. "I've been better. Everything hurts, but I'll be OK. I think Marci got it worse than me."

Marci said "I can't laugh, cry or breathe without pain. It's amazing how much two broken ribs can hurt, but at the time I hardly felt it. That and a gash that took twelve stitches to close."

Christine sat on the ground and her hand instinctively stroked Jasmine's hair. "And your babies are all right."

"I'm not a baby!" protested Jasmine.

"No, you sure aren't," soothed Christine. "You did great." Christine returned her attention to Marci. "Did the police question you about the attackers?"

"Sure did, for five whole minutes. Then later the FBI questioned us for an hour about how the people at the reservation knew to send help. We played dumb as best we could. I think they finally just got tired of hearing us say 'I don't know' and left us alone." Marci brushed back her hair. "I doubt that they will even try to find the people who did this."

"Did they question Jasmine?" asked Christine.

"They tried," said Alicia, her admiration showing in her voice. "She remembered everything we told her. No matter what they said, she just clamped her thumb in her mouth and played scared. She was great. They gave up quickly but not until she cleaned them out of two suckers and a pack of gum." Jasmine grinned with pride.

Christine paused, afraid to ask for what she really wanted. She looked up at Marci. "Do you think it would be all right if.... There is so much I want to know and need to tell you, and words just seem so inefficient anymore."

Marci gingerly sat down next to Christine. "That's up to Jasmine and how she feels."

Jasmine caught on to the request. "It's OK, mommy. We'll just be real careful. If I get too scared, we'll stop." Jasmine patted the ground beside her. "Sit down 'licia."

Alicia used her good arm to ease herself to the ground. "Ow! I keep finding new things that hurt."

Christine reached out and squeezed Alicia's hand and then felt her mind rush to join Jasmine's. Christine witnessed the attack through their eyes, one at a time. Each feeling the terror again. Christine then brought them up to date on what was happening in Washington and her last interrogation by the FBI. Christine then asked Jasmine what Carla had meant with the note on her hand. Jasmine slowly laid it all out for her, Kathy wasn't dead, she was just sharing Carla's body. Christine knew that the union of their minds accepted this as fact but her individual mind refused to accept it. How can that happen? How can they share? Christine felt another presence with her, one she hadn't met before.

"Hello, I know that you have some difficulty accepting my existence but here I am. I'm Kathy."

Then Christine felt another presence that was similar but definitely not the same. "And I'm Carla. We knew that this little girl was special but we never realized how special. If you think you're confused, look at it from our side."

"It's real hard to get just one of them," said Jasmine, "but I can sometimes."

Christine felt all of her questions being answered without asking them. The girls no longer considered themselves alone. Now it was always we instead of I. There was no resentment on Carla's part about giving up her life to live as part of this bizarre Siamese twin. Jasmine had no idea how she really did it and wasn't sure if she could have done it if they were not twins. Jasmine explained that she had connected with Rae Ann only once to explain what had happened and to show her that Kathy was still alive but she wasn't sure that she really believed her. It was Alicia who finally interceded and said they had to break the connection. As odd as it seemed, they needed to finish preparing the grave for the funeral of someone who was still with them. They all reluctantly slid back to themselves.

Christine was impressed at how good Jasmine had gotten at this. Gone was the sudden jolts of the past. Now it was just a smooth slide and she was alone again. Christine stood and helped Marci up. Alicia pushed herself up with her one good arm. "I don't think I'll be playing my guitar for a while," mused Alicia. "And I was just getting a couple of Tom Petty songs down. Now I'll have to start over by the time I get out of this thing."

"Can I help?" asked Christine. "With the preparations I mean. I don't think I'd be much help with your guitar." The three women arranged the flowers, then spread the cloth over the table that was to be used as an altar.

They had just finished when they saw the pickup approaching with what appeared to be the entire population of the reservation, nearly six hundred souls, walking behind. Carla and Rae Ann sat in the truck bed with the crude plywood box. Marci and Alicia walked down the hill to meet the truck. They joined several others who lifted the casket and carried it to the grave. You could see the pain in their eyes but it was not clear if it was emotional or physical. Still, no one tried to stop them from helping.

A woman who was a minister in her life on the outside performed the service. Rae Ann refused the chair offered to her. Carla stood by her side. After the short service, the casket was gently lowered into the ground. Rae Ann dropped a flower on the casket and whispered "Good-bye, honey. I'm not going to forget." Carla followed dropping her flower. Each person filed by giving their last respects for a young woman they had never met, yet each felt a intimate bond. In one way or another, they had all experienced the violence. Finally it was over. Rae Ann picked up the shovel and started throwing shovel fulls of dirt down on the casket. Carla and others picked up the remaining shovels and helped.

The minister approached Rae Ann and offered to take the shovel. "I think you best just sit down over there out of the way, Reverend," said Rae Ann. "You've done your job today. Now it's time for me to do mine." The people slowly filed away back to their jobs. Rae Ann attacked the mound of dirt with her shovel. Carla and the others cautiously assisted, keeping an eye on her, not sure what to make of her. One woman mentioned that the backhoe was available to finish filling in the grave but Rae Ann stared her into silence and then went back to shoveling. The job was finally done. Rae Ann stood next to the mound, sweat running off her face in the cold afternoon sun, gazing at the pile as if it held some great mystery that she couldn't quite understand. Then she dropped to her knees on the grave and cried. Carla stood beside her for a few respectful minutes, then helped her to her feet and guided her back toward the compound.

Wednesday, October 23

Christine had planned for an initial population of one thousand to work for sixty days to prepare the reservation for the tens of thousands to come. She estimated a maximum population of five thousand for the first winter with the main influx to start in the spring. Fenton had other ideas. The week that Christine arrived, the army clerks at the front gates processed eleven hundred new residents. Christine was furious but there was nothing she could do. Instead of being able to plan and integrate the newcomers into constructive work groups, everyone was overpowered by the tasks of feeding and housing those who came in after them. When Christine protested and requested a week moratorium to allow suitable living space to be prepared, she was informed that the staff at the front gate was being doubled to handle an increased load of refugees.

Christine was in a foul mood when one of her greeters, people who processed in the people on the Monoecion side of the fence, ushered in a middle-aged man whose red beard was streaked with gray. "I'm sorry to bother you, Mrs. Landis, but this guy said he had to talk to you. We checked him, he's not carrying any weapons."

Christine looked at the man over the top of her glasses. "Well, you're here so what do you want and make it quick. We don't have time for polite conversation around here."

"It's got little to do with what I want and everything to do with what you need. I've got four semi flatbeds outside the gates loaded with two-by-fours, sheet rock, plywood and other assorted materials."

"Whoa!" said Christine. "Where is this stuff from and who ordered it? I'm not the person to be talking to about this. You need to talk to the folks in receiving. Besides, I don't remember approving an order like that."

Undaunted, the man continued "You didn't. I also have two other men and one woman with me who are all experienced builders just like me. All I need is for you to tell me what to do with it and assign a crew to work with each of us."

"If I may ask, who is paying for all this stuff?" Christine eyed him suspiciously.

"We've already been paid, in full." He tossed down a manifest showing the list of materials on the trucks outside. At the bottom was her mother's signature.

Christine sat back in her chair and rubbed her forehead. He didn't look like the same man now that he added the facial hair. He looked much thinner than she remembered from TV. "I hope you know what you're getting yourself into."

"I could say the same to you, ma'am." He stood quietly at her desk waiting for her approval.

"What do I call you?" she asked already knowing his name.

"Just call me Chet, ma'am.... At least for now," answered Charlie Wilkens. "Do I stay or go?"

Christine didn't like the idea any more now than she did before but she sure needed the help and she had made the commitment to her mother not to stand in his way. "Have one of the greeters guide you to the main hanger at the airstrip. I'll track down our lead engineer, Robin Willey to meet you there and get the trailers unloaded. She will help you organize some crews and get things planned out today. That should allow you to get started first thing in the morning."

"Sounds like a good plan to me. Is there anything else?"

"Be careful. I don't want any on the job injuries." Christine rose from her chair and offered him her hand.

He took it in his and shook it, not as a beggar accepting a hand out. Charlie had come to make amends, not beg forgiveness. "I certainly will. It would be a wasted trip if I wasn't."

Thursday, October 31

As the population doubled again the next week, Christine created her cabinet. She added to it as required by the shifting sands of the current situation. This week she appointed the education chairperson who was charged to create a school system from scratch with no books, no money and no supplies. She added the utilities chairperson who was responsible for building and training a team to maintain the power, water and sewage systems.

The housing chairperson had been the first appointment when people started arriving and Christine had made it over the phone. Now she had to replace her. The woman had too much compassion and wasn't tough enough to make hard decisions. In their current situation, no one was happy with the housing decisions because all the choices were bad. She needed someone who could stare down a person twice her size when necessary. Christine asked Rae Ann Baird to take the post. "This is the most thankless job there is here. I can guarantee that you will probably be the most hated person on the reservation. It's not much of a recommendation but you're the best person for the job. Will you take it?"

Rae Ann said "I was really hoping for a position in the security area. I think I'm much more qualified there."

"I know," said Christine "and I considered that. You may be more qualified there but I need your skills and reputation more in housing. I can get several people who can do the security job but you are the only one I know who can handle the housing without cracking in a week. Right now we need people who can handle emergencies and isolate the planning team from the day to day activities. When we get out of the crisis mode, I promise you I will consider you for a security position. Fair enough?"

Rae Ann nodded her head. "Fair enough. There is one thing I would like to do if it's OK with you. We have all been victims long enough. I want to start training anyone interested in the martial arts. It will keep them in good physical condition and help fight the boredom that is sure to strike this winter."

"That's a great idea. Anything that will raise morale makes this place a little more livable. Just make sure they don't start using it on each other."

Rae Ann had other ideas than turning this into a ladies aerobics class. She planned on selecting her best students to train others, to make them hard, to create a force that would not be pushed around anymore. Rae Ann focused on the future, on revenge.

Chapter 32

Friday, November 1

The one area that hadn't gotten off the ground was the area of economic development. Dorothy was still in DC and was being very successful in bringing in money and supplies that were sorely needed but that did little for the long-term economic health of the reservation. Without a source of income, the reservation was destined to become just what Fenton wanted it to be, a ghetto. They had gotten quite good in the building trades and were now exporting some products such as custom trusses for local consumption in Elko but it was too little to have much overall effect.

Christine was still struggling with the problem when Alicia came to her with a proposal. "I have tracked down a collection of computer programmers here at the reservation that are top notch. We have already talked about putting out a product to be sold on the outside and I'm sure that we can do it. Between us, we have enough contacts on the outside who can market the products to industrial customers to make a go of it."

"Do you think they will buy it? It will already have two strikes against it coming out of the reservation," Christine pointed out.

"Our target will be the smaller industrial clients. Their biggest concern is a bug free product that performs as advertised at a rock bottom price," said Alicia, "not who wrote it."

"Sounds possible," said Christine. "What's the product?"

"We set up initially as an engineering firm doing the rent-an-engineer thing. The sales folks on the outside do the client contact functions, meeting and specification development. We do the software development and assist in debugging during installation via remote connections. In most cases we can work from here just like we are sitting in the factory control room. While we are working the contract engineer end we keep our eyes open for products that are needed that we can develop here and sell as end products. We have pros lined up in SCADA, graphics and database development in numerous industries and manufacturing methods, utilities too." Alicia paused for a moment. She knew that she wasn't explaining it well to someone with a non-technical background. "It's kind of hard to explain to a lawyer."

"Sorry," said Christine, "I've spent most of my career in law libraries and government offices. I think I follow you. We rent out our talents until we can create our own products worthy to compete on the market. How soon do you think you can get started?"

"We have contacts on the outside already looking for ways to sell our capabilities. They are small outfits with a few engineers on staff that now can draw on a team of twenty automation and I&C experts to augment their staff. I didn't think you would have a problem with us freelancing." Alicia added "Sorry, I&C is instrumentation and controls."

"What are the space requirements?" asked Christine.

"That's the good news, darn little. We are used to working in cube farms with people stacked up like chord wood. We also have our own computers and most of the software we need."

"Go with it. You are now in charge of the startup. Just make sure all operations are squeaky clean. I don't want any pirated software questionable business practices." Christine's thoughts moved to the future. "How long would a product of our own take?"

"That's the problem," said Alicia. "The normal software development cycle would be about twelve months for a product the size and complexity that we're thinking of. That's about eight months longer than we can live with. But with a little special help... I think we can shorten it to under six months."

Christine knew where Alicia was heading with the special help. The mental boost from a link with Jasmine could do wonders for her schedule but it was risky. "I can get you and your team released from your work details and set up some office space. Let me know if you need anything."

"With the contacts we have, we can probably get most of the industrial stuff we need on loan for the short time we'll need it, but we may need to buy a PLC for test purposes. We can get a DCS on loan. We will need to concentrate on the major lines first, Allen Bradley, GE Fanuc, Modicon. We can pick up the smaller players as we go."

Christine looked at her with a blank stare. "Are you and I speaking the same language? Because if we are, I lost you a ways back."

"Sorry," said Alicia. "Marci says I expect everybody to be an engineer. A DCS is a device..."

Christine held up her hands. "I don't want to know. I just want to know if you think this will make money? We are looking for maximum return on investment, that's what is important to us now."

"Yes. Industrial control pays well versus commercial where you have to make your money on volume. And it's an easier market to penetrate if the product is good. Of course the market is much smaller so don't expect to sell a million copies. But if you sell a thousand copies at a thousand dollars a copy, it adds up quick."

"OK, do it," said Christine. "As far as our own product development, pick your people, no more than three and yourself, and let me know their names. They will be assigned to you as soon as you can use them. Get me a list of what equipment you need, estimated cost and when you need it. Don't ask for it any earlier than you absolutely have to have it. Anything else?"

Alicia was ecstatic. "Thank you. All I came to ask you for were weekends and an occasional afternoon off to try to get the programming effort off the ground."

"We need income. Everything we get from the outside is coming from the government or private donations. They have complete control of this reservation because they control the flow of goods and supplies into it. Until we can become self-sufficient, the Feds will continue to call the shots and I want that ended as quickly as possible." Christine had made this speech a hundred times before but she couldn't help herself. "Your product will work into our middle and long term goals. I think you're on the right track with your efforts. Our only natural resources are our people. Intellectual property is our ticket to self-sufficiency and we need to develop it."

Alicia was nervous as she listened to Christine. She wasn't sure how to approach the next subject. When Christine paused Alicia asked "Is there any way to check out the people on my list? You know, make sure they are reliable. They will be working so close with me and my family."

Christine knew she was talking about Jasmine. "I don't know how I could help. I'll let you know anything that I hear but we don't have any way to find out anything about the people who come through the gate. I'm afraid you are on your own." Christine whispered the words "Be careful."

Alicia nodded and left the office. She had been planning this for a while now and she knew the dangers she was facing. Alicia had conceived of using Jasmine's ability to tie people together for the purpose of scientific advancement and project development since it first happened. The surge in mental capacity screamed to her to use it. But along side the tremendous benefits, Alicia realized the equally great dangers. What if one of the members talked and Jasmine was discovered by the Feds? She would be gone in a flash to be tested, prodded and exploited. What if the constant use of her power affected her mentally or physically? How could she face causing harm to her daughter even if it was out of ignorance?

All of this had been discussed with Marci for hours on end. Marci was dead set against it at first but Alicia had finally won her over to her side. The argument that tipped the scales in her favor was a simple question. Why was Jasmine given this ability if not to use it. They talked of what end it was to be used for and could come up with nothing nobler than to help the reservation survive.

They needed Jasmine to know what all the risks were and let her make the final decision, not alone but with them all connected where they could really examine the idea and share their concerns. The Mind seemed to have a life of it's own and often resisted being controlled and guided. Each person maintained their own component and could exhibit limited control but the Mind would sometimes leap and dart about to seemingly unrelated paths. After studying the problem from every angle, it was finally decided by one simple thought from Jasmine, "I want to help."

Sunday, November 3

Alicia was the one who created the population database when she first arrived. As people entered the reservation, greeters entered the usual information, birth date, children, and martial status. It also contained work histories, education and special skills. Alicia had been through the database searching for the right people to help her in her project. She then made a point of meeting them at their work assignment or bumping into them at the mess hall so she could feel them out to see if they would fit in before she ever raised the idea of her project to Christine. Now that Christine had approved her idea, it was time to make sure that Jasmine could work with the people she had selected.

Jasmine walked hand in hand with Alicia from the mess hall, staying back a safe distance from the woman they were shadowing. "Do you see her, honey? The one in the blue coat and red hat."

"I see her, she's looking back now," said Jasmine.

"That's right, she's looking back over her left shoulder." Alicia looked at Jasmine to make sure she was tracking the right person.

Jasmine stopped suddenly, her eyes focused on the departing figure. "OK, I can find her now. What's her name?"

"Her name is Ann, Ann Yates."

Ann lay in her bunk reading a book. She could feel her skills fading each day and the only way she had found to slow the draining of her talents was constant study in what little spare time she had. She felt the tickle inside her brain. She suppressed a gasp when she realized she wasn't alone.

Jasmine was as gentle as possible as she slid into Ann's conscious mind. She had to be as careful as she could be to explain what was happening without revealing her identity. "It's OK, you're not going crazy," reassured Jasmine.

"Great, I have someone else in my head telling me I'm not going crazy. Now doesn't this seem just a bit odd to you?" Ann asked her other presence.

"No," Jasmine replied matter of factly. "That's pretty much how everyone reacts when I first come to visit."

"Oh, that makes me feel much better," Ann's mind reacted sarcastically. Jasmine exposed a piece of herself and Ann understood what was happening, she didn't believe it yet but at least she understood it. All the reasons that this visitor was being so cautious with her became clear. Ann understood the danger that her visitor was placing herself in by making contact with her. "You need to know what I'm like before you can trust me to keep your secret. I understand what you want but I'm not sure how to convince you that you can trust me."

"Just show yourself to me. Show me who you are." Jasmine watched as Ann began to think of her work at Intel, the research at the institute, the long hours of study at the university. "No, that's what you do at work. I want to see what you are inside."

"I'm not sure how to show myself to you." Ann struggled to think about what she could show this visitor that would expose her essence.

"Think happy. Just choose a hallway and open all the doors," replied Jasmine.

Ann felt her mind flooding with images of her father, of her birthdays with her dad behind the camera always filming. She saw the father's day gifts that she made as a child and felt the rough morning beard and warm hug when she brought him breakfast in bed. She froze as she suddenly encountered her mother's death, once again so fresh and painful.

"I'm sorry," said Jasmine. "Sometimes you have to be careful about how quickly you open the doors."

"It's all right. It was wonderful to feel her again even if it was saying good-bye." Ann watched in amazement as Jasmine slowly revealed herself. In real time it only took seconds for Jasmine to unfold her life to her.

"My God," thought Ann, "this is amazing. You're a child!"

"You ain't seen nothing yet," said the new presence in her mind.

"This is my dad," Jasmine passed on to Ann. "Do you remember Alicia?"

Ann saw Alicia come into focus. This was the person who asked her if she was interested in working to develop some software project for the reservation. "Oh yes, I remember you. I'm still not sure that I'm not dreaming all this."

"That's the idea. We chose to do this at night just before you went to sleep so if it didn't work out you would convince yourself that it was all in your head. If you hadn't noticed, your mind is running on a new level. That's what happens when we connect like this."

"So I've noticed. It's like there are two of me, one is still out there reading the text book and one is in here with you. But the one in here isn't just me, it's like a blurring of me and you and the little girl, a mix."

Alicia exposed her plan to Ann. "As you can see this is a rather ambitious plan but I think that with the help of the Mind, we can do it. Are you game?"

Ann's mind gave up trying to make logical decisions and just decided to go on gut instinct. If she was mad, it didn't make any difference. If not then this was going to be one hell of an adventure. Ann jumped in with both feet.

Ann Yates was a graduate of MIT. She had finished her masters in physics and was working for Intel when the story broke. She went to her boss and explained her situation a few days later and was told to get back to work, they would handle things. The government unfortunately had other ideas. She refused the offer to have the surgery and turned in her notice and left for the reservation as soon as it opened. She jumped at the chance to work on Alicia's project because it was more challenging than working as a plumber's assistant. Alicia selected Ann not only for her qualifications but also because she was single and uninvolved. Alicia knew it would be tough not to share this secret with a spouse. But then, they had all been trained from birth to keep secrets.

Gina Gooden had just taken a sponge bath and was sitting on the edge of her cot when she screamed. Jasmine made a quick exit. The people in the bunks next to Gina asked if she was all right. Gina shook it off and explained that she just had a really weird feeling, and that she was OK now, it had passed. She laid back and tried to figure out where the feeling had come from. Jasmine slid back into her mind again. "Please don't scream again, you scared me."

"Oh my God, I'm hearing voices. Oh my God. Oh my God." Gina began to tremble. With ever improving skill, Jasmine soothed her way into Gina's mind. In a few moments Gina learned everything that Ann had learned the day before. She agreed to join the team on the condition that Alicia walk up to her the next morning and say "rhubarb." As much as she wanted to believe that this was really happening to her, she still needed this proof that she hadn't gone mad. After Alicia and Jasmine left her, she pulled out a scrap of paper and wrote *rhubarb*. She then tried to sleep with little success.

Gina Gooden held a masters degree in micro-biology and a minor in computer science. She had learned early that the computer was a critical tool in her field and decided to master it to make full use of its capabilities. She had been graduated a little over a year before the discovery of the Monoecion race became public. When a cousin went public, she followed suit. Her employer immediately laid her off. Like Ann, Gina was single but there was a special guy who had been in her life until she made the decision to enter the reservation. She still dreamed he would show up at the reservation gate someday and join her.

Monday, November 4

The next morning, Gina trudged down the street to her work assignment trying to clear her head. She felt so groggy from the lack of sleep that she had almost convinced herself that it was all a nightmare. Even the slip of paper with the one word written on it, shoved inside her mitten, was beginning to lose its power to convince her. Gina had expected to meet Alicia outside the barracks but no one appeared. Now she was past the halfway point and still nothing. The wind blew the biting cold across her face as she lowered her head against it. She looked up from her feet just in time to avoid collision with another person coming the other way.

The person stopped right in front of Gina and pushed the hood of her coat back. "Gina?"

Gina valiantly tried to stop the butterflies in her stomach that were straining to lift her off her feet. "Yes," she answered cautiously.

"Hi, remember me from last night?" asked Alicia as she held out her good hand. "I believe you wanted me to say 'rhubarb'."

Gina jumped on Alicia, wrapping her arms around her neck, nearly knocking her over. "Thank you, thank you, thank you! I'm not crazy!" Gina hugged Alicia so tight she could hardly breath. "I'm not crazy!"

Alicia winced as pain shot up through her left arm. Alicia carefully eased Gina back on the ground trying to protect her mending arm. "No, you are not crazy, but you will be dead meat if my spouse sees you do this. She's the jealous type. Come on, you're off that work detail and you've been transferred to mine as of this morning. I have to go explain it to your supervisor. Have you had breakfast yet?"

"No," replied Gina. "I'll grab it on the way since I go right by the kitchen on the way to work. Let's go, it's freezing out here." Gina practically vibrated as she and Alicia walked to the mess hall.

That night, Alicia and Jasmine tracked the last proposed member of Alicia's special team. Jasmine reached out and touched her mind. A troubled look came over Jasmine's face. "I can find her now," said Jasmine timidly.

Alicia heard the tension in Jasmine's voice. "Is something wrong, Jazz?" asked Alicia.

"I don't know," said Jasmine. "She just kinda feels funny. It's OK." Alicia wasn't so sure. They went back home and had a cup of hot chocolate. It was the closest thing she had to a special treat at home. At nine o'clock at night Jasmine sat with Alicia and started to reach out to her target.

"Get away from me!" screamed the woman's mind. She cursed the voice in her head with such hatred that Jasmine recoiled in fear.

Jasmine withdrew from the woman's mind as fast as she could. Tears started down Jasmine's cheeks. "I'm sorry 'licia. I think I scared her real bad."

"Don't try again, honey," soothed Alicia as she held Jasmine. "It's OK. Not everyone is a nice person inside. Maybe she just couldn't cope with feeling someone inside her head."

"Do I have to do any more?" asked Jasmine, her fear showing in her voice.

Alicia knew that this experience had bothered Jasmine deeply but she still wanted to help. "No, it's all done for now. We're not going to contact anybody new, just the people that you know. OK?" Jasmine nodded her agreement and the tears dried, leaving silvered tracks on her cheeks.

Tuesday, November 5

The team sat down together in the office that Dorothy had assigned them. There were three computer systems and an inkjet printer networked together. Two tables, a beat up file cabinet and a couple of desks completed the office decor. "Welcome to the worker's paradise," greeted Alicia with a bow. "Get a cup of coffee or tea. We are going to get started soon. As you know I have a team of engineers who we are using as a 'rent-an-engineer' outfit. As we can get work for them, they will work projects with firms on the outside and hopefully provide a revenue flow for us. You are the hand picked team to help me conceive and develop our own product that can be produced and supported here to provide another revenue stream."

"What are the constraints?" asked Gina.

"I just gave them to you." Alicia smiled and continued. "If we can do it and it will provide income then it is an option. What we need to do is pick the best option. Making a billion dollars doesn't help if it takes three years to get the first dollar. In the same way, being able to get an immediate return is not worth the effort if it is so small that it doesn't make an impact on our bottom line. So check out the machines, load your favorite editor and put your thinking caps on. We're going to start with a planning session and then we will get to work on a functional specification for the best ideas if we end up with more than one worth looking into." Alicia looked at her watch and held up five fingers. "And we will try to do this in the most efficient manner possible." Gina and Ann nodded to show they understood. Alicia had already let them know that they were never to discuss Jasmine's abilities out loud. The assumption was that the entire compound was bugged and had live video in process. If they kept alert and treated it that way, they were reasonably safe. If not, they were putting themselves and Jasmine in grave danger.

They made small talk for the next five minutes while they checked out the computers, waiting for the connection to happen. Alicia could tell they were nervous but that was expected. It's an unsettling feeling to have someone just pop inside your head. When it came, it was smooth as silk. Alicia realized that Jasmine's skills were constantly improving. Alicia felt Ann and Gina join the Mind. Everyone greeted Jazz, who was treated as another member of the team. Alicia also felt the Mind immediately start pulling away, wanting to go it's own direction. Alicia issued her instructions. "This thing we call the Mind is the union of all four of us. No one person controls it so to accomplish anything, we must all focus on the task at hand or we may end up creating a really good stew recipe instead of a great new industrial automation control system. It's a lot like herding cats. We can control the general direction it goes but it has a tendency to make a few unexpected turns so we have to stay alert."

Alicia described her vision of a possible project, feeling it being modified as it was presented by the Mind's new experience base. She watched it grow in complexity as it strained to become all things to all people and then felt it start shedding the frivolous features until there was a solid core, well-defined and workable. "That's one possible target," was the pronouncement of the Mind.

"That was a nice week's worth of work," announced Ann. "It took just over forty-five seconds. I timed it. So when we complete this project, what are we going to do this afternoon?" They all laughed but they also understood the limitations of the Mind. They could design and create with amazing speed, they could pass a complex concept between themselves in a millisecond but the grunt work of creating the product, of writing the code, compiling, linking, and testing would still of necessity be done at normal speed. The final product would be months away. Ann suggested that they each share their work experience and particular skills with each other. Ann started and the Mind bucked and bolted at every interesting topic.

When Ann came to her experience in graphics data compression Alicia became excited. She opened her experience in audio compression. That was all it took for the Mind to gallop away on a tangent. It took all of their efforts to bring it back to focus mostly because one of the members was fighting in the opposite direction.

Gina finally got the rest of them to listen to her. "Did anyone else see what I saw there?" No one had. "Humor me for one minute. I want to go back where we just came from. I have to look at this one more time to see if I really understand it. If it is what I think it is, we may have another possible product." The team agreed and retraced their steps. From the outside, the three team members appeared to be studying their computer screens intently. Inside the mind, they were totally engrossed by what they saw coming into shape before their mind's eye.

Chapter 33

Winter came early to northern Nevada. Temperatures dropped and snow swirled over the plateau. This was both good and bad news for the reservation. Even Senator Fenton couldn't keep the gates to the reservation open when any new residents would be forced to live in tents. The population peaked for the winter at fifteen thousand residents, three times the number Christine planned but less than what Fenton had hoped.

Construction moved from the outdoors to inside the various buildings. The old married housing apartments were completely full and functional. All the barracks were also functional and filled with tenants. Three large hangars were rapidly being converted into two floors of efficiency apartments. When they were complete they would house an additional seven hundred fifty people who were currently living in the gymnasium, offices, tents and any place else that could be pressed into service.

Living conditions were poor at best. The cold drafty buildings were packed to capacity. Privacy was almost non-existent. Some of the people couldn't take it and decided to leave the reservation. Christine knew this would happen but was disappointed at each departure. She guessed correctly that Fenton would make a big deal of the number of Monoecions choosing to leave in favor of the surgery. The percentage of Monoecions choosing surgery over the reservation doubled during early November. Christine needed a winner.

Thursday, November 21

Rae Ann looked over the housing charts trying to find a space for a woman who had walked the last twelve miles when her car had broken down. Even though the reservation was officially closed until spring, they continued to take in special cases as others left or as new construction created space. Rae Ann was lost in thought when a voice startled her from behind. "Excuse me."

Rae Ann whirled around. "Sorry, I didn't hear you come up," she explained as she regained her composure. "Can I help you?"

"Yes, I'm sure you can," drawled the woman. "I'm Victoria Lane and I live in housing unit seventeen of the Hastings building. We had a person leave yesterday and you moved a new woman in today."

"Yes, I remember. Is there a problem?" asked Rae Ann.

"Yes there is. I can't live with that woman. You need to put her somewhere else."

"I'm sorry," said Rae Ann cutting her off. "We don't have the luxury of changing housing assignments because of personality conflicts. You two will have to work out your differences on your own." Rae Ann returned her attention to her housing chart.

The woman held her ground. "You don't understand Ms. Baird. We could talk all we want but it still won't change her color."

Rae Ann returned her attention to the woman. "What?"

"She is black. I can not live with a black person."

In the more than two and a half centuries since the first Monoecion was born, almost all races had become affected. There were residents in the reservation of all creeds and colors. "I understand your problem," said Rae Ann sympathetically.

"Then you will take steps to correct the situation?" queried the woman.

"I'll take care of the housing reassignment myself," assured Rae Ann.

That evening, when Victoria Lane returned from her work detail, a pile of possessions were outside in the hallway. She smiled to herself as she entered her room. Inside, Rae Ann was helping a new woman unpack her things. "Ms. Baird, I'm afraid you are making a mistake," said Mrs. Lane.

"Again?" said Rae Ann. "I don't think so."

"Well, yes. You see, that is my bed there," she said pointing to the bed covered with the new woman's possessions. "I think she is moving into that space over there." She pointed to the bed on the other side of the room.

Rae stood up straight and faced her. "No, Mrs. Lane, a black woman has that bunk. You found it disagreeable so I reassigned you. Your things are outside."

"So where am I supposed to sleep," demanded the woman.

Rae Ann handed her a slip of paper. "This is your new housing assignment."

Mrs. Lane looked at the paper. "This is a tent!" she exclaimed.

"That right," said Rae Ann. "And it's the farthest tent from the food facilities, bathrooms and showers I could find." Rae Ann tore into the woman. "Irrational prejudice is why we are all here. I can't erase it but I sure don't have to put up with it. Now pick up your things and get out of my sight!"

"But..."

"Move it!" yelled Rae Ann. The woman pulled her hand back as if to slap Rae Ann. Rae Ann didn't move a muscle. "Please do. I haven't had a good excuse to kick somebody's ass in days."

The woman backed out the door. "You haven't heard the last of this!" she cried as she picked up her bags.

The next morning, Christine called Rae Ann into her office. "I just received another complaint on you," she said reading over a grievance sheet.

"That's not surprising," responded Rae Ann. "Is it a problem?"

"No," smiled Christine. "I just called you in to let you know how happy I am with the job you are doing. She dropped the sheet of paper into the trashcan. "Do try not to break any bones."

"Yes ma'am," smirked Rae Ann and excused herself.

Saturday, November 23
Alicia finished the testing with the audio and video files. The results were the same as with the database files tested yesterday. Ann hung over her shoulder. "How did it go, Alicia?"

"The same as yesterday, half the size of any other program output and twenty percent faster." Alicia's smile could light a room. "We now have a product that will compress data better than any product on the market. And not just marginally better, we are talking by a factor of two!"

"Cool," said Ann. "How many files have you put through it so far?"

"Five hundred in the last test. Look at these numbers! This is better than I ever expected. When is Gina coming in? She's got to see this. Christine is going to freak when she sees these results," Alicia said. "This is exactly the opposite of what I said we were going to do. This project was supposed to be industrial software, sell a few copies at high prices and be ready in a year. Instead it's commercial software that should sell a million copies at a few dollars each."

Gina burst through the door and slammed it behind her. "It's freezing out there." She saw Alicia and Ann looking at her with broad grins. "Did it work?! Let me see, let me see!" Without pausing to take off her coat she ran to the screen.

"It buried everything on the market. We kicked their binary butts." Alicia handed Gina and Ann each a cup of coffee and took her own cup in hand. "Ladies, we are in business," she announced and clinked cups.

Ann looked dismayed at the cup. "I hate coffee. Don't we have anything else to toast with?"

"Shut up and drink," said Alicia. "You can take time to brew your tea later. Right now it's time to toast." They again clinked cups and drank, although Ann had a sour look on her face. "OK, enough celebration. Let's get back to work. We need this recompiled and tested for Linux and Mac by the end of the week."

The Attorney General tried to maintain his temper even though Senator Fenton obviously could not control his. "This is a simple matter of dollars and cents. We have a limited budget and we must use it where we get the maximum return for the public welfare."

"Since when is preventing the destruction of the human race a poor return on investment?" Fenton threw a folder on the conference table. "Look at your own reports. Twenty percent of the Monoecions identified between the ages of eighteen and thirty have disappeared. One in five is not choosing to have the surgery or report to the reservation. They are going underground. And it's going to cost a hell of a lot more to track them down later than it is now."

"Tell me, Senator, what is the current lead time to get the surgery?" asked the Attorney General.

"I believe it is about six weeks. What's that got to do with anything?"

"Let me bring you up to date with your own agency figures. The wait for surgery is sixteen weeks in Atlanta, and that is the shortest wait time we could come up with. It's over twenty in Los Angles and Chicago. The Monoecions aren't going into hiding, they are moving. They're not hiding from the police, they are hiding from the street thugs who use them as punching bags because they know no one cares."

"You sound just like the bleeding hearts I have to deal with every day." Fenton jabbed his finger out at the Attorney General.

The Attorney General continued calmly, "I don't care if they run. They can't hide. We have a simple blood test that will identify them. It is required for marriage certificates and hospital admittance. It's the same all over the United States, all over the world. They are not a threat anymore."

"That's exactly what they want you to think," sneered Fenton. "These creatures have laid low, growing their numbers. They have lied and cheated to conceal their true abilities. All for one purpose, to eliminate mankind and claim the world as their own."

"We have had hundreds of agents on this investigation for four months and have not turned up one shred of evidence of any conspiracy to subvert the government or eliminate mankind. Hide, yes, subvert, no. This is a public health issue, not a criminal investigation."

"What about the evidence of telepathic ability way beyond what was admitted to Congress, or isn't lying under oath a crime anymore?" countered Fenton.

"We don't have enough evidence to put in your eye. You have a couple of coincidences that you have managed to blow all out of proportion." The Attorney General stood and closed his briefcase. "All of the agents are reassigned as of today."

"You can't do this. The American public won't allow it," stammered Fenton.

"You show me the threat to national security, conspiracy to commit murder or defraud the public, and you will have the full support of the FBI. But so far I have seen nothing to support having half the FBI field investigators assigned to this project. You can keep the staff of researchers only until the completion of the family tree, and understand that their cost comes out of your budget." The Attorney General walked to the door of the conference room. He looked back over his shoulder. "You get some solid evidence then let me know. Until then, don't call us, we'll call you."

"I'm going to enjoy watching you eat those words," snarled Fenton. The Attorney General ignored him and walked out the door. Fenton burned all the way back to his office. He stormed in and slammed the door. Staff members instinctively faded into whatever cover was available, attempting to become invisible. "Tell Lindell I want him in my office. Now!" Three people lunged for telephones.

Lindell arrived a few minutes later, obviously irritated at being called in on short notice. "Senator, I have a meeting in fifteen minutes and I was hoping to use this as preparation time. Can this be covered later?"

"The FBI is pulling out. Dropping the whole investigation. I just got the word from the Attorney General himself."

Lindell wasn't surprised. He had seen the writing on the wall as both parties jockeyed for position in the budget cutting battles. He couldn't see why the Senator was acting like it was a surprise. He tried to show some sympathy. "They're not even tracking the delinquents?"

"No, that's being left to the local authorities. Damn, if they just would have waited a little longer we would have had the evidence they wanted. I can feel it." Fenton wasn't really surprised, just upset at missing what he considered a golden opportunity to seal the fate of the Monoecions once and for all. "The Attorney General told me he wanted evidence and that's exactly what I plan to give him. I want Robert Landis out to that reservation watching his wife. He's delayed here long enough. You make sure that he understands that either he gets his butt in the game or we will put it in jail.

"I know the American public. They get all worked up about something like this, they can see the issues and they react. But then time passes and their resolve to finish the job starts to waver. Within five years the need for the reservation will start to be questioned. Ten years from now it will be closed, the creatures will be right back on the streets, breeding and carrying out their plan. They know human nature too. They know that all they have to do is wait. It's our job to expose them for what they are. To give the American public the proof it needs to justify in their own minds the need to wipe these creatures off the face of the earth."

"I'll take care of lighting the fire under Mr. Landis," said Lindell. "I'll arrange to make sure his house sells and his job here is terminated. He will be much more cooperative then."

Fenton had spent his anger. Now his mind began to focus more clearly on the target ahead. "Just make sure we get the evidence we need, even if we have to be creative. And we still have our ace in the hole. Find out what she's been doing. We have had her in deep cover for months and we haven't got jack shit from her."

Saturday, November 30

"Rae Ann Baird is brutal!" complained Dorothy. "I thought I was in pretty good shape but that woman worked us till we dropped. And she hadn't even broken a sweat yet."

"Don't over do it," said Christine. "I need you in one piece. We have too much work to do to have you too sore to move."

"Yeah," said Dorothy lost in thought, an edge of sadness in her voice.

"Are you OK," asked Christine.

"Oh yeah. I was just thinking about Rae Ann. It must have been tough to loose a daughter. You can feel it in her. She tries not to let it show but there are times when you can see the anger and hate."

"Yes," said Christine, "it worries me sometimes. I was hoping that it would start to fade by now but it hasn't."

"You can't complain about the job she has done since you put her in charge of housing though. She has exhibited good planning and has been fair and consistent. I haven't heard about any complaints that had any merit."

Christine had to agree. Rae Ann had done an excellent job both in housing and in morale building. Her self-defense classes went over big. There was a major building of pride going on in the reservation and the self-defense training was giving the people a feeling of control and self-determination.

It helped that the average age on the reservation was much younger than on the outside. The Monoecions who chose to come here were typically under forty with most being in their twenties and early thirties. It was true that some had come here and had not been able to cope with the hardships but the numbers were fewer than Christine had feared, less than ten percent so far. And there was a waiting list of new residents wanting to take the place of those leaving even it meant living in a gymnasium until the housing was available.

Christine couldn't complain about the heart of her "tribe" as she called them. But they needed more than heart to survive. They needed an economy. As long as the reservation was a drain on the budget there was always the chance of the government reversing it's decision and shutting it down, forcing the residents to undergo the surgery. That was why Dorothy was in her office on an early Saturday morning. Christine was hoping it was good news.

Dorothy opened the business with, "You had told me that a software design team led by Alicia Inman was in the process of designing a new industrial product that would be available within a year with some pieces ready in a few months. You also told me that this would be an expensive product with limited market potential."

"Yes, that's what they told me. Have you had a chance to talk to them on this?" Christine responded.

"Yes I have and I have found out that they were way off the mark." Dorothy watched Christine cringe.

"How bad is it? Or don't I want to know?"

Dorothy reached in her briefcase and pulled out a computer CD. "Their pricing was optimistic. They mentioned a pricing structure of four to ten thousand dollars but my research shows that this program will actually sell for around twenty dollars."

"What?!" Christine cried. "Are you sure? This doesn't sound right for Alicia to be so off in the weeds. She has a good head on her shoulders."

"She was also way off on the development cycle and the projected sales. The software is already complete. Here it is," she said laying the disk in front of Christine. "Oh, and I estimate the first two months of sales will exceed two million copies." Dorothy broke into a wide smile. "I know it's still a few weeks early but Merry Christmas."

"You witch! You scared the hell out of me." Christine started to smile then the math dawned on her. "Did I hear you right? Are you saying that this software will provide forty million dollars in income over the next two months?"

"That's gross, of course," responded Dorothy calmly. "The best that we expect to net is half that. We have the patent and copyright in progress and copies are already in the reviewers hands for the biggest computer publications. We'll catch the minor ones next month. I'm leaving to help with negotiations with at least three fortune 500 companies for sight licenses to get the ball rolling. This software will become the de facto standard for file compression in no time at all."

"Is it really that good?" asked Christine.

"I know damn little about software development but I do know that compression software is used in all kinds of other software. The test results that Alicia showed me were enough to convince me. I think that every company that ships software and wants to reduce the number of CDs and DVDs it has to ship will be using our product if they have any brains at all. Not to mention the hardware cost reduction because of the smaller disk space required for large databases."

"How about protection. Are we covered legally?" asked Christine.

"They have already applied for the patent and copyrights. We should be all right there." Dorothy's tone of voice conveyed more worry than her words let on. "I'm a little concerned about how much flak they will get from the government but as long as Fenton keeps his nose out of it we should be OK."

"That's a big if," mused Christine. "Try to put push it through with as little fuss as possible. The less attention we bring to ourselves, the better."

"All the paperwork and marketing is being set up through an outside company created by a friend of Alicia's. As long as they don't investigate, the patent should be in our hands before they realize it belongs to us."

"Is it all legal?"

"Squeaky clean. Nothing is concealed, we're just banking on no one taking the time to investigate. Cross your fingers."

Todd Lindell watched the woman walk to the drinking fountain, set down her newspaper and briefcase, and take a long drink. She picked up her briefcase and quickly walked away, leaving the newspaper behind. Lindell watched it for several minutes before walking over and setting his briefcase on top of it. He took a drink also and picked up the newspaper with his items and walked back to his car.

Once in the car, he sifted through the discarded newspaper until he found the half dozen sheets of hand written notes. In tight neat letters the pages gave a day by day description of Christine's life on the reservation. Every meeting of any interest was described. Almost all of it was useless administrative detail. Finally on the fourth page he found a note that caught his attention, Check out patent applied for computer software by DataComp Technologies - These ladies are sharp! After it was a list of companies. Lindell ran the yellow highlighter over the text. He finished the rest quickly and went back to the office wondering what the reference meant.

Thursday, December 12

Alicia received the phone call from Zak just after lunch. He explained what was happening with the patent as Alicia's temper rose. Gina and Ann listened to the one side of the conversation and knew immediately that it meant trouble. Alicia promised Zak to get back to him as soon as possible and hung up the phone. "We are being screwed again. Fenton got his grimy little fingers on our patent application and is claiming that we can't be awarded one because we're not human and the patent system was for the protection of human intellectual property only."

"That asshole!" exclaimed Ann.

"You said it," said Alicia. "He has filed suit to block the award of the patent on those grounds."

"He can't stop us from selling can he?" asked Gina.

"No way I know of," responded Ann. "Let's get Dorothy over here. She might know how we can handle this."

"I'll call her," said Alicia. "I'll also see if we can get Christine Landis to come with her. This can affect our economy in a big way so I'm sure that she's interested. She is also an attorney so maybe she will have some answers for us."

Dorothy and Christine arrived a few minutes later. Alicia started to fill them in on what Zak had told her. Dorothy was mad. "This is irrational. I think he's just trying to cause any problems he can just for the sake of causing problems."

"No, this is directed straight at our economy. He knows exactly what he is doing," Christine explained. "He wants us destroyed and he is willing to gamble that the public will go for forced sterilization if the reservation becomes too costly. The quicker the cost of maintaining the reservation climbs, the quicker the public gets fed up with supporting us, the higher the probability that Fenton's choice will be followed. The longer we succeed in living in peace with the outside world, the harder it will be for Fenton to justify our extermination. His program costs money too."

"This product would also give us name recognition too," added Ann. "People would see that we are productive in ways they can use and think twice about seeing us as the new Evil Empire."

"This doesn't stop us from selling our product does it?" asked Gina. "All it does is delay us getting a patent, right?"

"As far as selling individual copies," Dorothy answered, "that's true but when we try to sell the technology to major corporations, they will not be interested in paying money to someone who may not own the product. If someone else gets ownership of this then they can sue for royalties. The same thing can happen to major distributors of the individual packages."

"You haven't heard all that Zak told me yet," Alicia broke in. "He said that he called his contacts at the corporations that we are negotiating with to provide the bulk licenses for product distribution. He only got through to two of them. One just said they were looking into the situation but the other told him something very disturbing. They told him that they had been told that our product was being investigated as a possible tool of sabotage. Supposedly we are using this software to pass secret communications to our 'underground sisters' and that possibly this is really a time bomb virus."

"What a bunch of BS," exclaimed Gina.

"That's what Zak told them and they agreed," said Alicia. "They had already taken our code apart and checked it thoroughly themselves to see how it worked and were very satisfied with the safety of our product. They also said they had pressed the informer for where this information came from and who was investigating it and the guy couldn't come up with an answer."

"That's the key to this war," said Christine. "We are going to have to go on the offensive as quickly as possible. Dorothy, I want you and Zak to contact everyone as soon as possible. Lay out exactly what we have heard and reassure them that all the charges are groundless. Make sure those reviewers don't pull the articles for their magazines. We must get this product on the store shelves as soon as possible."

"And remember that we don't need store shelves," added Alicia. "Zak is just about set to have it available on the Web. Anyone with Internet access and a credit card will be able to download within a few days. The only thing he is waiting for is getting the automated credit card payment system set up."

"Great," said Christine. "I'll get an attorney working on breaking the patent block. Fenton may be able to slow down the flow of money coming in but I don't think he will be able to stop it. We need to do everything possible to maximize it. We also need to document everything that is happening. Some time in the future, we may be able to swing the tide in our favor by demonstrating how Fenton's COMA has forced us to be a drain on the budget. If we can turn this into a Fenton blunder in the public eyes, we just may get him replaced by a moderate."

"Fat chance," grumbled Gina.

"May be," said Christine "but it's a better chance than just rolling over and playing dead." The session had started pretty down but they all went back to work with some hope that they could beat the problem. Christine was pleased, not with what had been done to them but with how her people had responded, and with how she had handled the situation. She began to hold out some hope that someday she would learn to lead. She didn't realize how much she had already learned.

Fenton and Lindell looked over the article reviewing the new software that had been produced at the reservation. Nowhere was the mention that it was designed and produced by the Monoecions. "These people are playing right into their hands" snarled Fenton, throwing the magazine across the room. "Everyone is forgetting what's at stake with these creatures! Did you tell them that we wanted them to remove the article?"

Lindell nodded. "The publisher told me that they couldn't. It's already at the printers and in process. They couldn't make their release date if they removed it." He shrugged his shoulders. "There isn't much we can do at this point."

"No, there probably isn't much that we can do, but I can think of someone who can." Fenton spun through his Rolodex and pulled out a card. He jotted down a name and phone number and handed it to Lindell. "Strictly off the record, I think it would do a world of good to have a boycott of this product organized by a concerned citizens group."

Lindell looked at the slip of paper. "And this is a concerned citizen I take it?"

"Definitely," said Fenton. "We can't have anything to do with this so make sure there is no trail leading back to us. Just get him all the information he needs. Funding shouldn't be a problem but if it is, see what we can do to make sure he can afford to mount an effective campaign. None of the money can come from us directly but we can get him in contact with people who can help."

"What do you think will work best, ads in the trade publications?" asked Lindell.

Fenton thought for a moment. "That would help but I think a show of public indignation would be most effective. You know, protesters marching in front of the companies using the product, organized boycotts against the company's products. If the corporations that use the Mono's stuff start to lose sales and get negative publicity, they will drop it like a hot potato. Has our inside agent had any problems keeping us informed as to the Mono's business dealings?"

"Not so far," said Lindell "but she started asking me questions as to what was going on with the patent thing. She said that so far she has found no signs of criminal wrong doing."

"What we do with her information is not for her to worry about." Fenton didn't completely trust their mole in the Monoecion organization. Sometimes she did not appear to be properly motivated. "Remind her that she only sees a piece of the puzzle. She needs to leave the policy decisions to us."

"I'll make sure that she keeps the flow of information coming," said Lindell.

Robert and the children arrived at the front gate. The Federal clerks processed them through, taking their pictures, checking the girls COMA identification cards, verifying his identification and searching their belongings. Robert found the whole experience humiliating and told them so. He was ignored.

Their pictures were taken for new identification cards. As residents of the reservation they were required to have them on their person at all times. The whole process took two hours. They were eventually allowed to enter the gate where Christine waited on the other side. "Hello strangers!" she called to her daughters as they ran to her. She hugged them as they surrounded her.

Robert looked at his wife's face as he approached. There were bags under her eyes and she had lost weight. "Hello back. They don't make it easy to get in here do they?"

"You should see how hard it is to get out." Christine pulled her husband to her. "I'm so glad you are all here." After a ceremonial kiss she pointed to a waiting pickup. "Toss your bags in the back. The driver will deliver them to your luxury accommodations."

"I recognize sarcasm when I hear it," commented Robert dryly. "I just want to know if it's better than that hotel we stayed in on our way through Kentucky."

"Absolutely," assured Christine. "The bugs are much better behaved."

"Gross!" exclaimed the girls in unison.

Chapter 34

Monday, December 30

Charlie Wilkens stood proudly in front of the apartment building. On the outside it still looked very much an aircraft hangar, but inside snuggled sixty-four apartments designed to hold four residents each. It wasn't high class but it would be heaven to the families who had been living in the community center, the gym, the church and anywhere else a sleeping bag could be spread.

"Happy New Year, Chet," said the architect. "We said we could do it by the first of the year and, you know, I think Mrs. Landis had her doubts. I do believe that the woman owes us an apology."

Charlie just looked at it and smiled. Half of the units were already full with this new half already having people assigned, just waiting to move in. "Yeah, we made it with a full," Charlie looked at his watch, "thirty-eight hours to spare." The last of the finishing crews had straggled out only minutes before. "There's something about building. It's good for the soul."

"It sure is," agreed the architect. "I just can't wait until we can start building something from scratch, buildings that will stand for the next fifty or hundred years rather than stopgap living spaces. I want to be building homes."

The two construction foremen that had arrived at the reservation with Charlie came out of one of the apartments and trudged over to him. You could read the bone tired fatigue in the way they moved but they were smiling. "We're going to have to get going now, Chet. Thanks for bringing us along for the ride."

Charlie shook each of their hands. "Thanks for coming with me. I know that you want to get back to your families for a while. Sorry about missing the holidays."

"Hell, we made that decision. Nobody held a gun to our heads. We'll be back again as soon as we can afford the time." They said good-bye to the architect and climbed into a pickup already loaded with their personal belongings.

Charlie watched as they made their way toward the front gate. "Come on, I'll buy you a beer. Just don't tell my wife."

"Deal."

The lone clerk sat at her desk, huddling close to her space heater, her biology book propped up on a stack papers. She liked doing the night watch because there was little work to do and she could concentrate on her studies. Even though they didn't have a true university, several professors had started study groups to keep the college age students from falling too far behind while a real school and curriculum was created. Even though the books had to be shared among two or three people, the system was working. This was supplemented with online schooling where possible. She started back at the beginning of the chapter on sexually transmitted diseases and tried to maintain her concentration. Only a textbook could make sex this boring she thought. When the door opened she instinctively jerked in her chair, it was unusual to have visitors this late.

A man dressed in army fatigues entered the office. "Sorry to bother you this late but there is a family at the gate who said that they were to report in and we don't have any record of the arrangement. Just wanted to see if you had anything."

Boy, that's a switch, she thought, they are actually being civil. Usually they would just turn the people away and say tough luck, you didn't fill out the right forms, come back tomorrow. "I don't know of anything but let me look. There could have been something and they forgot to tell me. Let me see if there is a note." She dug through the pile of papers in the in-basket looking for any entrance forms or notes that may have been left for her. "I can't find anything here that....." She looked up just in time to see the club on it's downward arc, there was no time to react, just time to recognize what was happening. The blow shattered the left side of her skull and knocked her off her chair.

Her arm struck a bottle of white-out that she had been using, knocking it to the floor with her. As the bottle hit the floor, it splattered into the space heater. Flames immediately erupted jumping three feet high out from under the desk. The man was so startled that he ran for the door and stumbled outside. His noisy exit caught the attention of one of the army sentries on the outside of the gate.

The sentry eyed him suspiciously. Then seeing the flames through the window shouted "What's going on over there?"

The intruder looked frantically for another exit but knew there was none. "The place is on fire!" he yelled back as he ran toward the sentry. "Do you have an extinguisher?!"

"Yes, there's one inside!" The sentry ducked into the guard shack to retrieve it. The intruder sprinted through the gate into the darkness. The sentry dashed back with the extinguisher in time to see the man fading into the night. He yelled for his partner to give chase while he ran with the extinguisher to the burning hut just inside the gate. He started spraying the flames as he entered and then saw the girl on the floor, her head in a pool of blood and her clothes smoldering.

Robert roused at the pounding on the door. He swung his legs out of bed and stood unsteadily. "I'm coming," he muttered.

Christine lifted on one elbow. "What is it?"

"Who knows? At this time of night it can't be good." He banged his shin in the cramped bedroom "Son of a.... I'm coming already!" He crossed the living room and stood at the door. "Who is it?"

"It's Angela. There's been an attack. The girl on front gate security has been hurt real bad," came the voice from the other side of the door.

"Open the door, Robert. I know her." Christine turned on the light as Robert let the woman in. "Who was it that got hurt?"

"I don't know," replied Angela. "One of the Army front gate sentries found her and drove her to the hospital. I didn't see her. The doctor sent me here to tell you. The doctor said it was real bad. I don't think she expects her to live."

"I'll get my coat," said Christine as she hurried back in her room.

"Do you want me to come with you?" asked Robert as Christine quickly pulled on some clothes.

"No. You better stay here with the girls." Christine pushed her feet into her boots without bothering with socks. "I don't know what's going on and I don't want them left here alone. I'll be back as soon as I can." Christine grabbed a sweater and a pair of socks from her drawer and rushed for the door pulling on her parka as she went.

"Call me as soon as you can." Robert watched her scurry down the steps and dive into the waiting car. This was her world. Back in Washington, he was the dealmaker. He could put together the right amounts of powerful people, money and inside information and make money for all concerned. But here, he felt helpless as he closed the door behind the fading figure of his wife.

When Christine arrived at the hospital she saw that there was already a small crowd forming in the front entry. She nodded to them as a nurse's aid lead her back to the operating room. The injured girl's sister was waiting, pacing back and forth, pausing to peer in the small window in the operating room door and then repeat the cycle. Christine recognized her but couldn't place her name. "How is she doing?"

"She's not dead yet," responded the young woman. "The doctor said the injuries were very bad. Even if she does live, she will probably have some brain damage."

"I'm sorry. My family will be praying for her." Christine extended her hand. "I'm Christine Landis. I'm not sure that we have met."

She took Christine's hand. "Everyone here knows you. That's my little sister in there." Christine sat and talked with the woman for a few minutes. Little scraps of information came out with the hospital staff as they moved in and out of the operating room.

Finally the doctor came out and addressed the injured girl's sister. "We have her stabilized for the moment. If she remains stable for the next twenty-four hours then she will have a fighting chance."

"Can I see my sister?"

"In a few minutes, after she's been moved to Intensive Care. We'll set up a cot next to her so you can stay with her if you'd like," replied the doctor.

Christine excused herself and headed back to the front to call Robert and let him know what was happening. Then she bundled up and headed for the reception shack to view the scene of the crime and get an update on what was happening with the investigation. Her security chief was there watching over the two highway patrol officers who were conducting the investigation.

"What's the story?" asked Christine.

"We are not sure about the details, I'll tell you what we do know. About two twelve AM one of the sentries saw a man rushing out of the reception shack. He noticed that the man was wearing a military style uniform with a camouflage jacket."

"One of the Army personnel from the unit here?" asked Christine.

"Not likely. The sentry said the uniform was an old camouflage style not issued anymore. Probably purchased from a surplus store or it was a hunting outfit. He said the man yelled that the building was on fire and asked for an extinguisher." The security chief scanned her notes and flipped the page. "The sentry said he then saw the flames through the window and entered his building to get the extinguisher. When he came back out a few seconds later, he saw the man running out across the open field outside the fence. He told his buddy to chase him and came in to extinguish the fire. That's when he found the body. At first he thought she was dead but took the victim's pulse and discovered that she was still alive. He then tried to stop the bleeding with a piece of a blanket he found with the victim. He put her in his jeep and drove her to the hospital."

"Did the other sentry see anything?" asked Christine.

"Not a thing," said the security chief. "He never even saw the guy. He ran in the direction the first sentry pointed but never made visual contact. As a side note, it looks like the fire was accidental. It appears to have been caused by a small bottle of correction fluid. That's probably what scared off the attacker before he finished the job. Is she still alive?"

Christine nodded. "The doctor said that the next twenty-four hours will tell."

"Amazing. I was a cop in Dallas for more years than I care to admit and I never saw that much blood from a head wound at the scene and have the victim live."

"She's not out of the woods yet," reminded Christine. "What's the plan from here?"

"As soon as we have enough light, we will search the area for tire tracks or footprints." No one raised the question of motive, the pattern was all too familiar. It had all the markings of a typical hate crime. "Oh yeah, there is someone waiting to talk you. Rae Ann Baird showed up about fifteen minutes ago looking for you. I told her that you were probably at the hospital but she didn't want to bother you there. The last I saw of her, she was over talking to one of the Army sentries."

"Thanks," said Christine. "Try to make them do their job right. I would really like to catch this guy. This is going to scare everybody to death. They came here to be safe from this kind of stuff and now it happens right inside the fence."

"I'll do what I can." The security chief headed back in the direction of the reception shack.

Christine looked for Rae Ann and found her talking to one of the army sentries near the front gate. When she saw Christine she broke off and walked to meet her. "Christine, can I talk to you for a few minutes? I want to see if we can work out a way to keep this from happening again and I have a few ideas that I want you to hear."

Christine was feeling the cold penetrating her clothes and she knew she could offer little assistance to the investigation. "Sure, as long as it can be done indoors, I'm freezing out here." Rae Ann nodded her assent and they walked in silence to the jeep Christine had borrowed from the hospital. "What was it you wanted to discuss?" asked Christine as she started the motor.

"Is this your vehicle?" asked Rae Ann.

"No, I borrowed it from the hospital. Why?"

"I just didn't want to discuss this in anyplace where they have a bug," responded Rae Ann. "I want to install a security system to act as an early warning alarm. I've been thinking about this ever since we talked in your office about me taking the housing administration job."

"What are your ideas," asked Christine.

"From what we know now, the guy who committed the assault appeared to have been working alone. He just slipped past the army sentries, walked in the gate and tried to kill one of our people. He probably would have tried to kill a few more if he hadn't caused the fire accidentally and was spotted by the sentry. These people are our main threat. If a few fanatics got in here with serious intent, they could really wreak havoc before the police or military could get anyone in to help."

"I agree with what you're saying so far. What do you think we should do about it?" Christine asked.

"We have to have two elements to counter the threat," said Rae Ann. "First, we have to know that it is happening. We need an early warning system to alert the entire compound when someone has broken in. We can't afford a high tech system so the best is using what we do have, people. I'd like to see two people at the front gate at all times. If one is attacked, the other can sound the alarm. I would also like to see us institute regular patrols with radios so we can watch over our people and alert the whole reservation in case of trouble."

"That sounds reasonable," said Christine. "We do have some funds that can be put towards security equipment. If we really need a motion sensor in a particular location, we could probably swing one or two of those too."

"That would be great," agreed Rae Ann. "Another thing we need is warning horns that can be heard by everyone in the reservation. I don't want someone killed in their sleep just because they didn't know of the threat."

"I agree," said Christine "but I don't want the damned things going off every night because of false alarms. We need to make darn sure that we have an intrusion before the audible alarm gets triggered. It needs to be a manually triggered system. Anything else?"

Rae Ann took a deep breath. She knew this was going to be the hard item to sell. "We need a self-defense force. We need a trained militia who can fight back to protect the rest of the population if we are attacked."

"What? You want me to start an army?" exclaimed Christine.

"No, not an army, more like a swat team," explained Rae Ann.

"A swat team?" Christine shook her head. "That's about all they could do to the attackers is "swat." You do remember that we are not allowed to have guns inside the reservation?"

Rae Ann made her main argument. "My people don't need guns. If someone is trying to sneak inside the reservation, they aren't going to do it with guns blazing. The first shot ends their advantage of surprise. In a case like that, a trained team can stop or at least force a retreat of the attacking party before they can cause major damage or cost more innocent lives. I have a handful of students and instructors that I would put against anybody that the Marines could offer. There is another thirty or so who can hold their own in any bar brawl. With a little more training, these people could be molded into a potent fighting force, ready to respond at a moment's notice. And if we get four of five fanatics busting through the front gate intent on fire bombing our homes, I'd sure rather have a trained team meet them than a bunch who's only training came from an article in the Ladies Home Journal."

Christine shook her head. "No, I don't like the thought of that. We would be asking a group of unarmed civilians to go up against some shotgun toting maniacs. You of all people should know the results of that."

Rae Ann held firm. "If it hadn't been for our training, all of us would have ended up dead. If the others had been trained then we probably would have made it through without any casualties."

Christine listened to Rae Ann's arguments. They made sense but she didn't want to put anyone intentionally into harms way. But then she would rather have someone who was trained in combat situations than someone who wasn't. "OK. We will give it a try under the following conditions. One, the training will have to be on their own time and participation will be voluntary. I don't want anyone to think that they are being forced into participation. Two, the team will be under the control of the security chief. You will be responsible for training but the orders for deployment come from security."

"Deal," said Rae Ann. "The watch teams will need to be released from their normal duties but everything else should not impact the work crews."

"I still don't like this," said Christine. "I don't want anyone placed in a position where they can get hurt unless it is absolutely necessary to save lives. Do not risk people for property." Christine let herself slide back into her political persona. "It may help our people to sleep a little better at night with our own security force, especially after this happened. And the government sure can't complain because we are trying to defend ourselves."

"I understand." Rae Ann also understood that there were limitations to the martial arts. She knew that for her force to be truly effective that they would need more than just their hands and her training. Nightsticks help but in an emergency, a ranged weapon is needed. Several guns had already been smuggled into the reservation and stashed in various hiding places. Rae Ann had already created an underground network to make those weapons available to her people for use in an emergency although once they were used there would be hell to pay. It would play right into the government's hand to give them an excuse to run regular search and seizure raids whenever they wanted. And, unknown to anyone outside her hand-picked students, they were already receiving training with other ranged weapons that were not banned. "Don't worry, I'm not out to become Rambo," she assured Christine.

Saturday, January 4

The sunshine was unusually warm as the trio of programmers walked to the mess hall for lunch. The Mind had been unruly this morning and it had taken their full concentration to keep it on track for the thirty minute session. "Did you notice how hard it was to keep focused this morning?" asked Gina. "We couldn't stay focused if our lives depended on it. I was beginning to think that we wouldn't get anything accomplished."

"I noticed but I just figured that you had a hot date tonight and you couldn't think straight," Alicia chided. Gina stuck her tongue out in response.

"As much as I'd like to blame our young colleague here, I must agree that the Mind definitely had a mind of its own today," whispered Ann.

"See," said Gina in her best elementary school voice, "I told you so." Everyone walked quietly for a few minutes. Gina added in a whisper "What was really interesting was where it wanted to go. I really wanted to just sit back and watch it travel wherever it wanted. Have you ever done that Alicia?"

Alicia shook her head. "No, I don't think it has ever been done." They arrived at the mess hall, collected their food and found a table alone.

"Why don't we?" whispered Ann. "I for one would really like to know where it would lead, especially with all the horsepower we can muster."

Alicia cut her off, indication that no discussion was to take place there. On the walk back to the office after lunch, Alicia thought about Christine. The more people who knew that she knew about Jasmine, the more she would be in danger. After all, Christine testified under oath to congress that Monoecion telepathy was limited to pain and strong emotion. She could easily end up in jail if it came out the she knew of Jasmine's abilities. Carla Baird was also a possibility but Alicia really didn't want Ann and Gina to know what had happened with Jasmine and the twins. That would require some preparation to keep from shocking them. Rae Ann Baird was out. Jasmine had made it clear that she did not want to connect with her again because of the way that she rejected Jasmine after the joining of Kathy and Carla. It had hurt Jasmine deeply that Rae Ann considered her a freak. Alicia said in a low voice "Well, with the three of us, Marci and Jasmine, that's five, and maybe one or two more, it would be the most powerful union yet. I'll have to check to be sure before I commit for anyone."

"When could we do it?" asked Gina eagerly, "later today?"

"No, I want to sleep on this one," Alicia said. "I want to talk it over with Marci and Jasmine to make sure that we have looked at all the dangers involved. The decision is really up to Jasmine."

They all agreed to take it slow but an atmosphere of excitement prevailed for the rest of the day. Every few minutes one of them would think of some new angle that they hadn't thought of yet and write a note to the others. Alicia finally agreed to try to set it up for early the next morning if it was a go. They knocked off early for lack of progress, all of them excited about the possibilities of the next day.

During dinner, Alicia whispered in Jasmine's ear. Seconds later, Alicia, Marci and Jazz were linked. Alicia presented the idea to them and waited for the reaction. Marci wasn't sure about the idea but Jasmine could hardly contain herself. She found the control that the adults kept applying to be frustrating. Jasmine managed to convince Marci with those unique begging talents found only in five year olds. Alicia contacted Christine and Carla that night and they agreed to join although Christine would do it remotely. The others made arrangements to meet at Alicia's apartment in the morning. For better or worse, the decision was made.

Sunday, January 5

Marci set out a plate of pastry and a large pot of coffee on the table next to the cups and napkins. Alicia came out of the bedroom and looked at the spread. "Fancy. You qualify for the Emily Post competition to be held later this week. Do you have some hot water for Ann's tea?"

"All ready. I just wasn't going to take it off the stove until she got here." Marci looked at the table with concern. "It looks pretty meager to me."

"These are pretty meager times. It looks great. They aren't coming here for a party, this is a work session." Alicia picked a piece of frosting off the coffeecake and popped it into her mouth.

"Keep your fingers off of that!" exclaimed Marci. She pulled the towel from over her shoulder and threatened Alicia with it. Alicia held her hands up and backed away from the table. Marci holstered the towel like a gun.

A knock sounded at the door and before Alicia could make a move, Jasmine flew out of the bedroom door, cleared the couch and flung open the front door. "Carla!" Jasmine jumped into Carla's open arms. Carla tossed Jasmine over her shoulder like a sack of feed, carried her back into the apartment and plopped her unceremoniously on the couch. Jessica peeked out of the hall to see who the visitor was and then hustled to Carla for her share of attention.

"We made it, on time even." Alicia wondered again if it was a good idea to have them present but it was too late to turn back now. "Are we the first ones here?"

"Afraid so," chirped Marci. "Lose one social point."

The knock came again. Alicia reached out and grabbed Jasmine as she flew by again. "I'll get it this time." Jasmine stood still and stuck her lower lip out as Alicia opened the door. Gina and Ann came in together and each gave Jasmine a hug as they passed. Marci made the introductions.

They made small talk for a few minutes nibbling on the coffeecake. Marci carried Jessica back in the bedroom and plopped her down in her crib with a bottle. Alicia checked her watch and announced "Why don't we start with a relaxation exercise to get our minds clear." They had been using the yoga exercises as a cover for their sessions with Jasmine since the beginning of the project. It provided a perfect reason for the few minutes of silence.

"I had a hard time sleeping last night so if you hear me snoring that just means I'm really into the relaxation exercise," quipped Ann.

Alicia arranged everyone in a circle in the cramped living room, sitting Jasmine between herself and Marci. They closed their eyes and began to breathe deeply. Jasmine linked with Alicia and Marci first followed by Carla. They could feel her apprehension.

"You will be OK," soothed Marci. "You're with friends here," giving Carla a reassuring hug.

"I'm ready. Let's do this," said Carla.

Ann and Gina joined the Mind. "You said we had one more. Who's is she?" asked Ann.

"I thought we would leave that for a surprise. She will join us from her office," said Alicia. Seconds later Christine slid into the group.

"Hello everyone. I hope I can stay. I thought the office would be empty but there were two others here working when I got here. I told them I had to study a report and closed the door. That should give me a few minutes of quiet."

Gina reacted with shock. "You're Christine Landis! Jasmine, you do have friends in high places."

"I'm nobody special here. In this world Jasmine is the special one. So what do we do now?" asked Christine.

Alicia pushed her thoughts out to the group. "We all know why we are here. Let me say now that this has never been done before with this many people and I'm not sure what to expect. If anyone does not feel up to this, now is the time to say so. That means you too, honey," pushing special encouragement to Jasmine. "If you don't want to go through with this, it's OK. I will understand."

"I want to," affirmed Jasmine. "I'm a little scared but I'm excited too, like when we rode on the Ferris wheel."

"I think we all feel that way." Alicia again addressed everyone. "We have all felt the pull of the Mind in the past but this time, we are going to try not to control it, just to let it go wherever it pleases. If it gets too intense then it may take everyone's full effort to pull it back. Is everyone ready?"

Marci mentally shook her head no, and then nodded yes. "But first we have something to show you." Alicia wrapped a hug around Carla. "There is something that you all need to know about before we go on. Alicia opened up the experience of the attack on the road to the reservation. Ann and Gina watched the attack unfold. They saw the shotgun blast rip into Kathy. "Carla, just open your mind so they can understand."

"My twin sister's body died that day." They all felt her pain as they watched it happen, "but Jasmine helped save her." Again they felt another join them. "This is my sister Kathy. You don't see her here because we both share my body."

Jasmine could feel a mixture of fear and wonder coming from Ann, Gina and Christine. Jasmine showed them what had happened as best she could. She felt their fears subside somewhat but the wonder continued to grow. Jasmine could feel concealed areas in Kathy and Carla, things that were not to be shared. It was OK, everyone had secrets. "We just wanted you to understand what the Mind can do. Do you still want to continue?"

"We've come this far. Let's go for it," they replied still awed by the power they were dealing with.

Now it was time to release the Mind. They waited in anticipation. Nothing happened. They felt as if they were in a powerful racecar with the engine roaring but no one had put it in gear. Marci kicked the gear shift lever with "How do we survive?" The Mind roared off, all participants mentally holding on with all their might. They found that the Mind was still a product of each individual and as such was influenced by their concerns and experiences. It spent a great deal of time determining the strategy of Senator Fenton and what should be done politically. Hundreds of different paths were examined and discarded, always coming back to one primary strategy; make the reservation self-sufficient and the Monoecion race indispensable to mankind.

The Mind made a sharp left turn into "Is there a God?" This took the participants by surprise but they soon realized that it was all quite logical. If God did exist then there was some kind of master plan and they were just along for the ride anyway. At first it drew heavily from Christine who had studied theology as a sideline in college but threw away most of the knowledge keeping seemingly scattered and unrelated pieces to mull over. The Mind then performed traditional scientific analysis of the data available but threw the approach away as irrelevant to the question. No one could understand why but all felt it was the correct conclusion. As the Mind ran into roadblocks to definite proof, it decided that this line of thought was useless at this time and stored it for future evaluation when it had more information.

At the same time it was contemplating the existence of God, it was also evaluating the chromatic scale. Alicia suddenly understood it for the first time, not just the mechanics but the reason the ear reacted to it. Pieces of music floated through the Mind, some old, others created on the spot. New scales were created in keys that until this moment had never existed.

The Mind leaped from concept to concept with no apparent connection. Isolation, what if the reservation could be sealed off from the outside world completely? A force field shield to prevent any army or weapon from penetrating their boundaries. It was possible but only with the availability of vast amounts of power and time to develop and deploy. The idea was trashed.

Then a dark vision appeared. If humans refused to allow the Monoecions to exist in peace, one solution would be to eliminate the human race. A simple deadly virus that would only strike humans would not be difficult to create. Even if it was only ninety percent effective the world would be much too busy to deal with the minor problem of the Monoecions. Everyone recoiled from the picture of mass death and destruction but the Mind chastised them. "You created me for answers. Do not criticize when they are provided." Justice? Such a weapon would destroy the sinner and the saints alike. Thousands of humans had risked their lives and liberty to protect their Monoecion friends from harm. Most humans confused by the government propaganda just didn't understand. The Mind rejected the slaughter of innocents but like all living creatures, it did not reject self-defense. Mankind was destroying the planet. The population had grown well beyond the ability of the world to support it with global warming and pollution. Soon famine would be the logical result.

The Mind slid out of the dark and back to the concept of making mankind dependent on the Monoecions. If man needed what the Monoecions could provide, one problem was solved. But what could they provide? The answer was simple, technology. The human race had become so completely dependent on technology that without a constant flow of new developments, it could not survive. As the population grew, new methods were required for food production, energy, and communications. The software created by Alicia, Ann, and Gina was only a speck of sand. They needed a brick, something to build a foundation on for years to come. With enough time, the human race would become comfortable coexisting with the Monoecions.

The Mind began to examine concepts and compare the resources available to the knowledge required. They each felt the Mind probing their brains, examining, evaluating, collecting or discarding. Alicia felt humiliated as the Mind tossed aside some of her most cherished skills but then pounced on something she never considered important. Slowly the concept began to build, each piece layering on top of the last. Cold fusion was possible. A power plant the size of an automobile capable of supplying a major city. The Mind followed the path down the chain and suddenly dropped it completely, darting off in a new direction.

Ann was the first to recognize the new path because her training was in physics. It took the others a bit longer. The fragments began to focus to a single point, a flexible material with superconducting properties at room temperature. If it could be created, the value of such a material would be in the hundreds of billions of dollars.

Power transmission losses would cease to exist, motor sizes would drop by ninety percent; the list would be endless. There were still many holes in the knowledge available but it looked promising. This would be their ticket to freedom, the item that would change Monoecions from menace to partners in the eyes of mankind. The Mind laid out its plans for gathering the information and supplies that they would need to create the material. It would take some time but it was possible now that a target was set.

A question was posed, would the creation of a superconducting material also make possible weapons of mass destruction that could bring the world to an abrupt end, thus eliminating the benefits of saving the Monoecion race? Since mankind already had all the power necessary to accomplish that task, the Mind ignored the question. It did take a fraction of a second out to observe that in a tactical situation against a superior force, disabling an opponent was good, but disabling an opponent in a way that required another opponent to care for them was twice as effective. Kathy and Carla would have sworn that the Mind whispered "Curare" to them.

Jasmine was beginning to feel the fatigue of holding the group together but the Mind was not ready to yield yet. There were so many things it had not examined so many paths to be followed. Jasmine attempted to let her mother know that it was time to quit but Marci never received the message. Jasmine began to panic what if the Mind never let them pull apart? "One bright day in the middle of the night," she chanted to herself. Her confidence returned with the knowledge that she was the conduit. Slowly she began withdrawing, the power of the Mind fading as she pulled back. Soon she again felt each connection as a separate entity. As Jasmine closed each one, the members slid back to reality. Jasmine released everyone but Marci and Alicia so she could give them a glimpse of what had happened when she had tried to stop the Mind. They decided that great care would have to be taken in future to ensure that the Mind did not get the upper hand in the contest for control.

The sharp edged clarity of thought slowly faded but they each remembered their assigned tasks. If the theory they had glimpsed was correct, their safety would be assured in a very short time. It would take time to collect the equipment and to get the components but after that the answers would come quickly. They must be absolutely sure of their finding before it was used as a bargaining chip.

Christine again sat alone in her office. 'We have experienced enough in the last few minutes to keep a hundred philosophers and engineers busy for the rest of their lives,' thought Christine. 'There has been a gift bestowed upon us. We must do everything in our power to use it wisely.'

With great reluctance they started to stir. Carla stood, then bent down and hugged Jasmine. "I have to get back. Mom has plans for me helping with the security systems." They talked for a while making general plans for the week's work sessions.

"It's been nice meeting you," said Ann. "I'll stay here and eat some more of Marci's coffee cake."

"It's a dirty job but somebody has to do it," grinned Alicia.

Marci yelled "Hey!" and smacked Alicia on the arm.

"Did you see that! Domestic violence," reported Alicia.

Carla turned her back. "Didn't see a thing, that wasn't justified anyway." She slipped out the door into the bright morning sunlight.

After an hour the rest followed at intervals until all the visitors were gone. Alicia, Marci and Jasmine sat for a few minutes together. No one spoke, gentle touches were all the communication that was required. Jessica stirred in her crib, sat up and demanded attention. Marci went to the bedroom and carried out the sleepy-eyed toddler. Alicia put on her coat, gave Jasmine a hug, ran her fingers through their baby's hair and gave Marci a long deep kiss. "I'll see you tonight. I've got a lot of things to do at the lab."

Chapter 35

Monday, January 6

The electronics technician demonstrated the alarm system to Rae Ann. "There are two buttons, one at each end of the guard shack. Press either one and the alarm system will trigger in the main office building and in your barracks. The big emergency button by the desk will turn on a siren mounted on the roof."

"Is it loud enough to alert us at night?" asked Rae Ann

"This thing is loud enough to alert everyone who isn't dead," responded the tech. "All the stations around the compound are tied in together so any of them will trigger the alarm."

"And the emergency backup system?" asked Rae Ann in a hushed whisper.

"Battery powered laser aimed at a receiver on your barracks. The button is hidden here by the door. It's completely silent here but will activate in your room."

Rae Ann examined the hidden switch. "Make sure all the guards know that this should only be used in extreme emergency. If this button gets pressed, we're going to come out fighting. No one, and I mean no one, other than the guards and my security team is to know of this button's existence."

"I understand. They've all been briefed."

Rae Ann smiled. "Maybe next time it will be the other side who is surprised when they come visiting."

Saturday, February 15

Daniel Nash checked in at the guard shack outside the reservation gate and obtained an entry pass. The young Army private directed him to the reception hut just inside the gate. Nash entered the reservation and a woman approached him and asked him the purpose of his visit. Daniel smiled and flashed his press identification. "I've come here to interview Charles Wilkens."

The woman did not find the request humorous. "I see. I'm afraid he's not in right now, did you want to talk to Adolf Hitler or Attila the Hun."

Nash ignored her sarcasm. "No, I really would prefer to talk to Mister Wilkens. I realize that he may be using another name but I have it on very good authority that he is here on the reservation and I would like to talk to him if you don't mind."

"Are you serious?" asked the woman.

"As a heart attack," replied Nash. "You have some contractors who are working here on a volunteer basis. If you would be so kind as to direct me to the construction sites, I think I can find him myself."

The woman eyed Nash with suspicion. "No, I don't think so."

"Then may I speak to your supervisor," asked Nash politely.

"Oh yes," assured the woman. "That's exactly who you are going to speak to. Follow me." The woman led Nash into the small reception building. She told her partner to watch the gate while she called the head of security.

Nash listened as she recounted the story to the security chief. After a long exchange, she hung up the phone and told him to follow her to the administration building. There he once again explained why he had come to the reservation.

"And you really believe Charles Wilkens is here on the reservation?" asked the security chief in disbelief.

"I wouldn't be here if I didn't. I checked all my sources very carefully and I know there's a story here." Nash pulled out a photograph of Charlie Wilkens that had been touched up to add a beard and mustache. He handed the picture to the security chief. "Do you recognize this man?"

She looked it over carefully. "I'm not sure." She tucked the picture in her pocket. "Please wait here while I check this out."

"If you don't mind," injected Nash, "I'd like to accompany you. I don't want Mister Wilkens spooked until I have a chance to talk with him."

"You can stay here or you can be escorted back to the front gate," said the security chief firmly.

It was obvious that there was no room for negotiation. "I'll wait here."

The security chief hustled down the hall to Christine's office. "I'm sorry to bother you but we have a situation here."

Christine motioned her into her office. "What's the problem?"

The security chief closed the door behind her, then handed the photograph to Christine. "Does he look familiar?"

Christine examined the photograph. She knew where this was leading. "Yes, I'm sure I've seen him. He's one of the builders here isn't he?"

"I believe that we know him as Chet Walker. There's a reporter here who claims he is Charles Wilkens. The reporter says he wants to interview him."

Christine cradled her chin in one hand as she studied the photograph. "Find Mister Walker and bring him to me. Bring him in the back way so he doesn't cross paths with the reporter. I want to talk to him first." The security chief left Christine sitting at her desk holding the photograph.

Daniel Nash was growing impatient. "Where did she go? How long is this going to take?"

"I'm sure she'll be back as soon as she can. Just because some reporter claims something to be true doesn't make it so. She'll be back after she confirms your story," explained the gate guard.

"I want to talk to him while he's still alive," added Nash sarcastically. The guard ignored him.

The security chief returned with Chet and escorted him into Christine's office. "You wanted to see me?" he asked.

"Yes, Mister Wilkens, I did."

Charlie caught the reference immediately. "That's Walker, ma'am."

Christine looked him in the eye. "There's a reporter down the hall who says your real name is Charles Wilkens, *the* Charles Wilkens. He wants to interview you."

Charlie's shoulders sagged. "I see," he said quietly. He knew that Christine knew who he was all along but he did not want to create more problems for her than she already had. "I'm sure you already know why I did this. I wanted to try to repair some of the damage I've caused."

"I appreciate what you are doing," explained Christine "but I hope you understand why you must leave the reservation. I can not guarantee your safety now that your identity is known." Charlie nodded. "Do you want to talk to the reporter?"

"Not right now," said Charlie, "I need to get my thoughts together."

"I sympathize but if you don't talk to this one reporter, the story will be out and there will be twenty to replace him. If you do talk to him then it will be old news by tomorrow and you may be spared the other nineteen."

Charlie considered Christine's words. "Tell him to wait while I pack my things. I may change my mind."

Christine addressed the security chief. "Go with Mister Wilkens and assist him in packing up. Take a couple of others with you to help out, just in case."

"In case of what?" she asked.

"News travels fast here," explained Christine. "If there are any signs of trouble, get him outside the gate fast. I don't want an incident."

Christine walked down the hall to where the reporter was waiting. She was surprised to see Daniel Nash there; she hadn't thought to ask the name of the reporter. "Hello Mister Nash."

Daniel gave her a sour smile. "Are you going to sick the FBI on me again?"

Christine's face reddened with embarrassment as she remembered their last meeting at her front door. "No, not today. I must apologize for what I did to you back in DC last fall. If you hadn't kept your head, I could have gotten you killed."

"No shit Sherlock," Nash replied sarcastically. "Have you ever been searched by two pissed off FBI agents? It's not on my top ten list of favorite things."

"As a matter of fact, I have and I agree with your assessment. Charles Wilkens has asked that you wait here a bit longer. He hasn't decided yet if he wants to talk to you. He's thinking it over now."

Charlie packed his clothes and personal belongings into boxes that were carried out to his truck by the security team. It took him forty-five minutes to empty out the small workroom that had been his home for the last few months. He looked around at the collection of tools spread around the room. He collected his hammer and level off the workbench. "Give the rest of the tools to Nancy, my head foreman. She can distribute them as she sees fit. You folks need them more than I do."

One of the security guards opened the door and poked her head inside. "Mister Wilkens, there's some people here who wanted to talk to you before you left. They are from your work crew. Is that OK?"

Charlie paused for a moment and then nodded his assent. Five women came inside the cramped room. Charlie recognized them all.

One of them stepped forward and handed him a photograph. "This is a picture of Phyllis, my sister. She was beaten to death outside a grocery store in broad daylight. The police said there were no witnesses." She stepped back behind the others. Charlie tried to control the trembling in his fingers cradling the photograph.

The next woman approached and handed him another picture of a smiling youngster. "This is Amber, my daughter. She was beaten by her own classmates so severely that she has permanent brain damage. A bunch of twelve year old kids..." The woman's chest began to heave so hard that her remaining words became unintelligible.

Tears formed in Charlie's eyes as each woman stepped forward, handed him a photograph and told her story. Then they quietly filed out of the room. Charlie was openly crying when his foreman, Nancy, came in the room. "Chet?" She paused, embarrassed. "I know that's not your name but I've known you as Chet for so long I can't think of you as Charles," she explained. "We understand why you did what you did. We have forgiven you. You didn't know. But you have to understand that we cannot forget. We must never forget." She hugged Charlie for a long time. She pushed away from him. "I can return the pictures for you."

"If you don't mind, could I keep them for a little bit?" asked Charlie. "There's a reporter waiting to talk to me and I would like to show them to him. I think they can tell him more of why I'm here than anything I could think of to say. I'll give them to someone at the front office when I'm done."

"Sure," Nancy nodded.

Christine walked with Charlie after he had finished talking with Daniel Nash. "Mister Wilkens, I think history will view you as a man who was true to his convictions. You did what you thought was right. That applied to when you revealed our existence and it applies to why you are here now." She held her hand out to him.

Charlie warmly shook her hand. "Thank you for the opportunity to pay off some of my debt to your people. Give your mother my love when you talk with her next." Charlie drove to the front gate, wisps of snow swirling in his path.

Tuesday, March 4

Ann rubbed her eyes and looked at her watch. She had been on the Internet for six hours straight but she had finally found what she needed, a lab capable of slicing the ceramic material they had been creating to a thickness of five ten-thousandths of an inch. She stretched and rubbed her neck with the heel of her palms, attempting to push the stiffness out of her body. Ever since the first "Free Mind," session with the group, the hours had been long and hard. The ten-hour days of the data compression software development effort felt like a vacation when compared to the last eight weeks.

The weather had improved steadily the last couple of days and the design team was fighting an attack of spring fever. The real problem was that with the approach of warmer weather came the pressures of COMA. Hundreds of thousands of Monoecions were waiting to enter the reservation and Fenton was pushing to reopen the gates even though there was another good month of winter left. The Army was already constructing two more tent cities, each designed to house nearly ten thousand people. New legislation was pending that would make it a crime to give birth to a Monoecion child outside the reservation.

On the brighter side, the campaign to destroy the public support for using their compression software seemed to be a failure. Sales had been slow at first due to claims of a subversive plot and secret viruses, which industry quickly put to rest when the obvious benefits, and profits, were realized by having data take only half the space as previously required. The Monoecions now had royalties flowing in from nearly every software publisher, half of the Fortune 500 companies, and individual sales doubling each month. The development team felt more confident all the time that if they could produce a product that was crucial to economic growth, corporate America would dictate the rules to government, not the other way around. They would finally be free of the fear of extermination.

Ann finished writing a request for a quote for the ceramic slicing process and e-mailed it to the lab. She looked at her watch. It was after nine o'clock. No one would be reading it today she thought to herself. She shut down the computer and wearily stood, shaking her limbs to regain the blood flow to her fingers. Ann pulled on her jacket and trudged into the dark, heading for the cafeteria, the cold night air helping wake her. She almost immediately bumped into Christine in the dark. "Hello, running a bit late aren't you?"

"Look who's talking," replied Christine. "Didn't I see you already at work this morning at six-thirty?"

"Yeah," said Ann, "I got here at 6:15."

Christine could see the fatigue in Ann's movements. "Be careful. I know the importance of what you are working on but don't burn yourself out. We need you in one piece, physically and mentally."

"I'm trying. Care for a bite? I'm just on my way to the cafeteria." The two women walked across the compound making small talk. Then Ann told Christine something that had been bothering her for quite a while. "You know how easy it would be for us to create a virus that only attacks humans. What if the government is doing just that with one that would attack us?"

"I don't have an answer for that," responded Christine. "I guess we just have to trust that they would reject the idea just as we did." They approached the door to the cafeteria. "It is scary how simple it is to develop a virus that targets humans...." Christine saw the shadow of someone standing just inside the door and stopped in mid-sentence and gave Ann a concerned look. She opened the door and there stood Dorothy with a cup of coffee.

Dorothy gave a little start. "Hello! You surprised me. I was just reaching for the handle and the door popped open."

"We didn't mean to scare you," said Christine. "It looks like you had the same idea as we did."

Dorothy had a confused look for a second and then said "Oh, yeah. I need some of this black goo to keep my heart pumping." She took a sip of her coffee and pushed out the door. "See you in the morning."

Christine and Ann slipped inside and looked at the selection. "Thank God I'm not a connoisseur," said Ann. "I'd starve to death."

"I really need to meet with them face to face to be able to close this deal," explained Dorothy. "It would mean another fifty-thousand a month in sales to add this distributor and get our foot in the door for additional products down the line."

"Great," said Christine. "You just took me by surprise on this trip. I didn't even know you were negotiating with this company. You'll be back the day after tomorrow?"

"That's right," confirmed Dorothy. "I just didn't want to get your hopes up until I really felt we had a chance to land this contract. I'll get you a copy of my schedule before I leave this morning." Dorothy turned and opened the office to leave, revealing two visitors waiting outside. "Hello, may I help you?" asked Dorothy.

"Oh," said Marci, a little embarrassed as she struggled to hold Jessica still in her arms. "I didn't want to interrupt. I was just passing by and thought I'd drop something off for Mrs. Landis."

"You're not interrupting, Marci," called Christine from her office. She came forward to make the introductions. "Dorothy Joyner, this is Alicia Inman's spouse, Marci McBride, and their daughters." Jasmine smiled and looked up at Dorothy, then her smile faded and changed to a question mark.

"It's nice to meet you but you'll have to excuse me." Dorothy turned to Christine. "I'll stop by on my way out." She hurried into her office. Jasmine watched her intently as she left.

"Come in, and to what do I owe the honor of this visit?" asked Christine.

"I was just on my way to take Alicia her lunch and you seemed to appreciate my breakfast roll, unlike a certain spouse," Marci extricated her earring from Jessica's grasp , "so I thought I would drop you off a piece."

"Why, thank you," accepted Christine. "I thought it was delicious. It's obvious that Alicia has great taste in people but a poor appreciation of the culinary arts."

Jasmine tugged on Marci's arm to interrupt. "Why isn't Dorothy like us? I thought the people that work here were like us."

Marci looked at Jasmine, not understanding. "What do you mean, honey? What's not like us?"

Jasmine knew that she wasn't supposed to talk out loud about these things. She made a quick connection to Marci. "Dorothy isn't like us," repeated Jasmine. "She's not Monoecion."

"I don't know." Marci knew that to be seated on the Administration Council, you must be Monoecion. "Bring Christine in with us and we can ask her." The instant Marci expressed this thought, Christine was with them.

"There has to be some mistake," expressed Christine. "Everyone that comes here to stay has to take a blood test and I'm sure that Dorothy tested positive."

Jasmine made it simple. "I don't know about blood tests but I have my own test. I can touch someone if they are really a Monoecion." She looked out the window at random and touched a woman walking down the street. Both Christine and Marci felt the touch, saw the woman turn and look over her shoulder as if she suddenly felt she was being watched. "I can't do that to Dorothy," conveyed Jasmine as a solid fact. "Your blood test is wrong."

At first Christine couldn't accept the truth but in the cold light of the Mind's eye she had little choice. The logical deductions flowed immediately, "Is there a flaw in the test and Dorothy just thinks she's Monoecion?" That was immediately rejected as very unlikely. The next logical step was that the test was faked, that some how the test was fooled to show positive intentionally. "Why would someone want to lie about being Monoecion?" One did not have to be a Monoecion to come to the reservation but it was required to be on the Administrative Council. "The most likely explanation is that she's a spy placed here by the government."

They all felt Christine's great disappointment. She loved the people she worked with, Dorothy included, and to think that one of them was a traitor was almost too much to bear. Thoughts went immediately to what to do about Dorothy. They quickly came to a decision to do nothing. If they exposed Dorothy, the government would insert another spy that they don't know. Plus it would be hard to show how they found out she wasn't Monoecion without exposing Jasmine's talent. There was nothing illegal that they were doing that she could report so the best idea seemed to be to keep her in the dark on sensitive items. It could also be useful to feed her false information to keep Fenton and COMA off balance. They breathed a collective sigh of relief that Dorothy knew nothing of the superconductor project. The trio slid out of their union and time returned to normal.

Dorothy felt nervous. She couldn't put her finger on why but something had changed. When she met with Christine on her way out of the reservation she could sense a tension that wasn't there earlier in the day. She carefully watched the crowd in the airport for anyone suspicious, anyone who was paying a little too much attention to what she was doing. She carefully blocked anyone's view of the keypad as she dialed the phone. A secretary answered "Mr. Lindell's office, can I help you?"

"Is he in? This is Mrs. Haber," said Dorothy using her operation handle. The secretary knew that her calls carried top priority.

"No, I'm afraid that he's not here right now. He is in the building but it will take a few minutes to track him down. May I take a message?"

Dorothy weighed her options. If what she suspected was true then immediate action was required, if she was wrong then she would be wasting a lot of people's time. She decided to err on the side of caution. "Yes, tell him I need to meet with him right away. My plane arrives in Richmond Virginia, at eight thirty-five tonight on Delta. I'll be staying at the Comfort Inn on the I-295 bypass. This is important."

"I'll see that he gets the message," assured the secretary. Dorothy hung up the phone. She picked up her carry-on bag and took a seat at her gate. While seated, she bowed her head in prayer, first, that she was wrong, and second, that if she wasn't wrong that she was in time. The commuter flight was on time but the flight to Atlanta was delayed. She arrived with just enough time to switch concourses and run to her departure gate. She was the last person to board. The plane took off into a steady drizzle which had upgraded itself to a downpour as the wheels of the MD-88 touched down in Richmond.

All during the flight, Dorothy had begun to doubt herself. She didn't have nearly enough to go on to have Lindell dragged out to meet her. 'It's too late now,' she thought. 'I'm going to get my butt chewed for this one.'

She had picked up her suitcase at baggage claim and was headed for the car rental counters when a man she didn't recognize approached her. "Mrs. Haber? Your car is waiting out side. Follow me please." Dorothy didn't question him, she just followed outside to a champagne colored Buick parked at the curb. The man opened the back seat door and Dorothy got in.

Lindell was inside. "I hope this is important. I had to give up my daughter's piano recital for this." What he didn't say was that he would rather be anywhere than at the recital.

"I hope this is just a waste of your time, but I felt I should report it right away," said Dorothy.

"Well?" said Lindell.

Dorothy took a deep breath. "I overheard a fragment of a conversation between Christine Landis and Ann Yates, one of the scientists responsible for the compression software they have been putting out. It sounded to me to be referring to a new project.... the development of a virus that attacks only humans."

"Holy shit!" exclaimed Lindell. "What did they say?"

"I only caught a tiny piece of it, it might be nothing at all. It was late last night and I was in the cafeteria on my way out when I heard Christine's voice outside. She was commenting on how easy it was to develop a virus to target only humans and then they opened the door and saw me standing there. She quickly changed the subject." Dorothy ran her fingers through her hair, pushing it back off her face. "I don't know if this was some innocent conversation, talking about the flu or the development of a weapon to use against humans. I didn't hear enough to be able to tell."

"Have you found any other evidence?" asked Lindell.

"I just heard it last night and flew out this morning. It's not like I had a lot of time to research this," said Dorothy a little frustrated. "I did go back to the office and tried to check out the area where Ann Yates and the others work but it was locked up tight. There were several things that didn't make sense before but would if this is true."

"Such as?" questioned Lindell.

"First, the team. Every other project team on the reservation is a mix of Monoecions and humans. This team is strictly Monoecion. Second, I'm in charge of economic trade and they won't even let me know what they're working on. Landis is the only one outside the team that knows. And third, the stuff that's coming into them sure doesn't look like software tools to me. They're supposed to be a software development group but the hardware that's coming in looks like no computers I'm aware of. It reminds me more like chemical process equipment. I'll try to get some additional information when I get back to the reservation but I'm going to have to be careful. I can't say for sure but Christine was acting funny towards me this morning. She may be starting to suspect me."

"Have you asked what they are working on?" asked Lindell.

"The direct approach was shut down a while ago. I was told that it was a "need to know only" project and I was told that I didn't need to know yet. I was told that it would blow the socks off our competition. That's all I could get out of them."

"OK, you did good," assured Lindell. "You did real good. Don't do anything to blow your cover yet unless you can prove this is for real. I have the tendency to think that it was just talk but we need to make sure."

Dorothy took the opportunity to give Lindell a full report on the more mundane activities on the reservation, it had been sometime since their last contact. After an hour they dropped her back at the airport to pick up her rental car.

Fenton was actually gleeful when Lindell told him the news. "Biological warfare, I wouldn't think it was possible to split the hair that fine. She really said a virus that attacks only humans?" Fenton paced rapidly around the office, keyed up to the point where he couldn't possibly sit still.

"That's what she said but it's just conjecture right now" responded Lindell cautiously.

"They finally did it," Fenton nearly giggled. "They crossed the line! This couldn't have happened at a better time."

"It's possible but there's no guarantee," warned Lindell again. "We're going to need more evidence than one scrap of overheard conversation."

"I'm fully aware of what we need," chastised Fenton. His face manner became deadly serious. "Regardless of what the President might say, I am in full control of my faculties. We are going to need sufficient proof to justify a full investigation, and we don't have it, not yet."

"We need to find out if this is real or not," said Lindell. "I've got our inside person pushing as hard as she can without giving herself away."

"Our main thrust," said Fenton, "needs to be an investigation to collect enough circumstantial evidence to justify a raid on the reservation. If we can do that, we'll find all the evidence we need to put them out for good."

"And if we're wrong?" asked Lindell. "Another major investigation will cost the taxpayers dearly at a time when you are already being blamed for the current cost of the sterilization and reservation programs. If the investigation does not net sufficient evidence then you can kiss the primaries goodbye. It will also convince some of your supporters that the other side may be right, the Monoecions may be a bunch of harmless mutants. Your opponents will have a field day."

"And if we are right and do nothing?" posed Fenton. "If this initial investigation does not yield enough evidence to warrant a full investigation we would have to pull back. Then at a later date, if evidence surfaced that there was a plot, I would be accused of incompetence and shown as an indecisive leader. There would be no shortage of people who would come forward claiming that they had urged me to pursue the leads but had been ignored." Fenton realized that he may be able to get some mileage out of a stalled investigation if a leak was generated at the right time, just before he had to kill the investigation. Just a rumor that the Monoecions were being investigated for such a heinous crime would peak the public interest. It might also flush out an informer with enough evidence to bring things to a head.

"We can step up security in the reservation," said Lindell.

"Absolutely not!" said Fenton. "I don't want any visible indications that we are suspicious. I want them to get careless. What we will need is a list of everything that has gone in or out of the reservation, and that includes electronically. They can't create something like this with a kid's chemistry set. There would have to be telltale signs, equipment, supplies, chemicals. And we're going to need some experts who can identify those telltale signs when they see them."

"That can be arranged. When do we bring in the FBI?" asked Lindell

"When Hell freezes over! They had their opportunity. If we can prove the Monos are developing a virus, I'll have the Attorney General's head on a stake on the front lawn, and that's just where I want it. We'll get the proof and then rub their noses in it." Fenton paused in thought. "This has to be kept in absolute secrecy."

"I understand. If this leaked out, there would be panic."

"That's right and we don't want that to happen." Then Fenton added with a smile "Not until we are ready. It's all a matter of timing. If the public finds out about the Monoecion's plan to unleash a horrible disease on mankind the same instant that we raid the reservation, the end will justify the means. John Q. Public will be scared shitless that the Monos almost pulled it off. The public will clamor for their immediate destruction. There will also be plenty of praise for the agency that prevented this great disaster."

"And that puts you at the head of the polls for the first presidential primary."

"Exactly," smiled Fenton. The Senator again became deadly serious. "I don't want even a peep of this out until I say so or, so help me God, I will crucify the responsible party."

Fenton sat in quiet thought long after Lindell had left to get the ball rolling. He knew he could order a search of the site at any time but a team of agents knocking on the front door and politely requesting entry would provide the Monoecions enough time to destroy the very evidence he so desperately needed. No, this would have to be a lightning raid and take them completely by surprise.

If he was already too late to stop the release of the virus then mankind was doomed. He would be proven right in his treatment of the Monoecion population but it would be a useless victory. There would surely be sufficient time to slaughter the creatures at the reservation but there would be no way to exterminate the entire Monoecion population before the end came. He dropped this line of reasoning since it was a no win scenario and Fenton did not like to lose.

The outcome he feared most would be to go ahead with the raid only to find little or no evidence of any attempt to create a biological weapon. The result would be a long and costly investigation, probably followed by an investigation into his own performance as head of COMA by any number of his political rivals. This was a result he could avoid if he could be sure that there would be proof there to find. There was only one way he could be absolutely positive that it would be there, but that action carried its own risks.

Every item that had entered the reservation was logged by security as it entered to prevent banned materials from falling into Monoecion hands such as weapons, bomb making materials, and the like. This was the starting point of the search for evidence of a biological research project. Every item that could be used to this end was cataloged and entered into the growing database. The task was made more difficult by the fact that the researchers were not allowed to know exactly what they were trying to find for fear of a leak to the press. The massive list was narrowed down to a few hundred items. This compressed list was then supplied to the few experts who had been let in on the facts of the case. At first they scoffed at the idea of a credible threat coming from such primitive conditions as were available on the reservation. Then the list started shaking out. On it were materials necessary for constructing a clean room, micron air filters, breathing apparatus and related equipment supposedly slated for a high tech assembly room. A centrifuge was delivered for use by the hospital for diagnostic work.

What concerned one of the researchers most were some strips of ceramic material that had been cut by a lab in Massachusetts from a special block sent to them from the reservation. He had worked in the U. S. government programs during the eighties where they had used similar thin strips of ceramics as filters in the government biological warfare program.

This concern was magnified when a careful examination of the reservation population revealed that a world class microbiologist and a top-notch bio-engineer were current residents. Each piece of evidence by itself could be explained but as a whole, it began to look suspicious.

Dorothy managed to corner Gina alone in the hall. "Hello, I hardly see you folks stick your heads out of the lab lately. You have really been putting in the hours."

"Tell me about it," replied Gina. "I'm getting to the point where I get nostalgic about sleeping more than five hours."

"So when do I get to hear about your new project?" asked Dorothy. "Everything has been so hush-hush that you have piqued my curiosity."

"Soon," said Gina. "We have made some major breakthroughs but we are still not ready to let it out."

"Can't you even give me a hint?" begged Dorothy. "Remember that I have to sell this creation after you're done with it and I need to start researching markets just like you have to research the product. We need to maximize our return on any product created here if we want to stay alive."

"I wouldn't worry about that," said Gina. "If all goes according to plan then this one could take care of our worries for a long time to come. We don't want anyone to get wind of this before we are ready to release it. You understand."

"Yes, I guess so." Dorothy watched Gina head down the hall back to the lab. The entire conversation was taped on her pocket recorder and later transmitted with a narrow beam transmitter. Someone outside the fence received the transmission but she never knew who. Dorothy just aimed the beam at a specified spot and hit the transmit button. She didn't dare use a radio frequency transmitter since the offices were swept on a regular basis now to keep it clear of bugs.

Chapter 36

Friday, March 14

Marci finished her shift at the day care center, collected Jessica and Jasmine and bundled them up for the walk home. Jessica had other ideas. Despite her growing vocabulary, the only word she cared to use this evening was "No." This applied to attempts to get her to stand so Marci could put on her coat, to keeping her hat and mittens on, and to anything else that did not involve playing with the toy dump truck she had focused her attention on. Marci eventually succeeded at dragging Jessica out of the door with most articles of clothing still attached to the proper body parts. Jessica was not pleased and made it clear with her scowl.

Jasmine on the other hand had cooperated completely but only did exactly what she was told. Her mind didn't seem to be on the same planet as her body. When Marci told her to put on her coat, she did, but she made no attempt to put on her mittens, boots or hat. She wasn't misbehaving, she was just preoccupied.

By the time Marci had herded her wildcat and zombie out of the building, she was in no mood to spend the next hour accomplishing the ten-minute walk home. She picked up Jessica and carried her. This seemed to help appease her wildcat somewhat.

The zombie however was still mentally comatose. After Marci was forced to grab Jasmine by the collar for the third time to keep her from walking into the street without looking, Marci burst out "Where is your mind today?"

"I don't understand gravity," Jasmine stated plainly as if it explained everything.

"What?" said Marci.

"Gravity," replied Jasmine. "Miss Ann tried to explain it to me but I don't understand."

Marci felt a gnawing seed of pain growing in her stomach. Jasmine had been changing over the past weeks, maturing in the topics she discussed with her parents and drifting away from children her own age. Sometimes the childhood wonder came through at a new simple discovery but now more often than not, her conversations were way beyond her now six years. "It's the force that holds us to the ground. Everything has it and the bigger it is, the more force it has," explained Marci.

"I know that," responded Jasmine as if she was the adult and Marci was the child. "I mean it doesn't act like a particle or a wave the way Miss Ann explained it. I sort of understand how they work. Gravity is a force. It's different."

Marci felt the seed in her stomach grow a little more. "Well, you are already past what I know. I learned some of that wave and particle stuff in high school but I forgot it just as quick. I wasn't big on the sciences."

"You know a lot of biology," corrected Jasmine.

"Yes, that's true but I liked biology. I didn't like physics."

"And does it have a speed?" There was an excitement in Jasmine's voice. The zombie was gone, banished by an aching desire to know everything. "You know, like light or sound has a speed? It can't just go from here to there without taking some time, can it?"

"Is that what you've been so preoccupied with today?"

Jasmine didn't answer, she knew that her mom didn't like it when she thought about things too much. She looked down at the ground. "I like learning new things" she said defensively.

Marci knelt down and hugged Jasmine. "I know you do, honey. I'm afraid I can't help you with this one."

Jasmine hugged back. "That's OK, mom. I'll figure it out eventually. There's just so much I don't know."

After the exchange Jasmine reverted back to being six years old, skipping, laughing and acting silly. "I want to open the door," she yelled as they climbed the flight of stairs to the second floor apartment. Marci fished the key out of her pocket and handed it to Jasmine. With great concentration, Jasmine inserted the key and turned it. She turned the knob and bumped the door with her shoulder.

"Not so hard," warned Marci. "I just fixed it, remember?"

"Sorry, I forgot it doesn't stick anymore."

Marci dropped her things on the small dining room table next to a note from Alicia. Marci picked up the note and read it.

I had to go back to the lab to set up for tonight's test. Don't wait up. I'll be late. Give the kids a hug for me. I love you.

Me

"So what's new," muttered Marci and dropped the note in the trash. She squatted down and helped the girls with their coats. "Alicia wanted to make sure you got this," she said flatly as she hugged them both.

"Does Alicia have to work again?" asked Jasmine.

"Yes, that's what the note said. Go play for a few minutes and I'll get dinner." They scattered like puppies after a nap. Marci leaned back against the wall and slowly slid down to the floor. She sat there for several minutes trying to blot every thought out of her mind. She didn't want to think any more today.

Jessica waddled back out and looked surprised to find mommy sitting on the floor. She came over, dropped to her hands and knees and crawled the last few feet to come to rest with her head in Marci's lap.

Marci began to absently stroke Jessica's hair. She felt her head lurch, the world swung and tilted then slowly righted itself. Despite the abuse her mind was taking, Marci managed cohesive thought. 'This isn't Jasmine. My God, its Jessica!' she realized. Even at her earliest, Jasmine had been smoother making a connection, but then Jasmine had been much older. Marci reached out with a mental hug. Jessica seemed satisfied and the connection disappeared with another sickening jolt.

The question had been answered, Jasmine wasn't an aberration. "Jasmine, come here!" Marci called excitedly, "Hurry!"

"What?" she yelled as she ran out of the bedroom.

Jessica lifted her head out of Marci's lap to see what all the commotion was about. "Jessica just connected with me!" Marci squealed.

Jasmine just nodded "Uh-huh." Then she waited for the exciting news.

"Do you understand?! Like you do, she connected to me!" repeated Marci.

"Uh-huh. But she's awful rough," said Jasmine with a bit of irritation.

Marci's mouth opened but for several seconds she couldn't form the words, just sputtering gasps. "You... You mean... You mean she's already connected with you?!"

Jasmine knew immediately that she had done something wrong but wasn't quite sure of what it was. She began to look worried, then slowly nodded her head.

"Why didn't you say anything?" asked Marci incredulously. "Why didn't you tell us?"

Jasmine wore a wounded look and responded in proper six-year-old fashion. "I don't know."

Ann double checked the power lockout as Alicia confirmed that all power at the transformer was dead. "Power is dead and locked out," called Ann. They lived in constant fear of accidents. Their work schedule created a perfect breeding ground for careless behavior. Long hours, tight schedules, repetitive tests, and dangerous equipment resulted all too often in injuries and they knew it. So far they had managed to avoid accidents by enforced safety checking during all tests.

Gina placed a tick mark on each step of the checklist as they proceeded. "Mount the sample." Alicia carefully placed the H shaped wafer in the fixture. By testing very tiny cross sections of the material, they could limit the amount of current required to test the samples to destruction. Even at the low voltages they used for testing, the power required was tremendous. In theory, if the part was a perfect superconductor, even the smallest piece they could make would be able to handle all the current they had available. They were still far from making a perfect sample. Each new piece improved on the last but would also present new challenges to overcome before the next experiment could proceed.

Ann carefully focused the infrared camera on the latest sample as Gina double-checked that all the data logging programs were running and synchronized. "Ready," called Ann.

Alicia asked, "Ready to remove lockout?"

Gina looked down the list for any unchecked boxes. "Ready, turn it on."

Alicia removed the padlock and threw the large breaker handle. "We are running hot. Keep your fingers out of the sockets, ladies."

Ann checked the clear blast shield security and then manned her station. "Ready and clear," she called out.

Gina checked the calibration of the power source one more time. "Ready and clear."

Alicia took her station at the breaker. "Ready and clear. Let's get started or we'll be here all night." The testing cycle took three hours, starting at low currents and gradually increasing. Right from the beginning, this sample showed great improvement over the last one.

Gina recited the values as the screen counted up. "We are looking good gang. Approaching two-hundred percent of last maximum current with no measurable voltage drop."

"Thermal is flat and cold," recited Ann. A blinding flash filled the room as the thin wafer disintegrated. The current, suddenly having nowhere to go, converted itself to voltage, growing until it triggered the spark arrestors. Unfortunately, the spark arrestors were not up to the job and an arc leaped across the now vacant gap where the now vaporized wafer had been clamped. It had all happened in a few microseconds. All three women yelled in unison. The breaker reacted and tripped just as it was suppose to. The miniature bolt of lightning blew holes in the electrodes and spattered the safety shields with tiny droplets of molten metal. The computers shut down the test automatically.

"Damn!" yelled Ann. "Is everybody OK?"

"I'm all right," said Alicia.

"Me too," responded Gina "but I'm not sure I can say the same for my pants. I may never wear them again."

"Double Damn!" spat Ann.

"What's wrong?" asked Gina.

"What do you mean what's wrong!" exclaimed Ann. "This, the test! Didn't you see what happened?"

"Yes, we doubled our last current capacity. And we were treated to a rather brief but spectacular light show. So what's the problem?"

Ann looked at Gina as if she were a preschooler trying to understand relativity. "The failure mode. I was flat with no hint of a problem, then BANG! This does not match up with what was predicted for the failure mode at all."

"That means," injected Alicia, "we have a brand new opportunity."

"Yes, to go along with our old list of yet unsolved problems," Ann caught herself and nodded at Alicia, "sorry, opportunities."

"You're right," soothed Alicia, "but look at what else happened. As Gina said, we doubled our load carrying capacity. That proves that we are licking our old list of problems. We'll lick the new ones too."

Ann was frustrated and angry but she knew that Alicia and Gina were right. "Yeah," she conceded glumly, "I'm just so darned tired of *opportunities*. I was really hoping for a major breakthrough, not an incremental improvement." She added after a pause "But it was a hell of a light show while it lasted."

"Let's try not to have any more of these light shows though," remarked Gina. "I don't have enough pants as it is."

Alicia broke in. "I really don't want to know if any of this equipment is destroyed until I've had a good night's sleep and a relaxed breakfast. It's after two AM now. I say we go home, have a nice long sleep and do a half-day tomorrow. Even if it is broken, we can't order parts until Monday anyway."

There was total agreement. They shut down the equipment, started the automated backup of the data recorders and went home.

The process had become routine by now. Each new test yielded reams of computer recorded data that under normal circumstances would have required a team of scientist months to analyze. The full group of Marci, Alicia, Ann, Gina, Christine, and Carla/Kathy linked through Jasmine, released the Mind to examine the data. Usually only Alicia, Ann and Gina were in the lab, the remainder found their own place of privacy to conduct the sessions that lasted anywhere from five to thirty minutes.

The chaff was separated from the germ of the collected data and a new path was plotted for the next experiment. Most of the minor technical hurdles had been cleared, but with each step the remaining problems became more complex. A simple clean room had been constructed and had improved their results significantly. But now the Mind's pronouncement left them stunned. We need to perform the doping process in zero gravity.

The conscious parts of their minds scoffed. "I suppose hijacking the space shuttle is out of the question?" The Mind paid no attention as it broke down the process into its component parts. Only one portion of the process required zero gravity and it took only a little over one second to accomplish. Options were examined and discarded. The use of an aircraft was examined and rejected. The simplest solution was adopted, drop the process from a height inside a vacuum and perform it in free fall.

Fenton examined the photographs. "What is it?"

"We don't have a clue," responded Lindell. "That's what has everyone worried. It appears to be a pipe, eighteen inches in diameter, ninety feet tall, erected with great care next to their water tower. All we know is that it has something to do with the virus team project."

"It looks like a water pipe."

Lindell pulled out more photographs. "That's what we thought too but the word from the engineer who constructed it was that it had to be perfectly vertical to within one-tenth of an inch over the full height." Todd pointed to the top of the tube where a small platform was mounted. "There is an access chamber here and at the bottom of the tube. In this picture you can see one of the team members loading a cylinder in the tube."

"What do they do with the cylinder?" asked Fenton

"Apparently it's dropped down the tube. We don't know why or what it contains. We did just find out that there is a vacuum pump attached to the tube so one of our people thinks that they are using it as a zero gravity chamber."

"What are the other opinions?"

Lindell shrugged his shoulders. "No one else is willing to hazard a guess. From the conversations we have managed to record of the team members, it appears that they are getting very close to their goal."

"Can zero gravity be used in the manufacture of material for germ warfare?" Fenton asked concerned.

"I can't get any consensus from our people. They seem to be split evenly, some saying it's possible, others saying it's useless."

"The bottom line is they don't have a clue," berated Fenton. "It's time to shit or get off the pot! I want a meeting this afternoon with the whole bunch. It's time for them to make up their mind."

The first test was conducted with only load cells in the cylinder. The load cells could sense the slightest brush with gravity and record the critical breaking phase forces. The cylinder had to drop straight down or it would touch the side of the tube with disastrous results for the test pieces inside. Several braking methods were tried until they settled on a coil of high tensile fishing line and a constant force brake to slow the cylinder at the end of the fall. They attained three perfect drops in a row and decided it was time for a live drop.

Marci refused to watch any of the test drops because of her fear of heights. She couldn't stand to watch Alicia climb the water tower ladder and step out on that tiny platform. But now that this was the real thing, she came out for moral support. "I'm still not going to watch," she told Alicia. "I'm going to sit here and stare at the ground until you come back down."

"Don't worry. The whole thing doesn't take thirty minutes." Alicia kissed Marci gently and walked to the ladder where Gina and Ann waited with the cylinder.

"OK," briefed Ann, "one more time. When you get tied off to the platform, drop the lift rope and we will attach the cylinder and pull it up to you. Remember, no sudden movements or bumps."

"Yes, I know," said Alicia. "I'll stabilize the cylinder and allow fifteen minutes for all movement to die down. You will signal me when the tube is evacuated to the required level and I'll trip the release. Let's get going before I freeze to death out here." Alicia started the long upward climb. Marci started, true to her word, by staring at the ground but finally couldn't resist the urge to watch.

Alicia again checked her harness at the top of the ladder and attached her safety line. She stepped out on the narrow catwalk and dropped the line after feeding it through the pulley. After the cylinder rose to her, she carefully placed it inside the tube and sealed the opening. Alicia returned to the main structure of the water tower and tried to remain perfectly still for the long, cold wait until it was time for release.

Finally, Ann called out "All set! Release on count. One...Two...Three!"

Alicia triggered the release and the cylinder plummeted. The absence of gravity triggered the process inside to initiate, shut down and prepare for braking. The line reached the end of the coil and the brake engaged. But instead of the gradual slowing of the cylinder, the brake jammed full on. The fine line could not take the strain and snapped, allowing the cylinder to drop the last twenty feet uncontrolled. Alicia felt the impact all the way at the top of the tower. There was a round of very unpleasant expletives as the participants examined the wreckage of their first real drop and Alicia wearily climbed back down the ladder.

The sample inside had been completely destroyed but careful dissecting of the remains proved that the process had worked without a hitch. The failure of the brake was caused by a knot in the line that must have occurred while it was unreeling. It took three days to get the break reel mechanism modified and to prepare a new sample for the next drop.

Fenton pulled a thumb drive out of his drawer and walked down the hall to the staff area. The room was empty and dark at this time of night. He pulled on a pair of latex gloves, flipped on a computer and waited as it booted, the screen illuminating the room in a pale glow. He plugged the drive in to the USB port and the auto executable file did the rest.

A file transferred to an FTP server in Bolivia that then moved the file through a maze that would be impossible to track. Fenton formatted the thumb drive and pulled it from the computer. He shut down the computer and smiled. The destination server that he had just used could not be tracked back to him or anyone else. The file that he just sent was encrypted using tools that made the data completely indecipherable to anyone without the code to unlock it. Fenton returned to his office.

Harry looked at the message in his inbox. He was a little surprised to see another request for his services coming in from Fenton. The Senator had been really pissed after that little mix-up in Boston. But there it was, big as life and twice as ugly, a new request for services. Harry entered the code sequence to decode the message. The message broke into a series of individual files.

Harry started logically enough with the one titled ReadMeFirst. A raid was to be staged on the reservation in two days. Fenton wanted to make sure the raid was successful, meaning he wanted to be positive that evidence of wrongdoing would be found. The only way of being absolutely sure it would be was to place some evidence ahead of time. Harry looked over the timetable and checked the list of items that he was to plant at the site. It didn't give him much time to prepare the package and deliver it.

Harry looked at the other files that Fenton had sent him. The files included a detailed timetable for the raid on the reservation, a list of raid objectives, building layouts of the office he needed to break into, maps of the reservation, reservation security procedures, and details of the computer systems used in the office. He brought up the plans to the building and looked for the best way in. At least the old fart is thorough, thought Harry. He again examined the timetable and checked the airline schedules. He checked the equipment list against his inventory.

"Looks good, Herbert," he said to his cat as he scratched its head. "It's clean and simple and this time I don't have to kill anybody. And the money isn't bad either." Harry sat back down at the keyboard and returned a message to Fenton. It was a simple post to an online blog with the first word "Go". The rest of the message didn't matter. That first word was all Fenton would need to see to know that Harry accepted the contract. Tomorrow, there would be a fifty thousand dollar down payment deposited in his bank account. Harry pulled out a thumb drive and transferred the directory of false test results detailing the process of attempting to create a biological weapon aimed at mankind. All he had to do was slip into the building, copy the files into a hidden directory on one of the computers in the lab, and leave the rest up to the investigators. In the raid, the computers would be confiscated and the files would be discovered during the analysis. Harry booked his flights.

Ann and Gina stood on the ground with their fingers crossed. Alicia huddled on the water tower with the trigger in her hand. "All set! Release on count. One...Two...Three!" shouted Ann.

Alicia pressed the trigger. The cylinder seemed to drop forever before she heard the faint click of the break engaging the whir as the line played out, dropping in pitch as the cylinder slowed in its dive. Finally, the whir stopped completely, the cylinder had stopped. Alicia looked down at the figures on the ground who were feverishly examining the readout on a notebook computer screen. Gina looked up at Alicia and gave her a thumbs-up sign. Alicia let out a whoop and waved.

"Be careful!" yelled Marci, "and get down here."

"I'd be delighted," shouted Alicia in return. She unhooked her safety line and started down the ladder.

Fenton met with the head of the regional office of the ATF. "I want you to understand what's going down here. We have confirmed information that the Monos are stashing weapons on the reservation, nothing major, just a few rifles and pistols, no heavy stuff."

"If you don't mind me saying so, it doesn't sound like they pose much of a threat. Why are we bothering with this?" He usually didn't get such high-ranking visitors for such a minor item. "I can raid just about any rancher in the state and net higher fire power that that."

"Yes but the Monos are banned from having any guns of any type on the reservation and we plan to enforce this to the letter," emphasized Fenton.

"I understand that but this sounds like a job for the local authorities. Why are you involving us here at the ATF in this?"

Fenton lowered his voice to conspiratorial whisper. "Because there is something much more sinister going on at the reservation. We have a person in deep cover on the inside who has uncovered a terrorist plot that we must prevent from going further but we can't act on the real threat without blowing her cover. She has provided us proof that at least some weapons are being stashed in the same building that we need to investigate. The weapons charge provides us an excuse to get in the building."

"So what is this threat? Will my men be in danger?"

"Sorry, I can't let you in on what it is at this point in time, a matter of national security and all that crap. Our person on the inside has not been able to get absolute proof of the suspected activity. As far as your men, they won't be in any danger. All we need is for your team to secure the building. My experts will enter the building and conduct the search for the evidence of the plot. Your men will just handle security of the building and possibly assist in the search for weapons in other locations later. If a few guns are all we find, the raid is still justified in the public eyes."

"I want to be clear", the regional director told Fenton. "I don't want any rookies putting my men in danger."

"Don't worry. My people will not enter the grounds until all is secure," Fenton assured. "My people will arrive in ATF uniforms and conduct our search, you just secure the building."

The regional director was still far from convinced. Every time some other bureaucracy tried to tell them what to do, it ended up a screwed up mess. "We will support you, but if things turn ugly in there after your people are in the building, I can't guarantee their safety. We are only going in with a small force."

"We want the Monos to believe this is just a raid to find a few light weapons. This would fall under your jurisdiction and we need to make it believable. We can't show up with tanks and half the National Guard without them destroying the evidence before we can get close to the building." Fenton again covered the details.

"I need just a few agents, eight or ten, to silence the guards at their gate, go into the compound about four blocks and secure a building. The building and the streets will be empty. Once we know they can't enter the building, my search team rolls in and does its job."

"I'm going to need their security details."

"Everything is right in here," said Fenton patting a folder on the desk. "They work late in the lab, sometimes well past midnight. That's why our person on the inside said the best time to go in is at three AM. They will have no time to get anyone there to destroy the evidence. Get your plan to me by tomorrow morning. Remember, everything that we have discussed is top secret. None of your men are to know that this is anything but a raid to confiscate a stash of arms. Got it?"

"Yeah, I got it." It burned his butt to be dictated to by this pompous politician but he already had his orders from Washington to cooperate fully with Fenton. "You just remember that when this goes down, I'm the man in charge. After the site is secure, your boys can look around all they want. Until then, I call the shots."

"I wouldn't have it any other way," smiled Fenton.

Chapter 37

Wednesday, March 26
Dorothy walked by the lab again. She had seen them leave early tonight and they had not returned. It was after 11 PM and she saw no sign that they were coming back. She went back to her building and climbed the stairs. A few minutes later she had sent the all clear.

Marci was furious. "It's almost midnight! What are you thinking of?"

"I know very well what time it is. And you know we can't run these test during the day, we would blow our power distribution system sky high," explained Alicia.

"That's not the point and you know it," said Marci. "She's a little girl, not a workaholic like you. Start treating her like the six-year old she is!"

"Jasmine is the one who suggested this. She took a long nap this afternoon because she wanted to do this tonight. She wanted to see one of these tests with her own eyes," explained Alicia.

"So now you're leaving these decisions up to a six year old?" Marci was close to tears. "She's not equipped to handle the stress that she's being put under."

"I am watching over her. We all are. I know this is hard on her but she is handling it well. She lets us know when she gets tired and we stop." Alicia understood how Marci felt, she felt the same way. Each time Jasmine linked them to bring forth the Mind she could feel a tiny portion of Jasmine's childhood slip away. Jazz was growing up in a way no child had ever grown up before. "We won't be gone long."

"I'm just so scared," cried Marci. "I lost you and now I'm losing my little girl."

Alicia was dumbfounded. "What do you mean? You haven't lost me."

"Haven't I? When's the last time you touched me? When's the last time we just sat together and held each other? When's the last time we made love?"

Alicia became defensive. "I haven't exactly been on holiday. If you hadn't noticed, we are fighting for our lives here!"

Marci withdrew. "I just hope that what's left is still worth saving when you're through." Marci turned away from Alicia. "You better get going. You're late already." Her voice was emotionless and flat. Alicia tried to kiss her good-bye but Marci did not return the kiss.

Harry hugged the ground as a spotlight danced over him and moved on. The Jeep didn't slow down on its rounds of the reservation perimeter. Harry didn't move a muscle until the taillights were completely out of sight. Harry clipped two more links of the fence and wriggled under dragging his bag behind. He headed for the compound at a quick trot, staying low, using the terrain as cover wherever possible.

He carefully skirted a large complex of tents. At first he thought they were empty but then heard children's laughter followed by stern words in a male voice. Harry froze in his tracks, staying motionless until the voices subsided. He moved on to the nearest building. Tucking the bag close to his body, he boldly walked down the back streets of the compound. Bundled up with his hat pulled down, he could pass easily as a resident. He met only one other person on the walk to the lab. They exchanged a single hello in passing. She never looked back over her shoulder at him.

Ducking into a narrow walkway between buildings, Harry emerged next to the lab entrance. He waited several minutes listening under a window to be sure no one was in the building, at least in the portion he had to enter. The instructions had warned that other parts of the building might be occupied by residents since nearly every square foot was used for temporary housing. As he waited, he pulled on a pair of surgical gloves. Satisfied that there was no movement inside, he moved to the front of the building and tried the door. It was locked as he expected. He slid the key supplied by Fenton into the lock and turned. It worked perfectly.

Once inside, he locked the door behind himself. Harry had memorized the layout. He walked quietly down the hall, stopping at the third door on the left and placed his ear against it. No sounds could be heard from inside. Harry tried the second key he had received. This one didn't work. He expertly worked a pick in the lock, feeling each grove and pin, taking care not to leave any telltale marks behind. No evidence of forced entry could be left behind. Fenton had been very specific on this point. In thirty seconds, he slipped inside and closed the door.

Streetlights faintly illuminated the room through the window coverings. He looked around the room for the computer systems. There were three of them tied into various pieces of equipment. Harry chose the nearest one and powered it on. The screen added an eerie glow to the room. After checking the type of operating system, Harry rummaged through his bag and selected the proper boot disk, putting it into the CD drive. He shut down the computer and restarted it. The machine booted to a command prompt and he typed in a single command. He watched the messages scrolling down the screen as files were transferred from the CD to the Monoecion's computer system.

The file transfer process would take several minutes and he had no time to waste. He located the ceiling ventilation duct and, standing on a chair, carefully removed the louvered grate. Dust fell over him as he lowered the grate to the floor forcing him to suppress an almost overpowering urge to sneeze. Regaining control, he reached back into his bag, still slung over his shoulder. He removed the pieces of an AK-47 assault rifle. Still perched on the chair, he silently slid the rifle parts into the open vent. After it came a nine-millimeter semi-automatic pistol and two boxes of ammunition.

'That should give the ATF boys all the evidence they need,' thought Harry. He was starting to sweat. The warm clothing served him well on the trek in but was now getting uncomfortable in the confines of the lab. He wiped his brow with his sleeve as droplets of saltwater stung his eyes.

Harry reached down for the vent grill but with blurry eyes, he misjudged. He felt it tick off the back of his fingers. He grabbed wildly for it, missed, then froze. In slow motion, his wide eyes watched it arc toward the floor. He stopped breathing. His heart stopped beating. The grill landed on a rolled up cable with a gentle thud. Harry slowly exhaled, saved by a power cable. He took a few seconds to calm himself, and then recovered the grill. Quietly, he screwed it back in place.

He returned to the computer and checked the screen. The file transfer was just about complete. Harry checked his watch and started his cleanup. He frowned as he noticed the dust surrounding the chair he had used to get to the ceiling vent. He quickly brushed off the chair as best as he could and returned it to its original position. Using his bag he further attempted to disperse the dust. He surveyed the room. It wasn't perfect but it would have to do.

The file transfer had finished. He ran a quick check of the drive. All the files he transferred did not show up. He ran the check again looking for hidden files, all the files appeared. Harry smiled to himself. That should give Fenton's boys all the evidence they need and earn him another one hundred and fifty grand. Instantly, every nerve snapped to attention. He had heard the sound of the front door to the building opening. He hit the power button on the computer, grabbed his bag and moved silently to the back of the lab crouching behind some electrical equipment.

"I was beginning to think you'd forgotten us," said Ann as they came into the lab.

"No, Marci and I had a few things to discuss before Jasmine and I could leave," explained Alicia.

"Oh," said Gina. "I can tell by the tone of your voice that it wasn't good."

"No, not very," agreed Alicia.

"Look," said Ann, "we can run the test. For that matter, it can wait until tomorrow. Why don't you two go home and patch things up."

"Thanks, but Jazz really wanted to see a test herself." Alicia gave Jasmine a little reassuring hug. "What I really could use is a baby sitter for an hour or two tomorrow. Just so Marci and I could get out alone and get some things worked out."

"I can do that," volunteered Ann. "I don't mind. I love spending time with your kids."

"Thanks. I really appreciate it. Now lets get this test done so we can go home. It's all set up so it shouldn't take half an hour."

Jasmine spoke up. "If you want to we could analyze the data while you test it. Just us, we don't need the others right now."

Ann looked from Jasmine to Alicia. "It's your call. We've never done it during a live test before."

Alicia squatted down with Jasmine. "Are you sure you are rested enough?" Jasmine nodded. Alicia looked at the others. "OK I guess."

Harry's chest burned as he strained to remain absolutely motionless behind the electrical service cabinet, breathing ever so slowly. He listened intently to the footsteps as they moved around the lab. All it would take is one of them walking to the end of the cabinet and he would be in plain sight. He thought of just saying to hell with it and making a break for it right now but that would screw everything up. The evidence that he had carefully placed would become suspect because he had been seen there. No, he would stay put until they left. If they discovered him then he would make a break for it but not until.

Harry concentrated, trying to identify the separate voices as they moved through the lab. There seemed to be three women and a child but the child sounded strange.

Her voice was that of a child but her words were much older. He found by moving his head a few inches, he could see a tiny portion of the room through a small crack between mounting panels. He watched intently as they seemed to be setting up some kind of test. He saw two different adults pass his tiny window into the room but that was all.

"Man," said Gina, "this place is a mess. We need to get this cleaned up soon or we're going to contaminate every sample in here. Look at all this dust!"

"We'll take care of it tomorrow," said Ann. "Lets just get this test done so Alicia and Jasmine can go home." Ann powered up her computer. "What the..." she exclaimed as her computer started booting from the CD. Ann opened the tray and removed a CD from drive. "I wish you guys wouldn't leave a disc in the drive, especially a bootable one."

Alicia looked over at the CD Ann was holding up. "It's not mine. I use the ones with the blue stripe."

"Don't look at me," said Gina defensively. "I label my disks."

Shit, Harry cursed himself. He was going to retrieve the disk from the machine on his way out when they came to the door. If they examined the disk it would be obvious it didn't belong to them. And that would lead them to examine the computer it was in. He tensed himself to make a break for the door.

"That's right. It just walked in here on its own." She dropped the disk on her desk. "Come on, let's get the show on the road. Is everyone set?"

Harry relaxed slightly. He returned to concentrating on taking slow, silent breaths. The conversations had stopped, they were obviously engrossed in something.

The Mind examined the test set, noticing minute patterns of dust. Dust. The Mind returned its focus to the test. Data flew by, magnetic eddy patterns, thermal imprints, voltage drops, and dust. Alicia struggled to maintain the focus on the test. Alicia chastised Gina, Forget the dust and get back to the test!

Me? I thought it was you! With a great deal of difficulty, they dragged the Mind back to the test data being collected.

Harry felt the cabinet he was pressed against slowly coming to life. The hum from its innards grew louder, a vibration swelled as he felt the hair on his arms rise and dance to the tune. Whatever they were doing in here sure takes a lot of juice, he thought. This information may be useful to Fenton, and thus, valuable to Harry. I wish they would start talking again, he thought. At least then I would have a clue as to what was going on.

The Mind again abandoned the test. Dust. The patterns were all wrong. Where did it come from? The Disk! It is foreign. No one here used that brand. But what does that have to do with dust? The Mind felt itself being pulled away. Wait! Your conscious minds have handled the test before, let them do it again. Just give Me a little more time. The dust pattern would come from...eyes raised to a ventilation grill. Eyes returned to the floor, dust patterns, foreign disk, patterns... A footprint!

Fenton and Lindell squirmed in the corner of the command vehicle, vying for space in the cramped van. They were parked behind a low rise, five hundred yards from the entrance as the field commander finished the last minute briefing. "OK, listen up! Operation start is exactly five minutes from now," he said checking his watch. "Everyone keeps to their schedule and this will go off without a hitch. Keep your assigned team members in sight at all times and notify at each objective. Good luck and keep your heads screwed on straight. Any questions?" All eyes remained fixed on the field commander. "Then get moving."

The two unit leaders left the van to rejoin their teams. Fenton breathed easier as the van emptied and the space available improved. The assault teams were huddled outside trying to stay warm. Fenton heard one of the men called out "Hey Cap, did you ask if we can keep any cute ones we catch?" The reply was cut off when the van door closed.

"I hope your inside information was right. If anyone catches hell over this operation, it isn't going to be me."

"Don't worry," assured Fenton, "we will find what we're looking for." Fenton was sure of it because he had just browsed to a website that would have passed as any other blog on the web. But the Senator knew exactly where to look for the keyword that signaled that Harry had successfully planted his evidence. "I guarantee it."

One ATF agent slipped quietly into the Army guard shack. "You guys ready?"

"Yes sir," they responded. They had just received their orders to cooperate a short time before. They were taking no chances on a security leak. One Monoecion guard was in the entrance hut on the other side of the fence while the other paced by the gate itself. "Go over and keep her busy. After you open the gate, be sure to keep her back to us."

The soldier nodded, picked up his rifle and walked out to the gate. "How's it going," he called to the young woman on the other side of the fence.

"Cold," she called back as she watched him unlock and open the man gate.

He stepped inside. "I'm bored out of my skull. My mom sent me some cookies. Would you like one?" he asked holding out a bag.

She recognized him. He had been assigned there about a week and he had talked to her through the fence a few times. "Sure, why not. I just wish they were hot. It is cold tonight." She looked over at the entrance hut. When the front gate opens, a buzzer would go off inside. Sure enough, there was a face in the window watching her. She waved to the face in the window to signal that she was OK. A wave in the window acknowledged hers and after a few seconds the face disappeared.

The soldier stepped over to a trash barrel and leaned his gun against it. He dug inside his coat and pulled out a paper bag. He opened it and offered it to the girl. "I have to warn you, my mom's not a great cook."

She reached in the bag and took out a cookie. Carefully, she took a small bite. "Mmm. Not bad. Of course after eating the food in here anything..."

Her words were cut off as powerful arms grabbed her from behind and a hand clamped over her mouth. A badge appeared in front of her face and a voice whispered in her ear, "Federal agents. Keep your mouth shut and we won't have to get rough." Two men handled her like a sack of feed as they carried her out the fence to the Army guard shack. There they taped her mouth shut and handcuffed her, shoving her roughly to the floor in the corner. The agent curtly addressed the guard. "Keep her down and quiet. We'll be back with the other one in a minute. Got that?"

"Yes sir." He watched the agents leave and returned his attention to the woman on the floor. He could see the wild fear in her eyes. "It's OK. Nobody is going to hurt you," he assured her. He returned his attention to the scene outside.

Four agents crouched outside the door as the face reappeared at the window, looking for the now missing gate guard. The first agent burst through the door. "Freeze, Federal Agent!" The woman dived for her desk and the alarm siren button mounted on the wall next to it. The agent caught her leg in flight. She crashed down just out of reach of the button. She felt herself being jerked back and slammed into the wall next to the door. "For God's sake be quiet!" hissed one agent to the others now in the room.

She remembered the silent alarm button hidden inside the insulation of the open studded walls only inches from where her face was now being held. One arm was jerked down and handcuffed behind her. She had to act now. With her remaining free hand, she poked her finger between the paper-backed insulation and the two by four stud. For a split second she panicked, it wasn't there! Then she felt the smooth head of the button. Just as she pressed, her arm was jerked away behind her to be cuffed. She didn't know if she had triggered the alarm or not. "My nose is bleeding," she cried and tried to free her arm from their grasp.

The cuffs snapped closed and a piece of tape sealed her mouth. "Don't worry. We'll take care of it." Again, a squirming body was carried out the gate and deposited in the Army guard shack.

The alarm clock next to Rae Ann's bed beeped furiously. She slapped the snooze button but it refused to stop. Rae Ann's heart began to beat double time as she realized what was happening. She leaped from her bed and started shaking the bunks within reach. "Let's go! Let's go! This is not a drill!" Bodies of the handpicked team that shared her tiny makeshift barracks rolled out of bed began pulling on their night gear.

Each person kept a set of clothes at hand for use during action. Until now they had only used them in drills. Rae Ann pulled on her black sweatshirt, sweatpants, and shoes. She instinctively checked the time, forty-eight seconds from first alarm. She dashed to the weapons locker and opened it as the other nine women finished dressing. Each person grabbed their equipment from the cabinet, teamed with their partner, and made for the door.

"We don't know what's happening other than the alarm came from the front gate," called Rae Ann "and it was the silent alarm." Everyone knew that the silent alarm was only to be used in the case of someone breaching the perimeter. It meant that the guard was in fear of her life. "Get to your positions. You know what to do. Good luck." Now it was up to their training and how well she judged their character. She grabbed a knife, her bow and a quiver of arrows. Carla was standing next to her, ready to go. They exchanged a quick look that made words unnecessary. It was their job to check the front gate. They ran out the door.

Fenton heard the call come in. "The gate is secure. Element of surprise is still intact. First squad is proceeding now."

"Acknowledge that," answered the field coordinator. "So far so good," he said to Fenton.

The lead squad made up of two teams of two men each made its way up the street, only one team moved at a time while the second team swept the streets looking for any movement. The backup squad of four men held for sixty seconds at the gate, then followed the lead squad using the same crab-like advance.

The plan was for the foot squads to silently penetrate the compound to the lab building without being detected. The first squad would move straight down the street four blocks, turn left and proceed three more blocks. That would place them in front of the lab. The second squad would stop one block short on the first leg and turn left, stopping in position at the rear of the lab. At this point the main vehicle gate would be opened to allow the inspection van to enter. The element of surprise would be gone as the ancient motorized gate made enough noise to wake anyone within a hundred yards. They would announce themselves, ordering everyone to stay where they were. One team of the lead squad would enter the building and secure the lab while the other three teams watched the building so no one could enter. After that it was up to the inspection teams. They had made plans on being there all day.

The two Army sentries remained in position to operate the gate and guard the two captives. They watched the ATF agents move out from the gate area. The moon gave snatches of illumination to the scene as it found cracks in the low cloud cover.

The lead squad reached the turn point. The captain looked back to confirm the backup squad had reached its turn point one block behind them. He gave them a hand signal to confirm that all was still going according to plan, the reservation was sound asleep. The two squads advanced in parallel, one block apart, on their target building.

As Rae Ann and Carla approached the front gate, they saw several men carrying guns move up the main street from the front gate. Rae Ann pulled a small flashlight from her pocket. The narrow beamed light was equipped with a red filter lens and a shroud to prevent anyone other than the intended receiver from detecting the signals. She flashed it twice in the direction of where her next security team should be. A few seconds later, she saw two flashes in return.

Rae Ann had worked out a simple communications scheme. On deployment, each team moved to a position that was in direct line of sight with the other teams spaced at wide intervals. If any person could confirm the threat, they would give two blinks of their shrouded flashlights to notify the next team. This would be acknowledged and passed on down the line. After that point, each team was on its own to gain a position of advantage. If friendly teams were close enough to coordinate, three flashes signified intent to strike. As soon as it was to their advantage, someone would trigger the audible alarm. That should be enough to scare off all but the most determined attack.

Rae Ann and Carla held back in the shadows letting the teams pass them by. Their job would be to take out the tail end group of the intruders. They followed the intruders at a safe distance looking for an opportunity to get into a striking position. As she watched them turn down a side street, she had an idea. She signaled Carla to follow and ran quietly down the alley that paralleled the street the intruders had followed. At the intersecting alley she peered around the building. The lead two men were there by a dumpster looking down the street. Cautiously Rae Ann and Carla moved forward taking shelter behind some concrete steps. In a few seconds the pair of men moved on. In that instant using the sound of the men's footsteps to cover their own, Rae Ann and Carla sprinted up behind the dumpster. Seconds later, the second pair of men moved into the shadow of the alley. As the men moved into position behind the dumpster they were jumped. Rae Ann drove the head of her target into the side of the dumpster with a loud clunk. Carla swept the feet of her opponent out from under him and put him out with a single kick to the head. It was over in less than two seconds.

The lead team of the backup ATF squad heard a clatter twenty yards behind them from the alley they had just left. The captain turned and hissed, "Be quiet damn it!"

"It sounds like Fuller ran into the dumpster," snickered his partner.

A helmet peeked out from behind the dumpster and a gloved hand waved for them to come back. "Damn it. That jackass Fuller is so clumsy I wouldn't doubt that he broke his frigging neck," cursed the captain under his breath. The two men trotted back to the alley, watching the street over their shoulders. As they ducked back into the alley they found themselves staring into the barrels of two recently liberated M-4 rifles.

"Just put your guns on the ground nice and easy so we don't have to blow your heads off." Rae Ann tried to sound menacing. It worked. The men set their guns on the ground. "Your pistols too."

"Look ladies. You are in a mess of trouble, threatening federal officers," he looked down at his two incapacitated officers. "Make that assault. I think things will go a lot better for you if you hand over those guns."

"And I think you will live a lot longer if you drop those gun belts of yours and face that wall." Rae Ann tightened her grip on the M-4 to emphasize her point. Both men unbuckled the belts and let them drop. Rae Ann nodded at the wall. The two agents turned and put their hands on the wall. She nudged Carla "Pull their radios, get their hand cuffs and chain 'em to the dumpster. Do the same to the two on the ground."

"I don't think you understand the trouble you are in," said the Captain.

"How many more agents are in the compound?" demanded Rae Ann.

"So you can take them hostage too? I'm done talking to you unless you want to discuss returning our weapons and surrendering. You are interfering with federal officers in the line of official duty."

Rae Ann got in the captain's face. "Listen, moron," she whispered through gritted teeth, "we got a silent alarm. That means there are intruders in the fence with intent to do bodily harm. We have our teams out looking for those intruders now with the intent to do unto them before they have a chance to do unto us. My people don't know that you are Federal agents any more than we did when we took these two out. I can't guarantee that the other girls will be as gentle as we were. So unless you want some of your friends, and possibly some of mine, to end up dead you better tell me where they are and how many there are so we can get this stopped before it gets out of hand."

Rae Ann saw another self-defense team that had been tracking the same group and signaled them over. "Get back to the Administration Building and trigger the audible alarm. These guys are Feds. For heaven's sake, don't kill any of them. And get Landis. She is going to be needed to defuse this situation." The two women acknowledged and sprinted for the corner.

"Command and control. This is A squad, over."

The field commander smiled. "They're right on time." He picked up the mike. "Go ahead."

"This is team one. We are in position in the front of the building. We have visual contact with team 2 but we have not seen B squad for two blocks. They were tracking with us but now they have disappeared. They should have been at the back of the building by now."

The field commander frowned. B squad should have reached the back of the building at the same instant the first squad reached the front. "First squad, hold your position for one minute. I will advise. B squad, do you copy?" There was silence. "B squad, do you copy?" The field commander looked at Fenton.

"Could it be equipment failure?" asked Lindell.

"I doubt it. There's a radio on every man." The field commander thought for a second. "I'd say it's more likely that they tuned to the wrong frequency except we double-checked communications before they left."

The radio came to life again. "This is A squad. We are moving into position to attempt to establish visual contact with B squad. I will confirm in... Shit!" A clipped scream ended the radio transmission.

The field commander keyed his mike "What's going on?! What's happened?"

"Two men down! Two men down!" came an anxious voice. "I didn't hear a thing, they just dropped screaming!"

Three self-defense teams had been tracking the first ATF squad much the same as Rae Ann and Carla had done, by running parallel in the alleys. When the two pairs of men had stopped at opposite corners of a building, the women had taken positions across the street from them staying hidden in the shadows of the alley. "Get your bows ready," the group leader whispered to the three others with her. "If they step back out on the street we're going to eliminate this pair. They will be wearing body armor. Aim for their legs then back off fast in case they are still capable of firing back." Each one nocked a razor sharp cross bladed arrow into their bow and sat back to wait.

They hardly had time to prepare when the two men moved back out on the sidewalk and started back in the direction they came from. Three out of four of the first volley of arrows struck home, dropping one of the men hard on the concrete screaming. The other sagged back against the building, recovered and sprayed the area where the arrows came from with a burst of rifle fire. He then started to drag the downed man to cover.

The four women had already flattened themselves to the ground for cover from the flying lead and splinters of concrete. There was no more return fire from the two men who had been struck but the two men at the other corner of the building started firing wildly in their direction.

Chapter 38

Fenton heard a frantic "I'm hit! I'm hit!" followed by bursts of automatic rifle fire. A few seconds later sirens screamed to life and lights went on all over the reservation. "Son of a bitch," cursed Fenton.

"I got one!" yelled one of the remaining two men. They had taken refuge in the gap between the buildings.

"Cover me," said the other man. "I need to see if they made it to cover." He crawled to the edge of the building and peered out, trying to ascertain the condition of the two men fallen in the street. Two arrows sliced through the air, one striking him on top of the shoulder, the other glancing off the wall inches from his face. His team member fired in the direction the arrows appeared to come from.

"Damn that was close." He inspected the arrow jutting from his body armor. The tip had just broken the skin, drawing blood but not allowing the arrowhead to penetrate. The captain pulled the shaft back enough to allow pushing in a compress bandage and snapping off the arrow. "Man that hurts like hell. No wonder we didn't hear them. They're using god damn bows and arrows." Peering over the pile of trashcans they had taken refuge behind, he saw a shadowy movement and fired off two quick rounds.

"Hold your fire unless you have a definite target. We've got limited ammo." There was a woman's voice from behind them and they both turned and fired.

Rae Ann and Carla ran hard toward the sound of gunfire. Carla led as they reached the alley where the shots seemed to come from. "Hold your fire! Hold your fire!" she screamed. The firing stopped. Carla laid her gun against the building and stepped out in view with her hands in the air. "We have just..." Shots again rang out and Carla's body jerked and collapsed.

Rae Ann screamed "Noooo!" She raised her rifle and fired into the alley emptying the clip. She picked up Carla's gun and put it to her shoulder.

A scared voice came from the alley. "Please don't shoot! I give up!"

"Get out here. Now!" screamed Rae Ann. "Hands over your head!" She looked down at Carla as she lay on the cold asphalt moaning. "Somebody get a car! My daughter's been hit!"

A lone man staggered out of the alley, leaning on the wall to steady himself. Two of Rae Ann's defense team arrived to assist. "Is there anyone else in there?" demanded Rae Ann.

"J-Just my captain but I think he's dead," the man stuttered. Then his legs gave out and he collapsed.

Rae Ann saw the broken arrow dangling from the top of his shoulder pad. "Check it out," she said to one of the others as she pressed a pistol into the woman's hand. "Just be careful. I don't want any more casualties." The woman nodded and crept cautiously into the alley. Rae Ann handed her rifle to the remaining woman. "Cover her." Rae Ann turned back to her captive. The muscle relaxant that was delivered by the arrow would still take several minutes before it would suppress his ability to breath. "I should let you suffocate," and knelt down to Carla.

"It hurts mom!" cried Carla. "It hurts real bad!"

"I know, honey," soothe Rae Ann as examined her wounds. One shot had gone through her right arm but appeared to have missed the bone, another had grazed her side just inches from the old knife scar. A much more serious wound was in her left thigh. Her leg felt as if it was broken.

"You know," Carla sobbed. "We are really getting tired of being shot." She tried to smile but it was cut off as a new round of sobs racked her body.

"Where's a car?!" screamed Rae Ann. "We need to get her to the hospital now!" Just as she spoke headlights rounded the corner. The car stopped next to them and they carefully lifted Carla into the front seat. Another woman lay in the back seat. She didn't appear to be breathing.

"I don't know her. She's not on the team. We think she just came out at the wrong time and they shot her."

"Get to the hospital," Rae Ann ordered the driver. "I'll be there soon, honey," she said to Carla. "I have to do a couple things first and I will be right there."

"Don't let him die," Carla choked out.

"I won't," she promised. Rae Ann closed the door and the car sped off.

The woman sent down the alley by Rae Ann staggered out and vomited, leaning against the building.

"Is he dead?" asked Rae Ann.

The woman lifted her head and nodded. "His head..." She again started to retch.

"Go back and get his guns and ammunition. We're going to need them," commanded Rae Ann. The woman looked at her in horror. "Move it. We need them now!" reinforced Rae Ann. The woman took a deep breath and reentered the alley.

Rae Ann's team started collecting around her. "Is anyone else hurt?"

"None of us, just that lady we found in the street. The other two Feds only have minor wounds but the tubocurarine chloride in the arrows really did the trick. Those guys turned into a couple of rag dolls after a few minutes. They're on their way to the hospital right now. They should live as long as they get the shot to reverse the effects. They know what to do. Did you know about the other guy in the alley?"

"Yeah," said Rae Ann. "OK, take a team and haul this jerk down to the hospital too. He was hit by an arrow in the top of his shoulder," she commanded, pointing to the ATF agent still lying on the ground. "There are four more handcuffed to a dumpster down the block. Make sure to search them completely. Carla and I didn't have time to do it." Rae Ann pointed to the next in line. "You, collect all the rifles, ammunition and get them to people that know how to use them. We need to get to the front gate or we're going to have the bastards crawling all over this place. Let's move!" Rae Ann reclaimed her rifle and started running for the front gate.

Rae Ann went over the odds. She had captured eight M-4 rifles and some pistols. In a few minutes she was sure that the compound was going to be overrun with a few hundred troops with heavy weapons. It was going to be a very short uprising.

Robert had been awake since before one AM when Christine had received a call. She hadn't explained what the problem was. She just said she had to go and would call as soon as she could. He was sitting at the kitchen table cradling a cup of coffee in his hands when he heard what sounded like firecrackers in the distance. He bolted from the table and opened the front door. Standing on the landing, he heard the sounds of automatic rifle fire from the heart of the main compound.

He closed and locked the front door, then tuned in the reservation emergency radio station. There was nothing but a marker signal being transmitted. He thought about waking the children but that decision wasn't necessary.

The wail of the emergency sirens started and all three girls burst wide-eyed from their bedroom. "What's happening, daddy?"

"That's what I'm trying to find out!" He fiddled with the radio dial even though he knew he had the right station.

"Where's mom?"

"I don't know. She left over two hours ago. She promised to call but she hasn't yet." The gunfire had stopped as quickly as it had started but Robert was taking no chances. "Get down!" he commanded. "Down here on the floor. I want you low, below the windows. Don't turn on any lights."

"What happened?" asked Melissa, his oldest.

"There's been gunfire in the compound. Right now, that's all I know." Robert repeated his instructions. "I want you to stay below the window sill. Do you all understand?" The three girls nodded. Robert cautiously peered out the window, looking for any signs of movement. He could see lights in other housing units go on and off but saw no one in the streets.

The radio finally came to life. "Attention! There are intruders in the compound. Everyone please stay where you are and take cover. Keep your lights out. Defense teams, report to your assigned locations. This is not a drill. Defense teams, report to your assigned locations." The entire message repeated two more times.

"Get dressed," whispered Robert to his daughters. "Stay low, put on warm clothes. If we have to make a run for it, I want you ready." The girls scurried for the bedroom. "Stay low!" hissed Robert. The girls dropped to their hands and knees and crawled into the bedroom.

They emerged a few minutes later, dressed but carrying their shoes. "Get your shoes on," said Robert. He stood and went to the closet, pulling out hats, gloves and coats. "Keep these in your hands. If I say go, I don't want you searching for them."

The radio now played music, interspersed with the same message that was broadcast before. The four of them sat huddled together, listening for anything new.

"Come in anybody." There was no reply. The field commander keyed his mike again. "Lead team, respond."

"What the hell is going on?" demanded Fenton.

"You tell me! I thought that this was a simple task of going in and securing a building. Isn't that what you said, Senator?"

The operations officer interrupted his boss. "Do we go in after them?"

"We have no idea what their current condition is. All we know is that the team was ambushed, took hostile fire and are likely captured or killed." He brushed his hair back with both hands. "We need intelligence. Get some teams to probe the perimeter. I don't want to be surprised by an assault. Let's try to find out what is going on. I want them to just do a limited recon with constant communications."

The operations officer reminded the commander "Only about a dozen of the remaining men are our guys. The others are the Senator's scientists."

"I know that. Tell the damn scientists to get the hell out of the way. We won't be needing their services for quite a while now. And change our communications settings. Our opponents probably now have eight of our radios and will be listening if they can."

Fenton jumped in. "Get the State Police in here and the National Guard. We have to get into that building before they have a chance to destroy the evidence."

"I'm putting in a call right now for support." He leaned down to the map and addressed his operations officer. "Get a hold of the Army unit that's building the new tent city. I want them over here NOW! Tell them to come armed and ready for action."

Rae Ann was directing her people into defensive positions when Christine and her security chief found her. "OK, what happened?"

"We were just defending ourselves."

"No smart answers, just the facts," demanded Christine.

"Well I'd love to sit and chat with you but I'm a little busy setting up a defensive line at the moment. Come back in a few minutes."

Christine turned to the security chief. "Get them positioned. Make sure they understand that they are only to fire in self defense." She returned her attention to Rae Ann and held out her hands.

Rae Ann realized that Christine wanted her rifle. "I've got a job to do," Rae Ann said defiantly.

"Yes, you do and it's waiting for you at the hospital. Your daughter needs you now, not later. Come on, I'll drive you and you can brief me on the way." Christine could see the indecision in Rae Ann's face. "Carla needs you more than we do right now."

Rae Ann looked around her as people ran here and there. She handed the M-4 to the security chief. "Be careful with them. I don't want to lose any of my team. They're like my kids."

Christine listened to Rae Ann's story on the way to the hospital. "Did they ever identify themselves as police officers?"

"Only after they were captured," said Rae Ann.

"After this is all over, I'm going to need written statements from everybody involved. You better get inside." Christine watched Rae Ann hustle into the hospital front door, put the car in gear and headed back to the administration building.

"Is this all the armament you've got?" demanded Fenton.

The Army lieutenant tried to explain to the Senator. "We didn't come here to fight sir. We came here to put up tents and dig latrines."

Fenton looked at the handful of men with disgust. "Get them out there and at least cover the main gate. And keep the patrols on the perimeter. I don't want any of the murderers slipping out the back door."

"I have already coordinated with the ATF field commander, sir. We are reinforcing the perimeter to provide some security from attack. At this point that is all we can do with the resources we have." He led his men over the small rise separating the makeshift command center from the road in front of the reservation.

"What's happening with that National Guard unit?" asked Fenton.

"I just got off the phone with them," replied Lindell. "They said that they were getting the armored personnel carriers ready now and should have them up here by seven thirty. The State Police said they had six cars on their way now with more coming to control the roads in and out of the reservation."

"Come with me for a minute," Fenton said to Lindell. "We need to talk." They stepped away from people milling around the van. "We need to determine how we're going to handle this with the press. Any minute now, they're going to be coming up this road looking for answers. We need them blocked from any access until we have time to prepare releases. Make sure they get nothing other than prepared statements until we can get a lid on this thing."

Lindell muttered "Fat chance," under his breath.

Christine sat at the head of the table with some of her staff members and Alicia. Ann and Gina waited outside the conference room. "That's the current situation," summed up Christine after laying out what she knew.

"What was the raid all about?" asked the Education Director.

"The ATF agents we captured said it was to secure a building where we were supposedly storing a cache of firearms. But that is not the real reason. The real reason was to collect evidence of something much more heinous," said Christine. She then added a cold edge to her voice "Dorothy, or whatever your real name is, would you care to tell us what that is?"

Dorothy looked scared, then tried her best to change it to a look of surprise. "What do you mean? How would I know?"

"Can it!" shouted Christine. Dorothy shrunk back in her chair. Christine continued calmly "I've known about you for some time but thought it would serve us better to ignore you and know who the spy was rather than expose you and have you replaced by someone else." Christine could tell from Dorothy's reaction that so far she had been on the mark. "You see," she said addressing the others at the table, "Dorothy has been working for Fenton." Murmurs arose around the table. "She is also human, not Monoecion."

All eyes came to rest on Dorothy. "By the way, how did you fool the blood test?" Christine asked lightly.

"A blood transfusion right before I entered the reservation," Dorothy replied sullenly, "We tested it on the outside to make sure it would test positive."

"Very clever." Christine's voice rose as she spoke. "Since you're so clever maybe you can explain why we have two bodies in the morgue and several more in serious condition at the hospital?"

"I don't know..."

"That's a lie and you know it!" 'Right about now the judge would be telling me to quit badgering the witness,' Christine thought. "Fenton didn't send these guys in here on a lark. He was looking for something and he was pretty sure he was going to find it. What I don't understand is why he didn't just walk in the front gate and call an inspection?"

Dorothy remained silent. "Tell me, Dorothy," continued Christine, "what is the procedure for the guard when an outside inspection is called? You should know, you helped draft it."

Dorothy recited, "Cooperate fully, call security to escort them to anywhere they wish to go, contact you immediately."

"It sounds pretty damned simple to me," said Christine. "So why weren't we allowed to follow it? What was the idea of the swat team approach?"

"I assume that Fenton was afraid that you would destroy the evidence if you knew they were coming," responded Dorothy.

"Oh," Christine responded in mock horror. "Then we must be involved in something pretty dangerous. The agents have been very cooperative. They informed me that their target was to secure the lab where Alicia, here, is working."

Alicia stood and picked up a small vial from the table. "The fruits of all of my team's efforts are in this vial. And it's ready for release now." Alicia waved it in front of Dorothy.

"Maybe Dorothy would like to tell us what Fenton thinks this is." Christine paused and looked at Dorothy for several seconds. The fear was obvious on Dorothy's face. Christine snorted in disgust "I guess not. Alicia, would you like to demonstrate its effectiveness on our human subject."

"A virus, deadly only to humans." Dorothy blurted out in a panic.

Christine shoulders fell. "Alicia, open the bottle and show our spy what you have."

Dorothy screamed as Alicia opened the bottle.

Alicia carefully removed the thin ceramic shape from the vial. "This little piece of material can carry a thousand amperes of current. It will allow motors to drop to one-tenth their size today. It will allow subways to operate at nearly zero energy loss. It will allow power companies to move vast amounts of energy across the nation with no line losses. In short, it's a room temperature superconductor. And with a little more development, it can be manufactured at a cost less than the copper cable it's replacing."

"Now you know," said Christine with a great sadness in her voice. "I hope it was worth the two bodies in the morgue."

"I didn't know," stammered Dorothy.

"That's precisely the point," said Christine. "Now our goal is to make sure no one else dies because of what you didn't know."

Christine's office assistant stuck her head in the conference room door. "I've got a line established to the ATF command center outside."

"Thanks," acknowledged Christine. "Dorothy, we have to diffuse this situation as quickly as possible to eliminate the chance of any more casualties. I'm going to negotiate the return of the dead agent's body. You will accompany it and get to whoever is in charge on the outside."

"I think Senator Fenton is here. Mr. Lindell told me that he wanted to direct this operation personally," explained Dorothy.

"I know he is. The agents we questioned confirmed it. It's no wonder the operation was a mess," said Christine. "What I need is a face to face meeting with him. You need to arrange it but you need to be convinced that we are telling you the truth. Alicia will take you over to the lab so you can see for yourself what's being done there. Get moving. You have ten minutes."

The emergency radio station updated its report. "The reservation is secure. The intruders have been captured. The intruders were Federal agents who had not identified themselves as such. The situation is still tense with armed agents at the main gate and around the perimeter of the reservation. Please stay where you are until the situation has been stabilized. One of the Federal agents was killed and several more wounded. One reservation resident was killed and another wounded. Identification is being withheld pending notification of next of kin."

Robert listened as the message repeated. He turned up the volume on the television and searched for news from the outside world. He had already tried to call Christine at the administration offices but was told that she couldn't talk now. One of her aides briefed him with as much as she knew.

A CNN reporter gave a short report about a firefight that had occurred in the early hours of the morning but details were sketchy. The reporter told of an Army unit being deployed and showed filmed footage of armored personnel carriers being loaded for transport to the reservation.

"This is insanity," muttered Robert. "They are going to come in here and blow us away." He realized his daughters were staring at him, frightened at what they had seen on the TV and more frightened at his words. "Don't worry," he tried to reassure them. "I'm going to protect you. I'll get you out of here somehow."

The sun was just beginning to poke over the horizon as the pickup rolled to a stop next to the main gate. Dorothy and three others walked along side. Dorothy directed as they slid the stretcher with the body bag off the bed of the truck. They carried it through the pedestrian gate and two soldiers accepted the load. It was placed on a set of sawhorses and scanned carefully for booby traps before being moved inside a waiting ambulance.

Dorothy watched the other three women reenter the compound as the soldiers eyed her with suspicion. "I need to talk to Mr. Lindell."

"Yeah? And who are you?" asked a soldier.

"I work for him. Tell him Mrs. Haber needs to see him," replied Dorothy.

"Wait here." The soldier disappeared over the small rise separating the gate from the command center. A few minutes later he reappeared and waved for her to proceed. One of the soldiers escorted her to the command center.

Lindell met her at the communications van. "What are you doing here?"

"Mrs. Landis sent me. They knew I was a spy the whole time."

"Great," said Lindell sarcastically. "So they've been running a disinformation campaign the whole time."

"No," said Dorothy, "that's the point. They just let me continue on in my role to try to prove to us that nothing underhanded is going on."

"What about the lab?" demanded Lindell.

"I've been through it. I was wrong. I told you at the time that it might be an innocent conversation and it appears it was."

"Shit!" exclaimed Lindell as a news helicopter flew low overhead. "Get them the hell out of here!" he yelled at an ATF agent nearby. "This is a restricted area and I want them outside of it, now!"

"I'll try," the agent shouted back over the noise.

"Mrs. Landis wants to set up a meeting with the Senator, face to face."

"Tell her to call him on the phone."

"No good. She says it has to be face to face and alone," said Dorothy. "She says that the crisis can be resolved without further incident if they can meet."

Lindell thought for a moment. He knew Fenton was already at work on a press release that placed the blame for the deaths squarely on the Monoecion administration. To make it work, the situation had to be extended for a while longer. "I don't think the Senator will go for it, at least not yet."

"She said she would be willing to release the wounded agents in exchange for the meeting," added Dorothy.

Lindell looked around at the people nearby. "I'll talk to him. Wait here." Lindell disappeared inside the van.

"Who knows of Mrs. Landis's offer to release the wounded men?" asked Fenton.

"I'm not sure. There were a couple of men near enough to hear our conversation but I'm not sure they did," replied Lindell.

"I don't want to go into this until we are operating from a position of strength. Where are those armored personnel carriers?"

Lindell checked his watch. "They're due here in half an hour. It will take a few minutes more to unload them and get them ready." A knock came on the van door. "What is it?" called Lindell.

A man stuck his head in the door. "There's a news story running on TV. It seems they're interviewing some people inside the reservation."

"I thought we had all their phone lines cut off!" stormed Fenton.

"We do but they're doing the interviews over short wave radio."

"Make sure you record everything being said," Lindell instructed the man. "Then get a hold of the network and tell them that they are jeopardizing our efforts out here. God damn idiots." As the man disappeared out the door Fenton shouted "Send Mrs. Haber in. I want to talk to her."

Dorothy entered the vehicle a few seconds later. "You said you toured the lab?" asked Fenton without bothering with pleasantries.

"Yes. I didn't have much time but one of the engineers showed me the equipment and told me how they were testing there."

Fenton became intense. "I need you to be absolutely sure on this matter. Were there computer systems in the room?"

Dorothy thought and said "Yes, there were at least three that I saw. You know, the normal desk top kind."

Fenton leaned back in his chair. "OK, we are going to go with the meeting but delay it with security measures. I want those armored personnel carriers and our inspectors ready to go in the moment I come out of this meeting."

Two ambulances waited while the main gate slowly ground open allowing them to enter the compound. Once inside the gate the attendants opened the doors and allowed a Monoecion guard to search the vehicles. From there, a jeep led them to the hospital. The three wounded agents were gingerly loaded while the attending physician detailed the procedures already conducted and handed over the charts showing all medications administered.

Christine's security chief approached her as she started out to the front gate to meet with Senator Fenton. "There's a crowd gathering behind our defensive line."

"Well, get them out of there," ordered Christine. "If something goes astray, who knows what will happen. I don't want civilians in the line of fire."

"I already tried. They demand to be let out of the reservation," explained the security chief. "They say they didn't come here to be murdered by tanks like at Waco. They say they are leaving with or without your permission."

"My God. If they rush the gate, all hell will break loose!" Christine didn't see any options. "Tell them that they are free to leave but only after the people outside the fence have been notified and agree to accept them. Send an envoy to arrange it. Let them know that they will probably not be allowed to return by the authorities, their decision may be final." Christine continued to the front gate.

As the ambulances arrived again at the front gate on the return trip, Christine walked out and stood next to the reception hut just inside the gate. The Monoecion jeep remained motionless blocking the gate.

"What's the holdup?" asked an Army guard nervously.

"I'm here, where is the Senator?" asked Christine politely.

"I don't know, Ma'am."

"When he is here with me, the ambulances can proceed." Christine assumed a relaxed stance. "I can wait a long time. I'm not so sure about the men inside those ambulances."

The guard went back to the Army guards shack and transferred the message. A few seconds later Fenton, Lindell, and two agents walked cautiously to the gate. Christine signaled the jeep driver who immediately pulled back out of the way of the gate and the ambulances proceeded out of the compound.

The two armed guards advanced on Christine and were greeted by the sound of bolts being pulled back. Christine raised her hands to signal her people to relax. "We have to search you for weapons, ma'am," explained one of the agents.

"I understand but my people would feel better if you left your arms back there," said Christine, indicating the gate.

The guards looked back at Fenton for approval. He nodded and the Army guards rested their rifles against the fence. They again approached Christine, patted her down and checked her pockets. "We will need to look in your briefcase also." She opened it and they inspected the contents. "We also need to check the room."

Christine waved her hand in the direction of the door. "Be my guest. My security chief will assist you incase you *accidentally* drop something during your inspection." The agents entered followed by Christine's security team and after a few minutes emerged and gave a thumbs up signal. The Senator and Lindell approached the reception hut. Christine signaled one of her guards forward. "Senator, I'm sure that you understand that we need to establish mutual trust."

"I assure you that I am not carrying any weapons," blustered Fenton.

"Open your coat please, Senator," said Christine politely but firmly.

Fenton made a big production of unbuttoning his overcoat and holding it open. The Monoecion guard ran the wand over him. It beeped wildly. "He's wired," announced the guard.

"Remove it," ordered Christine. Fenton angrily yanked out his shirt tail and pulled the transmitter off his chest where it was taped. "Thank you," said Christine. She nodded to her guard "Again." A second much smaller bug was located inside his shoe and removed. A final check revealed no additional listening devices. "You can go inside."

Lindell stepped forward and opened his coat. "That isn't necessary," said Christine. "This meeting is one on one, remember."

"I am just attending as an observer," explained Lindell.

"I believe that the agreement was very specific. There will be no observers." Christine waved her hand as if to shoo off a puppy.

"If Mr. Lindell does not accompany us then the meeting is in jeopardy," said Fenton.

"If Mr. Lindell attempts to accompany us then more than this meeting is in jeopardy. The agreement was for the two of us to meet alone," said Christine sharply.

Fenton motioned Lindell to retreat back toward the gate. "This won't take long." The guards withdrew as Fenton and Christine entered the small guard hut on the Monoecion side of the fence. Once inside, Fenton did a quick look around, there was a single desk, a couple of chairs, a file cabinet and the usual assortment of office equipment. Fenton had learned long ago to seek out the power points in a room. If you were in a conference room with a table, take the seat at the head of the table. In this room there was only one point of power and that was behind the desk. Fenton did not hesitate as he crossed the small room and sat behind the desk.

Christine paused at the door, inspecting a small hole punched in the insulation backing. She strode over to the desk, pulling off her gloves on the way. "I would like to end this standoff without further loss of life," said Christine. She pushed the clutter on the desk to the side, leaving her gloves covering the intercom controls as her finger brushed the controls.

"That's simple," responded Fenton. "Have your people bring their weapons forward and leave them at the gate."

"We fully intend to do so after we have some guarantees."

"You want guarantees then I will give you some. If your people do not lay down their arms, we will take them by force," stormed Fenton.

"And if you try it then there will be a loss of life on both sides," assured Christine. "Let's stop the bluster and get down to facts."

"Facts? The facts are that an inspection team was sent into the reservation to perform a surprise inspection. Your people ambushed them causing the loss of life and preventing the inspection." Fenton slapped his palm on the desk for emphasis. "Those are the facts and your people will pay for these crimes."

"You sent in an armed group of people into the reservation without following procedures and without notification of the proper authorities. Because of that, an alarm was triggered identifying your people as civilian thugs attacking the reservation, which, as I am sure you are aware, has happened before. Your people were attacked as an act of self-defense. They were not identified as Federal agents until after they were captured."

"That's a bunch of bullshit and you know it," said Fenton confidently. "The alarm didn't go off until after they were ambushed. We have it all on tape."

"Oh really?" asked Christine as she stood. "Come here for a moment. I would like you to see something." Fenton eyed her with suspicion from behind the desk. Fenton stood but made no attempt to follow. "Do you see this hole?" Christine pointed to a small puncture in the insulation backing.

"Yes, I can see the hole," said Fenton.

"Inside, you will find the silent alarm button. That is the button that warns us of a hostile, illegal entry." Christine added "Have your people check it out. They will confirm it. You have two of our people in custody. Just ask them. One of them is the person who pressed the button."

Fenton brushed it aside. "It doesn't matter. Our agents were on a legitimate inspection and your people ambushed them." He dropped back heavily into the chair. "Those are the facts of the case. Let's get to the heart of the matter. Here are the terms and conditions of your surrender.

"First, as soon as we leave this room, the remaining hostages will be brought to the front gate and released.

"Second, all firearms will be deposited at the front gate for collection.

"Third, your people will step aside and permit a full camp inspection. And I promise all infractions will be dealt with severely.

"Fourth, all the criminals who took part in the assault on the federal officers will be turned over to the authorities to await prosecution. Those are the terms. Take them or leave them, but I advise that you take them. A full scale assault on the compound would have disastrous results for you and your people."

Christine made no response. She waited for a few seconds, eyes locked on Fenton's. Without breaking her eye contact, she reached in her pocket and pulled out an envelope. She tore it open, unfolded the single sheet of paper it contained and handed it to Fenton.

Fenton broke the stare and looked down at the piece of paper. It read:

If your people outside are using any type of listening device to eavesdrop on what is being said in this room, I advise you disable it now.

Fenton glared at her with open hostility. "I don't think you are in a position to dictate."

Christine's expression never changed. "Turn it over."

Fenton turned the sheet over. He turned white as he read the single sentence.

We have Harry.

Fenton fought to regain his composure. "What's this supposed to mean?"

"You haven't answered the questions on the other side," said Christine.

"There are no listening devices," said Fenton, all bluster was gone from his voice.

"Now that you have said your piece, it's time for me to say mine." Christine gave him no time to respond.

"First, as soon as we finish taking statements from our prisoners, we will release them to the proper authorities. You will do the same with our people that you have in custody. You will make your people available for questioning in the future just as we will make our people available to you. No one will be incarcerated unless convicted by a court of law.

"Second, we will be more than happy to turn over all firearms that were captured from your men during the aborted raid. I have no desire to have firearms inside the reservation. Your people will follow the same rules inside our gates. No firearms will be allowed inside the confines of the reservation and that includes your law enforcement personnel.

"Third, we will be more than happy to allow an inspection of our reservation. I am sorry to say that your team will find none of the evidence planted by your employee, Harry. We removed and destroyed the guns he hid on site and cleaned the hard drives of all of the files he placed to make it look like we were involved in biological warfare research."

"I don't know what you're talking about," barked Fenton finally regaining some of his composure. "I don't know this Harry you keep talking about and I have never had any involvement in the planting of evidence!"

"That's very interesting. Earlier this morning you visited his Internet site and collected a message from him by entering in a passcode. This happened about half an hour before your raid started. I believe the message was a simple icon of a flower being planted in a pot." Christine let the news sink in before continuing. "There are some wonderful pieces of software out there that allows tracking of the MAC ID of a device that accesses a web site. I do believe that this one leads straight back to you." Christine watched Fenton's face pale.

"Fourth, an independent investigation will be conducted on what happened in the raid today. That commission will find that there was a breakdown in procedures and communications. There will be new policies implemented to prevent it from happening in the future. No criminal charges will be placed on either side." Christine paused.

"How can I control what an independent commission decides?" said Fenton. "I'd have no control of that."

"Of course you would, Senator. By having control over who sits on the commission you can control what comes out of it. Don't tell me you haven't learned that in all your years in the Senate."

Fenton grumbled something unintelligible.

"And there is one last thing. You will not announce for the presidency."

"What?" exclaimed Fenton.

"You will express thanks to your supporters but you will decide that you can do more good in the Senate. Everyone will be disappointed but they will get over it." Christine continued "You see Senator, I can deal with a mad dog in the legislature but I draw the line at electing him President of the United States. This is no loss for you since after your role in this mess becomes public, you will have a hard enough time to keep your Senate seat."

"I think you are over playing your hand, Mrs. Landis. I can paint this just as it appears; an attempt to extort favorable treatment with trumped up evidence. You have provided me a few obstacles to overcome but you are far from holding all the aces. With a little work I can prove this is an extortion attempt by the Monoecion leadership to destroy my good name. You do not realize how powerful I am."

"Oh yes, Mr. Fenton, I do. I would be a fool to underestimate you," assured Christine. "I was thinking about that when we found Harry's airline tickets. So just as a lark we went back to mid September and checked with the airlines. I have a few contacts outside the reservation also. It seems that Harry took a trip to Boston at the same time my old pal Ben's friend was murdered. You did know we had reliable witnesses who had seen the murderer. I was assured that they would be able to pick him out of a lineup. Harry became even more cooperative when he learned this."

Fenton lunged forward. "You can't blame that one on me! I didn't tell him to kill him."

"Yes, that is true," confirmed Christine. "You paid him his standard rate for a hit and told him to make Ben Davis disappear off the face of the earth for an extended period of time. I think a jury might disagree with your assessment of the instructions. Harry kept very detailed records for his own protection.

"You see, Senator, I feel quite confident that you will agree to our terms because you are addicted to power. You would rather hold on to the power you have than chance losing everything."

"You're feeling pretty smug right now aren't you?" spat Fenton. "Why don't you release all this to the authorities and bring me down instead of cutting a deal?"

"Let's say it's a business decision. We would rather have someone in control of COMA that we have some sway over. It weighs the equation in our favor. Also, as I'm sure that your spy has already informed you, we have developed a rather amazing product that should remove us from the public dole for a long time to come. With cooperation, we can get it into production immediately, and I'm sure that some of the profits would find their way to the proper people."

"Are you offering me a bribe?" asked Fenton.

"Oh no, Senator. Let's just call it a political contribution. A guarantee of a very comfortable retirement could be arranged," responded Christine. Fenton sat back and stared at Christine without saying a word. "Do we have a deal?" she asked.

"And what happens to Harry?" Fenton queried with suspicion.

Harry will disappear through the fence at the first opportunity. After that, he is your problem. I don't plan to do your dirty work for you."

Christine locked eyes with Fenton. "I ask again, do we have a deal?" she asked. Fenton slowly nodded.

Christine pulled a typed copy of their agreement from her briefcase. "Check it over but I think you will find it per our discussions. Of course our side agreements will have to remain a gentleman's agreement. I don't think we need anything written up for those."

Fenton looked over the document, made minor changes in the wording and signed it.

Christine checked the changes, initialed them and signed at the bottom. "It's been a pleasure doing business with you." She stood and held out her hand. Fenton ignored it. Christine shrugged and left the reception hut.

Back away from the hut, hundreds of Monoecions had filled the streets. Robin stood outside in view wearing a headset whose cable trailed into an open window. As soon as she saw Christine she gave her the thumbs up sign with both hands. Christine returned the thumbs up sign and a cheer erupted from her staff.

Fenton came to the door and looked quizzically out at the commotion coming from the administration building. He squared his shoulders and walked to the gate where the ATF field commander met him. "Senator, I regret to inform you that you have been relieved of control of this operation."

"What are you talking about, you idiot. You can't relieve me of control!" exclaimed Fenton.

"No sir, I can't, but the Attorney General can. We have been in communication with him and that is exactly what he did. You need to come with us."

Fenton looked from man to man, none would look him in the face. Finally he saw Lindell coming over the rise, an ATF agent on each side. "You old fool!" Lindell screamed. "They broadcast the whole thing straight to the command vehicle who sent it straight on to the Attorney General's office. It is being played now on network TV!" Lindell shook his head. "You old fool," he muttered again.

Fenton spun and looked at Christine Landis. She stood firmly and stared back. There was no joy in her face, destroying a man's life did not give her pleasure, no matter how much he deserved it. She turned and walked into the arms of the crowd that awaited her.

Christine's oldest daughter, Melissa ran to meet her. "Mom!" she cried. "Tara and Stacy are gone. Dad took them out of the reservation."

"What are you talking about? When?" asked Christine confused.

"When the people were let out while you were in with the Senator," explained Melissa through sobs. "He made them go. He told me to also, but I refused. Then he tried to grab me and I ran into the crowd. I saw them go through the gate a little while ago."

Christine held her daughter and strained to pick them out in the milling crowd outside the gate. Tears ran down her cheeks. She had won a chance at freedom for the reservation but had lost her family.

Chapter 39

Sunday, May 4
"This is Henry Rogers with a WTRQ news update. Senator Gordon Fenton was found dead today at his home in Washington DC. Officers at the scene say it is being investigated as an apparent suicide. Senator Fenton was under investigation for his alleged involvement in evidence tampering and a contract murder. Details at six."

Late September
Jasmine walked home from school, the cool late September air letting her know that summer was gone. In another few days she would celebrate her one-year anniversary on the reservation. A lot had changed since they drove half way across the United States. Jazz liked her first grade teacher well enough. She was very good despite her slight speech impediment, the one lingering symptom of her head injury from the intruder's blow, many months ago. Jazz became bored with correcting her teacher all the time. It seemed to frustrate the teacher and the other kids kept calling her a "smarty pants". Even though she had the equivalent of three advanced degrees in her head, every day she found things that she hadn't learned yet, six-year-old things, like reading, writing and her best friend had recently taught her how to spit between her front teeth. Her mom got really mad when Jazz showed her. Jazz giggled out loud when she thought about how Marci reacted. Going to school with kids her own age seemed to make her parents happier too. They kept worrying that she was going to grow up all mixed up if she didn't spend time with other kids.

Jasmine still got to work with the team a few minutes every day. This was her favorite part of the day. She loved how much she learned each time they linked to analyze test results or design new methods to beat a problem. But what she loved the most was when they let the mind wander. It was like riding bareback with that feeling of almost being out of control while feeling the wind blowing through your hair. And then there was the time Jazz spent working with Jessica. It was different connecting with her. Jasmine couldn't tell you why, only that it was different. Her little sister was coming along but she had a nasty stubborn streak. Sometimes she would just refuse to learn something that Jazz would show her. It wasn't that she didn't understand, she just wanted to do it herself.

One cloud kept creeping back into Jazz's mind. How would the world take the revelation of the new Monoecion talent? She had seen how the humans reacted when the last secrets were revealed, even though much of the reaction could be explained by the *way* it was revealed. If her gift was revealed, it would raise the concern about a conspiracy all over again. There were several pregnancies to Monoecion couples already so it wouldn't be long before others shared Jasmine and Jessica's ability. But that time wouldn't come for another few years and until then the two little girls were very vulnerable, especially Jessica who's ability was just developing. Several times in their connected sessions the topic of how and when to contact the new parents was examined but no decision had been made.

This led her to contemplate one of her great questions. Jazz had a list of questions she carried around in her head. These were the things she wanted to know more than anything else. The one that slipped into her conscious thoughts now was 'Where does the Mind's power come from?' At first she thought it was from the combining of each person's mind causing the combined Mind to become more powerful. But lately she had been thinking of another option. What if it had nothing to do with their individual minds? What if each additional person joining in the connection increased their ability to connect to some universal mind? She wondered if this was a connection to God.

Jasmine grew tired of the whole thing and slipped back to six-year-old issues, like what was she going to eat for a snack when she got home. She skipped across the street to her apartment building and froze as she stepped up on the curb. Someone had just touched her. Not physically, it was a touch like she would do to check to see if a person was Monoecion. Jazz's mind raced. There were only two people in the world capable of doing this, her little sister and herself, and this was not done by her little sister. Jasmine unconsciously looked over her shoulder. By force of will, her feet started moving again and she entered her building. "This changes everything," she whispered to herself.

Major Characters in Order of Appearance

Rachel Delings
> The first person to exhibit the Monoecion genetic trait. Born in the early 1700's. An accident exposed her telepathic abilities to her community, causing her family to become ostracized, many believing them to be in league with the devil.

Dr. Irene Moore
> Chicago coroner and doctor who discovered her family's monoecious trait in the late 1930's. She became the first Monoecion to father a child.

Carol Ann Jacobs
> Spouse of Irene Moore. She became the first woman to be impregnated by a Monoecion.

Charlie Wilkens
> The contractor who discovered Dr. Irene Moore's journal during a house renovation.

Gloria Wilkens
> Wife of Charlie Wilkins. She helped Charlie with the initial research but later befriends Becky Lovett.

Becky (Rebecca) Lovett
> Youngest daughter of Dr. Moore and Carol Jacobs, mother of Christine Landis.

Marci McBride
> Jasmine's mother. Marci and Alicia became a couple in college.

Jasmine
> The first known offspring of a Monoecion couple. Marci McBride is her mother and Alicia is her father. Her telepathic powers prove to be compounded by this heritage.

Alicia Inman
> Jasmine's father. Marci and Alicia became a couple in college.

Jessica
> Jasmine's little sister.

Daniel Nash
> Reporter at the Nation's View tabloid newspaper. He is the reporter that broke the Monoecion story based on the information gathered by Charlie and Gloria Wilkins.

Christine Landis
> A lawyer for the justice department and daughter of Becky Lovett. She becomes the de facto leader of the Monoecions after the government pushes her into the position of their representative.

Robert Landis

Christine Landis' economist husband.

Senator Gordon Fenton

Senator Fenton has presidential ambitions and sees the Monoecion issue as a way to ride the wave of public outrage to the White House. He manages to become the head of Commission to Oversee Monoecion Affairs (COMA) where he can manipulate the government policy towards the Monoecions.

Todd Lindell

Senator Fenton's top aide.

Ben Davis

Christine Landis' former boss and her current legal council.

Rae Ann Baird

Rae Ann lived in Macon, Georgia, with her husband and daughters until she revealed she is Monoecion. Thrown out of the house by her husband, she takes her daughters to the reservation. She is a martial arts instructor who has trained her daughters since they were young.

Kathy and Carla Baird

Rae Ann Baird's twin daughters.

Robin Willey

Robin is a mechanical engineer that Christine chooses for the reservation site investigation team. She continues to be responsible for the site buildings and utility systems.

Dorothy Joyner

The reservation business administrator selected by Christine Landis.

Ann Yates

A graduate of MIT with a masters in physics. Worked for Intel when the story broke and moved to the reservation. Joined Alicia's team to work on product development.

Gina Gooden

Gina holds a masters degree in micro-biology and a minor in computer science. She joined Alicia's team to work on product development.

About the Author

Gary Aumaugher lives in Knoxville, Tennessee, along with the love of his life and two mutts. When not writing he performs research in the use of renewable energy and power distribution efficiency. All reader feedback is welcome. Contact him at gaumaugher1@gmail.com.

www.ingramcontent.com/pod-product-compliance
Lightning Source LLC
Chambersburg PA
CBHW060528180626
46817CB00002B/487